Dear Reader,

Beneath the prim and proper
exterior of turn-of-the-century England,
many dark and dangerous desires were
brewing. This is the story of how one
woman disappears without a trace—and her
disappearance sets in motion events that will
come to a climax one hundred years later. In
the present day, two people learn to believe in
the power of love—and discover that this
power is the only thing that can save
them. Step inside the Circle of the Lily,
if you dare. Because once you enter,
you may not want to leave...

St. Martin's Paperbacks Titles by Jill Jones

CIRCLE
OF THE
LILY

JILL JONES

St. Martin's Paperbacks

This is a work of fiction, as are all the characters and events therein. Any resemblance of characters to persons living or dead, or actions of the plot to real life is entirely coincidental.

CIRCLE OF THE LILY

Copyright © 1998 by Jill Jones.

ISBN: 0-312-96813-2

Printed in the United States of America

St. Martin's Paperbacks edition / November 1998

St. Martin's Paperbacks are published by St. Martin's Press, 175 Fifth Avenue, New York, NY 10010.

10 9 8 7 6 5 4 3 2 1

For my Florida critique group—

Eleanor Boylan, Jasmine Cresswell,
Maggie Davis,
Kathleen Drymon, Carol Gaskin, and
Virginia Henley—
with inexpressible thanks for your generous help
and support.

$\mathscr{A}$cknowledgments

As always, I have received invaluable help from many people in the research of this book.

For sharing their knowledge and personal libraries with me, I thank Robin Tolleson, Leah Atkinson, Jackie Chamberlain, and Carol Gaskin.

For their generous help with my research, I thank Ken Britton, Linda Leighton, and Sheila Keener who assisted me greatly during my visit to Stansted Hall.

For their continuing support and kind hospitality, I thank Alistair Scott and Mrs. Margaret Scott of London.

I wish to thank Caroline Wise, proprietress of the Atlantis Bookshop, London, which in *no way* resembles the fictional "Alchymical Book Shoppe" in this story, but which is a wonderful, mystical, and intriguing place.

In addition to these people, I wish to thank my husband, Jerry Jones; my daughter, Brooke Kurek; my friend and mentor, Maram Schuster; my editor, Jennifer Enderlin; my agent, Denise Marcil; and friends too numerous to name for supporting me in various ways that have allowed me the time, money, and confidence to follow my dream.

Author's Note

During the last four decades of the nineteenth century, England experienced a renaissance of interest in the occult, largely due to the publication in 1859 of Charles Darwin's *On the Origin of Species* which questioned the spiritual beliefs of many.

Myriad occult groups sprang up or were revitalized, including the ancient Rosicrucian and Kabbalistic societies, the Mystery schools, spiritualism, the Theosophical Society, the Rose+Cross, and the Hermetic Order of the Golden Dawn. Many of these claimed that their teachings were based on the wisdom of the ancients, secrets entrusted by unseen Masters only into the hands of highly trained adepts known as Priests or Initiates. The vehicle for the transmission of this occult knowledge was ceremonial magic.

Although this story is purely fictional, it is based on extensive research into the activities of these magicians of old.

$\mathscr{P}$rologue

IN THE SUMMER OF 1899, A MYSTERIOUS OCCURrence at Hartford Hall, the country manor house of a wealthy London merchant, caused a nearby farmer to report it to the police. He told them he'd seen a brilliant flash of light streak from the basement windows, followed by the sound of a thunderous explosion.

Upon investigation, the police were told by the lord of the manor, Nigel Beauchamp, that there had been a problem with the newfangled heating system he'd installed in the basement. Yes, there had been a minor explosion, he'd said, but no real harm was done.

The police noted the incident in their records and closed the case.

Friends of Eloise Beauchamp, the lady of the manor, called on her shortly thereafter, for it had been some time since she had been seen in the nearby village, and she had not responded to their invitations to tea and their dinner parties. They were informed by her husband, who appeared distraught, that she had fallen ill, and that he had sent her to recuperate in the family's villa in the south of France.

In September of that same year, Nigel Beauchamp, along with his young son, Joseph, left Hartford Hall. Friends assumed he was joining his wife in France and that in time, the family would return to their magnificent country estate.

But Nigel never returned. Rumors spread that he had committed suicide and that the boy had died of a fever. Eloise was never seen or heard from again. It was a tragedy and a scandal, for theirs had been considered an ideal marriage, and they had appeared to be citizens of extraordinary character. There was some talk that a curse seemed to have fallen on their lives . . .

Chapter One

Montlivet, Essex
1998

THE STORM HIT THE SLEEPING VILLAGE JUST BEFORE dawn. Vicious lightning ripped the dark morning air, striking the bell tower of the ancient church and shattering the quiet night with the sizzle of unharnessed electricity followed by the crack of earsplitting thunder.

Claire St. John bolted upright in her bed. Her menagerie of cats leapt from their respective sleeping places as well and ran about in a howling, squalling frenzy, pumping her already racing pulse. "Shut up!" Claire threw a pillow at Damien, a large black creature with piercing green eyes and the loudest voice of them all, then reached for the bedside lamp. Her hand trembled. "It's only a storm," she assured the animals. "Just regular lightning and thunder." The strike, however, had slammed into something uncomfortably close by, and she shivered.

Pulling on a robe, she went to the tall front window of her bedroom and looked out across the valley toward the village below. Wind howled and rain fell in torrents, but to her relief she saw no sign that the lightning had started a fire. She turned from the window and tripped over an orange tabby, who protested loudly and shot from beneath her feet to take refuge under the bed.

"For heaven's sake, calm down, all of you!" Claire was unsure who was more upset, herself or her brood of frightened felines, the beloved pets that were like the children she'd never had. "Let's make tea."

Padding downstairs in robe and slippers, Claire's heartbeat slowed at last. Silly of me to be so undone by a storm, she thought. As she passed the small breakfast table on her way to the stove, she caught a glimpse of the tarot cards she'd left there, still arranged in the pattern of the throw she'd done the night before, and her disquiet returned.

For there, in the position of the "Outcome," card number ten, lay the Tower, one of the darkest, most disturbing, and frightening cards in the deck. She picked it up and stared at it for a long moment, studying the image of a lightning bolt striking a tower, knocking the steeple off and throwing two terrified people into the blackness of the sky behind.

The Tower.

Symbol of violent change.

Not always welcome change, but a major change of one sort or another. The Tower could mean a divorce. But she wasn't married. It could mean loss of a job. But she was self-employed. It could mean the destruction of a dearly beloved something or someone.

Claire looked out the window through the lightning-illumined darkness at the land that stretched behind the old farmhouse, land that had been in her family for over a century. The land that she loved was being beaten violently by the wind and rain. Yes, a storm, she supposed, could be what the card indicated, although usually the Tower reflected more than a bad storm. Usually, she thought unhappily, filling the kettle with water and placing it over the fire, it meant a life-altering change was in store.

And life-altering changes were always scary.

Claire St. John was in no mood for alterations of any kind in her life. She was happy, settled, complacent. Content to live in the house where she had grown up, on the farm left to her and her twin brother, Cameron, by their doting father.

Cameron. Apprehension niggled at her. Did the Tower card refer to him? Claire loved her brother, but she worried about him. Ever since he'd taken a position with an aggressive stock brokerage firm in the city, he'd been increasingly obsessed with making a fortune . . . immediately. No matter what. He'd begun to run with a fast crowd of London's young, rich, and restless. Claire did not like the few she had met. Many of them had auras of a sickly gray-green, revealing hidden fears and jealousies and a general lack of the kind of character she could respect.

Unfortunately, she had not kept her opinions to herself. Knowing that Cameron had always respected and welcomed her advice, she had warned him off these new acquaintances, with the result that they had quarreled, and he had not spoken to her since. That had been a month ago. "What do you know?" he had sneered. "You never get out of your little hole here, except to engage in the folly you call a business."

His words had hurt, partly because they were flung at her in such violent anger and partly because she suspected he was right. She *did*—in a way—hide from the world, living alone with her cats in the familiar old farmhouse, away from the "real world" in nearby London.

As for her business, she did not consider it a folly, but she knew many people would. Psychic counseling. It wasn't exactly a profession of which her more urbane brother was proud. Nor one she had planned for herself, either. It had just sort of . . . happened. Because of her unique psychic abilities, she had always been able to understand people and discern their troubles. All her life she'd offered what had proven to be astute advice to her close friends, based solely on what she intuitively felt was going wrong for them. Although she had not sought a paying clientele, three years ago she had helped a stranger. The woman was brought to her by a friend and was so impressed by her work that she began to recommend Claire to her friends in turn. Claire's reputation had spread rapidly and unexpectedly, and the only way she could afford to spend the time necessary to help the many people who came to her for counseling was to start charging for her services. There had never been a single complaint, either about her advice or her fee.

Cameron had been supportive, too, in the beginning, until he moved to London and began to pretend to be someone he was not. Claire shook her head. She didn't understand why he was trying so hard to be one of *them*. He wasn't their kind.

But then, there was much about Cameron she didn't understand these days.

Although she loved him more than any other person in her life, aside from their twinship they had few traits in common. He was the dark one, their father had always said. She'd thought until recently that he'd been referring only to Cameron's coloring. Cameron took after their mother, a dark-eyed, dark-haired Italian beauty they knew only from the photos that still lined the mantel in the farmhouse. A war bride from a land of endless sunshine who, after a late-in-life pregnancy and the birth of the twins, had become ill and died in the cold, damp climate of her adopted England.

Claire resembled their father, who had raised the pair of them. Pale golden hair, light blue eyes, fair skin.

The light twin.

Only since Cameron's recent behavior had she begun to consider that her father's estimation of his son as "dark" might extend past his physical characteristics. Thinking back over their childhood, she was troubled by memories of Cameron's misbehavior at school and his tendency to bully younger, more vulnerable children.

Claire had never swayed in her loyalty to Cameron, ever believing she could influence him with her own positive outlook and shape him into the good person she knew he could be.

The Tower card glared at her from the table. Had she been wrong? Was some dreadful catastrophe about to befall her brother, perhaps *because* of the dark side of his nature? She stared at the cards. More likely her imagination was running away with her. The storm's fury must have charged her with all the sudden negativity she was feeling. Whatever, the reading bode no good, so with a swipe of her hand she gathered the cards from the table and placed them with the rest, tying the deck neatly in a silken scarf and storing it away in a plain wooden box.

Hoping that would relieve her troubled psyche, Claire went about the business of the morning. She poured a cup of tea and placed a slice of bread in the toaster. She rattled the bag of cat food and filled the various bowls on the floor. The sound summoned a flurry of fluff as her plump wards hurried in for breakfast. There were seven of them in all, adoptees—strays who had wandered into her life from the nearby fields and roads. Two of them were unwanted pets left on her doorstep by someone who knew of her inability to say no to a cat in need. She didn't mind. They were good company, smarter than a lot of humans, and they suited her quiet nature.

By mid-morning, the storm had passed, leaving only a pewter sky to shield out the sun. Silver droplets trickled from emerald leaves onto the backs of the livestock that grazed beneath the trees, oblivious to the storm's aftermath. Despite the calm, the wreckage was severe. From a back window upstairs, Claire could see trees that only yesterday had been tall and stately with more than a hundred years' growth, now lying like fallen giants, their muddy, shallow roots wrenched from the sandy soil.

"Oh, my God," she murmured, shocked by the devastation. Those trees were like old friends. She'd climbed their limbs as a young girl, peered into birds' nests cradled in their branches, scratched out the initials of her first boy-

friend in the bark of one uncomplaining trunk. Now they
were destroyed.

Swiftly, she ran into her room where she donned a rain-
coat and slipped into a pair of waterproof boots. She tied
a scarf around her pallid blond hair and glanced in the
mirror. The image did not please her. She ought to apply
some makeup, lipstick at least, to warm the paleness of her
skin, but she was in a hurry and expected to see no one.
She dashed down the stairs, unsettled by the discouraging
image in the mirror. It wasn't that of an old woman. Not
really. Raincoats and scarves could make anyone look haggish. Besides, thirty-five was not old.

Thirty-five.

She didn't want to think about it. Picking up an umbrella
from the stand in the hall, she pushed the image problem
from her mind and popped out into the rain-washed morning.

It was worse than she'd expected, even after having seen
the devastation from her window. A newborn calf lay dead
at the feet of its bawling mother. A large chunk of the
pasture had dropped into the creek below, as if it had been
sliced off the land by a giant's cleaver, leaving an ugly,
gaping scar in the landscape. The lilacs that yesterday had
been in resplendent full bloom were shredded to purple
rags, and a dying baby bird lay on the path beneath a tree
that had managed to remain upright. Blown from the nest,
Claire surmised with a lump in her throat, wondering if its
siblings in the branches above had survived. She started to
attempt to rescue it, but when she touched it she realized
it had no chance of survival.

She avoided walking across the high grass of the
meadow, not wanting to slop through the mud she knew
lay beneath. Instead, she made her way up the gravel path
that led to the old manor house that had once been home
to a wealthy merchant and his family. Hartford Hall had
stood empty for years, but she'd heard that it had recently
been purchased by an affluent Londoner who would soon

set about extensive restorations. She was glad of it. The place was a magnificent example of eighteenth-century Jacobean design, with a many-gabled roofline and fanciful red brick chimneys. She and Cameron had played in it many times as children, ignoring the NO TRESPASSING signs as well as the local rumor that the place was both haunted and cursed.

Claire wondered if the storm had wrought any damage to the hall, but she doubted it. It was made of stone and brick, and she guessed it would take the power of a cyclone to bring it down.

Not far along the path, she came to a tall tree that had fallen only a few yards away. Deciding to inspect it more closely, she left the smooth walkway and stepped carefully over the sodden soil. The tree's root system was enormous, a gnarled wooden fist clutching a ball of yellow-orange soil. Lying sideways on the ground, exposed to the unfamiliar daylight, the tangle of the root was twice as tall as Claire. The lump in her throat tightened into a knot.

Despite her grief for the loss of the tree, she had never seen anything like this, and she made her way through the wet grass to the foot of the uprooted leviathan. At first she didn't believe her eyes. But as her mind registered what she saw entangled in the roots, she gasped and a scream of horror tore from her throat.

It was a skeleton. A *human* skeleton. A bone that once supported an arm protruded from its gnarly cage and swayed slightly in the light wind. Sunlight suddenly broke through the pale clouds, and it glinted on something that was captured in the mud. Claire caught her breath and, struggling to contain her terror, took a tentative step closer. There, lodged on one bony finger, making a macabre and surreal fashion statement, was a golden ring.

"Looks like some kind of symbolic signet ring to me, the kind worn by members of those secret fraternal lodges." One of the police officers investigating the case turned the artifact over in the palm of his hand. "But I'm baffled. I've never seen anything like it. Or this case, either. Intriguing."

It was only ten o'clock in the morning, but Claire slumped into her favorite armchair, exhausted from lack of sleep and the intense questioning concerning the discovery of the skeleton. The two policeman had arrived at her house several hours before in answer to her distraught phone call reporting the grisly find.

Despite her distress and fatigue, however, she was as baffled and intrigued as the investigators. What on earth was a skeleton doing on her property? Who had been buried beneath the tree?

"Do you have any reports of missing persons? Any unsolved murders in the area?" she asked.

The lieutenant shook his head. "Not in our precinct. Of course, it could be related to a crime in another county. Do you have any thoughts on the matter?"

Claire knew she might be a suspect in any investigation of foul play, although when the police checked her reputation around the village, she was certain they would drop such a notion. But she wanted an answer as badly as they did. "May I see the ring?"

Besides being able to read auras, Claire's psychic powers included psychometry—the ability to divine information about people or events associated with an object simply by touching it. She could hold an item of clothing or someone's personal possession and almost instantly receive valuable information about the owner. She had no idea *how* it worked, but she knew from experience that it did.

She was not inclined to tell the police that she hoped to learn the identity of the corpse from the ring. They would think her daft. If she could pick up impressions of the dead person, however, perhaps she could guide their investigation in the right direction, although she was unsure if she could resonate psychically with the wearer of this ring. Did dead people resonate?

The police officer handed the ring to her. It felt cold

against her skin, and she was instantly overcome by a sickening feeling of fear and dread. She forced herself to study the odd symbol engraved on the circular golden surface. In the center was an eye, with six sunlike rays extending outward from a small diamond that formed the iris. The eye was enclosed by a triangle, and the entire image was then encircled by a graceful calla lily, its stem winding around the outside edge and coming back into the flower, like the mythical dragon swallowing its tail.

Acid rose in her throat. Whoever had owned this ring had been evil to the core. But to her surprise, she sensed that the ring did not belong to the person whose skeleton had worn it. Claire closed her eyes, forcing herself past her personal distaste to search psychically for the identity of the wearer, or the owner, but behind her eyelids, all she could see was red.

Blood red.

Suddenly convulsed by an involuntary shudder, she dropped the ring. Reaching beneath the chair, she grasped it and stood up again. Wordlessly, she held the piece on her open palm to return it to the policeman.

"Know anything about this symbol?" he asked, frowning slightly. "Does it mean anything to you?"

"No. No, I've never seen anything like it before, either."

He studied her a moment. "Are you sure? You seem a little upset . . ."

"I'm not upset." Her reply was short, hostile. Then she added more softly, "Not about the ring, at any rate. But, yes, it is upsetting to come across a skeleton almost in your own back garden." She sensed the officer suspected she wasn't being fully truthful with him, but she was not about to reveal that her shock and revulsion were psychic in nature. She didn't tell total strangers, especially policemen, about her unusual abilities.

Fortunately, he didn't press further. He simply secured the ring as evidence, handed her his card, and thanked her gravely. "We appreciate the strain this incident has placed on you, Ms. St. John, but we would be grateful if you would give us a call if you think of anything else that might help us resolve this case. Identifying a skeleton is not an easy matter. We will try to determine how old it is, how long it has been interred. The best clue to the person's identity we have at the moment is that ring.''

"I understand. But I assure you I have never seen that symbol before.'' Even as the words came out of her mouth, Claire realized they weren't true. Some memory deep inside stirred and rose faintly to the surface, but only enough to unsettle her once again. She did not grasp at the memory but rather forced it back into the darkness from whence it came.

Claire had just closed the door behind the departing policemen when she was summoned by the shrill double ring of the telephone. "Hello?'' she said as she picked up the receiver.

"Claire, it's Bitsy. Is your cottage booked? I have an American gentleman in the office who is looking for a place for a possible extended stay.''

Bitsy Flanagan, sounding unusually excited, spoke in an Irish brogue even though she'd lived in England for years. She was Claire's closest friend in the village, one who knew of Claire's psychic gifts and who shared her interest in the supernatural. They both, in fact, had recently been asked to join a séance circle that met weekly in town.

"Hi, Bits,'' Claire replied, her tension easing at the sound of her friend's voice. "No, it's not booked, but I've had a rough morning, and frankly, the idea of dealing with a tenant at the moment is not very appealing.''

"He is.'' Her friend's answer was given in a straight-forward voice, as if Claire had asked if the prospective tenant was interested in a week or longer. He was obviously sitting right in front of her. But Bitsy's meaning was unmistakeable.

The *gentleman* was very appealing.

Oh, for Pete's sake, Claire thought. Bitsy and her husband were forever trying to make a match for her. "Can't you find him someplace else?" It was Bitsy's job as hostess at the local Information Centre to help visitors find lodgings to their liking in the area.

"All the B and B's are full for the weekend. Besides, he's really interested in a self-catering apartment rather than just an *en suite* room."

"I see." Claire paused. She could use the money. An extended rental of the small apartment across the walk from her own house would give her enough to make badly needed repairs to the plumbing of both places without having to delve into her savings. "How long does he plan to stay?"

Bitsy covered the phone with her hand, asked her client the question, then returned to Claire. "Could be a week, could be a month. He doesn't know for sure."

Renewed fatigue settled around Claire's shoulders, and she suddenly just didn't have the energy to fend off Bitsy's enthusiasm. "Send him over then," Claire said with a sigh.

"He'll be there within fifteen minutes," Bitsy said aloud, then added with a whispered giggle, "You won't regret it!"

But Claire regretted it the moment she laid eyes on the American man. Yes, as advertised, he was appealing. Handsome in fact, with a strong, square chin, dark hair and eyes, and a tall, fit body beneath denims and a casual jacket. Perhaps it was the stress of the day, or the troubling images conjured by the mystical ring, or even her own overtaxed imagination, but the very sight of the man who stood before her struck her nearly dumb with terror. He frightened her more than the storm, more than the skeleton and the sickening resonance of the ring combined.

Part of it was his aura. It wasn't just somber or melancholy. It was black. As if he were surrounded by an unholy darkness.

Even more frightening, however, was a powerful, almost overwhelming attraction that drew her to him, as if his darkness were a forceful magnet commanding her light. She had to struggle to maintain control. This man was definitely bad news.

I have to get out of this obligation, Claire thought, panic-stricken. She couldn't let such a person stay in her cottage. It was unthinkable. For one thing, it would take weeks to clear the negative energies he was bound to bring into the place. If, that is, she survived the sheer psychic force of his presence. Or he didn't murder her in her bed, if his darkness were criminal in nature.

"Ms. St. John?" His deep voice, with a distinctly American accent, refocused her attention.

"Yes. Come in." Claire went through the motions of being polite but stopped short of offering her hand. She could afford no physical contact with this man. She would extend only the briefest courtesy until she could convince him he really didn't want to rent her cottage.

Once inside, the man turned and handed her a card. "I am Dr. Michael Townsend. I am, or rather I was until recently, a professor at Strathmore College in Virginia."

Claire took the card, willing her hand to cease shaking, but to no avail. The dark red ink raised against a creamy white background outlined a crested symbol of some sort, above which read "Strathmore College, Excellence for a Lifetime." Beneath was his name and department. But she felt tension held within that symbol. He was *recently* this professor, he'd said, sounding almost apologetic. The vibrations resonating from the card troubled her, and her doubts about him increased.

"What brings you to Montlivet, Dr. Townsend?"

He eyed her levelly and replied in an impassive tone, "I am writing a book. I've come here to do research."

She waited for more, wishing desperately that he would say or do something that would put her at ease, that would let her know he wasn't the Power of Darkness incarnate. But no such reassurance was forthcoming. "Well, then . . ." she said finally, filling in the awkward silence, her mind searching wildly and futilely for some way to divert him from his plans to rent her cottage. "Follow me," she said at last. She must show him his room. She had, after all, made a commitment through the Information Centre.

And for that, she swore silently as she led the man through her house and across the old stones of the covered walkway to the cottage, she would happily throttle Bitsy Flanagan the next time they were together.

Chapter Two

MICHAEL TOWNSEND WAS ACCUSTOMED TO LIVING IN a hostile world. His father had told him since childhood how it was. "Life isn't that proverbial bowl of cherries, y'know, boy," he'd warned. "The world's a cold and lonely place. Always expect the worst, and you won't be disappointed." For thirty-eight years he had lived with such an outlook and, for the most part, his father's words had proven true. So although he was a little nettled at her hostile attitude, he wasn't surprised that the woman who answered the door offered him no smile of welcome.

He was curious, however, as to why she seemed distinctly disturbed that he'd come, as if she were afraid of him. Was there something she didn't like about him or was it just his buzzard luck at work again, bringing him into the home of a misanthrope?

Michael didn't need the woman's affection, however. He needed her cottage. So he opted to ignore her inhospitable reaction and assumed his usual air of aloof detachment. Too bad he'd forgotten that the business card he'd presented was no longer valid, that he was no longer an esteemed professor of English and American literature, but rather a professional has-been, his tenure having been recently denied. The humiliation at having to alter his introduction to admit he was *recently* a professor deepened the bitterness that seemed his constant companion.

He studied the woman as she read the card. Claire St. John. The woman at the Information Centre had pronounced her last name the English way, "sin-jen," like the cousin in Charlotte Brontë's *Jane Eyre*. That sounded strange on his tongue, though, so Michael had called her "Saint John." She was not an unlovely creature, he decided as she returned his card. He noted that she handled it delicately, as if it burned her fingers. She might even be pretty if her features were not so drawn, her hair not so severely pulled away from her face and bound into a ponytail. As it was, a slight frown furrowed her brow and her face was grim. She seemed more the warden than the landlady. Her troubled demeanor, however, could not disguise the delicate line of her cheekbone and the appealing luminescence of her wide blue eyes.

Her brusque inquiry—what brought him to Montlivet?—rekindled his irritation. It was none of her damn business why he was here as long as he paid the rent. With practiced control, he maintained an implacable expression and made up some lie about writing a book. He didn't care. Maybe he *would* write a book someday. An autobiography. When he had the courage to face and to record everything that had gone wrong in his life.

It would make a good disaster story.

At last she seemed satisfied that he was worthy of staying in her cottage and beckoned him to follow her. She led him through a house strewn with cats and crossword puzzles. The very warmth and coziness of her surroundings belied the inhospitable nature she had shown him so far, raising his curiosity as to the reason for her unspoken animosity. But the idiosyncrasies of his landlady didn't really matter to him. He was exhausted from traveling, and all he wanted at the moment was a hot shower and a good bed.

The cottage was more than acceptable, although Claire St. John warned him that the water pressure was inadequate and that she had been unable to rid the attic of a family of mice that would likely keep him awake at night. It sounded as if she were trying to discourage him from renting the place. The redhead at the Information Centre had told him this was the only rental available at the moment in the entire village, however, and he was not going to turn it down. Besides, he was so tired that the world could burn down around him once he was asleep and he would never notice.

He gave the woman a hundred and twenty-five pounds in cash for the first week's rental and, regardless that the lodging was self-catering, made arrangements to have breakfast each morning. He wasn't much of a cook. Michael took the key, thanked her with a coldness that matched her own, then closed the door firmly behind him. Only when he was alone at last did he let down his guard and allow his repressed emotions their freedom. He slung his suitcase onto the bed with an angry oath.

What the hell *was* he doing here?

Research. He'd told Claire St. John he was here to do research. Well, I suppose I am in a way, he thought darkly, if uncovering one more betrayal counted as research. If finding one's mother fell into that category.

A mother, who in his mind had been dead for over thirty-six years.

Michael went to the window and stared out at the meadowland that stretched behind the cottage, ending in a wooded copse. He saw that trees had been blown down, probably by the storm that had delayed his landing at the nearby airport, and the wreckage reflected the chaos of his own life. Everything that had meant anything to him, everything he'd worked so hard for had been wrenched from him; his whole existence had been turned upside down, destroyed by a recent series of events fit for the script of a soap opera. The sudden death of his young fiancée a year ago in a car crash. The cruel betrayal of his former friend. The unexpected denial of tenure. And then his father's

death, which he did not really mourn, but which led to a
shocking discovery that he was still having trouble accepting.

After his father's funeral, Michael had come across a
locked box in Thomas Townsend's attic. Inside, among
some other strange items, he'd found a letter written by his
mother and had learned that Stella Townsend had not died,
as his father had always told him, but rather had left him
and her husband when Michael was only a small boy.

The revelation continued to stun him. When he thought
about it, he was able to forgive his father, if only for a
while, for all the times that Thomas Townsend had been
emotionally unavailable to him, for all the lonely years he'd
known as a child. At least now he better understood his
father's morose behavior, why he had told Michael there
was no such thing as love and that he should never trust a
woman.

Michael's eyes scanned the rooftops of the village. Did
she live somewhere near here? he wondered. His mother.
Mom. What the hell would he call her when—if—he found
her? Stella? Mrs. Townsend?

Deserter?

He leaned his brow against the cool pane of the window.
Why, after all these years, did he even care? He was a
grown man now. Maybe he shouldn't have come. He knew
if Mrs. Stella Townsend was still alive, she likely didn't
want to be found. She'd made that clear in the letter.

What was not clear, at least to Michael, was her reason
for leaving.

He moved away from the window and opened the suitcase fasteners with a snap. Inside, amongst his clothing and
personal belongings, nestled a long narrow box. From it he
took out a battered envelope, which contained a letter and
a black-and-white photo faded to sepia tones with age. He
held the photo at arm's length and stared at it. Staring back,
a pretty young woman with an outdated hairstyle stood beside a '51 Ford sedan. She was smiling, almost, although

the expression did not quite make it to her large, shadow-smudged eyes. His mother? He'd found the photo and the letter together in the envelope, so he assumed it was. It was the only image of Stella Townsend he had ever seen as an adult, for his father had burned all her pictures when Michael was still a small child.

He again read through the words penned nearly four decades before, searching desperately for understanding of an act that had changed forever the life of an unsuspecting two-year-old.

Dearest Thomas,

    It is with indescribable grief and anguish that I take my leave of you and Michael, but I do so out of love and the hope that my actions will protect you both from the curse I believe I have brought into our marriage. It seems I cannot find happiness in this country, no matter how hard you have tried to please me. I do not understand my continuing heartbreak—I should be the happiest woman alive, with such a loving husband and a healthy son at last. And yet it is not so. I weep constantly for no reason, and lately I have been hearing voices inside my head. I fear that I am going mad. I believe that, like my mother, I am somehow cursed in this life, and I pray that by taking my leave of you and our son, you and he will be spared that curse.

    You have already borne much sorrow since our marriage, and yet you have never blamed me. I cannot in good conscience ask you to bear with me any longer. Nor do I wish to inflict upon my son the memory of an insane mother. I leave Michael in your most loving and capable care, as I believe a boy should be with his father, and it is my prayer that by leaving him, he will somehow escape the curse that plagues this family.

    Please do not try to find me or ask me to come back. I give you my full blessing to file for a divorce, find another, better woman, and build a happier life than I can give you. As for our son, he is so young, he will not remember me. Perhaps it would be best if you just tell him that I have died, for in truth, Stella Townsend is dead. I am no longer the woman you married, but a terrified soul plunging into a darkness I can neither explain nor overcome. I beg your forgiveness.

The letter was signed with a single large swash of an "S," as if the writer were unable, or unwilling, to sign her full name.

But understanding eluded Michael once again. A *curse*, for God's sake! How childish and ridiculous. He wanted to crush the letter in his fist. More likely, Stella Townsend had suffered from chronic depression. Or an inability to accept motherhood. He studied the photo again, trying to find some compassion in his heart for this woman, the mother who had abandoned him, but it seemed his heart was made of stone.

There was no compassion, but there was curiosity. *"You have already borne much sorrow since our marriage ..."* What sorrows had his father and mother endured before he was born? Thomas Townsend had spoken little of his relationship with Stella. All Michael knew was that his father had met and married his mother when he was in the Air Force, stationed in England in the mid-1950s. Michael had not been born until 1959. What "sorrows" had transpired in the years in between? Had there been real sorrows, or had his mother made up sorrows in her mind to excuse the inexcusable—deserting her husband and baby?

Michael stuffed the letter and photo into the envelope once again and thrust it back into the box, slamming the lid as if that might make it all disappear. Was he mad himself, making this impulsive trip to England in search of a mother from whom he had never once heard over the course of his life? He had no known address for her, only the name of this village and county—Montlivet, Essex—

that he'd found scratched inside the cover of a curious old bookbinding from which all the pages had been torn. He'd found the shell of the book in this box as well, and although he didn't know whether the letter and the bookbinding were even related—the date in the book was long before his mother's time; before the turn of the century, in fact— Michael thought it possible and was working on the assumption that Montlivet might be the home to which his mother had returned.

It was precious little to go on, and he was probably foolish for pursuing it, but he wanted to know the truth. Had his mother been insane? Or only faithless? He wanted the information, feeling he deserved to know after all this time. He was less certain, however, whether he wished to actually meet Stella Townsend.

He had recently decided, somewhat bitterly, that he might as well spend some time on this particular ''research,'' as he had little else to do with his life right now. Denied tenure meant a major career move. Usually downhill. It wasn't a place he wanted to go, but he wasn't certain he had a choice. He was, in fact, not certain about much of anything right now. He felt powerless, like his life was out of his control.

He laughed at himself silently and with disdain. Maybe his mother wasn't crazy after all. Maybe she *had* been cursed and in spite of running away, maybe she'd passed the curse along to him nonetheless.

An absurd thought, of course. Irrational. Like this journey. Theatrical, like the puzzling items he'd come across in the same box in which he'd found the letter.

Michael glanced at the box again, but did not reopen it, for he simply did not know what to make of the objects that lay beneath the envelope. From his brief initial investigation, he had decided that they were magical props of some sort. Among other things, there was a lotus-tipped wand, a tarnished chalice, a large bronze disc engraved with a five-pointed star, a crown, and a short dagger with a wide blade. Most intriguing to Michael was a ring engraved with a curious mystical symbol.

He had no idea where the items had come from unless, like the pageless book that had accompanied them, they too were from Montlivet, Essex. Nor could he explain their presence in his father's attic. Thomas Townsend was not the magical sort. He'd been an accountant. A withdrawn, unremarkable, undemonstrative man who had provided for his quiet, studious son all that a child needs in life—with the exception of warmth, love, and paternal closeness.

Michael suspected that the props must have been left-overs from some bygone youthful venture into stage magic. He could not conceive that the ring or any of the rest of it might be paraphernalia of some kind of secret society any more than he could imagine that his father had been hiding some dark secret, other than that of his wife's desertion, behind his impenetrable reserve.

Michael shook his head. There was suddenly so much about his family he didn't know and was hungry to learn. Maybe having this unexpected "sabbatical" forced upon him was a disguised blessing. It would give him time to sort out this latest shock as well as to figure out what to do next with his life.

His mind still on the mysteries that had brought him to this place, he began to explore the possibility of a shower to rid himself of the grime of extended travel. It took some time to figure out the plumbing system in the cottage's tiny bathroom, but at last he managed to coax steaming hot water from the small, wall-mounted water heater. Unfortunately, the hot water was interrupted intermittently with shots of ice-cold water, rendering a shower not only uncomfortable but painful. He swore aloud, jumping away from the shower head and thinking that perhaps the St. John woman was somehow manipulating the temperature to convince him to find other lodgings.

That was ridiculous, he told himself, giving up on a

shower and running the hot and cold water together into the tub. Why would she want to do that?

Claire was so unnerved by the time she left Dr. Michael Townsend to himself in the cottage that she was shaking. She'd done her best to discourage him from staying, pointing out the worst in the accommodations, but he didn't seem to care. He'd paid her, and she'd accepted his money. He was staying.

At least for a week.

Claire gripped the bannister and forced herself to climb the stairs to her room. It was a place of refuge where she retreated to restore herself when she felt her psychic energies depleted, as they sometimes were after meeting with a client. But nothing, not the ambient scent of lavender, the presence of harmonizing crystals, or the fresh flowers in bowls, served to calm her.

She continued to tremble as she sank into the antique chair in front of her dressing table. She peered at her image in the mirror. She looked wan, ragged, worn out. No wonder. It *had* been a bloody distressful day, and it wasn't yet noon. She'd handled worse things than the discovery of the skeleton and the inquiry of the police, however. But it was not that incident, she was certain, that was causing her present distress.

It was the man.

Even though she'd consciously fought it, she'd continued to be attracted to him despite the darkness of his aura. It was a frightening and powerful attraction, an undeniably *sexual* attraction which both aroused her and left her quaking.

Claire leaned closer to the glass. Her face was so pale it seemed almost translucent except where two bright spots tinged her cheeks pink. Her lips were nearly colorless. Running both hands over the smooth skin of her face, she felt its coolness against her fingertips, as if she were nearly devoid of life. However, the pulse at her neck thrummed, echoing the fear that coursed through her veins.

Fear. Of the man.

She feared Dr. Michael Townsend, for his darkness and sexual magnetism seemed to have reached beyond her psychic and physical defenses, penetrating her spirit, draining her vitality. His dark essence seemed to have fed on the light of her life force, as if he were some kind of energy vampire.

Yet Claire knew that was nonsense. Dr. Townsend had done nothing—nothing!—to harm her. Nothing other than to unknowingly reveal the darkness of his nature to her simply by being in her presence. Still, a chill shuddered through her. No matter that the man was innocent of malevolent action. There was danger here. Very real psychic and physical danger. She must summon the strength to withstand his dark allure, to protect herself and her vulnerable psyche. Except she wasn't sure exactly how.

Since she had become a professional psychic consultant three years ago, she had studied the dynamics of psychic phenomena under the tutelage of some of England's most respected occult teachers. They had instructed her in the basics of self-protection, how to consciously surround herself mentally with a shield of holy white light and to repudiate with affirmations any negative influences that might be brought into her energy field. But those seemed sadly ineffective at the moment. She had never encountered anyone with such a surge of darkness as Michael Townsend.

Claire moved to the bed and sank onto it, grabbing a pillow and hugging it tightly. How she wished at times that she didn't have these powers. She certainly never asked for them and only in recent years had she sought to develop them. Maybe that had been a mistake, for in pursuit of understanding, she had also opened herself to this kind of distress. She glanced at the phone and considered calling Maeve Willoughby, her psychic mentor and good friend. She needed both advice and comfort, but remembered it was Maeve's day to give readings at the headquarters of the Spiritualist Association at Belgrave Square in London.

A small white-and-gray cat with only one eye but six toes on each paw jumped up next to Claire and began to purr loudly, as if he sensed her distress. "Hello, Lefty," she murmured, smiling and stroking the cat's silken fur. This pitiful little stray had become her favorite of them all, for he seemed to have an uncanny ability to sense her emotional needs and tried in his own feline way to meet them. It was as if the cat had a soul as compassionate as her own.

"What am I going to do, Lefty?" she whispered to the animal. "I mustn't be around that man. He could make me very ill." Claire regretted that Dr. Townsend had requested and paid for breakfast each morning, for she would be unable to avoid being in his presence.

She stroked the cat absently, thinking about the American who had so unhinged her. Was he truly evil? Or was there something else afflicting him so direly that it was literally blackening his aura? Suddenly, she was ashamed at her lack of a single thought of compassion for him. She was a healer, after all. At least, a healer of sorts. It was her job to help people sort out and get past their problems, and yet she had not stopped to consider that Dr. Michael Townsend might have problems or that she might be able to help him.

She rarely offered to help anyone unless they asked her, and she wasn't about to reveal to this complete stranger the unique powers she could tap on his behalf. He'd likely think her off her head.

It was out of the question at any rate. If she couldn't withstand his presence any better than she had today, her best bet was to steer clear of the man altogether.

Early afternoon sunlight shimmered through the window, and her stomach growled, reminding her she'd had nothing to eat since the pre-dawn tea and toast. Hunger, she reasoned, rather than an attack on her psychic energy, was more likely responsible for her pallor and unsteadiness. "Are you hungry, too, little one?" she asked her pet. Lefty, so named because his left eye was the one that still worked, gave her an affectionate and, she was certain, affirmative meow.

"Very well. Maybe we should both have a bite to eat." Removing the cat gently from her lap, Claire stood, but before going down to the kitchen, she stopped at the dressing table again. She brushed a light pink blush onto her cheeks and dabbed a darker pink over her lips. Her head was aching, so she released her hair from the rubber band that held it back and brushed it vigorously, letting it fall to her shoulders where it curled under slightly. She smiled at the results, feeling better already.

Claire St. John had no intention of allowing any darkness to hold her down for long. A sandwich and an apple followed by a cup of strong tea should restore her energy, and then she was determined to walk through town to the Information Centre to set the rest of her problem straight. Bitsy would simply have to find Dr. Townsend other lodgings. As soon as possible. Claire would happily refund his money for days not stayed at the cottage.

Turning the corner and entering the kitchen, she saw Lefty suddenly arch his back and hiss viciously. The hair on his spine stood straight up, then he let out an horrific screech and flew past her and out the door again. Before she could stop or register what had happened, her own momentum carried her headlong into something.

Something she could not see.

Something cold. And slimy. Lefty's bloodcurdling squall was tame in comparison to the screams that tore from Claire's throat for the second time that day.

Chapter Three

MICHAEL HAD BARELY FINISHED HIS BATH AND slipped into fresh jeans when he heard the screaming. It was not the sound of someone who had been merely startled. It was the alarm of someone who was terrified, the screams going on and on hysterically.

He buttoned the front of his pants and jerked open the door to the cottage, not stopping to put on shirt or shoes. Outside, the woman's screams were louder, emanating from the main house. Finding the back door unlocked, he opened it and ran to the kitchen, where he found Claire St. John leaning against the wall, sobbing spasmodically, her face deathly pale and her hand to her mouth.

"What's the matter? What happened?" He went to her, but she shrank from him as if she wanted to disappear into the dark wood of the walls.

"Leave me alone." Her large eyes were filled with the ferocity and fear of a cornered animal.

He stopped his advance but did not back off. "I won't hurt you," he said cautiously, thinking perhaps the woman was mentally unbalanced. "I heard your screams. What happened?"

She glanced over his shoulder, searching the room anxiously. Then she blinked several times and refocused on him. "Did . . . you see . . . anything?"

Michael looked around the room. It was empty except for all the normal things a kitchen contains. He shook his head. "What did *you* see?"

She didn't answer immediately. Then she straightened and pushed away from the wall, rubbing her forearms with both hands. "Nothing. I didn't see anything. It's just that . . . I'm very tired. It's been a taxing day. It must have been the cat that startled me."

Michael knew she was lying. This woman lived with cats. Lots of them. He doubted that a cat's squall, no matter how loud or unexpected, would spark the unholy terror he'd seen in her eyes. "Can I do anything?" Oddly, he wanted to comfort her, but he felt distinctly unqualified. What did one do to console a woman who only moments before had been screaming hysterically? For once, he wished he knew more about women.

"Please, just go. I mean . . . I thank you for your consideration, but . . ."

Determined to make sure she was all right before he left, Michael stepped closer to her instead, close enough to lay his hand on her shoulder in reassurance. He sensed she didn't want him to touch her, so he slid his hands into his pockets instead. "Shouldn't I call a doctor or something? I mean, you look so shaken."

She worked at pulling herself together. It took some effort. She drew in a deep breath, ran her hands through her hair, and gave him a tentative smile. He noticed that her hair was no longer bound behind her head, but swung freely at her shoulders. It was a flattering improvement. Her cheeks and lips, in spite of her fright, seemed more colorful than when he'd first knocked on her door. In the light-pink sleeveless shell she wore, she even looked pretty, in a pastel sort of way. She brushed past him and went to the stove.

"No. No, thank you." She clanged the teakettle against the stove. "I'm quite all right. I apologize for disturbing you, Dr. Townsend. I'm not normally so easily perturbed.''

He made no move to leave, but studied her from behind, getting the distinct impression that she did not want to turn to face him. Why? Did she have something against him? But that made no sense. He was a total stranger. Yet now, like when she'd shown him to his room earlier, he felt an almost palpable enmity.

At last she turned, and her features softened, relieving her face of the strain of her earlier fear and the frown of antipathy. ''Please forgive me. I don't know where I put my manners. I was about to make lunch. Will you . . . join me for tea and a sandwich?''

Michael knew she was only being polite, but his curiosity was piqued at her chameleon ways. Besides, he was hungry. He accepted with a nod. ''It's been a long time since that croissant on the plane. Are you sure it wouldn't be too much trouble? I will gladly pay . . .''

Something undefinable flickered in her eyes, and he hoped he hadn't offended her.

''Don't be silly,'' she said at last. ''But . . . perhaps you would like to . . . finish getting dressed.''

Michael looked down at his bare chest and feet. ''Yes, that would be a good idea. I was just getting out of the bath when I heard your screams.''

They stared at each other for a prolonged moment, and in that instant, something passed between them that Michael couldn't describe. Almost like an unspoken bond. He had seen her rendered helpless and vulnerable, and it had stirred him to protect her. He read the wordless gratitude in her eyes and immediately forgave her earlier hostility. He still wondered why she had screamed in such terror, but she obviously was not inclined to tell him. It was enough, he supposed, that she had been in no real danger and did not, after all, appear to be insane. ''Well, then,'' he said awkwardly at last, distinctly unsettled at the protective feelings she had aroused in him. He really ought to change his mind and keep his distance. He had too many other disturbing things demanding his attention at the moment.

But something about Claire St. John rendered him unable to decline her invitation. In spite of her recent fright, she had an air about her that he found peculiarly soothing. Perhaps it was the wide eyes that now appeared so guileless. Or her coloring, her fair hair and skin that even in the low light of the kitchen seemed almost luminous. She was like a balm for his chronic despair and ragged anger.

There was no harm in having a bite of lunch with her, he convinced himself. He could make sure she was truly recovered from her upset, and since she was a local, he thought she might be able to provide him with some information about the area. "Give me a few minutes."

Claire watched Michael Townsend leave the room, then turned to the stove again and gripped the handle of the teakettle so tightly her knuckles turned white. Had she lost her mind? What on earth had compelled her to invite that man to lunch?

The darkness of his aura had not changed, nor had her dangerous attraction to it. To him. She wasn't known for exhibiting such bad judgment. Nor for jumping at shadows like she had and becoming hysterical. It wasn't like her. Was she having a nervous breakdown? Had his dark force weakened her somehow? For the first time since she'd embarked upon her journey of psychic development, Claire began to harbor doubts, for when a person opened to psychic expansion, she also became vulnerable to influences beyond the normal range of human experience. Psychic growth could be dangerous if a person wasn't strong enough mentally, emotionally, and even physically to withstand the strain. Maeve had told her of several psychics who had gone over the edge.

She closed her eyes, trying to sort out what she was feeling, and the image that immediately arose in her mind's eye told her it was more than psychic strain that was disturbing her. It was the image of Michael Townsend's half-naked body.

Although she was inexperienced with men, Claire St. John was not a virgin, hadn't been since a disastrous youthful love affair had turned her off romance for more than a decade. It wasn't that she didn't like men. She had loved her father and still loved her brother. But as for the rest . . . well, she had trusted once and been burned. Badly. It would take someone very special to get her to take that risk again.

For longer than a decade, no one special had shown up. She didn't mind. Her life was easier that way. Set. Patterned according to her own cozy habits and preferences. She answered to no one but herself, and her teachers, of course, but that was part of her satisfaction with life. She had the time and freedom to pursue that which interested her without having to answer to the demands of a husband and family, the way Bitsy Flanagan did.

Only occasionally did she envy Bitsy.

She opened her eyes and released her death grip on the teakettle, suddenly understanding her sexual susceptibility to Michael Townsend. Part of her occult training demanded that she seek an understanding of herself, and she was wise enough to recognize that her state of celibacy, whether it was by choice or not, would render her sexually attracted to a man like him. She picked up a knife and began to make the sandwiches. Hers was a simple, feminine reaction. Any normal, healthy female would find him attractive, especially clad as he had been when he'd come running helter-skelter in response to her screams . . .

Her screams.

Claire's thoughts returned with a jolt to the incident that had brought him running, and she dropped the carving knife. It barely missed her toe as it clattered to the floor. She grabbed it up again and wielded it as a weapon as she looked cautiously around the room. What *had* she run into that had caused her to lose control so completely?

Only moments ago, she'd dismissed her hysteria as

"jumping at shadows," but upon recollection, she knew she had encountered something far more substantial than a shadow. She could almost feel the wave of tomblike air that had passed over her and the cold, slimy, invisible wall into which she had run. It must have been a wall, or at least something semi-solid. Otherwise, there would have been no impact. Yet she didn't feel as if she'd bruised herself. She ran her left hand over the upper muscle of her right arm and felt something crisp, like skin peeling after a sunburn. She examined her arm more carefully and saw that it was covered by a transparent film like a facial masque. Laying the knife on the counter, she carefully peeled the layer away. It flaked in places, falling to the floor in a shower of tiny white particles.

An unsettling suspicion came over her, and she shuddered violently. She wasn't certain—she'd have to ask Maeve—but she believed that right here in her own kitchen she might have encountered the ectoplasm of an earthbound spirit.

She'd bumped into a ghost!

Claire didn't know whether to laugh or start screaming again. She'd always declared that she wanted to see a ghost. In fact, that was her motivation for joining the séance circle. It was part of her continuing investigation into the world of the paranormal, her educational process as she stretched her psychic muscles. But now that the possibility of having encountered a ghost stared her in the face, she was a little frightened. Her home had never been haunted. Why would a spirit come calling now?

As it happened, she neither laughed nor screamed, for Michael Townsend re-entered the room, fully dressed now, his damp locks the only reminder of his former state of dishabille.

"Anything I can do to help?"

Although now fully clothed, his darkness and his maleness unsettled her all over again, but she'd be damned if she let him know it. "No. No, I'm fine. Make yourself comfortable in the sitting room, and I'll bring the things in straightaway.''

Her tenant, thankfully, did as he was told, and Claire hurriedly finished the preparations for lunch. Her mind skipped between attempts at remaining objective about the man in the next room and her burning desire to know if there indeed had been a spirit—a ghost—in her kitchen.

''Here we are at last,'' she said a little too brightly as she entered the sitting room and placed the large silver tray on the low table in front of the sofa. She was determined not to let the darkness of his aura plunder her vitality or his sexual attraction to set her off balance again. She handed him a plate with a large, sliced beef sandwich and potato crisps—potato chips, as an American would call them. Her own sandwich was much smaller, made of cheese and tomatoes, but she wondered how she was going to get it past the dry tightness in her throat.

''Thank you very much,'' he said, taking the plate. ''I'm afraid I'm imposing.''

''Not at all,'' she half lied. ''It's the least I could do to thank you for coming to my rescue, although I'm afraid I foolishly overreacted to my cat's yowling.''

''You live here alone?''

His question sounded innocent enough, and it was followed by the crunch of lettuce as he took a large bite of the sandwich. But Claire hesitated. Why was he asking that? The color of his aura made her cautious. A person's aura was part of the living being, and it usually changed hues even from moment to moment as emotions shifted, but this man's aura remained as black as ever. ''Yes,'' she replied, lifting her chin, ''but I have people dropping by all the time.''

He gave her a rather sardonic look, and she knew she'd read him wrong. His reason for asking wasn't to see if he would have privacy in which to chop her to bits with an ax. ''I'm sure you do, Mrs. St. John.'' He pronounced her name the American way, and somehow it sounded more interesting to her ears.

She grinned nervously, trying to relax, wanting to like this man of darkness, wanting to find out the source of his wound and heal it. "It's not Mrs. And you can call me Claire if you'd like."

His lips tilted in a small smile. "Claire, then. Are you from this area?"

"Lived here all my life." She eased her throat with a sip of hot tea. "In this house."

"That's interesting," he said, then added—wistfully she thought, "not many people have those kinds of roots."

"Where are your roots?" The moment she asked the question, she regretted it. The darkness around him seemed to intensify, and his face was bleak. "I don't know, really." He gave a short, cynical laugh. "It's the curse of being an American, I suppose. We all came from somewhere else. Actually, part of the reason I'm here is to . . look up my ancestors. I think they came from around here. Is there a local courthouse that would have records of births and deaths and marriages and that sort of thing?"

"Maybe the local vicar," she told him. "But most of the old church records are sealed to prevent them from deteriorating. Your best bet would be to go to Somerset House in London where all the records are stored."

He smiled and nodded his thanks, and she sensed he appreciated the information, but he fell silent and asked no further questions. The silence continued until she wanted to squirm in her seat. My God, this is awkward, she thought, searching for small talk. She recalled that he'd told her he was researching a book. "So, what are you writing about?"

He looked at her quizzically. "Writing?"

"Your book. You said you were writing a book."

He set the plate down on his knees and reached for the china teacup. In his large hands, it looked particularly feminine and fragile.

"Actually I'm doing research right now. I haven't started the book yet."

"Oh." She was only trying to make conversation, but his words were just short of curt, so she decided not to pursue it and dropped the subject with a final offer. "Well, if there is anything I can help you with just let me know. I have several friends at the British Library."

Michael Townsend had wolfed down the sandwich in spite of its size, and Claire was glad she'd offered it. The man obviously had been famished. He leaned back against the light gray-and-pink floral sofa, and for the first time she saw him, or rather, psychically, felt him, relax. She sensed he was both physically and emotionally exhausted.

"That is very kind of you, and I may take you up on it." He gestured to the wall of books behind her. "I see you have a quite a library yourself. I hope you will forgive me, but while I was waiting, I took the liberty of checking it out. Very . . . esoteric."

Claire felt the temperature in her face rise slightly. Although she did not advertise her interest in the occult, neither did she hide it when asked. At the moment, however, she was distinctly uncomfortable with the insinuation behind his words . . . that her library was somehow suspect.

"It must be obvious to you, then," she replied a little coldly, "that I am a student of the occult."

He showed little reaction, positive or negative, to her somewhat defensive reply. But a moment later, he surprised her again by leaning forward and asking, "Do you know anything about magic?"

While he was waiting for Claire St. John to join him, Michael had wandered aimlessly around the sitting room at the front of her farmhouse, surveying the furnishings and decor of the room, building his impression of the woman who lived here from the things with which she surrounded herself. Besides several hunkering and sleeping cats nestled into chairs and on windowsills here and there, the most notable aspect of the room was its floor-to-ceiling book-shelves that lined two walls and were filled to overflowing. His landlady was obviously an avid reader.

Upon closer examination of the titles, however, Michael's eyes widened. This was no ordinary library. Most of the books here were distinctly occult in nature. There were books on ghosts. Spiritualism. Psychic healing. Tarot reading. Angels. Alchemy. Something called psychometry. Astrology. Witchcraft. Hundreds of titles that took him completely by surprise.

Claire St. John did not appear to be the sort of person who would indulge in anything occult. In spite of his initial impression of her as a warden, he'd changed his mind and decided she looked more like a Sunday school teacher, pleasant and fair and appealingly tweedy in her herringbone slacks and pink sweater. She did not look like a witch or a sorceress. Certainly not like a gypsy fortune-teller. He turned and studied her as she entered the room with their lunch on a tray. Nope. She simply wasn't the type. Maybe these books belonged to someone else. A husband. A room-mate.

But she'd told him she lived alone and that she wasn't a Mrs. When he pressed her about the esoteric nature of her book collection, she had told him unblinkingly that she was a student of the occult. A thought had struck him suddenly. Although he hadn't seen a book specifically about it on her shelves, surely if she knew anything about the occult, she must know something about magic.

"Magic?" She looked up at him in surprise. "Why do you want to know about magic?"

He hesitated, not wishing to reveal his real reason for coming to England or to air his family's dirty laundry. "It . . . interests me," he hedged. "It's part of the subject I am investigating."

"What do you know about magic?"

"Nothing."

She stared at him, frowning slightly, and he could guess

her thoughts: how can a person write a book on a subject about which he knows nothing? "I always begin a project, whether it is an academic paper or, as in this case, a possible book-length manuscript, as close as I can to ground zero," he offered in impromptu explanation. "That way I come to it unbiased, and as I pursue my research, I can form more objective opinions." It wasn't exactly true, but he hoped it sounded plausible.

She must have thought so, for she only shrugged slightly. "I don't know a lot about it," she told him. "I myself am not a magician." She paused and shot a suspicious glance at him. "I'm assuming you mean real magic, not those silly stage shows where an actor uses sleight-of-hand to fool the audience."

Actually, he had thought the magical-looking paraphernalia in the box might have been part of just such a stage act. He frowned. "What do you mean, *real* magic?"

"You *are* starting at ground zero, aren't you?" She put her half-eaten sandwich on her plate and set it on the table. She closed her eyes for a brief moment, as if considering what to tell him, and he wondered in that instant what drove her interest in the occult? If she did not know much about magic, what was her area of expertise? Or did she have one?

"Real magic, according to what I have read, is the use of ceremony and ritual to focus the mind's power, which in turn supposedly causes external events to happen according to the magician's will."

Her definition summoned images of the abracadabra foolishness of children at play, of a kid waving a magic wand and expecting to turn a frog into a prince. Or of Mickey Mouse in the robes of the Sorcerer's Apprentice. In a word, childish. But she'd taken his question seriously and had answered it; so he concealed his feelings.

"I see. Does it . . . well, does it work?"

"As I said, I am not a magician. But there are many who believe it is powerful indeed. I know for a fact there are many ceremonial magicians in the London area. If you want to learn more, there's a store in London called the Alchymical Book Shoppe that has a lot of books and things concerning magic. I don't go there much myself, although it has a reputation for stocking everything that's ever been written about the occult. Frankly,'' she laughed uneasily, "I find the energy in there a little dark.''

Dark energy. Again he didn't understand what she meant. "Are you talking about black magic?"

"Not exactly. But black magic is one reason why I don't like to go there. I'm certain that among that store's clientele there are magicians who have gone black.''

The words to a song sprang to mind—"That Old Black Magic''—and Michael glanced at her, puzzled. "Isn't it all black magic?''

She gave him a patient smile. "Unfortunately, when most people think about magic, they think about either black magic or stage tricks. Sorcerers casting evil spells or rabbits out of hats.''

Michael gave her a wry smile. "What else is there?''

"Well, in my understanding, most magicians are nothing like that. Their magic is very spiritual, 'white,' if you will. It is their religion, their path to the One God.''

Michael was not a religious man, and this unexpected turn in her explanation of magic seemed beyond his requirements at the moment. He had no intention of becoming involved in a conversation about religion with this woman. Still, he was intrigued by the idea of white magic.

"Do you know any white magicians? I suppose I ought to interview both kinds, to give the full picture.''

She gazed at him intently, and he could almost feel her scrutiny. He knew she must be wondering what in the hell he was really up to.

"There is one, an old woman who lives in this area, but I doubt if you could get an appointment to see her. She's a recluse. I've only heard about her. I've never met her myself. Supposedly she is quite a powerful practitioner of white magic. She calls herself Lady Sarah.''

Claire stood and gathered the plates, and Michael took this as his cue to be on his way, too. He was sorry, for it meant a return to his infernal private torments and the shadows of his lonely existence. He grasped at anything that would extend the moment. "How can I find this Lady Sarah?"

She shook her head. "You would be better off taking the train into London and visiting the Alchymical Book Shoppe. They should be able to put you in touch with magicians of either bent."

Another thought occurred to him. "The place of records you mentioned. Can you direct me there?"

Claire opened a drawer in a nearby desk and brought out a map, which she spread on the dining room table. "You may borrow this, but I'd like to have it back when you're finished. My guests often need directions." She circled the locations of both Somerset House and the Alchymical Book Shoppe. "The major tourist attractions are all listed and numbered on the back, as is London's underground system, the tube, which is quite safe to use. Just take the train into the city and transfer to other means of public transportation. A day pass is the cheapest way to go. Now, if you will please excuse me, Dr. Townsend," she said with finality, signaling him that it was really time to go, "I have some errands I need to run."

Chapter Four

CAMERON ST. JOHN STARED AT HIS COMPUTER SCREEN. There must be some mistake. This could not be. The numbers were all wrong. There was no way this could be happening.

No way.

Panic rising, he shut down his desktop computer and restarted it in the unlikely event he had logged onto the main system improperly and this nightmare was a computer glitch of some sort.

But it wasn't a computer error. The stock he'd purchased, based on an insider tip, had plummeted nearly off the market. Not only had he invested heavily, he'd bought the stock using a client's account without authorization, and now that client was stuck with a substantial margin call. Unless the stock recovered later in the day, Cameron would have to find the money to meet the call immediately or get caught at his patently illegal scheme.

Sinking into his swivel chair, he buried his face in his hands, shocked that this could have happened. He'd been assured the aggressive stock was on the rise, and he'd expected to earn a quick, hefty profit that would impress the hell out of his new and potentially most important client, Delilah Mason. She was a powerful woman in London, and he'd been working hard for several months to gain her confidence and prove to her that he was a shrewd, daring, and savvy investment advisor. The best broker to handle her money. He believed if he was successful with her money—only a relatively small amount of which she had entrusted to him—she would not only increase her portfolio with him, but also recommend him to her friends. This would put him in control of some of England's oldest wealth. It was a heady thought. Powerful.

And it would make him a rich man.

But now. Oh, God, what was he going to do? He wanted to kill the "friend" who'd given him the tip in the first place. Cameron scowled, wondering briefly if he'd been set up. He'd never totally trusted Omar Solis, his fellow broker who sat even now only a few desks away in the large, undivided bull-pen office at Johnson and Howard Investments, Ltd. Why had he listened to him on this?

Because he'd been greedy, he acknowledged bitterly. He'd wanted so badly to make a big score with Delilah Mason, he had let his avarice overrun his good sense, and he'd made a very foolish and naive move. Now, unless he could cover his tracks quickly, he faced certain ruin. For if he got caught, he'd be thrown out of the brokerage, he would be ostracized by his new circle of friends, most of whom were also friends of Miss Mason, and he might even go to jail.

Cameron laughed nervously at these fearsome thoughts. Of course it would never come to that. He would not get caught. He would find a way to fix the situation. He would learn from this costly incident, and he damn sure would not make such a mistake again.

But where in bloody hell could he come up with that amount of money on such short notice? As he ran over the possibilities in his mind, he began to sweat profusely and his hands grew clammy. He doubted he could raise it by the close of trading today, and he could only pray that neither his client nor his supervisor got wind of it before morning.

Money. Money. He needed money. There was only one person he knew who had the kind of money he needed. His sister. He knew Claire still had every pound their father had left her squirreled away in some low-interest account. Claire never took a risk.

Could he find a way to access her money? He thought of asking her to give it to him as a loan, but the idea turned his stomach. He didn't want to ask his sister for anything. Claire had gone all funny since she'd become so involved in all that psychic crap. Cameron snorted and ran his hands through his thick, dark hair. He had to admit his sister had always had an uncanny ability to seemingly read his thoughts, but he'd ascribed it to their twinship, not to anything mysterious or psychic. As twins, they'd grown up so close that she knew everything about him and could anticipate his thoughts and actions.

That disconcerted him further. He had no intention of telling her why he needed the money, but would she be able to guess his secret? He had never been able to hide his emotions from her, and he was certain she would read his desperation at a glance. But that could work in his favor, he reasoned, brightening. She was protective of him, always had been, and he would likely be able to take advantage of that now.

Still, he hated like hell to ask for a loan from Claire. He couldn't face her syrupy goodness, nor did he like the idea of being financially obligated to her. Although she'd never criticized him explicitly, he knew she was shocked that he had run through his own inheritance, buying an expensive car and a first-class condominium in the Docklands. She didn't understand that having a certain image was vital to his career in the cutthroat world of high finance. If he wanted to *be* successful, he must *look* successful. What wealthy client would trust his investments to a bloke who drove a Toyota for God's sake?

He was also well aware that Claire did not like his new friends. She'd said she could see in their auras that they were shallow snobs without real character, even though they bore the surnames of some of England's most aristocratic families. She had been adamant that he drop them, and they had had a serious quarrel. Cameron hadn't been to see her in nearly a month.

What did she know anyhow? he growled to himself, shutting down the computer again and reaching for his cashmere jacket. She was probably jealous that he'd made it big while she languished in that dreary farmhouse, and she'd trotted out that ridiculous psychic mumbo-jumbo to make him feel bad.

Well, she hadn't succeeded. The only thing he felt bad about at the moment was his need for quick cash. In a large amount.

Then pure inspiration hit him. That dreary farmhouse. Half of it was his. Their father had willed it to the both of them, and he'd never asked Claire to buy him out. He reached for a pencil. What would half of that property be worth? He scribbled his calculations on a calendar pad, then eased back in his chair and straightened his tie.

Enough. It was worth enough.

And he would not have to grovel for a loan from his insipid, sanguine sister. Grabbing his briefcase, he looked at his watch. Two o'clock. He should have time to drive out to Montlivet, make his demand of Claire, and return in time for the evening's social events.

He *had* to make this work. He could not face the social scene tonight unless he knew his mistake was covered and that by tomorrow it would be rectified with no one the wiser.

Making his way hastily toward the door, he didn't see Omar Solis until it was too late to avoid him.

"Had a good day, Sin-Jen?" the swarthy man asked.

Was that a smile or a leer on his thick lips? Cameron glared at the other stockbroker, knowing in his gut that this man had set him up, but because he'd risen to the un-equivocally illegal bait, he could not accuse him of a thing.

"I've had better," he snarled.

That evening, Claire joined the small séance circle in Maeve Willoughby's large, old-fashioned living room.

"How've you been?" her mentor asked in polite conversation.

Claire glowered at her. "This has been the worst day of my life." She was sorry that her answer sounded so rude and abrupt, but she was nearly at her wits' end. She needed to spill her troubles, and she could trust these friends not to think her crazy. Bitsy Flanagan stood up to give her a hug.

"Poor Claire," she said, her voice dripping with mock sympathy. "I know it's difficult, housing that handsome hunk under your roof. But I couldn't turn him away, the darling. He'd come such a long distance to visit our little town."

Claire gave her friend a stony stare. "Couldn't you see it?" she demanded, wishing she had done as she'd planned and had this out with Bitsy beforehand. But one thing and then another had prevented her from taking her intended walk, the last of which was Cameron's most unexpected and upsetting visit.

"See what? All I saw was one incredibly good-looking man. Wearing no wedding ring."

"His aura is black, solid, unchanging black." Claire heard concerned murmurs from the others, and Bitsy instantly dropped her flippant attitude.

"What does that mean?" the petite Irishwoman asked. She was the least experienced in the group and had much to learn about psychic phenomena.

"Well, it's not good for him," Claire replied, turning to Maeve, "but I'm wondering if it could be harmful to me to have someone like that around."

Maeve looked concerned and indicated for Claire to take

a seat at the round wooden dining table where later the five psychics gathered there would attempt to make contact with the spirit world. "No wonder you look a fright," she said directly, but with concern rather than lack of tact. "Perhaps first you should tell me what this is all about."

Claire sat down, and a weight seemed to ease from her shoulders. Surrounded by her friends, fellow travelers into the world of the supernatural, she allowed tears of relief to spring to her eyes. "It's not just him," she told them, her words strained over the tightness in her throat. "It's the skeleton, and the ring, and the ghost . . ."

"Whoa! Wait a minute! Hold on!" Maeve said, shoving a cup of tea at her. "Want to go over that again?"

Claire looked at her pointedly. "Like I said, I've had a bad day."

She told them everything, starting with the discovery of the skeleton in the tree roots and the ominous resonance of the ring when she'd held it. "Then after all that, Dr. Townsend showed up with his aura all dark and eerie . . ."

"Oh, God, Claire, if I'd only known," Bitsy cried, genuinely distressed. "But I can't see auras . . ."

"I know. I shouldn't have jumped on you. It's not your fault."

"What was that about a ghost? I thought you mentioned a ghost," piped up Jim Amesbury, the only male medium in the group.

"I was getting to that." She told them all about her encounter, describing in detail the incident in the kitchen, but leaving out the part about her hysterical screaming fit and her tenant coming to the rescue. Those details were not, after all, pertinent.

"I'm certain that must have been an earthbound spirit," Maeve said when Claire had finished.

"But why in my kitchen? My place has never been haunted."

"It must have to do with that skeleton. The ectoplasmic energy was probably released when the wind toppled the tree. From your psychometric impressions, it's my bet that the person in question did not die of natural causes, and its spirit has not yet passed completely over."

Claire shivered. "You think somebody was killed and buried under the tree? But that tree was enormous. How . . . ?"

"Did the police say how old the bones were?"

Claire shook her head. "They were going to run tests. Why?"

"I think," Maeve said at last, "that someone might have been killed, buried, and a tree planted on the grave to cover it up. Must have happened some time ago since the tree was so large."

The small group sat in stunned silence. Montlivet was a quiet burg. Nothing much happened here. There was very little crime.

"Certainly something as sensational as a murder would have been remembered by the police, even if it happened a long time ago," Bitsy said at last.

"But no one ever knew about the murder," Claire replied in a low voice, getting a sudden and clear impression that this was the case, as if the soul of the victim was whispering in her ear.

"And the spirit won't rest until his—or her—story is at last revealed and justice in some way or another is served," Maeve finished, nodding in agreement.

"Maybe we should try to summon that spirit now," Jim said, but Claire shook her head.

"Please. Don't. I mean, I've just been through a hellish day, and I don't think I could stand to encounter that spirit again at the moment. In fact, I had already decided I shouldn't stay for the séance. Maybe you can contact the ghost after I leave."

"I don't think it would be wise in any event," Maeve told the others. "Such newly released energy is bound to be powerful, and we are, all of us, rather novice at this business of summoning spirits." It was true. Even though

Maeve and the Amesburys had been mediums for years,
none had ever successfully participated in a materialization.
"I would hate for things to get out of hand. And besides,"
she added, giving Claire an understanding smile, "I don't
want you to go. I think you need to be among friends tonight."

Claire was glad Maeve was an astute psychic and had
picked up on her feelings. She hadn't really wanted to go,
and she *did* need to be with her friends. "But what about
the séance?"

"There's always next week. Instead, why don't I do a
tarot reading? Let's see if we can get to the bottom of
what's causing your handsome visitor such stress."

"Thanks, Maeve." Claire grinned at her friend, grateful.
The rest expressed their enthusiasm for the change in plans,
and Maeve went to fetch her well-worn pack of tarot cards.
She was a talented reader, and Claire felt a twinge of excited anticipation as the medium shuffled the cards.

"The intent of the reading is to learn more about Dr. . . .
What did you say his name was?"

"Townsend. Dr. Michael Townsend."

"To learn what's up with our interesting Dr. Townsend." She finished her shuffle, allowing Claire to cut the
deck, then turned the first card face up.

The Hermit.

A trump card. One of the twenty-two cards in what is
known as the major arcana. The important cards.

"At the heart of the matter," Maeve said, reminding
them that the first card in a reading exposed the issue at
hand. "He's looking for something." The Hermit depicted
a cloaked figure holding a lantern. A seeker.

"He told me he was here to research a book," Claire
offered, but Maeve shook her head. "I'm not getting that
it's that kind of search. Let's see what comes up." She
pulled a second card.

The Ten of Swords.

"Cripes!" Bitsy exclaimed when she saw the card showing a man with ten swords stuck in his back, lying in a pool of blood.

"Obviously, he's very distraught," Maeve remarked wryly. "Some rather unpleasant things have happened to this guy. No wonder his aura is dark."

The next card indicated the hopes and fears of the man in question.

The Empress. Mother Earth.

"Another trump," Maeve noted. She studied the card a moment, then added, "It is a woman he seeks."

"Tough luck, Claire. He's probably after his runaway wife," Bitsy said, attempting a joke.

Claire laughed, but inside she was not amused.

The fourth card, in the position of events present or passing, was the Devil.

"Another trump," Maeve pointed out. "Three trumps could indicate that this search is a major issue for this fellow. And this particular card, especially in conjunction with the Ten of Swords, tells me he has been one bedeviled man. I wonder what's gone on in his life?"

"I always have trouble interpreting the Devil card," said Audrey Amesbury, who until that moment had spoken little the entire evening. "What do you make of it, Maeve?"

"Well, it can indicate 'bedevilment' of varying degrees, from small, annoying harassments to really big stuff."

"Dr. Townsend's bedevilment must have been serious to have darkened his aura like that," Claire said. "What kind of trouble could cause an aura to turn black?"

Maeve thought a moment, her hand and the next card poised in midair. "Oh . . . an emotionally upsetting event, like a death or a betrayal or a failed love affair could blacken an aura temporarily. However, a series of such events, or a curse of some kind, could make it permanent."

"A curse? Now we're sounding like a bunch of gypsies," Audrey objected. A little self-righteously, Claire thought.

"Curses exist," Maeve stated, unperturbed, and laid the

fifth card on top of the second. "Forces working for or against him."

The Queen of Wands.

"The fire queen. Another woman?" Maeve speculated.

"What's your sign, Claire?" Bitsy giggled. "Are you a fire sign?"

"You know perfectly well I'm a Gemini, an air sign," Claire replied, ruffled by her friend's continuing insistence that she should become romantically involved with Michael Townsend.

The next card, indicating events in the near future, was the Seven of Cups.

"Temptation is headed his way," Maeve predicted.

"That figure always reminds me of a stage magician," Bitsy said, pointing to the man silhouetted on the card who was looking at a sky filled with cups that offered him all kinds of things, both good and bad.

"He told me he was interested in magic," Claire recalled.

Maeve let her hand drop to the table. "Oh? How so?"

Claire shrugged. "He said he was researching it. That it's going to be the subject of his book. But he doesn't know anything about magic. I suggested he visit the Alchymical Book Shoppe."

"Ugh. I hate that place," Audrey said with a visible shudder.

"Well, this card could well indicate that he will get mixed up with magic in the near future," Maeve continued, tapping the card. "I just hope his heart is in the right place."

The next three cards indicated indecision, deception and confusion. "I wouldn't want to be in his shoes," Jim said, pulling a dour face.

Maeve placed the final card in the throw.

The Hanged Man.

The drawing on the card was of a man hanging by one foot from a T-shaped tree, and in Claire's experience, it represented a person whose entire life was going to be set on its heel. "His world is going to be turned upside down," Claire uttered, feeling tangible pity for Dr. Michael Townsend.

"Or it already has been," Maeve suggested quietly. "That could account for the aura thing. But my guess is, things are going to get worse for him before they get better."

Chapter Five

THE FOLLOWING MORNING, REFRESHED AFTER A night of sound sleep, Michael took the high-speed train into London as Claire had suggested. In his briefcase he carried all the items he'd found in his father's attic, except for his mother's letter and the curious empty bookbinding. It was only the "magical" items that concerned him, for he hoped someone at the occult bookshop could tell him what they were.

He planned to stop first at Somerset House to see if he could find any records concerning a woman named Stella Townsend. It was a long shot. He didn't even know for sure that his mother was from Montlivet, nor did he know her age or maiden name. He supposed she was born in the late twenties or sometime in the thirties. It would likely take time and patience and a lot of luck, but he reminded himself grimly that time was something he had a lot of these days.

Waiting for a stoplight to change, he spied a large hotel across the street. A hotel would have public telephones . . .

He knew this was an even longer shot than Somerset House, but he made his way through the bustling crowd and entered the lobby. A bank of pay phones lined a corridor. He picked up a London telephone directory and thumbed through the pages. Townsend. Townsend. There were plenty of Londoners named Townsend, he discovered quickly, but none listed as Stella Townsend. He'd had the same luck looking her up in the Montlivet directory as well. But then, he hadn't really expected to find her in either. That would have been entirely too easy. He returned the directory to its holder, left the hotel, and continued on his way.

It took most of the morning, but with the help of an efficient clerk, Michael obtained the record of a marriage between an Englishwoman named Stella Grisham and an American soldier stationed in the U.K., Sergeant Thomas Townsend. The record showed Montlivet, Essex, as the place of birth of the bride.

He also learned the name of his grandparents. Stella Grisham, the records showed, had been born in 1937 to Margaret Grisham, née Beauchamp, wife of Arthur Grisham of London. Michael had never heard of Margaret or Arthur Grisham; his own kin, yet people so remote to him they didn't even seem real.

There was no record on file of the death of a Stella Townsend. Or a Stella Grisham. Or any of the other names he'd guessed at in an effort to discover the alias his mother might have assumed upon her return to England.

If she had, indeed, returned here.

In short, even though he'd learned some things about his mother, he'd hit a dead end as far as locating her.

What next? Go to the old folks' homes and peer into the faces of the nearly dead to see if any of them resembled him? But he reminded himself his mother wasn't that old. She would be only sixty-one now, if she still lived. She'd been very young when she married Thomas Townsend.

"You might try the Salvation Army or the Red Cross," the clerk suggested when Michael asked where to turn next if one was searching for a lost relative. "They have a surprising track record for locating missing persons."

But Michael couldn't bear the thought that his mother

might have become a bag lady or some street derelict. If she had, he didn't want to know. Discouraged, he went to a pub, where he ordered a pint of stout and a meal and considered his next move. Maybe he should just go back to the apartment, gather his things and return to the airport to catch the next flight to New York. Searching for Stella Townsend was like looking for Waldo. London was an immense city. England was a populous country. His chances of finding her were slim.

Why was it so damned important that he find his mother? He already knew the truth of his life, that she'd deserted the family long ago. It had hurt when he'd discovered her betrayal in the letter, but he was a grown man. Get over it, he told himself.

But something inside wouldn't be silenced. Something that said that if he ever wanted to turn his bad-luck life around, he must find his mother. It made no sense to the rational, reasonable man he was, but it drove him nonetheless. He finished his lunch and set out for his second destination of the day.

The Alchymical Book Shoppe was housed in a nondescript storefront on a cobbled side street of London and was marked by a small, faded sign that hung out from the stone wall above the door. Stenciled on the plate-glass window were the words RARE AND HARD-TO-FIND BOOKS, OCCULT ANTIQUITIES, and interestingly, MAGIC SUPPLIES. He turned the brass knob and went inside.

The day was overcast, which deepened the gloom inside the musty shop, and Michael had to pause a moment to allow his eyes to adjust to the low light. He recalled Claire's description of this place as dark. It was dark, all right, but in a different sense than she'd meant.

He looked around for the owner or a sales clerk, but there appeared to be no one else in the shop. Perhaps he or she had stepped out for a moment. While he waited for someone to show up, he began perusing the books on the shelves along one wall. The volumes looked to be used books, some of them worn hardcovers, others tattered paperbacks. But it was apparent from the titles that Claire had steered him to the right place. *Mind and Magic. The Occult. The Dark Side of History,* subtitled *Subversive Magic and the Occult Underground.*

He noticed a section marked NOVELS and picked one off the shelf. *Omega.* The front cover captured his attention immediately. On it was a beautiful naked woman holding aloft the image of the earth on fire. He raised his eyebrows as he read the description on the jacket cover. It was about witches.

Dr. Michael Townsend suddenly felt very foolish and out of place. He knew there were a few students on campus at Strathmore who, embracing the current fad for paganism, had claimed to be witches, but he could never take such a thing seriously. Or magic, either, for that matter. The whole idea of occultism, he believed, was for fools. His briefcase filled with the magical instruments suddenly weighed heavily in his grasp.

He replaced the book, turned to go, and was startled to find himself facing a short, fat, balding man with bulging eyes. How long had he been there?

"May I help you, sir?" the man said.

Michael stared into his huge, hypnotic eyes and grew increasingly uncomfortable. Not only did the proprietor look odd, but he also seemed to radiate some kind of force or power or unseen energy that sent a chill up Michael's spine. He was dressed like a character from a movie, wearing a long, rust-colored sarong and sandals. His hair, what there was left of it, was pulled to the nape and braided in a single coarse, greasy-looking pigtail that almost reached his waist.

But as to the source or nature of the mysterious power of his presence Michael was uncertain. Was this the dark energy of which Claire had spoken?

Michael repressed his urge to push past the man and run back to the safety of the street and gathered his rationality around him once again. "Perhaps," he replied, straightening. He raised the briefcase slightly. "I have in here items that I found in my father's attic after he died. Although I have no idea what they are, I believe they might have something to do with magic. I was wondering if you or someone else knowledgeable about the subject of magic might be able to take a look at them and enlighten me as to their nature."

The proprietor of the store hesitated, then indicated for Michael to place the briefcase on a nearby countertop. Michael opened the lid and stepped away, watching as the man began to rummage through the items.

"These for sale?" he asked after a few moments, his expression detached, almost disinterested.

Michael had not considered that anyone would want to buy them. "I . . . well, I suppose they could be. But what are they?"

The man gave Michael a sideways look. "Are you serious? You don't know what you've got here?"

Michael shrugged. "I have only a vague notion that they might be props of some sort, maybe for a magic show."

The man shot him a scornful look, then went back to his exploration, taking each item from the box and examining it carefully. He held up the wand, twisted it and telescoped it to its full length. It measured about a yard and was divided into twelve equal bands of differing colors, the once-bright paint now faded. Secured at one end was a lotus flower, carved of wood and painted white and green.

"This was never used in any vaudeville act," he growled at Michael. "It is a true magic wand, the type once handmade and used by initiates of the O.R.R. Et A.C. and the Golden Dawn. Crowley and Yeats and those folks. Could even be of that era. Hard to tell."

Michael looked at the man, nonplussed. "I beg your pardon, sir, but I have no idea what you are talking about."

The man turned his gaze on Michael, his expression clearly skeptical of Michael's ignorance. "Magic. I'm talking about magic and those secret magical orders from the turn of the last century.''

He waited for a reply, but Michael was speechless, so the storekeeper returned to the box. ''This,'' he said, holding aloft a bronze disc about five inches in diameter and engraved with a pentagram, ''is a magical symbol. As are these . . .'' He produced two lamens, or badgelike ornaments, threaded onto faded ribbons, one white, bearing the image of a cross, the other black, showing a triangle.

A brass chalice was next, rather battered and tarnished, unremarkable except for the odd engravings on the bowl. The pigtailed man studied the designs intently for a long while, then gave Michael another suspicious glance. But without speaking further, he merely placed it next to the other items on the counter. He brought out a wooden-handled dagger. It was short, with a wide blade, and the hilt was painted yellow. The man spoke again at last. ''This is what is known as an athame. A ritual dagger. Where did you say you got this stuff?''

''It . . . was in my father's attic.''

''Was he a magician, your father?''

''I don't know. I don't think so.''

''You sure you don't want to sell these?''

Michael shrugged, but the man had already returned his attention to the box and was feeling around for the smaller pieces. There was a slender circlet, like a crown, some faded flags or banners with symbols sewn on them, and finally, he brought out the ring. Squinting, he examined it closely, and Michael heard an audible intake of breath.

Suddenly, the man jerked his head up, his fish eyes piercing Michael's even gaze. ''Who the hell are you?''

''Excuse me?''

''This ring. You claim this was your father's?''

Michael was bewildered at the incredulity on the man's face. What was the big deal?

''I found it in that box with the other things. I have no

further explanation than what I have already told you. Why? What's so special about that ring?''

The man's expression was shuttered instantly. "You're an American, aren't you? Who sent you here?"

"A . . . friend."

Michael saw the man make a strange gesture with his hands but did not respond except to stare at him in total incomprehension. The man eyed him darkly.

"I cannot help you further," he said as if suddenly coming to a decision. "You must speak with Delilah."

"Delilah?" Michael checked a grin. It sounded like the name of a saloon hostess in an old Western movie, and he decided the man must thrive on things absurd and theatric. "Who's Delilah?"

Without answering, the shopkeeper went behind the counter and reached for a scrap of paper and a pen. "I can say no more."

Michael persisted. "How can I find this Delilah?"

The man raised his head and narrowed his eyes. "You *can't* find Delilah," he replied. "But if you will give me your name and a telephone number, if she chooses to, she will find you."

Claire stood for a long while outside the bank, her mind and heart at war. Intuitively, she knew she shouldn't give Cameron the money he had demanded of her, that he would just do with it as he had the rest of his inheritance—squander it. But her brother was correct that they were co-owners of the farmhouse, and he had every right to ask her to buy out his half.

It would seriously deplete her savings, but she supposed she had no choice. Otherwise, he might insist they put it up for sale and divide the proceeds, and there was no way Claire was going to let that happen. Fairfield House was her home.

Although he hadn't told her why he needed so much money in such a hurry, she knew he was in trouble, and as always, her first instinct was to come to his rescue. However, his attitude on the phone had angered her thoroughly. It was his life, she thought grimly, squaring her shoulders and going into the building. If he wanted to ruin it, it should be no concern of hers. She was tired of always bailing him out. This, she vowed, would be the last time.

Less than an hour later, at home again, she heard the sound of a car in the drive and looked out through the lace curtains in the sitting room to see her twin getting out of his racy black Jaguar XK8. He was a handsome man, but today his face was drawn, and a scowl marred his features. Claire wiped her palms against her slacks and went to open the front door.

"Do you have the money?" Cameron asked as he brushed past her.

"It's nice to see you, too," she retorted, closing the door behind him.

He whirled and faced her with angry eyes. "Look, sis, I'm in a hurry. I don't have time for small talk. Let's get this over with."

Claire's heart constricted, not because of his rude attitude, but because psychically she felt, she *knew*, that he was in terrible trouble. She went to him and put her hand on his arm. "Cam, oh, Cammy, tell me what's going on. You know I want to help you."

He pulled his arm from her grasp. "Don't call me Cammy. I'm not a schoolboy. And if you want to help, give over the money."

Claire felt as if he had slapped her. He'd always been Cammy, as to him she'd been Clary. So what if those nicknames were remnants of their childhood? It was a childhood she cherished. Fighting tears, she went to the sideboard in the adjoining dining room.

"I have everything in order," she murmured, the muscles in her throat tightening. "My attorney couldn't be here on such short notice, but because he's aware that time is critical for you, he has agreed to warrant your signature in absentia, since he's known us both all our lives. He wants you to sign in these places." She indicated several lines marked with an "X" on the legal papers deeding her the house. "When the house is mine, legally, the money"—she held up an envelope—"is yours."

It wasn't like her to be so curt, but she was stung by his insensitivity to her feelings, and in a way she wanted him to hurt like she did. Cameron did not seem to notice, or care, how she felt. Hastily, he scribbled his name on the lines she'd indicated, then reached for the envelope.

"It is in cash, isn't it? As we agreed?"

Claire didn't reply, just watched as he opened the envelope and answered his own question. He took only long enough to count the notes, then stuffed the envelope into his jacket pocket and headed for the door. Just before he left, he turned and gave his sister a twisted smile. "Don't worry, sis. Everything's fine. It was just time to get this last piece of business between us done." With that, he was gone.

Claire knew without a doubt that everything was *not* fine. Her mind was drawn back to the presence of the Tower card on her kitchen table the night of the terrible storm, and she couldn't help but wonder if Cameron was about to be knocked off his own tower of power.

A part of her would have liked that.

She went into the kitchen and made tea, a ritual that often served to soothe her when she was upset, but today it didn't work. Her hand shook as she carried the cup and saucer to the window. Outside, the clouds were beginning to break up, and the sun shone down onto a meadow that was brilliant in its English springtime green. Claire allowed her mind to wander back through time to happier days, when she and Cameron had frolicked like wild colts across that meadow, creating adventures and being their own favorite playmates.

When had it gone so wrong between them?

But Claire realized her relationship with her brother had

been going wrong for a long, long time, and that she had just not wanted to admit it. In school, she had not wanted to believe that he was a troublemaker. She had come to his rescue time and time again, covering for him and making excuses, always hoping he would outgrow his mischief. She could see now that he had been her personal rehabilitation project for a long time without her really recognizing it.

And she had failed.

She bit her lip. Perhaps it was just as well that his most recent demand had allowed her at last to make a break from him. As far as she was concerned, Cameron was on his own now. She supposed she had been a fool to remain so blindly loyal to him, for it was clear to her that her brother did not reciprocate that loyalty, nor did he wish to be rehabilitated. It was her nature to try to help people. That was why she took in strays and worked with difficult clients. She truly believed she could help them, and in her altruism she'd never until today suspected that her brother did not want her help. He had simply used her.

Claire blinked back tears, forcing her thoughts once again into the moment, when suddenly she became conscious of a small noise, a hissing sound emanating from the direction of the plumbing beneath the sink. Curious, she set the teacup on the drain board and knelt to open the cabinet doors to investigate. The sound was louder, but she saw no sign of a leak. Maybe a toilet was running somewhere in the old house.

After making the rounds of the plumbing outlets in her house, she found nothing amiss. Still the sound persisted, and she was certain it was in the plumbing system somewhere. She tried to think. Was the plumbing to the cottage next door tied into that of the main house? She couldn't remember, but decided to check.

She did not relish the idea of coming into contact with Dr. Townsend again, having received warnings from all her friends the night before that he could possibly be dangerous to her psychic health.

She hadn't seen him all day. Hopefully, he'd gone out. She would knock, of course, but if no one answered, she'd use her own key to let herself in, quickly check on the plumbing, and then be on her way again before he returned.

She reached for the key where it hung on a hook by the kitchen doorway, thinking about Michael Townsend and the tarot reading of the night before. Strangely, in spite of her friends' warnings, her fear of him seemed to have dissipated, replaced by compassion. Her heart went out to him, for the reading had revealed that he was a person experiencing terrible difficulties. She wondered how she might help him, but suddenly she stopped herself short.

Was she looking for another rehabilitation project? What made her think he wanted her help any more than Cameron did? Or that she'd be any more successful?

"Fool!" she muttered, grabbing the key and heading toward the rental apartment.

It was late afternoon when Michael returned to Montlivet, and he came back only slightly more enlightened than when he left. The owner of the Alchymical Book Shoppe had confirmed the objects in the box were magical in nature, not stage props at all, but probably antiques that might have been used by *fin de siècle* occult groups in England. But he'd offered no further explanation other than to recommend a few books which Michael now carried in a bag: *The Occult: A History, Esoteric Orders and Their Work*, and one with the outrageous title of *The Legacy of the Beast,* a biography of the most famous black magician of Edwardian England, Aleister Crowley.

As eager as he was to delve into the books, which he hoped would shed some light on the mysterious connection between his parents and the magical antiquities, he hadn't taken them out of the sack to start reading them aboard the train on the way back to the village. This wasn't the type of material that he, a scholar and a rational man, wished to be seen reading.

Michael did not ring at the front door of Claire's farm-house, for he had found a path that led from the lane directly to the cottage behind the main house. He did not wish to disturb her or in fact to be disturbed himself until he'd had time to read at least one of the books and get a better grasp on the subject of ceremonial magic.

He would learn what he could on his own, for he was reluctant to ask any more questions of Claire. Although she had been gracious in offering him a sandwich the previous afternoon, she had been reticent to discuss the subject of magic and seemed uncomfortable when he'd asked about her interest in the occult. At breakfast, she had returned to the warden-woman of the day before, serving his plate in almost total silence. He was still drawn to her, but she remained an enigma.

When he reached the door to the cottage, he heard a commotion coming from inside. It sounded like a vacuum cleaner. This was supposed to be a self-catering rental, and he expected no maid service. Who was in his room? Turning the knob, he found the door unlocked. He opened it and was greeted by the sight of the rounded curve of a woman's hips clad in black slacks. Claire St. John was straining over a piece of noisy, heavy equipment, her back to the door, and she had not heard him enter. He hesitated a moment before making his presence known, enjoying the view. Then, scolding himself for such sophomoric behavior, he set his bundles on a nearby occasional table and cleared his throat loudly.

Claire jumped as if she'd seen a ghost. She whirled to face him, one hand at her throat. With the other hand, she turned off the machine.

"Oh, you startled me!"

"It would seem I have. Please forgive me. What are you doing?"

Only then did he hear a metallic clink coming from the direction of the small kitchenette. "Just about got it, Ms.

St. John,'' came a man's voice. ''Shouldn't take but a tad longer.''

''The plumbing is broken,'' she explained, a little out of breath. ''I'm sorry, but the carpet is soaked. I've tried to get the water up with this . . .'' She pointed to the shop vac. ''But I'm afraid it is going to take some time to dry completely. Look, I'll be happy to call my friend at the Information Centre and have her find you another place to stay . . .''

Michael was tired and irritable from his rather unproductive trip into London, and he did not want to move to other quarters. He was used to a hostile world, but he couldn't understand why this woman seemed to be trying so hard to get him to leave her cottage. ''What exactly have I done to offend you, Ms. St. John?''

She shifted her gaze to a far corner of the room. ''I'm sorry. I don't understand . . .''

He went to her and took her arm, turning her to face him. ''You don't want me here, do you? Ever since I arrived, you have made excuses—the plumbing being one of them—to get me to change my mind about staying here.''

She yanked her arm away and glared at him. ''Do you think I soaked this carpet on purpose? To get rid of you, a paying client?'' She was almost yelling, and the fear had returned to her eyes. ''I . . . I am not stupid, Dr. Townsend. I am simply a woman of integrity. I wasn't planning on renting this place out again until I had the plumbing fixed, for I suspected something like this might happen.''

Michael doubted that she was telling the whole truth, for she seemed truly unnerved. By him? Of course he had startled her when he came in, but it seemed her fear went deeper than that. Maybe the woman was paranoid or suffered from some kind of psychosis that made her chronically fearful. He recalled the incident in her kitchen the day before when he'd found her screaming her head off in terror over nothing.

''My apologies,'' he said, not wishing to add further to

her distress. Neither did he wish to have to find other lodgings. "I was out of line." He reached over and took the hose to the vacuum from her hand. "I can finish this. And you needn't find me another rental. I simply won't walk on the carpet until it dries."

Chapter Six

WITH THE TIPS OF HER IMMACULATELY MANICURED nails, Delilah Mason parted the silken draperies that covered the windows of her elegant apartment high above London and looked down on the city below. She could see boats on the Thames, the dome of Saint Paul's, the buildings of the financial district where every day her already enormous wealth increased. She had not only been successful in the stock market, she had invested heavily and profitably in real estate as well. From where she stood, she could count the buildings she owned, those she had sold, those she wished to buy.

Delilah Mason had it all. She was beautiful, a darling of high society who enjoyed wealth, status, and privilege. Everyone wanted to know her secrets, to learn how she was so enduringly successful. She was constantly fielding questions from the media, politicians, even royals. She didn't really mind. In fact, she rather enjoyed their attention. She found it amusing to insist with a demure laugh that she had no secrets. That she was just lucky.

She *had* been lucky, she supposed. One made one's own luck, after all.

That was what magic was all about.

The only secret to her success was that she had used

magic to build an empire, but it was a secret she wasn't about to give away.

But creating wealth no longer held a challenge for Delilah. All along it had been merely a means to a more important end. She was bored to distraction with practicing over and over the magical skills she had already mastered. She was ready for the greater challenge that awaited, the more interesting playing field.

She was glad the time was upon her at last. She was ready to begin the Great Working that was both her birthright and her destiny.

Going to the large desk in one corner of the room, Delilah removed twelve dossiers in manila folders. She shuffled through them, admiring the photos. They were all handsome men, younger than she, although her much-speculated-about age was among her closely guarded secrets. She had selected them carefully as potential initiates for her magical High Court, for in addition to being easy to look at, they must also have certain specific qualities if they were to serve her effectively.

They must be daring. Courageous. Adventuresome. Loyal. And discreet.

They must also be . . . amoral. Unoffended by the unconventional rituals used in the level of magic they would be practicing.

The men all knew one another, although she had been careful to choose those without loyalties to old school chums within the group. Their loyalty must be only to her. She'd picked them from among London's young, fast, and elite; the new breed who sought thrills, power, and money. If they were good boys, she thought with a smile, she would give them all that and more.

If they were not . . .

Well, regrettable accidents happened.

There was only one piece missing in the plans she had so carefully laid out. She had chosen her High Court, but not her High Priest. For none of these men whose photos lay before her were of the caliber she sought in her mate.

Her magical mate.

She did not doubt the right man would come soon, for she'd been told when traveling on the astral plane to make things ready. In three days' time she was scheduled to finalize the purchase of the property that the last Delilah had consecrated for the ancient Temple of the Circle of the Lily. She would meet with the architect later the same day. She would spare no expense, waste no time, for the clock was ticking toward the turn of the century, the turn of the millennium, and she knew from both experience and training that this time would be like no other. That in this time she, Delilah Mason, would effect the most forceful magic brought forth in a thousand years. Of all the Delilahs in the ancient line of her breed, she would be the most powerful, and through her, the forces of darkness would flow freely upon the earthly plane.

A thrill of excitement ran through her.

At last, she was to meet her destiny. At last, her discipline and training were to pay off. At last, the boredom would come to an end.

The shrill ring of the telephone pierced her reverie, and she glanced at it in surprise. It was her private line, the one she had forbidden her servants to answer. It could only be one person.

"Yes, Adrian, what is it?" Adrian Demos, the keeper of the occult store known as the Alchymical Book Shoppe, was her single magical contact in all of London. No one else had any idea of Delilah's interest in the dark arts, and she intended to keep it that way. Adrian knew if he betrayed her, he would be a dead man. So far, that had proven sufficient incentive for him to keep his mouth shut and his ears open.

Because of his extensive contacts throughout London's occult subculture, she had entrusted him to help her locate the right candidates for her plan—the resurrection of the secret magical society that had been destroyed by her inept forebear over a hundred years before.

The Circle of the Lily.

Adrian's voice sounded thick and heavy over the phone. "There was a man in the store just a short time ago . . ."

Delilah raised an eyebrow. "Oh?"

"He brought in a box of antique magical implements for me to appraise."

"You're calling me about a box of antiques? I don't buy old rubbish. I have my own consecrated tools . . ."

"That's . . . not why I'm calling." She heard the excitement in his voice, but she waited for him to continue.

"He . . . he had this ring, Delilah. It was exactly like yours. It was engraved with the emblem of the Circle."

Delilah sat straight up in her chair, feeling the blood begin to race through her veins. "You are certain it was the symbol of the Circle of the Lily?"

Adrian described what he'd seen in detail, and when he was finished, Delilah was satisfied that it was indeed the device of the magical order to which she was the contemporary heir. The order she was preparing to resurrect in the restored temple.

There was only one explanation for this seemingly coincidental event. It was no coincidence at all.

Her High Priest had arrived.

"You *did* get his number . . ."

Claire paid the plumber and showed him to the door, thoroughly rattled once again by the abnormal events that kept interrupting her placid lifestyle. Cameron's demands. The break in the plumbing. Most of all, the continuing presence of Michael Townsend.

Despite her sympathy for his plight and a desire to help him get free of whatever plagued him, he'd frightened her again when she'd turned and seen him standing behind her, surrounded by his darkness. She really did wish that he would just leave, and she guessed she had communicated that to him in some unspoken way, for he had become angry with her, accusing her of deliberately trying to get rid of him. She laughed nervously, wondering if her tenant was psychic, too, or if she had really been that obvious. Since she couldn't explain her fears to him, she knew that she had likely hurt his feelings. Claire, who never wished to hurt anyone, could hardly bear the thought.

She was also confused because she couldn't seem to discern her own feelings. She didn't understand her continuing attraction to Michael Townsend when she knew how dangerous it was. It bothered her that she had been unable to "read" him, to discover why his aura continued to be so dark or how best to help him.

Auras were an emanation of a person's life force. Typically, they flickered and fluctuated like the flames of a fire as emotions and physical experiences changed. She had often witnessed an instant change in the auric pattern when a client had a breakthrough, an epiphany moment, so to speak. When people discovered not only the source of their distress but the resolution to their problems as well, she had watched it literally "dawn on them." Their auras typically brightened from the gray-brown of despair to the bright yellow of hopeful thoughts and the vibrant orange of the action of change.

But throughout his short stay at Fairfield House, Michael's aura had remained consistently black, surrounding him like a shroud. She'd thought she'd seen a faint flicker of a lighter color above his head when he'd apologized to her, but decided it must have been a trick of the light, for when she'd glanced at him over her shoulder as she'd left the cottage, the blackness was sealed solidly around him.

Oh, God. What was she going to do about that man?

She shut her eyes and thought back over the little he had revealed to her in the past twenty-four hours, seeking a gateway into his psyche, but there was little to go on. He'd been distressed that he was "recently" a professor, which might mean he'd been fired. The tarot reading had indicated he was seeking something, or someone, and Bitsy's flippant remark might not be too far removed from the truth, that he might be seeking a runaway wife. She tried to stretch her imagination. Maybe he'd been fired because his boss was having an affair with his wife.

That would blacken anyone's aura. But not unwaveringly. She recalled Maeve's mention of a curse. Claire shivered. She disliked such concepts, not only because they represented the slimy side of the occult, but also because they were just too high drama for her taste. Still, she considered for a moment the possibility that Michael Townsend had had a curse placed upon him.

The idea struck her as rather ridiculous. He was a white, male, American college professor. Not a likely target for a curse. But she knew little about him. Perhaps he'd been to Haiti or Jamaica or even New Orleans, where traditional voodoo was still practiced. Maybe he'd angered the high priest . . .

Now her imagination was totally out of control.

Michael Townsend presented Claire with the most complex and intriguing case of her career, except that he wasn't her client. She had no business even contemplating the source of, or the solution to, his problems. He was her tenant, nothing more. Hopefully, he would soon find what he was seeking, finish his business here, and leave.

The phone rang.

"Fairfield House," she answered in a professional tone, as her cottage was advertised in a number of magazines as a vacation rental.

The throaty woman's voice that came across the wire sent through her a vibration as cold as ice, as powerful as electricity. "I wish to speak to Dr. Michael Townsend."

Claire felt the breath leave her. Her hands grew clammy on the receiver. She heard a ringing in her ears, and she was rendered speechless until the voice spoke again. "Hello? Is anyone there?"

"Yes," she managed. "I . . . I believe he is in his apartment. One moment please . . ."

Nausea overwhelmed her, and she wondered whether to try to call Dr. Townsend to the phone first or to run to the bathroom and be sick. She forced herself to stand very still in the middle of her sitting room. She inhaled several deep, calming breaths and at last regained her balance before summoning her tenant.

Whoever was on that phone line was powerful. And evil. Her heart began to feel sick as well.

What was Michael Townsend up to?

She knocked at his door and pointed him in the direction of the telephone, then made her way into the kitchen where she opened a bottle of mineral water and sipped at it, feeling its coolness soothe as it went down. She sank into one of the chairs at her small kitchen table, her embryonic sympathy for Michael Townsend vanishing beneath her renewed fear. She must steer clear of him. He was not her kind of person. As soon as he was off the phone and had left her house again, she would burn frankincense to clear his psychic impact on her personal space. Then she would call Maeve and ask for advice on what to do from there. Perhaps her friend could think of something to make him leave. Maybe there was some method of psychically reaching into his thoughts and implanting the idea in his mind that he must depart Claire's home. Immediately.

Claire could hear his voice as he answered the telephone, and though it was against her ethics, she was unable to overcome her temptation to listen through the door.

"Yes, this is Dr. Michael Townsend."

Prolonged silence.

"Yes, I am in possession of such a ring." Silence. "Tomorrow? I suppose I could meet you then. Where?" Claire heard the scratch of a pen against paper, then Michael's voice again. "Do you want me to bring the other items? Very well, then, just the ring." A pause. "Yes, I believe I can find the location. One more thing, though. Could you just tell me if this has anything to do with magic?''

Psychically, Claire heard the caller laughing, but it was laughter without humor. It was the sound of someone in power mocking another's ignorance. Suddenly she realized this was not someone Michael knew, and in fact, he was the intended victim of this woman's plot, whatever it was.

Her stomach knotted again, and she was torn by ambivalence. This was none of her business, and she should stay out of it. Whatever Dr. Townsend's involvement with this woman, it was his affair. She had no right, no reason, to intrude.

Yet it went against everything she stood for in her consulting practice not to at least try to warn him off this rendezvous. It was her job to save people from themselves. Without further consideration of what she was about to do, she barged into the main room of the house just as her tenant was replacing the receiver in its cradle. Unable to stop herself, she blurted out, ''Don't go.''

Michael looked up, startled to see Claire St. John gripping the back of a chair until her knuckles were white and begging him with those large, blue eyes not to go.

Go where? Had she overheard his conversation with Delilah Mason?

''I beg your pardon?'' he said, irritated.

''You . . . mustn't meet . . . that . . . that woman. She is . . . she means you harm.''

Claire St. John must be nuts, he decided, affirming his earlier suspicions. ''Do you know the person I was speaking to?''

''I . . . I don't need to know her. I *felt* her on the phone when I answered it.''

'' 'Felt' her? You must forgive me, Ms. St. John. I'm afraid I don't quite follow. How can you 'feel' someone over the phone?''

Her face turned bright pink, and he could see a war of

emotions being waged in her eyes. She let go of the chair and moved toward him.

"I know you must think me insane," she said at last, speaking slowly and softly, sounding for the first time like she might be in her senses after all, "but there is something about me you must know." She gestured to the books in their shelves. "I have told you I am a student of the occult. The reason for my intense interest in that field is . . ." She paused and drew in a breath before continuing. ". . . Is that I am what is called a psychic sensitive."

Whatever that meant, she was a little too unstable for his tastes. Michael started to reply inanely, "I see," but he didn't see at all. So he remained silent, waiting for her to continue. She spoke again at last.

"I . . . I've had these gifts all my life, if you could call them gifts. Sometimes they are a terrible burden. I have the ability to see the unseen. I can sense energies and some-times see the future . . ."

"And you can 'feel' a person by long-distance tele-phone?" He heard the cynicism in his voice.

Claire's head snapped up, and the previous distress in her eyes was replaced with clear, cold anger. "I know this sounds ridiculous to you, Dr. Townsend. After all, you are a man of science to whom likely all things must be proven analytically. If it isn't tactile, if it isn't of the five senses, it doesn't exist. Am I correct?"

Michael was startled by the depth of her anger. Sane or not, she seriously believed in her psychic . . . condition. But her anger relit his own. "I'm not a scientist, Ms. St. John. But I must tell you I don't approve of eavesdroppers or meddlers. Unless you have some reason that I can under-stand better than this nonsense, I would appreciate it if in the future you would stay out of my business."

He saw her recoil as if he'd struck her. Then, unexpect-edly, her eyes brimmed with tears, and he felt like the world's greatest schmuck. He went to her and put his hands on her shoulders. "I'm sorry. I didn't mean to be so rude."

She raised her chin. "It's all right. Most people don't understand." A tear escaped and rolled down one cheek, and Michael's heart fell apart. Without thinking, he pulled Claire against him and held her tightly in his arms. He had never meant to make her cry.

The warm softness of her body against his had an even more disconcerting effect on him than her earlier seemingly irrational words. He felt the gentle pressure of her breasts against the plane of his chest, he smelled the clean scent of lavender in her hair. Michael closed his eyes. This woman, insane or not, felt wonderful in his arms, and he wished the moment would last and last.

Without stopping to consider what he was doing, he raised her face and lowered his lips to hers. She did not resist the first tentative brush of his kiss, so he allowed his caress to melt into a deeper, more passionate exploration of the sweet taste of her. His senses overflowed with the beauty and delight of her. Never had he held a woman who so completely filled him with . . . what? He found no adequate way to describe the sensation of Claire St. John.

The only word that came to mind was "light."

But what was he doing kissing Claire St. John? Had he lost his mind? Reluctantly, he released her and held her slightly away from him. "I'm sorry, once again. I don't know what came over me. I didn't mean to . . . make you cry."

He couldn't tell if she was offended by his kiss or not, but the tears had not cleared. "You didn't make me cry, Michael. I was crying for what I see in store for you. You may think of me whatever you wish. I'm used to it. But I *did* feel that woman's vibrations over the phone, and they were so evil it frightened me."

Her use of his first name, spoken in a tender hush, along with her continued insistence on what had transpired psychically when she'd taken the phone call, made Michael rethink his earlier skepticism. Obviously, whether it was true or not, Claire believed she had these supernatural powers, and she was willing to expose herself to ridicule in order to warn him against something she considered to be dangerous. If nothing else, he was touched. Few people had ever cared enough about him to reach out as she had. He owed her a debt of respect.

"I will be careful," he told her, "and I appreciate your concern. Really, I do. It's just that I don't understand when you talk about evil coming across on the phone and seeing the future and things like that." He saw her glance toward the top of his head and then felt her pull away at last from his grasp.

"Michael, I know this may be out of line, an intrusion of your privacy," she said hesitantly, moving toward one of the bookshelves, "but have you . . . had a difficult life recently?"

Instantly, his emotional wall slammed back into place, and he shut out the tender feelings that had arisen in him during their embrace. "You're right, Claire. That is an intrusion."

She gave him a long, almost sad look, and then she nodded. "Very well, then. I won't pry further. But I would like to loan you this." She pulled a book from the shelf and handed it to him. "It's a basic handbook about the occult. Read it or not, it's up to you. But if you want to understand the things that seem strange and foreign to you, like psychic sensitivity and the concept of dark and light energies, it is an excellent book. It explains a lot about metaphysical phenomena." She walked toward him, passing only close enough to him to give him the book, then continued on into the kitchen, closing the door behind her.

Michael stared after her, emotions clashing within him. Shame for how he had treated her. Curiosity about her life and her claim that she was a psychic. Fear of becoming vulnerable to her guileless charm. And desire. Oh, yes, desire. It seemed that her tender kiss had opened a portal to his heart that had been barricaded for a long while.

He forced his thoughts in another direction, remembering

his brief but astonishing conversation with Delilah Mason. He had not felt anything dark or evil in her voice. She had seemed vibrant and excited when he had confirmed that he had a ring bearing the symbols she'd described. True, she had been more than a little secretive about her interest in that ring and had laughed, merrily it seemed to him, when he'd asked her if it had anything to do with magic, but she had in the end confirmed that it was a magician's ring.

Should he heed Claire's warning? Or should he keep his appointment the next day with Delilah Mason?

Michael could find no rational reason not to meet with the woman who had tantalized him with her interest in the ring. If nothing else, he might learn something that would aid his search for his mother. He shook his head. What possible harm could come from that?

Chapter Seven

CAMERON ST. JOHN COULD NOT BELIEVE HIS INCREDible good fortune. He'd had no idea when he arrived at the elegant penthouse suite owned by Delilah Mason that the gathering to which he'd been invited would be so exclusive. In fact, he counted himself lucky to have been included on her guest list at all, for she was one of London's top hostesses, and although she had chosen him to handle some of her investments, he hadn't thought himself to be of her social standing.

She was extraordinarily beautiful, one of the richest and most powerful women in London. Why had she invited him? There were only twelve guests at this strange little party. All men. Mostly from London's top families. He was the only one from what he thought of as the middle class. Perhaps she was pleased with what he'd managed to do with her portfolio so far.

Thank God she had no idea of the mistake he'd made. It had taken virtually all the money Claire had paid him to cover his tracks, but it was worth it. No one, especially Delilah Mason, would ever know of his near disaster. But he must be extremely careful in the future. He couldn't afford another incident like that one.

Cameron held up his empty champagne flute, signaling

the tuxedo-clad waiter for another. There would be no more mistakes, he assured himself. He was too smart for that. He'd been careless and trusted someone else. He would never again trust another rival broker. Somehow, someway, he would get Omar Solis.

He heard a murmur rustle among the small group gathered in the room and looked up to see Delilah Mason enter the room. She was dressed in floor-length black palazzo pants topped with an exquisitely beaded jacket bearing mystical symbols—stars and moons and spirals and crosses—in shimmering gold against glimmering black, obviously the product of one of Paris's most talented designers. Her fiery hair, by day drawn up into a sophisticated twist, tonight fell to her shoulders where it curled under slightly. Large but tasteful gold and diamond earrings adorned her ears. She was beautiful, but Cameron was attracted to more than just her physical allure. She radiated bold energy, implicit power. She was sharp, a woman of influence, someone who could open the right doors if she liked you. Cameron's mouth watered just looking at her.

"Good evening, gentlemen," she said, flashing a smile and moving into the group of men. She became the immediate center of attention, and the earlier cocktail conversation ceased. "I take it everyone has had a chance to refresh themselves at the buffet table." She swept an arm toward the lavish display of food on the sideboard. "If not, please help yourself over the course of the evening. I have let the servants go home, for . . . privacy's sake."

Her gaze moved slowly around the circle, meeting the eyes of each man in turn. "I'm glad you're here," she said in a low, throaty voice. Her lips lifted slightly as if in some secret amusement.

When she turned to Cameron, he could have sworn that something personal and private passed between them, something she had not conveyed to the others. At first, he got the uneasy feeling that she knew about his screwup with her investment account, but quickly decided that was impossible, choosing to believe instead she had given him a special look because she was uniquely interested in him.

"Gentlemen," she said at last, easing gracefully into a large Louis XIV chair and charming her audience once again with an arresting smile. "I have invited you here for a very specific reason. Please, come, sit, and I'll tell you what it is."

As if mesmerized, Cameron dropped into the nearest chair and sat on the edge of his seat. The woman was positively bewitching, and he was awestruck that he was among the group she had assembled. She had fame, fortune, and the easy power of a natural-born queen. What did she want with him?

Delilah continued. "This may come as a surprise to those of you who read in the tabloids about how exciting my life is, but the truth is, I'm bored," she said with a laugh that invoked empathy. "I feel in need of some more . . . interesting entertainment. I have invited you tonight, for I've heard that each of you has a streak of boldness and daring in his soul. That you are men who do not let the conventions of the world intimidate you. Is that true?"

As a group, the men, gratified at this compliment to their virility and manhood, assured her soundly in low, husky voices that they were Europe's most daring types. Delilah rewarded them with a nod. "Just as I thought." She paused, looking into their faces, her expression serious now. "I want to undertake an experiment," she said, "but I cannot do it by myself, and I was hoping that you might help me."

Cameron's pulse quickened in anticipation. He had no idea what her experiment might entail, but if it would improve his standing with Delilah Mason, he wanted to be a part of it.

"It isn't a difficult experiment," she went on, "but you must be willing to pledge your utter loyalty to me and keep what transpires completely secret." Cameron saw her tawny eyes turn to the sheen of burnished steel. "Do you quite understand?" Her voice was suddenly as hard as her gaze. "For unless you agree to swear both your loyalty and your secrecy, I must ask you to leave at once."

Not a man moved. Then boldly, Cameron rose and went to her, stopping several feet from her chair. He looked into her eyes, which had returned to a mellow golden hue, and they seemed to penetrate his very being. He knelt beside her. "You have my unconditional loyalty," he affirmed, feeling suddenly empowered by his brash commitment. "And whatever transpires between us shall remain a secret, a . . . sacred secret, forever. I swear it on my life."

He didn't know what possessed him to use the word "sacred," but he could see Delilah was pleased.

"Very well, then. You may be the first to join the adventure." She indicated a door to her right. "In the next room you will find your first instructions and appropriate attire. I plan to begin tonight. Go. Prepare yourself."

With that, she held out her hand for him to kiss, and as his lips touched her skin, a rush of exhilaration surged through him, for he sensed in some way the mysterious Delilah Mason was about to share some of her secrets.

Claire was restless, unable to sleep. She felt the presence of a current of great evil somewhere within the sphere of her life, but she was unable to pinpoint its source. Perhaps, she told herself, tossing on her bed in the midnight darkness, it was just residual negativity clinging to her from the vibrations of the phone call earlier in the afternoon. Or more likely, she was still charged with the dark energy she must have absorbed after foolishly falling into Michael Townsend's embrace.

How on earth could she have done that? She was well aware of the dangers he presented to her personal safety. But strangely, for those few moments when she'd leaned into his arms, she had felt nothing but the warmth and comfort of being held by another human being. She'd had no sensation that he was draining her energies as she did when she first met him. Nor had she experienced any kind of clash with the darkness of his aura. Instead, she felt as if she had somehow penetrated that darkness and stepped inside his barrier for a moment and found there a tender and caring man worthy of her efforts to psychically fight for him.

She was rationalizing, of course. Making up excuses for her behavior because she had enjoyed the feeling of being close to a man again. It was pitiful to think she had become so estranged from sexual contact with men that she would allow herself to become vulnerable to a man like Dr. Townsend.

She glanced at the clock. Twelve thirty-three. Unwilling to slug it out with her pillows any longer, for she did not feel sleepy in the least, Claire slid out of bed and donned her robe and slippers. She went to the window and saw that a nearly full moon lit up the meadow, illuminating the verdant pasture with a silvery sheen. Then she noticed a light shining from the bedroom window of the cottage. So Dr. Townsend was having trouble sleeping, too. Claire wondered, a little hopefully, if he was as unsettled as she was by their earlier and unexpected embrace.

Probably not.

Rather, he was probably reading the book she'd given him. Education did wonders for people like him, skeptics who believed only what was prescribed by conventional society. In the past when she'd shared her books and other reading materials with difficult clients, what they'd learned had often opened them to making much-needed changes in their lives.

She hoped she would have such luck with Michael Townsend.

Michael.

She'd called him Michael. He'd called her Claire. For one brief moment, they had been together not as adversaries or threats, but simply as man and woman.

And she had liked it very much.

Claire turned from the window, more perplexed and confused than ever. Her usual sensibilities were all befuddled, her rational thinking debilitated. If she were a drinking person, she'd resort to a tot or two. Instead, she opted for warm milk. That usually did the trick when she couldn't sleep.

Quietly, so as not to disturb her sleeping cats, who were ensconced in their favorite slumbering places throughout her bedroom, Claire tiptoed down the stairs and felt her way into the kitchen. Her eyes were accustomed to the dark, and she knew her way around the familiar room, so she did not turn on the lights lest she summon the ever-rapacious Lefty, if not the rest, in search of a midnight snack.

Before she reached the refrigerator, she was struck out of nowhere by an icy draft of air, and she stopped dead in her tracks, her heart pounding. Cautiously, she reached out and her fingers touched something cold and slimy and wet.

Ectoplasm.

The earthbound spirit had returned.

Gathering her wits quickly and refusing to give in to another fit of hysteria, she tried to think of what to do. Seeing a ghost was a rare opportunity, one that presented itself to few mediums, even those who tried for years to contact spirits. She mustn't botch this again.

But what did one say to a ghost?

At first she said nothing at all, but rather reached out to the presence mentally, sending a psychic message that she was a friend and wanted to help. Claire had no idea what to expect, so she held her breath and waited in the darkness.

Soon, she witnessed a soft wisp of fog gathering before her eyes. The wisp became a cloud, and the cloud then took on the shape of a person. Although the body was attired only in the filmy cloudlike substance, Claire sensed that it was a woman. "Who are you?"

The figure did not speak, but it did seem to turn to face Claire. She could make out large, sad eyes, and then suddenly a name resounded into her consciousness as clearly as if it had been spoken.

Eloise.

"Are you Eloise?" Claire dared to speak again. She thought she saw the figure nod ever so slightly. Then another message came indirectly, psychically.

Murdered.

The hair at the back of Claire's neck stood on end, and suddenly she lost her nerve and grew frightened. She clenched her fists, determined not to be ruled by her fear this time. She gathered her courage and pressed the ghost for more. "You were murdered? When? Who did it?"

But to her disappointment, the ectoplasm began to fade. Claire cried out again, "Who murdered you?"

Another fainter message glimmered in her mind.

Warn him.

Then abruptly, the air lost its chill and the wisp of fog disappeared into the dark of the night, leaving Claire both alarmed and ecstatic. She had seen a ghost! And, she believed, she had actually received messages from it. Wait until Maeve heard . . . !

No longer caring if she awakened her cats, Claire flipped on the lights, more to ground herself back into reality than to chase away any ghostly shadows. She knew the spirit had departed, at least for the time being.

She decided to copy down the words the ghost had given her, lest she forget them by morning like she often forgot her dreams. Opening a drawer in search of writing materials, Claire's hand came upon an unfamiliar object. She drew it out and stared at it in astonishment, certain she had never seen it before in her entire life.

It was a small golden crucifix studded with emeralds, rubies, and pearls.

Claire was not a Catholic. In fact, the only Catholic she knew was Bitsy Flanagan, but she doubted that Bitsy had casually left such a crucifix, or any crucifix for that matter, in Claire's kitchen drawer.

Suddenly, Claire began to pick up sensations from the object. She saw fire, felt like she was surrounded by flames, and she was filled with an overwhelming terror. She heard a sharp crack, as if lightning had struck nearby, and then her world collapsed into darkness.

When she regained consciousness some time later, she was lying on the kitchen floor, her arms outstretched, the crucifix just out of reach.

"It must be an apport," Maeve said, staring at the cross that still lay on Claire's floor.

Not wishing to disrupt her friend's sleep, Claire had managed to wait until dawn before calling Maeve to her aid. She had sat up the rest of the night, afraid to go to sleep, afraid to touch the crucifix again. As she sat at her table, absently stirring cup after cup of tea, she had pondered the appearance of the spirit, questioning whether she had really seen it and whether it had actually given her those messages, or if she had hallucinated the whole episode. She wrote it down to be sure she remembered it properly.

"Have you ever seen an apport before?" Claire wanted to know. She had heard of such things, but she'd always tended to disbelieve the reports as claims of overzealous mediums who, to prove their success in contacting the dead, insisted that spirits had brought them "presents" from the other side.

But apparently Maeve took them quite seriously. "Of course I've seen items that have been brought in by spirits," she replied matter-of-factly. "But I'm worried about this particular apport, however, or rather I should say, I'm worried about you handling this. Obviously, it is highly charged with that spirit's energy, enough to knock you down."

"She told me she was murdered," Claire revealed. "At least that's what I think she was trying to convey. After picking up those images of being surrounded by fire, I am inclined to believe her. I wonder," she added in a grisly afterthought, "if she were burned alive."

"What else did the spirit say?"

Claire frowned down at the paper where she had scribbled her notes. "She gave a name. It seemed like it was 'Eloise.' Then I got the word 'murdered.' Just before she faded, I could swear she tried to tell me, 'Warn him.' "

"Hmmm. Sounds like a nasty business, whatever happened."

Claire nodded morosely. "What should I do, Maeve? What can I do? I'd like to help that spirit, not just for her sake, but for my own as well. I don't want to keep bumping into her in my kitchen. But I can't very well go to the police and say, 'Oh, by the way, there was this ghost that stopped by my kitchen the other night and told me she was murdered. Can you please find out whodunit so she can move on?' "

They laughed, which dispelled some of the tension in the room. Then Maeve said, "How do you feel about playing sleuth?"

"What do you mean?"

"Well, a murder would be reported by the newspapers, so perhaps if you searched through the archives you might find some reference to her case."

Claire shook her head. "Even though she didn't convey it to me, I have the sense that nobody ever knew about her murder," she replied. "That's why she is still earthbound. She wants the truth to be known."

"Could be," Maeve agreed thoughtfully.

"What about the warning?" Claire asked. "Who would she want to warn? And about what?"

"She specifically said, 'Warn *him*'?"

Claire nodded. "Maybe that message is a holdover from what happened to her in the past. Maybe whoever killed her was going to kill her husband, too. Or her boyfriend."

Maeve gave her a meaningful glance. "Or still might be going to kill him. We are assuming this is an old crime, but we don't know that. Someone could be at risk even as we speak." She paused, shaking her head. "I still feel that the sudden appearance of this ghost in your house has something to do with that skeleton you found."

"And until we can resolve her mystery, she'll probably continue to hang around here," Claire added with resignation.

The night without sleep suddenly weighed heavily on Claire's shoulders, but she remembered that shortly she would be required to prepare breakfast for her tenant. No sense in trying to go back to bed until she finished that task. She decided she should freshen up and try to cover the dark circles under her eyes.

"Thanks for coming over, Maeve. Are you sure you won't stay for breakfast? I could at least make coffee or tea."

"Thanks, but I really can't stay. It was actually good that you called so early. I have a lot to do today." She knelt and picked up the crucifix. "I don't want you touching this," she admonished as if she were Claire's mother. "Shall I take it with me?"

"Well, I don't want to be knocked on my backside again," the younger woman laughed, "but I'd like to keep it for a while. Just put it where I can see it without having to touch it." Maeve laid it carefully on a shelf in the kitchen.

"Very well, then. I'll be off. Don't hesitate to call if you need me again. You have my pager number."

Claire knew that Maeve was a very busy medium, and she appreciated that she had taken time to come over at the crack of dawn. "Thanks. I'll let you know of any late-breaking developments."

Maeve turned as she reached the front door. "By the way, how are you faring with your handsome tenant?"

Claire felt her cheeks flush and knew she could never hide anything from this astute psychic. "He's still giving me fits," she admitted, making light of the matter. "See you later."

Not wishing her handsome tenant to catch her in her robe

and slippers, Claire hurried upstairs, took a quick shower, and put on fresh clothing and makeup. She felt better, but not rested. As soon as she got the breakfast ordeal over with, she promised herself she'd take a long nap before deciding what to do next to resolve the ghost issue.

Chapter Eight

AT HALF PAST EIGHT, MICHAEL KNOCKED SOFTLY ON the frame of the doorway between the kitchen and dining room. He was later coming in for breakfast this morning than he had been yesterday, and he wondered if he might have inconvenienced Claire, but he saw she was frying bacon on the stove and that breakfast was still in the making.

"Good morning," he said, and he saw her jump ever so slightly. She turned and greeted him, nervously it seemed. He didn't blame her for being nervous around him after his uncouth and indiscriminate behavior of yesterday. He was still embarrassed that he had been so forward as to kiss her. His embarrassment, however, did not lessen his attraction to her. He gazed at her openly, taking in the soft features of her face, the curves that hid just beneath the white cotton fabric of her blouse. She was lovely, the way the bud of a pale pink rose is lovely in both its purity and its promise. He longed to cross the room and release her hair from the band that held it tightly behind her head. He longed to feel the blond texture of it between his fingers. He longed . . .

"Would you like some coffee?" she asked. "The pot's on the counter, and there are mugs in the cupboard just above. I apologize for breakfast being so late."

Michael was glad she'd distracted him. His thoughts

were inappropriate and had wandered in a most dangerous direction. As they had most of the night. "I thought I was the one who was running late." He took a mug and filled it with hot coffee. "I stayed up late reading that book you loaned me, and I overslept." He took a seat at her kitchen table, and it seemed somehow natural, comfortable, like he was at home here. Michael had never felt at home anywhere, even in the house he'd shared with his father. He'd never felt comfortable, not in this way, being around a woman. She was like the family he'd longed for and never known.

She dished his breakfast onto a large china plate and turned, looking at him in surprise. "Do you want to eat in here? I was going to set your place at the dining table."

"Do you mind?" He didn't want to go to the dining table. Nor did he wish to eat breakfast alone. "I like it here."

He saw her hesitate slightly, then she placed the plate on the table in front of him. "Suit yourself. Do you take milk in your coffee?"

"No." He broke the yolk in one of the eggs that looked up at him. The plate held a traditional full English breakfast—a slice of meat that was like Canadian bacon, two small sausages, two eggs over easy, half of a grilled tomato, and several sauteed mushrooms. She brought him a rack that held several slices of toast and offered butter and orange marmalade. "Does everyone in England eat like this every day?" he asked, eyeing the plate, wondering if he could, or should, make it through the mountain of food. He'd been served identical fare the day before.

Claire laughed. "Of course not. I almost never have a breakfast like that. I usually have cereal and fruit."

"You just feed all this cholesterol to Americans you'd rather not have around too long." He'd meant the remark as a joke, but considering their argument of the day before, he wished he hadn't said it. He could see she'd taken it wrong.

"I'm sorry if somehow I've given you the impression that I don't want you here, Dr. Townsend." Her tone of voice was cool, stony. "You are welcome to stay as long as you like."

Michael decided the best thing to do was drop it and change the subject. "Thanks for the loan of the book. It was very interesting. I learned a lot, but I can see I have a long way to go. I never knew the term 'occult' covered so much territory."

She visibly relaxed and rewarded his efforts with a gentle smile. "That is a very grown-up attitude. Some people are put off by the mere mention of the word 'occult.'"

"Please. Join me for breakfast." Michael gestured to the chair across from him. "I'd like to pick your brain, if you wouldn't mind." What he really wanted was just to be around her, to believe that even for a moment she was his friend. Something had shifted inside when he'd kissed her, and he wanted to feel that light penetrate his soul once again.

Claire poured some cornflakes into a bowl, cut a banana in slices over the cereal, and added milk. She did not speak during the preparation of her simple breakfast, but Michael felt tension building between them and wondered if he'd made a mistake in asking her to sit at the table with him. But when she took her seat, she continued the conversation as if it were no big thing.

"You see," she said, taking a bite, "a lot of people mistakenly associate the term 'occult' with devil worship and such, when in truth, it simply means 'hidden' or 'unseen.' It also relates to ideas that are not generally accepted by a given society, especially if they are of a mystical or religious nature. Once paganism was the accepted form of worship, and Christianity was considered occult. Now it's just the opposite." She spoke softly and clearly, without a hint of defensiveness in her voice.

"That's an interesting way of looking at it." Michael considered her definition. "I've always thought the occult had to do with things like witchcraft and Satanism and other evil practices.''

She gave him a wry smile. ''You are not alone in your thinking, but you are missing the mark. Those things can be considered occult, but so can the practice of Spiritualism, which is Christian-based and one of the most loving and gentle of religious practices. And witchcraft, by the way, is not necessarily an evil practice. Only if the witch has gone black.''

Michael looked up at her and raised an eyebrow. ''Like magicians who have gone black?''

''Yes, exactly. There are white witches and black witches, just like there are white magicians and black magicians, like we talked about before. Those who practice witchcraft and magic for their own gain and in such a manner as might harm others are considered black, while there are many whose occult arts are most beneficial.''

''The . . . uh . . . *white* kind.''

''That's right. It's the same concept with dark and light energies. People who are surrounded by dark energy often behave in antisocial ways that reveal their inner anger and fear and negativity. Criminals generally have dark auras. And people who live with hate in their hearts. That's why when I see someone with a dark aura, I try to stay away . . .''

She broke off and raised her head abruptly, and he knew she had just revealed a secret about herself she would rather have kept hidden.

''You see auras?'' He doubted it seriously. He had read about the supposed phenomenon of the human aura in the book she'd lent him, but never having seen such a thing himself, he didn't really believe light emanated from human bodies.

Claire's face was a study in chagrin, and he could tell she was really angry with herself for what she had said. She shifted her gaze, looking above and beyond him for a moment, as if searching for some way to withdraw her slip of the tongue. When she made eye contact with him again, she didn't answer his question aloud, but simply nodded.

"Can you see my aura?" he pressed.

She swallowed hard and nodded again.

He waited, but she said nothing further. "Well, what does it look like?"

This time, she shook her head. It took her some time, but she found her voice at last. "It's . . . dark, Michael," she rasped at last. "Very dark."

Claire could have bitten off her tongue for revealing to Michael not only that she saw auras, but that his own was dark, just as she'd been describing a criminal's to be. However, she'd had no choice once she'd gotten herself into this mess.

She did not lie.

She could see Michael was disturbed by what she'd told him. The irony of it was that up until this moment, she had noticed that his aura had lightened perceptibly from the day before. When he'd come into her kitchen, she'd seen that although it was still dark, it appeared more the muddy gray color of pre-dawn than the black of midnight. As if he were becoming enlightened about things. It would stand to reason, since he'd read a book he admitted he'd found thought-provoking.

But the instant she told him his aura was dark, it returned to the blackness that frightened her so.

"Is that why you've been trying to get me to leave?" He pushed his plate away and glared at her.

"I . . . I have not . . . I mean . . ." She fumbled to soften the truth and failed. Finally she shrugged and looked him in the eye. "Yes. It is, Michael. And it's why I asked if your . . . life had been particularly unhappy lately. Your upper body, especially the area around your head and your heart, is surrounded by a layer of darkness. I don't pick up that you are a criminal, although at first I wasn't sure. It seems to me instead you are carrying around a great sadness in your soul and a raging anger with life."

His eyes burned suddenly with that anger, and she saw red sparks flare aurically from the blackness around his heart.

"Well, it must come as a hell of a relief to know you are not harboring a criminal in your cottage," he lashed out.

Although she was sorry she had caused him even more distress, from his reaction Claire knew she had read him correctly. Often, even clients who paid her to help them found it too painful to look at, or admit to the source of their troubles when she accurately psychically put her finger on them. Anger was a typical defense. And denial.

"I told you I was a psychic," she said, bracing herself for his wrath, but feeling compelled to finish what she had so inadvertently started. "Besides seeing auras, I have the ability to just . . . sense things about people. I sense that you're not a criminal, Michael, just a very unhappy man."

"You're weird," he said, standing to leave.

"I've been called worse."

Instead of beating a hasty exit, however, he surprised her by leaning with both arms rigid against the back of his chair. "Well, what else do you pick up about me?" His words held the edge of both doubt and challenge. "Don't you find your psychic snooping a little like invasion of privacy? I do."

Her own anger flared, but she suppressed it. He obviously wanted to challenge her abilities by demanding she tell him more about himself, but at the same time, he didn't want her to know his secrets. She understood his frustration. With a heavy sigh, Claire asked, "Is there something you really wish to know, Michael, or are you just trying to test me?"

He paused, eyeing her steadily for a long moment. Then he let go of the chair and headed for the door. "Never mind. Thanks for breakfast."

Claire glanced at his virtually untouched plate, then at

her own full cereal bowl. As far as breakfast went, it had been a disaster. And it felt like disaster somewhere down around her heart. "Damn!" she swore aloud, as if the word could place a barrier against the rush of disappointment that swept through her. She regretted with all her soul having let Michael in on the awful secret of his aura, and even worse, that it had occurred to him she might be able to discern his even deeper, darker secrets. She wished she hadn't been so eager for him to understand the occult, to accept her psychic abilities. It had all backfired on her. He'd even called her weird.

She didn't consider herself weird, but she *had* been a fool. A fool, fooled by the illusion of his kiss. She could not explain, psychically or otherwise, why that embrace had happened, but it had obviously left her senseless and vulnerable, and she could not afford to let it happen ever again.

As she cleared the table, she tried to clear her mind as well, but it was not an easy task. With all that had transpired in the past few days, her thoughts kept running into each other as they careened around her head. Everything was so extraordinary, she felt as if she had entered some kind of alternate reality. It was not one she was certain she liked, peopled as it was with unquiet ghosts, belligerent brothers, and dark strangers whose kisses shook her to the very core.

Suddenly, Claire felt it was she, not Michael, who must be the Hanged Man of Maeve's tarot reading, for her world seemed to have turned upside down, leaving her normal equanimity hanging by a thread.

She was the most disturbing woman he'd ever met. Michael stormed into the cottage and slammed the door behind him, not understanding why Claire St. John's psychic babble had set him off so badly. He went to the mirror and peered into it intently, striving to see the dark aura she claimed surrounded him, but all he saw was a very angry man with dark hair and brows that were drawn into such a frown they nearly touched in the center of his forehead.

Why? Why was he so angry? Was it because she had presumed to tell him that he was unhappy, that—as she had said—he carried around a raging anger with life? He didn't need a psychic to tell him either of those things. But there was something else she'd said, something that had touched a deeper nerve.

Something about sadness.

Michael sank onto the bed and lay back against the soft comforter. He was again bone-weary, but this time his fatigue seemed more related to Claire St. John than jet lag. He'd been unable to sleep most of the night for thinking about her.

Claire. At whom only moments before he had been raging with nearly out-of-control anger. Claire. Who claimed she could see what he could not, a sadness in his soul that somehow darkened his being. Suddenly, as if bidden, that sadness began to creep out of someplace in his heart where he'd kept it hidden for a long time. It was a scary thing, a deep, dark, gut-wrenching anguish, with roots sunk like poisonous tentacles into the nether reaches of his being.

It was a horrifying, accursed sorrow. He did not understand it.

And he did not want to look at it.

"Damn her!" He bolted upright once again. What business did she have meddling with the skeletons in his emotional closet? For he knew that was exactly what she had done. Even more distressing, he must have allowed her to do it. Beneath the tender power of her kiss, he must have inadvertently let down his guard and unknowingly handed her the keys to that closet, giving her access to those things he had so fiercely protected all his life.

His feelings.

For as long as he could remember, Michael had locked his feelings away, keeping them safe from an outside world that seemed daunting and merciless to a motherless boy.

From a father who would not offer love. From others his age, who instead of asking him to join in their games had made fun of his studious habits. Only twice had he dared take the risk of sharing his feelings with others, and twice he had been betrayed. Once, it had been the betrayal of a cruel universe, the other of the only man he had ever called friend.

It was a risk he was unwilling to take again.

No matter how powerful she claimed her psychic skills to be, Michael vowed he would find a way to prevent Claire St. John from ever looking into his heart again. He would simply build the wall even higher.

He looked at his watch. It was half past nine. His appointment with Delilah Mason was at noon. If he missed the ten o'clock train into London, he would have to wait an hour for the next one, and he thought it might make him late for their meeting. Burying his disturbing thoughts about Claire St. John, he went to his closet and took out the single business suit he had brought along. He was not certain about the type of person he would be meeting at this interview, but he intended to treat this like any other normal business engagement. Although she had called him because of the mystical ring he'd found, he'd had about more than he could stand of paranormal jibberish. He was looking for historical data. Hard facts. He would find out what this Delilah Mason knew about the symbolism and origin of the ring, then be on his way again. He had no time in his life for the nonsense of psychics and magicians.

He made a mental note to stop by the Information Centre on his way back and see if any other lodging had become available. He wanted to remain in Montlivet, but not around the woman who claimed she could see inside his soul.

Chapter Nine

CLAIRE STARED ABSENTLY THROUGH THE LACE CUR-
tains of the sitting-room window, not seeing the world outside, but rather the torment on Michael's face when he'd
stormed out of her kitchen. What was his story? What was
the source of his deep, underlying sadness? Most of all,
why did she even care?

A large, lumpy feline jumped onto the windowsill and
began nuzzling her hands. "Gingerbread Boy," she murmured and began scratching his ears affectionately. Claire
did not know what she would do without her cats. They
never demanded anything of her other than food and water.
They never got angry with her or caused her any distress.
They simply *were*, and let her simply *be*. She wished it
were so with Dr. Michael Townsend. But he had stirred up
confusing feelings deep within her, and she doubted that
they would let her be until the moment he left.

A movement caught her eye, and when she focused her
attention on the mundane world once again, she saw Michael come around the house and head up the lane toward
the road. He walked briskly, with determination. He'd
changed into a navy-blue business suit and looked more
like a banker than a college professor. He carried an umbrella with him, as black as his aura, and she surmised he

was going into London. To meet the woman who had called him yesterday?

Claire followed him with her eyes, and her heart grew heavy with apprehension. He was headed for some terrible trouble, she was certain, and she wished there were some way she could protect him, steer him away from that dark destination.

She stepped away from the window. What she ought to do was leave it alone. What Michael Townsend did was none of her business. But he had no concept of the kind of power she'd sensed coming over that telephone line. How strong it felt. How evil. He had no idea how insidious such power could be. She believed he could fall into that woman's snare and never know what happened.

With sick certainty, Claire also believed that she'd just psychically seen the future.

She bit her lip. Yes, she ought to stay out of it, but she could not. Suspecting what she did, that he was about to become a victim of the darkest kind of evil, she could no more allow Michael Townsend to become prey to that woman than she could let a cat starve.

It made no sense for her to try and save him. The man was dark and dangerous, and she was nothing to him except a bother. She suspected he would resent her intrusion if he were to find out. However, those arguments did not sway her from what she was about to do. She let out a quiet laugh. If she didn't know better, she'd think she'd fallen in love with the man.

Impossible.

She'd only known him a few days. Besides, he was distinctly not her type.

She put those disquieting thoughts to one side and faced another, more pragmatic problem. Because of Michael's inquiries into magic, she surmised that the trouble he was walking into had something to do with magic, likely black magic, and Claire knew very little about magic of any kind. Were there ways to counteract the forces of evil that might soon surround Michael like a spider's web? Would she have the power to prevent him from being ensnared? She knew of only one person nearby who might answer those and the many other doubts and questions Claire had on the subject of magic.

Lady Sarah.

She stood very still for a long moment, trying to talk herself out of becoming embroiled in Michael's affairs. Objectively, she knew there was no rational reason for her to put herself in jeopardy on his behalf. But on a deeper, emotional level, she knew if she didn't try, and something terrible happened to him, she would forever blame herself.

No. The choice was clear, and she was overcome by the sense that she must act quickly. She didn't know how to get in touch with Lady Sarah, but she raced to the phone and dialed Maeve's number. Her friend answered on the second ring, and breathlessly, Claire filled her in on what she believed was happening with Michael Townsend.

"That jibes with the tarot reading," Maeve remarked calmly. "In the position of the near future, we had the seven of cups."

"And Bitsy said the man on the card reminded her of a magician," Claire recalled. "Oh, Maeve, I just know he is headed for some kind of disaster. That woman's voice was so filled with evil it literally made me sick. Do you think Lady Sarah could give us some idea of how to protect him?"

Maeve hesitated, then asked, "Claire, are you sure you want to get involved? Have you asked him if he wants you to?"

Claire felt her face grow warm. It was one of the tenets of their psychic work that their powers were used on behalf of another only when asked or given permission by that person. "No. I haven't mentioned any of this to him. It just came to me as I saw him leave the house. I'm not sure I *want* to get involved, but, Maeve, I'm not sure I can stay out of it."

"You're in love, aren't you?" Maeve's tone was wry but understanding.

Claire started to automatically deny it, but couldn't. "I . . . don't know," she squeaked, not wanting to face the fact that Maeve, a very astute psychic reader, had likely pegged the truth. "I just feel strongly, intuitively, that I must do something. I'm thinking that there must be some skills of white magic that could counteract any black forces he might confront. Wouldn't Lady Sarah know what to do?"

A protracted silence stretched between them. "I'm not sure Lady Sarah will help us out. She is terribly reclusive."

"Please, Maeve, you've met her. Would you give her a call?"

She heard Maeve let out a sigh of resignation. "Lady Sarah has no telephone. We'll have to go there in person."

Lady Sarah came out of her trance and sat quietly in the well-worn chair she used when traveling on the astral plane. Its tall back and comfortably padded arms supported her in the difficult undertaking of leaving her body and moving onto another plane to the place where she'd learned to go to fight the darkness that incessantly threatened to engulf her.

She had sat in this chair and made this journey almost every day since beginning her magical training nearly three decades earlier. That training under the aegis of the Watchers had taught her much about the natural but hidden forces of the Universe, the polarities of good and evil, the nature of power, its use and misuse. In the beginning, she'd had much to overcome, but she had succeeded and then gone on to become a high white magician, serving as an anchor for the forces of good on the material plane of earth.

Several days ago, as she was traveling on the astral to the Palace of Light, she had encountered a force of darkness the strength of which she'd never before experienced in her magical work. She'd felt the evil—heavy, palpable, and very close. She had not run, or even flinched, but stood strong in the knowledge of her own power. However, she was aware that some vast, awesome dark force was now afoot and she understood that soon she would be summoned to the battle for which she had so long prepared.

She actually smiled as she re-entered the world of human consciousness, glad that soon it would be over. Her commitment to the Watchers had cost her dearly, but she was determined to emerge victorious. She *would* put an end to the darkness.

But she could no longer do it alone. Her power was strong, but she was aging. She needed help in this fight. Although she could serve to link the material world to the invisible and be a channel for the energies it would take to combat the evil, she needed someone on the Earth plane to support the work in the physical. More than one person, if she could find those whom she could trust.

Having been reclusive for many years, she was out of touch with the occult community. Now she needed help immediately. So today, before leaving the astral plane, she had expressed to the Watchers her desire for deputies, and she knew that it was only a matter of time before the right parties came to her.

In spite of successfully catching the early train, it was nearly noon when Michael arrived at the address he'd scribbled on one of Claire's notepads. He had not noticed the length of time he'd spent on his journey, however. His mind had been too filled with crazy, mixed-up thoughts about Claire St. John. Michael wanted to deny everything she'd said about him, to deny even that she had psychic power. But he couldn't deny that she had been devastatingly accurate in her assessment of his emotional state. Being brutally honest with himself, he acknowledged that he *was* chronically sad, disillusioned with the world, disappointed in life to the point that if something didn't change soon, he thought he might explode in frustration and anger. He wanted to take charge of his life, but for some irrational reason, he seemed powerless. No matter how hard he tried, it seemed that bad things just kept happening to him.

He thought of his mother's letter, her mention of her own despondency, which she'd blamed on a curse, her remark about sorrows. Maybe he had sorrow in his genes, he thought grimly. The only time in recent memory that he'd felt the slightest ease of the tension that coiled inside him was when he'd been with Claire St. John. A woman he hardly knew, yet a woman whose very presence seemed strangely to soothe him and bring him a kind of quiet inner peace. He liked sitting at her kitchen table. He liked watching her prepare breakfast. Hell, he even liked her cats.

He wished she liked him as well, but he knew she was afraid of him and his dark aura. He frowned. How, he wondered, did one go about getting rid of a dark aura?

His destination proved to be a high-rise glass and chrome structure that soared upward from the heart of London. Access to the upper floors was guarded by a dour-faced concierge who detained him in the lobby until he was given instructions by Delilah Mason to escort her guest to the elevator and send him up to the penthouse floor.

Then he turned surprisingly apologetic. "Sorry I had to make you wait, sir. I'm not supposed to let anyone in here without Miss Mason's consent." He shrugged. "I guess that's her prerogative. After all, she owns the place."

Michael stepped off the elevator on the top floor into a plushly appointed private lobby. Before he could knock at the ornately carved door made of rich mahogany, a uniformed servant opened it and beckoned him inside. He followed the man down a narrow hallway that might have appeared tunnel-like except that it was fully mirrored, even the ceiling above him. Michael could see his image reflected into infinity, and it gave him an eerie sensation, as if he were passing from this world into another dimension.

They came to a large living room expensively and dramatically furnished in colors of black, white, red, and gold. He was offered an elegant cut-crystal glass filled with an amber substance. "Sherry, sir? Miss Mason will be with you shortly."

He accepted the proffered drink and tasted the richness of the nutty-flavored liquid. Left alone, he wandered around the room, noting the luxurious antique tapestries, the ornate and expensive furnishings, the contemporary accent pieces that wove a modern touch into the design. He paused a moment at a large vase containing an array of exotic flowers and read the gift card that stood for all to see: "Yours forever, CSJ."

Michael decided he must indeed have slipped into some other world. College professors, no matter how esteemed in their own little book-lined, ivy-covered kingdoms, were not normally guests of the likes of Delilah Mason. Although he had yet to lay eyes on the woman, her surroundings revealed she was a person of incredible wealth and power. Obviously, he surmised from the flowers, she had a lover. What on earth did she want with him? The only connection between them was the mysterious ring. Was it so very valuable . . . ?

"Good afternoon, Dr. Townsend." A deep but unmistakably feminine voice startled him, and he turned to see an incredibly elegant woman standing in the doorway at one end of the long room. She was dressed in a conservative business suit, gold trimmed with black velvet. Expensive looking. Her red-golden hair was twisted atop her head, revealing an angular but attractive facial structure and a lovely slender neck. She had about her a certain confidence, an air of class and breeding. "Did you have trouble finding me?"

Momentarily unable to find his tongue, Michael only shook his head in reply. He'd seen this woman before, he was certain. On the cover of some magazine or something. Maybe on TV. Who was she? A model? A celebrity?

"I hope I didn't keep you waiting too long," he stumbled at last, thinking from her question that maybe he was tardy for their appointment, although he could have sworn he'd arrived at the proper time.

She laughed, and he recognized the sound that he'd heard the day before over the phone. "I've been waiting for you for a long time," she said, coming toward him, arms extended. She took his hands. "At least I think I have, if you prove to be who I suspect you are."

Before Michael had time to try to discern the meaning in her confusing statement, all sign of merriment vanished from her face, and she held his gaze with penetrating golden eyes. "Did you bring the ring?"

Startled first by her unexpectedly warm welcome and the intimacy of her claim that she had been waiting for him for a long time, Michael was thrown off balance again by her sudden shift in demeanor. She made him distinctly uneasy, but he'd come here to find out what he could about the mysterious ring, and it appeared she was ready and eager to talk about it. He dug into his jacket pocket and brought out the well-worn relic, handing it without a word to Delilah Mason.

He caught the flicker of keen interest in her eye as she took it and wondered again what it was about the ring that was so important to this woman? Surely not its monetary value. He was certain she must have other, far more precious jewelry.

She slipped the ring onto the slender forefinger of her left hand and held it up, studying it carefully. Then she brought her right hand alongside her left, forefingers touching, and to Michael's astonishment, he saw she wore an identical ring on her right index finger.

After a moment that seemed to go on forever, she lowered her hands and turned to Michael, a slow smile easing onto her lips. "You *are* the one," she murmured in an excited undertone. "You have come at last."

Delilah had indeed waited a long time for her High Priest to appear. Lifetimes, it had sometimes seemed. She had never doubted, however, that when the time was right, he would come to her. That time was now, and the man was here. With him she would work the magic that would at last make her the most powerful woman in all the world.

She had not expected that he would be such an innocent, although she was aware even before meeting him that Michael Townsend knew little about magic. Adrian had told her that Townsend had not even recognized the secret magical sign the bookseller had made toward him in the shop, and from his open face, she could tell that the man who stood before her held no knowledge of the secrets of the ancients.

Ah, well, she thought, training him would be a delicious task, although she had no intention of giving away her real secrets. The last Delilah had done that, with disastrous results. No, this High Priest would be a figurehead only, used to generate the raw physical power she would need. For that, he would serve well. He was handsome and virile, taller than she, with broad shoulders and a narrow waist . . .

She mustn't move too quickly, she reminded herself. She must take her time, gain his confidence. She did not want to frighten him off, and she knew that to one unschooled in the magical arts, the kind of magic she was about to introduce him to could be alarming.

Actually, Delilah decided, it would be better if he knew nothing about magic, for she would not have to change any misguided beliefs and could train him to her way of thinking. First, however, she must learn as much about him as she could, discover the traumas of his life, the manifestations of the curse she knew surrounded him if he were the true heir to the High Priesthood. For the curse was the key to her power over him. When she knew the extent of the curse's influence, she would know how to manipulate him and bend him to her will.

"Would you care for lunch, Dr. Townsend? We have much to discuss."

Seated next to Michael at the large dining table that

stretched along a wall of windows that overlooked the city, Delilah waited until their plates were served, then poured champagne into a tall flute and handed it to her guest. She could feel the heat of his body where their legs nearly touched. It was a pleasant sensation. It had been a long time since she'd been with a man, for although many wanted her, Delilah was extremely discriminating. To her, sex was more than a physical mating. It was a sacred magical act, used to raise power, and only the perfect mate would do.

She eyed Michael, speculating whether he would indeed become her magical mate. Before she decided for sure, she must find out how he had come by the ring. He must be of a particular descent to become her partner in magic.

"I know you must find this all very curious," she said, clinking her glass to his to disarm his obvious anxiety. "Please, relax, and I will tell you what I know about the rings."

She adjusted the ring on her finger and held it up once again. "They were designed by my ancestors centuries ago and worn in connection with their religious ceremonies. There were once thirteen in existence, but all except this one I wear had been lost over the years." She laughed and leaned forward, touching his arm in a friendly, intimate manner. "So you can guess my excitement when my friend at the bookstore called and described the ring you had found."

Michael gave her a twitch of a smile. "Yes, I can imagine. What I *can't* imagine is how it came into my father's possession."

Delilah wanted to know that, too. She hesitated, then looked up at him with guileless eyes. "Adrian told me the ring was with other items, magical paraphernalia you'd found in your father's house. Was he—your father—a magician?"

She saw a dark expression mar his good looks, and he gave a bitter laugh. "Hardly. My father was an accountant.

A quiet, very plain man. Although we weren't close, he raised me, and I would have known if he'd been playing at some kind of hocus-pocus.''

She winced inwardly at his reference to magic as hocus-pocus. She would have to teach him to have more respect for their work. But Delilah also heard the anger behind his words and discerned immediately that Michael did not like his father very much. The curse at work? He'd said the father had raised him. Where was the mother? Were his parents separated? A divorce could be indicative of the curse. Her hopes mounted, and she wondered about the condition of Michael's psyche. Had he grown up feeling alienated? Unwanted? Powerless? She probed further.

''What about your mother? Did she practice magic?''

Michael's jaw tightened, and he sat still as a stone. When he spoke, his voice was like ice. ''I've never known my mother. I don't know where she is, or if she's even alive. Excuse me, Miss Mason, but I don't see the relevance of your questioning. As far as I know, neither of my parents had anything to do with magic.''

At his defensive reply, Delilah knew she'd struck a raw nerve that had to do with his mother, and she felt with certainty it was the mother who had inherited the ring.

And the curse.

''Oh, please, you must forgive me,'' she apologized, affecting remorse, hoping to defuse his resistance. ''I know this is really none of my business. I'm just curious as to where the ring has been over the past years. You see, Dr. Townsend,'' she added slowly, baiting her hook, ''I believe your ring may hold great power.''

He shook his head as if bewildered. ''Power? What kind of power?''

''I told you my ancestors created the rings for religious purposes. However, theirs was not a religion in the traditional sense. My ancestors were ceremonial magicians. Theirs was the power of . . . magic.''

She said the last with deliberate emphasis and watched

closely for his reaction. She was disappointed to see a hint of amusement in his dark eyes.

"Are you a magician, Miss Mason?" His voice bespoke clear skepticism. It looked like this one wasn't going to be so easy after all. Not like that fawning Cameron St. John.

"Please, call me Delilah. I dislike being so formal." She took the ring from her finger and twirled it against her palm. "May I call you Michael?"

"You may."

"Then tell me, Michael, what do you know about magic?"

He pushed away from the table slightly. "In truth, nothing. I bought some books on the subject from your friend at the Alchymical Book Shoppe, but I haven't had time yet to read them."

Delilah traced the edge of her ring with a polished nail. "Let me fill you in a bit then. See this outer circle? It is formed by the stem of a lily. The early magicians chose this lily as their symbol, Michael, because the lily stands for purity. It represents pure power, in its rawest form. Magical power." Delilah eased herself from her seat and went to the window, gazing out over the rooftops of London. "Power," she murmured, "is a wondrous thing." Then she turned and gave him an inscrutable smile.

"Do you have power, Michael?"

Chapter Ten

IF MICHAEL HAD BEEN UNCOMFORTABLE TALKING about the metaphysical with Claire, who had been hesitant to proselytize her views, he was acutely distressed now, for it was clear Delilah Mason embraced the power of magic and was trying to convince him of it as well. Although this woman fascinated him, she also made him very uneasy, and he could not help but suspect that she might be just a little bit demented. If she were indeed a magician, as she seemed to be claiming, he decided she was likely of the black variety that Claire had told him about.

"What do you mean, do I have power?" he asked, standing as well. "What kind of power?"

She came to him and raised her eyes, looking deeply into his. "I mean the kind of power to make anyone in the world do your bidding. The power to control fate."

Michael laughed self-consciously. This woman was standing way too close. "I guess not," he said, moving to the window she'd just left. He thought about it for a moment, then added, "That's impossible. A person can't control fate. Things . . . just happen."

"Only powerless people allow themselves to be controlled by fate."

He raised his chin abruptly and glared across the room

at her. He didn't like her insinuation that he was powerless.
"I have control over my life, if that's what you mean."

"Do you?"

Her tone challenged him openly, forcing him to consider
his state of affairs, and suddenly it was apparent to him that
he *didn't* have much power over his own life. If he had, it
wouldn't be in such a mess. He wouldn't have been denied
tenure. His fiancée wouldn't be dead. He wouldn't be
searching for a mother who'd deserted him. But it was impossible for him to have control over matters like those.
"Look, Miss Mason . . ."

"Delilah, please."

Michael didn't want to call her Delilah. She was too
close, too intimate already. He needed some distance from
her. At the same time, he was intrigued by her talk of
power. "Do you have the power to make people do as you
wish? All the time?"

She laughed, but her mirth had a cynical ring. "Look
around you, Michael," she said, turning, one arm extended,
holding her champagne flute between slender fingers.
"Does this look like the dwelling of a powerless woman?
Not only do I own this apartment, I own the whole damned
building. In fact . . ." She grinned at him over a sip of
champagne. ". . . I own a great deal of this city."

"Money is powerful," Michael agreed, put off by her
boastfulness. Still, he couldn't help but be impressed.

"You have that backwards. It isn't money that brings
power. It is power that brings money. Or fame. Or whatever
it is you want."

He was confused. "I guess I don't understand your definition of power. Are you talking political power?"

She shook her head. "You have so much to learn," she
replied in a more gentle tone and moved to take a seat in
a large overstuffed chair. "Come, sit by me, and I'll help
you understand power."

Feeling a little childish, Michael sat where she indicated
on the cushioned ottoman near her feet. She took his hand

and placed his right palm against her left one. At first, her skin was cool against his, but in an instant, heat began to radiate from where their palms touched. Then he saw a glow light up their hands, reddish at first, then brightening to a brilliant gold. Delilah pulled her hand away, taking with it in her palm a small globe of light the size of a golf ball.

Michael held his breath and stared at the light, amazed and skeptical at the same time. It seemed like a parlor trick, and yet an astounding feeling surged through him. A feeling of deep and intense . . . power. Then his skin began to tingle and grow warm, and to his surprise and consternation, he felt himself growing sexually aroused.

"Did you like that?" she asked, as if she knew what he was experiencing.

"It . . . that was impressive," was all he could manage. Abruptly, he drew away from her. "How did you do that?" he challenged.

She appeared unoffended. She waited until the light on her palm dimmed into nothingness once again, then she spoke quietly. "That was the power of magic, Michael, and it is your legacy if you came into possession of that ring through your lineage. If you are the one I believe you to be, you have until now lived a cursed, wretched existence. I am here to change all that."

Michael was both irritated and dumbfounded. "How did you know . . . ?"

Her eyes were serene, and she nodded as if he'd just confirmed something in her mind. "I know many things. It is not important how. The question is, wouldn't you like to change your life? I can lift the curse that defeats you. I can teach you the power of magic, show you how to use it so the world and everyone in it will indeed do your bidding, and you will never be without power again."

Her promises hung heavily in the air between them. Michael knew he should run for his very life, but he remained glued to his seat. Delilah leaned forward, and he caught the cinnamon scent of her body. Her eyes locked on his in a mesmerizing gaze.

She was a sorceress, he thought wildly, an enchantress taking him under her spell. Or more likely, a madwoman. But somehow she was making him want her and the power she offered. He was overcome by desire—for love, for happiness, for all that life had cheated him out of. He didn't truly believe she would be lifting some kind of actual curse, but with the power she promised, he would never again be vulnerable and at the mercy of others.

"What . . . exactly . . . does that entail, learning the power of magic?"

He saw her lips curve upward, but he didn't care that he had momentarily succumbed to her will. He didn't view her as his adversary, but rather as a means to an end. She most assuredly held power, potent power, and he did not care if its source lay in magic. He wanted to own that kind of power, too. He wanted to regain control over his life, to change his miserable existence. She promised all this, and at the moment he wanted nothing more than to learn Delilah's secrets.

"I am preparing to enter a new, higher realm of magic than I have practiced in the past, and you were sent here to be my High Priest." She stood and drew him up beside her with a firm grasp. "As your High Priestess, I will teach you the secrets of the Circle of the Lily, and together we will create power the likes of which this world has never known. It's up to you. Will you serve?"

Michael teetered on the brink for a moment. He sensed that Delilah's magic was fraught with danger, but what she offered was salvation from the curse of his sorrowful, angry existence.

He thought about Claire St. John and her disdain for the dark side of the occult. But she'd also told him that his aura was dark, like a criminal's, that he was a deeply angry and unhappy man, and she had treated him as if he were the Prince of Darkness himself. She was afraid of him, and in spite of the sense of peace and comfort he felt when he was around her, he knew she could not help him out of the darkness.

For that, he would need the resources of Delilah Mason.

Lady Sarah lived in a modest cottage at the end of a dirt lane about ten miles from Montlivet. The house was isolated, surrounded by pastureland on all sides. Claire parked the car in the yard, noting that there were no trees, although flowers bloomed in the garden close to the house. She turned off the ignition and peered at the strange dwelling in front of her.

"Look at that," she murmured to Maeve who was in the passenger seat. "Everything's white." The whiteness started at the roof, which was covered in white tile. The stucco walls were painted white, and the shutters at the windows, instead of being a contrasting color, were white as well. The stones in the pathway leading to the front door had been whitewashed, and even the flowers all bore blossoms of white.

Claire exchanged glances with Maeve. She'd been forewarned that Lady Sarah was an eccentric, but this was more than eccentric; it was bizarre.

"She's a white magician." Maeve shrugged and gave her a grin. "What would you expect? Come on. Let's see if she'll talk to us."

As the two women made their way up the walk, Claire got the feeling that someone was watching their approach. Maeve gave a stout rap at the door, but at first no one answered. After several long moments, Claire was about to lose her nerve and give up when she heard the sound of a lock clicking open. The hinges creaked as the door swung slowly inward. Claire barely glimpsed the figure of the woman who greeted them before she stepped back into the shadows so they could enter.

Lady Sarah was thin and pale, gaunt almost, with large dark eyes that seemed filled with a curious mixture of peace and pain, like a saint's. As soon as Claire was inside and her eyes adjusted to the lower light, she noticed immediately that the woman's aura virtually shimmered in shades of the deepest blue, the color that usually surrounded persons of a highly spiritual nature. She wore a flowing white gown that draped in heavy folds around her thin frame, and her hair was long, wavy, and very, very white.

"Welcome," she said, her voice barely more than a whisper. "I have been expecting you."

Claire gaped at her, but Lady Sarah ignored her and closed the door behind them. Then she turned to them with a small smile and said, "Please, make yourselves comfortable."

Maeve settled into a high-backed chair upholstered in a well-worn ivory brocade, while Claire took a seat on a white-cotton-covered sofa. Everything around them—every article of furnishing, every pillow, every picture frame—*everything* was pure white. There was even a pair of white doves chortling from an ornate white cage in the corner.

Claire felt encompassed by a sense of power that was as pure as her white surroundings. It was a deep and quiet power, mystical, holy almost, and it held her awestruck, unable to utter a word. She was glad when she heard Maeve at last find her voice.

"Thank you for inviting us in, Lady Sarah," she said, and Claire heard the awe and respect in her voice. Her friend felt the woman's power, too.

"I have been expecting you," the woman in white repeated. "I am glad you have come, for I need your help."

Claire shot a glance at Maeve, then spoke to Lady Sarah. "I . . . I'm afraid I don't understand," she began. "We . . . uh . . . I came to *you* seeking help."

The wizened woman gave her a benevolent smile. "That is usually the way it works. We must help one another. I suspect that our needs are somehow related. Why don't you tell me first what I can do for you?"

Claire was startled by the woman's conviction that this

visit was predestined, but she decided that Lady Sarah was likely a powerful psychic, and she was curious as to how exactly she and Maeve could help the magician. Still, she was pleased that the favor she was about to ask could be reciprocated.

"My name is Claire St. John. I own Fairfield House in Montlivet. I recently rented a cottage adjacent to my house to a man who . . ." She glanced nervously at Maeve, then continued, ". . . Who is surrounded by an aura that is almost completely black. He . . . he seems a nice enough sort, except that in my psychic vision I can see not only the black aura but also sometimes flashes of red anger around his heart. I sense strongly that he has led an unhappy, maybe even disastrous, life."

"Why is he any concern of yours?" Lady Sarah asked bluntly. "Is he just a tenant, or is there some other relationship?"

Claire blushed deeply. "He is just a tenant," she asserted, but the older woman shook her head.

"No. There is a deeper connection."

Claire caught the edge of a smile on Maeve's lips. "I think my young protégée here has fallen in love with this man of darkness," she explained to Lady Sarah.

"Yes. I can see that." It was an analytical statement, completely free of judgment, and Claire knew the woman was only gathering facts, as Claire herself always did when beginning to work with a new client. "Continue," the woman said.

"He told me when he first arrived that he was here to do research for a book, and he asked if I knew anything about magic. I referred him to the Alchymical Book Shoppe in London." For the first time she saw a shadow of a frown cross Lady Sarah's face. "I . . . I know that might have been a mistake, but I know nothing about magic, and you . . . well, you seemed unavailable."

"It is not important," Lady Sarah replied. "Go on."

"The afternoon that he returned, he received a telephone

call at my house, which I answered, and . . .'' She broke off and cleared her throat, feeling again the horrible evil she had sensed across the phone line. ''It was a woman's voice, and it was so . . . vile, it made me ill. I admit to overhearing part of their conversation, and he made an appointment to meet with her today. Earlier I saw him leave, I assume heading for the train station, and I felt a strong psychic sense that he was about to get involved with this woman, and that she personifies evil and power of the darkest kind.'' Claire raised her eyes and looked directly at Lady Sarah.

''I don't understand why I feel so compelled to try to help this man, but if I don't make an effort, and if he is lost to the darkness, I will blame myself forever.''

Lady Sarah's face softened. ''Love is a powerful motivator.'' She stood and went to the mantel where she picked up a box of matches. Then she returned and lit a large, white candle in the center of the low table that stood between their seats. ''I have felt a strong disturbance on the astral plane for several days now,'' she spoke at last, gazing into the flame. ''It was at first only a current. But two days ago, I felt the power strengthen. It is magical power, and whoever is working it is a strong magician indeed, but unfortunately, one who has taken the Left Hand Path. I have already set about taking protective measures.''

Claire's eyebrows shot up. ''Left Hand Path?''

''The dark side of magic. Some call it black magic, although I find that term offensive.''

She grew quiet and focused on the flame of the candle. ''I have spent a lifetime working to overcome the powers of darkness,'' she said after a few moments. Her voice was low, ragged, and Claire again read a deep sorrow in her hollow eyes. ''I had hoped the evil had been banished. But now I know it was only held in abeyance.''

''What is happening?'' Claire felt the hair stand up along her arms.

''I see a renaissance, if you will, a rekindling of an ancient evil. You were right to fear for this man. He is in grave danger.''

Claire's stomach knotted. "What can we do?"

Lady Sarah turned her grave eyes to Claire. "We must wage war to destroy this evil once and for all.''

"Wage war?" She was appalled. "What kind of war?"

"A war of wills. We must overcome the forces of the Left Hand Path by asserting the influence of the Right Hand, or white, Path both in the astral and here on the physical plane. I cannot do it alone. I am old and my magic is not as strong as it once was. I need help. I suspected that our needs were related. In truth, I believe they are intertwined. I can help you, but only if you can help me.''

Claire grimaced and gave Maeve a look of dismay. She'd come here for some simple advice, never expecting to become involved in what appeared to be some kind of magical war. She found the idea distinctly distasteful. "What would I have to do?"

"You will have to learn the basics of my magical practices, of course, but mostly I need the strength of your psychic powers. The more power we can join together, the more likely we are to succeed.''

"I will commit mine as well," Maeve offered, "and I believe the others in our séance circle will work together in the effort. Perhaps I can enlist the powers of my friends who work at Belgrave Square as well.''

"Very well. That will be of immense help. We must begin work at once. But I must warn you," she said, turning to Claire, "your . . . uh . . . tenant may be in even greater danger if he is caught in between the forces of good and evil. You must try everything in your power to bring him to the Right Hand Path, for if he remains in the path of darkness, and we are successful in destroying it, he, too, will be destroyed.''

"Maeve, I'm frightened." They had taken their leave of Lady Sarah after receiving specific instructions for employing the psychic powers of the members of the séance circle and for setting up their personal magical defense systems. The white magician had involved them in a special ritual of protection and given Claire an amulet to shield her from the darkness of Michael's auric field. Lady Sarah had warned them that the war they were about to wage was serious—deadly serious. "I had no idea we were getting into anything like this," Claire murmured.

Maeve shot her a slightly amused look. "Of course you had an idea on some level that you must fight for the one you love or else you wouldn't have sought help from Lady Sarah. But don't fear, Claire. Fear is your worst enemy. Believe in yourself and your powers and your will to overcome Michael's darkness. It will give you the strength and courage to face anything."

Her words gave Claire heart. She did believe that what she was doing was best for everyone involved. "You're right, of course. I just wish I knew more specifically what I could do to persuade Michael Townsend to steer clear of that woman."

"You fight fire with fire," Maeve returned with a grin.

"What do you mean?"

"Lady Sarah told us she's seen the sorceress who is working the black magic out on the astral plane, and that she is very beautiful and very seductive. I imagine that combination gives her great power over men. You could have that power, too, you know."

Claire looked across at her friend, not believing her ears. "I don't get it. What are you suggesting?"

They had reached the village, and Maeve invited Claire to have a cup of coffee at the local cappuccino bar. When they were settled at a table in the patio garden behind the shop, she continued. "Claire, you are a very attractive woman, but you don't seem to realize it. You dress nicely, but if I may say so, you look prematurely . . . well, matronly."

Claire was taken aback. This was so unlike Maeve, who

normally had more cosmic things on her mind. "I beg your pardon?"

Maeve laughed and took Claire's hand. "Please, don't take offense. Hear me out. It's only a suggestion. You can take it or leave it. But if Michael is enticed by the siren song of a beautiful sorceress, wouldn't it make sense to counteract that attraction by being just as beautiful, or more so?"

"I . . . I'm not the beautiful type," Claire protested, her face burning.

Maeve shook her head. "You are beautiful. Inside and out. You just need to . . . showcase your beauty."

Claire thought about it a minute and recalled how she had looked in the mirror just before going out to survey the damage of the storm. Haggish. That's how she'd described herself. She glanced at Maeve. "Do I look that bad?"

"No, my dear. But with just a little attention to detail you could look stunning. I sense psychically that Michael Townsend is already somewhat taken with you, but if that other woman gets her claws into him and you don't fight back . . . well, all this could be for nothing. I'm not exactly sure of the scope of Lady Sarah's magical war, but I know that if you want that man, you'd better pull out all the stops."

Chapter Eleven

MICHAEL WAS EXHAUSTED FROM THE AFTERNOON spent with Delilah Mason. Her high energy seemed to wear him out. But she also intrigued him. If nothing else, she was an intelligent, well spoken woman, and her talk of the history and mechanics of magic, no matter how outrageous he found it, had held him rapt the entire time.

Over the course of the afternoon, as they'd gotten to know one another better, she'd managed to draw the story of his life from him. He'd even shared with her the reason he had come to England, and she'd surprised him by saying that she had the feeling that his mother was still alive. She'd even offered to use her contacts to help him in his search.

Although she had argued hard to get him to accept magic as something real, the rational, academic side of him rejected the concept out of hand. But her knowledge of the mythical subject was deep and authoritative, academic in its own way, convincing, and at last he conceded that he would consider it as a possibility.

She'd asked him to stay the night, using her guest room, but he did not wish to remain in the intense atmosphere of her presence. She fascinated him, and he wanted to know about her power, but he couldn't shake his sense of danger.

Her secretive intimations that their magical relationship, if
he became her High Priest, would involve certain sexual
practices alarmed him, and her relentless attentions had
drained him.

She had not told him directly what she really wanted of
him as her High Priest, only that she wished to personally
instruct him in the ways of magic rather than have him
learn it from reading books. She had not asked for the ring
but rather had insisted that he wear it, claiming that the
rings forged a magical bond between them that not even
time could sever. She was prone to the dramatic, he'd
noted. At any rate, he wasn't sure he wanted such a bond
with Delilah Mason, and as soon as he'd left her apartment,
he'd slipped the ring into his pocket once again.

He was disappointed that he had learned little that would
explain the presence of the ring and the other items in his
father's attic. Delilah had made mention of his "magical
lineage" and thought that possibly Stella Townsend had
been a practicing magician at one time. Magicians, she'd
told him, required much time alone for their work and suggested that as a possible motive for Stella's desertion. Michael was tempted to grasp at it as an explanation for the
inexplicable, except for one thing—Delilah claimed that
magic created power. If Stella had had power, why didn't
she use it to overcome the demons, real or imagined, that
apparently had haunted her?

Michael's head pounded as he stepped from the train
onto the platform at Montlivet. He needed a drink and some
time to think everything through. At least Delilah had not
sent him home with a textbook to read. He was still somewhat overwhelmed by the material in the volume Claire
had given him, and he didn't want to face more homework
again tonight.

Recalling the book brought his thoughts to Claire St.
John. When he'd left for the city earlier in the day, he'd
been determined to find another place to rent upon his return. He had not wished to give her further opportunity to

probe into his psyche or to discover his personal emotional secrets. But suddenly, he found to his surprise that he wanted to see her, very much wanted to be with her. Strangely, he realized he had actually missed her today.

How odd that in his life, which until now been rather devoid of involvement with the opposite sex, he would find himself in the company of two very appealing women. They were like opposite sides of the coin, however. Claire shone like silver, while Delilah emanated a darker attraction, like the promise held within the base metals that alchemists once sought to turn into gold.

Michael had walked as far as the main intersection in the village and contemplated dropping into a nearby pub, the King's Arms, before returning to his apartment. But not having eaten much of Delilah's elegant lunch, he found he was hungrier than he was thirsty. It was just six o'clock. Uncharacteristically, he made an impulsive decision. If Claire had not already prepared her evening meal, he would ask if she'd like to have dinner with him. He owed her that much as an apology for his earlier rudeness.

He knew it wasn't mere good manners that inspired his decision, however. He wanted to be with Claire again. He wanted the peace and serenity that surrounded him when he was with her.

Upon reaching Fairfield House, instead of going down the path to the cottage at the back, Michael knocked at Claire's front door as he had just two days before when he'd first arrived. Would her welcome be any warmer today than it had been then? The way he'd been behaving, there was no reason to think so.

When she opened the door, Michael didn't think it was the same woman. Not only did her eyes light up when she saw him, but her entire appearance was dramatically altered. Instead of being severely pulled back, her hair was styled in loose curls that teased and played in casual disarray around her cheeks. Her eyes were pleasingly accented with touches of eye shadow and mascara, and her lips shimmered in a frosted raspberry color. Instead of the gentrified casual attire and pale colors he had seen her in before, she wore a long skirt of a crinkled silken fabric and a matching sleeveless top, both in a shining sapphire blue. Around her neck was a pendant on a golden chain. It looked to be a large wedge of quartz crystal.

Michael's heart sank even as he admired her. She must already have a date. "I'm intruding," he said.

"You're not," she replied. "Please come in."

He followed her into the sitting room, unable to take his eyes off the sway of the long skirt over her hips. "You look beautiful," he said as she turned to him.

She lowered her gaze. "Thank you," she murmured demurely.

"Are you expecting someone?"

Her eyes raised again and met his.

"You."

Michael was astounded. And pleased. He took a chance and placed both hands on her shoulders. "I knocked on your door because I wanted to know if you would have dinner with me tonight."

Her cheeks were high with color. "I bought this new outfit, in case I needed something to wear to dinner tonight."

"You must be psychic."

As if it were the most natural thing in the world, Michael lowered his lips to hers, and equally as easily she opened hers to receive him. He moved his hands to her back and felt the coolness of the silk fabric against his palms. She was like the silk, liquid in his embrace. He ran the fingers of one hand through her platinum curls, luxuriating in the texture and the scent released by his touch. Her looks, he realized, were not all that had changed since this morning. She exhibited no sign that she feared him. He had no idea what had brought about this astounding change, but he felt as if his heart would explode.

She drew away from him, and he released her gently, his

eyes quizzing hers to see if he had overstepped his boundaries. But she glanced briefly toward the top of his head, and a smile formed on the lips he longed to taste once again. "What? What is it?" he asked.

"Your aura," she whispered. "It's brightening."

"If you like Indian-style cuisine, this place is excellent," Claire told Michael as he held the restaurant door open for her. She still could not believe everything that had transpired during the day, most of all that Michael had actually sought her out to invite her to dinner.

The ambience of the restaurant was exotic, with decor that summoned images of the mysteries of the Far East. Sitar music played in the background, and a fountain trickled near the entrance. Claire felt as exotic as her surroundings. Beautiful even.

At first she had been slightly offended when Maeve suggested that she needed a makeover, but then, upon fair consideration, she knew her friend was only telling her what she had already been feeling, that she'd let her appearance lapse, and that she looked older than her age. Once she'd crossed that hurdle, accepting that she could use an image update, she and Maeve had had a heyday in the shop of one of Maeve's clients who specialized in wardrobe, hair, and makeup design. First, the artist had trimmed and shaped her hair, clucking over its lackluster plainness and severity and styling it into a swishy, sexy coiffure that would be both easy to care for and far more flattering to her face. Claire had been astonished at the change she saw in the mirror.

The stylist then performed another miracle with the application of just the right touches of makeup. Claire protested at first that she never used makeup, but Maeve gave her a very pointed look, and she acquiesced, remembering that change was why she had come here. She was not sorry. Her face took on a new glow, her eyes looked brighter, her lips fuller.

"Even Morgan LeFay had to put on the glamor to enchant the young King Arthur," her friend joked, recalling the old tale. "In fact, the word 'glamor' originally meant to cast a magical spell or enchantment."

After her makeup session, Claire had gone through the adjoining boutique with the wardrobe specialist who advised her to wear more vibrant colors. "Pastels make you fade away," she'd warned. "But don't wear bright red or stark white or black, either. They would be too harsh. Choose jewel tones instead."

And she had. Lots of them. She knew she might regret it when her bank statement came in, but at the moment, she was glad she had spent the money on the new items of clothing and accessories, including the blue skirt and blouse she had been trying on when Michael came to the door. It had been worth the cost of it all to see the look on his face when she'd answered his knock. Yes, she knew she had indeed put on the glamor, and she hoped her first enchantment would be strong enough to attract him away from the sorceress in London.

Still, her heart beat heavily beneath the crystal pendant. This game was very new to her, and she wasn't exactly sure how to play it. She had never been a seductress. She fingered the pendant nervously. Lady Sarah had told her it would protect her from any forces of darkness that might be hovering around Michael, including his aura. Claire didn't know if the amulet had such powers, but she chose to believe that it did.

They ordered drinks, and the host handed them each an oversized menu. She looked up from it to find Michael's eyes boring into her. "What . . . what's the matter?"

He gave her a curiously sad smile. "Nothing. Except . . ."

"What, Michael?" Normally, she might have been able to sense what was troubling him, but her romantic feelings toward him appeared to be blocking her psychic channels tonight.

He took her hand. "I'm almost afraid to be here with you," he said at last.

"I don't understand."

"You said you saw darkness in my aura. I don't know if I believe there are such things as auras, but I do know that you were right about my life. It's been one bad turn after another all along the way, and everything I've touched seems to have turned to disaster. I . . . I'm afraid that somehow I might bring you harm . . ."

Claire wanted to reassure him that his fears were groundless, but she could not. He very well might bring her harm. At least she'd thought so until her visit to Lady Sarah's today. Now, she feared, it was she who might bring harm to him.

"Do you want to talk about it?" she asked quietly. "All that's gone wrong in your life, I mean. I'm a good listener, and sometimes I can help people resolve their dilemmas. It's what I do for a living."

"What do you mean?"

"I'm a . . . counselor, Michael, although I must tell you I use different techniques than most psychologists and social workers."

She saw a shadow cloud his face. "I don't need a shrink."

She squeezed his hand. "I'm not a shrink. But I could be your friend."

The waiter brought their drinks and took their dinner order. Michael remained silent for a long while. "What techniques?"

"Sorry. What?"

"You said you use 'different' techniques. What are you talking about?"

"I'm a psychic counselor, Michael. I use my sensitive perceptions, sometimes with psychometry, to get to the root of people's problems."

He thought a moment. "I read about psychometry in

your book, but could you explain it to me? How does it work?''

Encouraged that he seemed to be opening to things out of the ordinary, Claire explained how she could get messages about people by touching items belonging to them. ''I don't expect you to believe in all this,'' she told him. ''It's . . . not for everybody. And I certainly don't want to force my beliefs and opinions on anyone.''

He didn't seem to hear her last comment. ''You mean if I gave you an item, say a piece of jewelry, you could tell me who it belonged to? Or where it came from?''

Claire was surprised by his sudden interest. She shrugged. ''Maybe. It depends on how old the vibrations are.''

Curious, she watched as Michael fished something out of his pocket. A small item. He took her hand again and turned it palm up on the table. In it he placed a golden ring. Claire looked at it closely, then gasped and began to tremble.

It was the ring she'd held only a few days before. The ring worn by the skeleton she'd discovered in the roots of the tree in her pasture.

''Where did you get this?''

Michael was shocked by the intensity on Claire's face when he handed her the ring. He didn't really expect her to pick up any resonance from it, but he thought perhaps she might recognize the symbol. He was hoping that it was far more common than Delilah had claimed. He did not really buy the woman's story of being descended from a long line of magicians. He had, in fact, wondered more than once during the afternoon if the woman known as Delilah Mason was not a borderline lunatic.

''I found it,'' he answered Claire's question.

She gave him a skeptical look. ''You aren't with the police, are you?''

It was his turn to be confused, but she continued before

he could find out why she would ask such a question.

"No. Never mind. This isn't the same ring, although I'm certain it is the same symbol."

Wondering what she meant by "the same ring," Michael held his breath and watched her study the piece. An amazing array of expressions crossed her beautiful face. She was obviously feeling something—many things, it would seem. At last she spoke.

"Oh, Michael, this ring is just like the other one. It virtually trembles with . . . a terrible evil. Where on earth did you get it?"

"I found it," he reiterated, not wanting to tell her where. Michael found himself suddenly at a crossroads. He'd taken a risk in showing Claire the ring, hoping her psychic impressions would give him a shortcut to its history. Did he dare tell her more? What would she think of him if he told her that he'd spent the day with a black magician and was considering becoming her pupil, if only to learn how this ring related to his life? Or that this ring that "trembled with evil" might have belonged to his mother, who possibly also practiced the black arts?

"Do you recognize the symbol?" he asked instead.

She nodded and eyed him speculatively. "I saw a ring just like this only two days ago. It, too, resounded with evil vibrations. Michael, what is going on here?"

The arrival of their succulent, curry-scented dinners interrupted them momentarily, and Michael considered dropping the subject. But it was critical that he know the history of the ring. He decided to answer her obliquely. "I found that ring along with some other odd things in the attic of my father's house after he died. Can you tell me anything about it? How old is it? Who has owned it?"

Claire closed her fingers around the ring and shut her eyes. "The trouble that is passed with this ring goes back many generations," she told him at last. "It has been like a . . . a curse to your family."

It wasn't the kind of history Michael had been expecting.

He stared at her. "A curse? What are you talking about? There's no such thing as curses."

"Michael," she returned, her tone exasperated, "you asked me to read this ring, and I'm telling you what I'm getting. Please, don't make light of what I'm telling you. Curses exist. I don't know much about how they work, but my friend Maeve can tell us."

Michael recalled the words Delilah had uttered to him that afternoon: *I can lift the curse that defeats you.*

He ran his fingers through his dark hair, his appetite vanished. He shouldn't have involved Claire in this business. It was a shameful, shadowed affair and best dealt with by the likes of Delilah Mason. Not wanting to despoil the beauty he found in Claire St. John, he decided he would take his darkness and crawl back under his rock. He must protect her—from himself.

He held his hand out for the ring, and she returned it. "Forget it, Claire," he said, putting it back in his pocket. "It's just silly superstition."

She gave him a skeptical look. "Is it? Then why is it bothering you so much?"

He slammed down his napkin. "I'm not bothered."

She grinned. "You could have fooled me, and I'm psychic." Then she reached for his hand. "Come on. Let's forget it and enjoy our evening."

But for Michael, the joy was gone.

When they'd finished their meal, which they'd eaten without becoming involved in further serious conversation, Michael and Claire returned to the street and strolled in the gathering twilight along the cobblestones, past store windows replete with tourist-tantalizing goods ranging from antiques to comic books. He would have liked to take her hand as they walked, but her talk about curses had made him uneasy. If he was cursed, could he somehow contaminate her? He quickened his pace, angry with himself for even considering such nonsense. Curses didn't exist, no matter what she said. Neither did any chance exist for closeness between him and Claire St. John. The sooner he returned her home, the better.

As they reached her garden gate, a full golden moon edged up over the roof of her house, and Claire stopped and stood transfixed, her hands clasped like a little girl staring in wonder at some childish delight. Michael's heart twisted. How he wanted to be close to her, to share her delight. Her ease with life. But he was becoming more and more convinced that when the gods had cast his lot, they'd chosen him a fate that did not include such things as closeness and ease and delight.

She turned to him, her eyes shining. "Oh, Michael, isn't it beautiful?"

"Yes, it is." *And so are you,* he wanted to add.

At his clipped reply, she frowned. "What's the matter?"

What was the matter? Only that he wanted her and all she stood for—beauty, truth, light—but likely he would never have any of them.

"It's getting late. I'll walk you to your door."

She did not move toward the door. Instead, she came to him and slid her arms around his back. She leaned into him, pressing her breasts against him, and he could feel their softness on either side of the hard crystal that nestled between them. He wished she'd take it off.

She raised her head. "Kiss me, Michael."

Oh, God, why was she making this so difficult? What had happened to her fear of him? Didn't she know he was dark and dangerous and not worth knowing? But his lips had reached hers, and his thoughts blurred as she drew him even more tightly into her embrace. There must be magic in the moonlight, he thought briefly, feeling himself dissolve in her arms.

Magic, and she was the ultimate enchantress.

Chapter Twelve

CLAIRE WAS FAR MORE UPSET OVER THE VIBES SHE'D received from the ring than she'd let on to Michael, but she did not want to spoil the evening or dampen her efforts to lure him into the influence of her positive energy. If anything, what she'd felt convinced her even more strongly that she must work with all her power to keep him from falling deeper into the darkness.

There was nothing she could do about what she'd psychically received, at least not until morning when she would call the police and see what they might have learned about the symbolism on the ring. Perhaps it would give her a clue as to what she should do next.

When they reached her door, she invited Michael in for tea or brandy, but he declined, giving some vague excuse which left her feeling foolish for the overt advance she had just made toward him by the garden gate. What had gotten into her? Was she smitten by the moonlight?

No, she sighed, climbing the stairs to her room. She was smitten by Michael Townsend. Slipping out of her skirt and hanging it carefully in her closet, she decided it was just as well that he hadn't accepted her invitation. She needed time to sort out her thoughts, her feelings toward him.

Did she love him? she asked her image in the mirror, an

image that looked back at her in an unfamiliar yet undeniably radiant beauty. Intellectually, she didn't see how that
was possible. She barely knew him. But she couldn't deny
that she seemed to care very much about him. Was it love?
Or was it just her usual penchant for bringing in strays?
Was he just another project, like Cameron had been?

Still, both Maeve and Lady Sarah had at separate times
psychically perceived her feelings toward Michael Townsend to be love. Claire laughed. It was sort of like that old
joke about the two psychics who ran into one another on
the street, and one said to the other, "Good morning. How
am I?" Psychics often could perceive another's state of
mind better than their own.

Claire considered putting on the silken chemise night-
gown she'd purchased. She had seen no need for it, but
Maeve had insisted, "Just in case." Well, there was no
need for it tonight, she thought glumly, so she donned a T-
shirt, her normal sleeping attire, and headed for bed with
several books Lady Sarah had given her about the elements
of magical power. However, since she'd never taken the
nap she'd intended, fatigue and her unsettled thoughts
about Michael stole her concentration. The book fell into
her lap as she nodded off . . .

*A noise sounded in her consciousness, a drone, like
the sound of a thousand bees swarming in a hive. It
grew louder as she hurried along the corridor of the
basement toward the forbidden room. Her heart beat
so hard she thought she might faint, but she would not
allow herself one thought of failure. She must be
strong. For Nigel. For their young son, Joseph. She
must rid her home of the evil that Nigel in his foolish
yearning for power had brought into their lives. Banish forever the wicked ones who crept into the basement of her stately hall under cover of darkness, too
cowardly to proclaim their filthy deeds before God and
countryman. This was a battle for God, she told her-*

*self, to save her beloved family, and the only weapon
she had was the small golden crucifix she grasped so
tightly in her hand it threatened to cut her skin.*

She reached the enormous double doorway that led
into a chamber she had never been allowed to visit.
The sound was now very loud, a chant in a strong,
rhythmic vibration. What did they do in this room?
Nigel had created it in great secrecy, allowing only
one person to enter during the construction, a vile
woman with flaming red hair and a cloak of crimson.
Watching from one of the tall windows in the gabled
upper floor of the mansion, she had often witnessed
the woman's arrival in a fancy coach and had seen
her husband rush eagerly to greet her and, when like
a queen she'd held out her hand, kiss her fingers.

She felt the sin of jealousy wash over her. She hated
this woman whom she had never met. This woman who
was slender and beautiful, elegantly but licentiously
dressed, flaunting her body openly toward Nigel, while
she, plump and unpretty, was ordered to the upper
floors, where she huddled in the nursery, holding her
young son, afraid for their very lives. Was that woman
behind these doors tonight? She had not seen her arrive, but she was certain of her presence. The very air
seemed to crackle with evil.

Clutching her cross, she took a deep breath and
slowly twisted the large knob in the center of one of
the huge oaken doors. Surprisingly, it was unlocked.
As she eased it open, the sound of the chanting resonated through her entire body. Deep, male voices, repeating strange words over and over. Her stomach
clenched, but she did not lose her resolve. Quietly, she
slipped into the room, leaving the door ajar. The scene
before her shocked, revolted, and terrified her.

The room was round, and carved into the stone of
the ceiling was a circular image, a mystical symbol of
some sort, although it was difficult for her to see it in

the darkened chamber. The only light was cast by candles placed at intervals around the walls, and by the flicker of their flame, she could see figures clad in long red robes. Men, walking slowly around the circle, chanting, chanting, ever louder. As they walked, she could see their feet were bare, and she felt certain that beneath the cloaks they were naked.

But it wasn't the circle of men that filled her with revulsion and despair. It was what they were circling around. For there in the center, lying naked and writhing in sexual ecstasy upon an altar, was the flame-haired woman, her long legs encircling the waist of the man who was also engaged in the act . . . her own husband, Nigel.

No one had seen her enter the room, for the entire company was entranced by what was transpiring. She stood frozen for a moment, looking on in horror and disbelief. And then she gathered her courage. She must save him. She must save Nigel from this incredible evil. Her Christian God was with her, and His cross was more powerful than any heathen magic.

Raising her arm and brandishing the crucifix, she screamed at the top of her voice, "In the name of God I command you to cease! In the name of our Holy Mother Mary, take your wickedness from here! Begone!"

The chanting stopped immediately, but the man and woman on the altar appeared unaware of what was happening. They continued their sexual union with the abandon of wild animals. Again she cried out, "Nigel! Run! Run for your life from her! She is the devil's own bride! Nigel!"

At the sound of his name, her husband raised his head. His eyes were heavy-lidded, his look dazed. And then he saw his wife, and his entire body seemed to turn to stone. He appeared unable to move. She took a step closer to the circle. "Leave her at once!" she *ordered. "This is not your fault. God will forgive your sins. But you must leave now!"*

She moved still closer to the edge of the circle, when suddenly Nigel pulled himself from the woman and screamed, "No. Don't come nearer." He held his arms out, his hands splayed, warning her of danger. On one finger, she spied an unfamiliar golden ring. She knew nothing about the kind of wickedness in which her husband was involved, but she did not for a moment doubt its power. The room fairly hummed with some unseen force.

Then she looked at the woman, who had not moved from her bed upon the altar. Like a sexually sated whore, the wicked one leaned on one elbow and flaunted her voluptuous naked body by stroking herself from breast to navel. On one finger, she wore a ring identical to Nigel's. The woman's tawny eyes flickered in the firelight, taunting her, daring her to attack.

That was all it took. With the power of a lioness determined to protect and defend what was hers, in the name of righteousness and all that was holy, she charged toward the woman . . .

A crack sounded, like air split by lightning, and Claire bolted from her bed. She was shaking uncontrollably and drenched in sweat. Tears burned her eyes. It took several moments for her to realize it had only been a dream, a horrible nightmare.

She went into the adjoining bathroom and splashed cold water on her face, ordering her mind to clear, her nerves to calm down. It wasn't easy. This had been no ordinary dream, not even your run-of-the-mill nightmare. It had been instead like a vision, an insight into things past. And present. And future. Claire shuddered.

In a few moments, however, she managed to regain control, and when she did, it was with determination to look at the dream objectively. Quickly, she scribbled down what she had seen and felt, and as she wrote, she suddenly remembered the crucifix. It had been the same, she was certain, as the one she'd found in her kitchen drawer. The apport brought to her, so Maeve believed, by the ghost who called herself Eloise.

"My God," she uttered. "Was that . . . did I dream I was . . . Eloise?"

She flew down the stairs and into the kitchen, turning on all the lights, not wishing to invite the ghostly presence of Eloise into the room. She grasped the crucifix, half expecting it to send her reeling as it had done before, but although she psychically felt it trembling, it remained benign. Claire closed her eyes. Yes. This was the same crucifix as in the dream. And she knew with certainty that what she'd seen in her nightmare had been history, not dreamstuff.

Murdered.

The ghost named Eloise had believed she was murdered. But concentrating, thinking back into the dream, Claire was not sure. It seemed to her more like a terrible magical accident. Either way, could such things happen?

Was the power of magic strong enough to kill?

Delilah Mason did not sleep that night, indeed never thought about sleep. She was too wired about the sudden and unexpected progress of her magical plans.

Wired, and worried. Because of the ring, she believed that Michael Townsend was her man, the High Priest she had awaited for so long, but she harbored some serious concerns about him.

In the first place, she could not tell if her discourse on magic had had much impact on him. He'd seemed keen enough even though what she'd revealed had been elementary, a quick broad picture intended to tantalize him further with intimations of the power that could be his. Although his questions had been intelligent, she caught no sense of passion, no hungry curiosity about the subject.

It had crossed her mind that perhaps he had come by the ring purely by accident. Perhaps he was not the one whose legacy it was to join her in recreating the Circle of the Lily. That was possible, she supposed, although the very coincidence of the timing of his arrival made her believe that her astral contacts had delivered him to become her High Priest just when she was ready for him.

Another problem was that although she had offered him ample invitation through her body language, he had not made any sexual advances toward her. He might have just been practicing gentlemanly conduct; certainly he had shown a great deal of restraint. But a High Priest must take the lead in the kind of magic they were about to share—High Sex Magick. She was particularly piqued when he'd refused her invitation to stay the night.

Delilah was rarely refused anything. And she was not pleased.

Before she could implement her plan, she must be sure he was the right man and that she held him spellbound in every respect. She could not work effective magic with a halfhearted partner. She must have a partner who fiercely desired her sexually. For it was only High Sex Magick that could generate the kind of power she sought.

Quit worrying, she told herself, pacing. You've only just met him. He has no idea that this is his destiny. He's still the most innocent of initiates. Don't be impatient.

But Delilah was impatient. She wanted right now what she had awaited for so long, what she believed was rightly hers . . . immense personal power that would allow her to influence heads of state, religious leaders, princes of commerce. With her strength, magically raised, she would be able to manipulate the manipulators, to make them—as she'd told Michael—do her bidding.

Other magicians in history had approached such power but had fallen short of creating it. The ancients in Egypt, who had discovered the language of magic, had used it to attempt to gain immortality. The popes and kings of the

Renaissance had resorted to magic and alchemy to emerge powerful from the Dark Ages. In more modern times, occultists had turned to magic for a more personal kind of power, repulsive religious uses for magic in Delilah's opinion.

None, however, had succeeded in obtaining the full power inherent in and available only through the practice of High Sex Magick. Only she, Delilah Mason, would know that ultimate success. She who had trained more carefully under the auspices of the Dark Masters in the astral than any other. She who had earned the right. She who was disciplined. Dedicated. Determined.

She was not about to lose now to the lassitude and naivete of the High Priest who'd been sent to serve her. She would conjure all the power she controlled at the moment, and it was considerable, to bring Michael Townsend into line.

Immediately.

Delilah knew what steps to take. Entering the secret, forbidden chamber, she laughed to herself. Outside of her newly formed High Court, no one knew, not a single person suspected that she—urbane, witty, charming Delilah Mason—was also a potent sorceress. No one would believe it, either. It simply wasn't a twentieth-century skill. She wondered briefly if she would be able to effectively train the boys, as she thought of the young men in her High Court, or if they were only going along with her for a lark.

She hoped they were serious, for she had no patience with dilettantes.

In the low light of her private temple room, she approached the altar where she took up a book, a handwritten magical diary with yellowed pages and no cover. She turned the well-worn pages deftly and reviewed the spell, much as a chef might review a recipe.

Satisfied, she took five red candles from the supply cabinet and placed them in a five-pointed arrangement upon the altar. Lighting them one by one, she called aloud as the flames flared, invoking the most masculine of all energies, the warrior god Mars, commanding his power to overcome Michael's hesitancy.

Releasing the buttons on her silken robe, she let it slide off her shoulders and onto the floor. Standing naked, she raised her arms and stared into the flames and began to chant. The words were as ancient as time. Powerful words, used to summon an errant lover. As spells went, this one rarely failed.

In the flame of one of the candles she saw him, his dark hair silhouetted against a white surface, likely a pillow given that it was long after midnight. She saw him awaken, and she smiled. He'd heard the call. She chanted again and focused her entire mental power toward the image in the flame. She summoned him with every ounce of her will. Her magic was powerful. He would return to her this very night.

On the astral plane, there is no day, no night. There is, in fact, no time and all time. Yesterday and tomorrow coexist with today, but all are an illusion. The astral plane is a doorway into the more refined dimensions beyond. It is a mental realm, accessible to humans who quest with their mind to break through the confines of the physical and delve into the mysteries of the universe.

There are beings who dwell in the astral, and just as on earth, not all of them are nice. Lady Sarah had learned this the hard way in the beginning of her training as a magician when she'd been psychically attacked by a discarnate spirit of darkness who challenged her entry into his "territory." She had quickly learned how to create safe passageways for her travels to avoid encountering the malevolent ones, and if she happened upon them nonetheless, how to protect herself from their influences, both in her astral travels and on earth. Recently, she had also learned the difficult art of becoming invisible to astral beings and other travelers to this realm, thereby enabling her to observe while not being observed in return. It was this unique ability that had allowed her to witness the dark workings of the sorceress named Delilah.

It had been many years since Lady Sarah had begun developing her abilities under the auspices of the Watchers, the ones who in the occult hierarchy are responsible for the safety and well-being of the world. In the beginning, she had thought she was going mad when she'd heard them speak to her, calling her into service. But once she'd made her initial passage into the astral and had been greeted and blessed by the great Beings of Light who met her there, she knew she must join and follow their Order.

For theirs was the cause of Light over Darkness. And theirs was the magic that offered redemption from the midnight torments of her own soul. For the Watchers she would become a lookout, a guardian of the Light on the Earth plane. For their cause she was willing to become a warrior when the time came, because she believed that by conquering the continuing threat of universal evil, she would also at last be able to break the spell of darkness that had taken such a toll in her own life.

Now that time had come.

She had known it intuitively when she began to feel the unusually powerful tremors of evil in the astral. They had strengthened so much in the past few days that she had been prompted to call for her psychic reinforcements. As she had increased her travels to the astral in preparation for the coming challenge, she had on numerous occasions observed the sorceress. Until now, Lady Sarah had only perceived of Delilah as an archetype, a myth, a shimmer of dark power. But recently she had seen her in her resplendent human form and watched her summon forth the spirits of the dark in support of a great magical working that she had planned.

Lady Sarah knew it was her destiny to fight this working, but she did not understand exactly how her fate was connected to the evil one. If she were being called upon to fight Delilah, perhaps even to the death, she wanted to know why.

She had petitioned the Watchers for this enlightenment, and they had responded. The place they had sent her to learn the answers was more awesome and holy than anything she had ever experienced, and she trembled at the threshold.

Of course she'd heard of the Akashic Records. Anyone in occult practice, any mystic or spiritual seeker was familiar with the concept of the existence of a vast universal "library" wherein the record of all existence—past, present, and future—was written. Now, as she entered these great halls, she was flushed with the anticipation of learning more about her enemy, the sorceress named Delilah.

Delilah.

As the name flashed through her mind, she was transported to a chamber wherein stood an enormous table that reached as far as she could see in either direction. Upon the table rested an equally enormous book. Lady Sarah stepped up to the volume and saw that it was open to the name she sought:

Delilah. The energy of the ancients most associated with power. The Delilah energy first incarnated in Atlantis and wrought havoc upon that civilization through her conscious and deliberate abuse of the powers entrusted unto her, resulting in the ultimate destruction and disappearance of that world. The Delilah energy was reborn into the modern world with Delilah the Philistine, whose unfaithfulness and betrayal ended in the torture and imprisonment of her husband, Samson, as well as great losses to the land of Israel.

Delilah has been known by many names as her energy incarnated in the race of humans on earth in different times and cultures. She ruled ruthlessly as one of the Cleopatras in Egypt, she murdered for power as Caligula's wife in Rome, she manipulated princes and popes as Catherine de Medici in France. She has reappeared as many lesser-known but equally power-hungry entities throughout time. Wherever she appears, she is the face of madness reflected in an undying quest for power. Little can stop her as her power is strong, and it strengthens with each incarnation. Only forces of greater power, those committed to the protection of the worlds known as the Watchers, hold sovereignty over the Delilah energy and the underforces she commands.

It will come to pass at the turn of a millennium that a great battle of wills must commence between the Watchers and the Delilah force wherein the fate of the Earth and all its beings will be determined . . .

Lady Sarah stared at the page. "But who is she, today, on the earth?"
The answer flashed before her on the page.

Delilah Mason, sorceress and power broker in London, High Priestess of the Circle of the Lily.

"When was her last incarnation?"

She last lived on the earth plane as Delilah Freeborn, a black magician in London from 1868 to 1899. She established the black lodge known as the Circle of the Lily and became its High Priestess with the intent of raising immense power. Her plans were thwarted by the wife of her High Priest.

Lady Sarah quaked as she posed her final question: "How is my destiny connected with the Delilah energy?"

The answer that came was lengthy, detailed, and gruesome, but at last she understood. It was an unhappy discovery, but it strengthened her resolve not to fail in her service to the Watchers. She must be an agent for the Light, in this time, in this place. She would fulfill her destiny, no matter what the cost.

For it was written here, in the Book of All Time, that she had been chosen and given the rare power that could dispel the Delilah energy for all eternity.

Chapter Thirteen

NO BREAKFAST THIS MORNING. GONE TO LONDON.
Michael.

When Michael had not shown up for breakfast by nine o'clock, Claire decided to knock on his door and discovered the note. Why would he have left so early? she wondered, deeply troubled.

She leaned against the doorsill, dismayed and disappointed. She had failed. The new clothes, the hairstyle, none of it had been strong enough to hold him. But then, she should have known that. It took more than chic to attract a man like Michael. He must be surrounded by beautiful women. She had never thought of herself as beautiful. What had made her expect him to find her so?

She wandered dejectedly back into her kitchen, more confused than ever. She was also acutely embarrassed at the way she had thrown herself at Michael the night before. "Damn," she murmured into the empty morning, but no one heard except the cats, who had begun to gather for breakfast.

What should she do now? Michael was likely with the woman in London, the one Lady Sarah had described as a beautiful sorceress. How could she compete with that? Maybe she should just drop her involvement with Michael and write off her feelings for him as naive infatuation. She probably ought to do exactly that. Make her excuses to Maeve and Lady Sarah and wash her hands of the whole business. Obviously, Michael did not much appreciate her interference. He'd even called her psychometric reading of the ring "silly superstition." How could she help him if he didn't want her help? Shades of Cameron.

She made herself a breakfast of tea and toast and sat at her kitchen table for a long while, pensive and on edge, thinking about Michael, the rings, the skeleton, the ghost, the crucifix, and the dream. Undoubtedly, they were somehow all interconnected since each was related to the mysterious symbol. Finally, after much soul-searching, she concluded that she, too, was part of the picture and that it was unlikely she could extricate herself entirely from Michael's affairs even if she wanted to. She glanced at the crucifix that lay on a shelf nearby, her present from the ghostly Eloise. She had been summoned into this mystery by someone who needed her desperately. Someone who was calling on her, depending on her, to right a terrible wrong.

Claire took a deep breath and let it out slowly. This wasn't just about Michael. It was about defending the forces in the universe that she called upon almost daily to effect her healing for others. Psychic forces that she used for good but which could be used for evil as well. Was there, as Lady Sarah warned, about to be a confrontation between the powers of darkness and those of the Light for command of these forces? Were her psychic powers needed, as Lady Sarah had insisted, to do battle against evil of the nature she'd just seen in her nightmare?

Lady Sarah. Now there was an enigma. Who was she? Claire remembered the white magician's comment that she'd spent her entire life fighting the forces of darkness. Why? She recalled the haunted look on Lady Sarah's face, the ingrained sadness. What was her real name? Why was she so reclusive? Was this magical war she spoke of real, or just the obsessive mania of a madwoman?

Either way, Claire felt compelled to delve further into the mystery that had been presented to her, by the skeleton, the ghost, Lady Sarah, and Dr. Michael Townsend. Her first thought was to telephone the police investigator who had left his card with her to see if he'd learned anything about the symbolism of the ring or the identity of the skeletal remains. But then some memory flickered from her dream.

The symbol. She'd seen it in her dream, on the ceiling of the circular temple room.

Claire's pulse quickened. She was certain she had seen it before as well, in childhood, in the great country manor house nearby, Hartford Hall. If she remembered correctly, it was carved into the ceiling in the strange round room in the basement of the building.

She would go there first. Now. This morning. If her memory proved correct, she would come home immediately and phone the police. Perhaps they could put the two together— the ring and the room—and come up with some answers.

But what about the second ring? The one Michael had shown her? Should she tell the police about it? Claire hedged, fighting with her conscience. She didn't want to involve Michael in this, but the fact that he had such a ring might mean he was very much involved. She'd wait, she decided at last, and see what she learned about the symbol.

Shunning her usual slacks and shirt, Claire slipped instead into a pair of new curve-hugging leggings that she'd bought at the boutique and topped it with a sleeveless, flowing tunic of deep ruby. She made a few swipes at her hair with a brush and from habit, started to pull it back into a ponytail, then gave herself an abashed grin in the mirror. Her haircut was performing as promised, and it fell in loose curls around her face in a flattering and natural style. She left it that way. Whether Michael was in her life or not, she was determined not to slip back into the image of a frump. Before leaving, she put the crystal pendant around her neck. She would not likely need it to protect her from Michael's dark energy, but as a talisman, it would increase in power the more often she wore it.

Anxious now to check out the basement room at the manor house she thought she recalled, she took the steps downstairs from her bedroom two at a time and darted out of the house into the brilliant late morning sunshine. The world looked friendlier out here, and it gave her courage. She turned down the path that led across the meadow to the derelict Hartford Hall.

It had been years since she'd been inside the spooky old house where she and Cameron had played as children. No one had lived at Hartford Hall since the seventies when the last owner, an ancient, reclusive man, had died. Apparently he'd had no heirs and died intestate, and the various government agencies had been confounded ever since as to how to dispose of the property. Local gossip had it that someone at last had purchased the grand old manor and was planning to restore it.

Walking at a leisurely pace, she reached the hall in less than fifteen minutes. From the outside, the huge old house looked much as it always had—steep, awesome, forbidding. Ivy clung to the red-brick walls, covering them to the chimney pots in some places with thick, dark-green leaves that provided a perfect habitat for spiders and other crawly things. Claire looked up at the ornate, many-gabled facade and shivered, wondering if the ghostly Eloise was watching from one of the windows high above.

Swallowing her trepidation and ignoring the NO TRES-PASSING sign, she marched boldly to the front door. She had not expected it to be open, but when she pushed on it, the heavy wooden door squeaked on rusty hinges and yawned for her to come in.

She entered the large front parlor, the walls of which rose from worn planked floors to an ornate ceiling nearly twenty feet above. They surrounded a vast and forlorn emptiness. Claire stood in the very center of the room and slowly surveyed her surroundings, grieving for the long-ago grandeur that had decayed beneath the ravages of time, weather, and neglect. Whoever had bought this place certainly had his work cut out for him, she thought gloomily. It would cost a fortune to renovate.

She closed her eyes for a moment, trying to visualize how she and Cameron had made their way into the basement all those years ago. It seemed as if she should go through the doorway to her left. She followed her instincts and pushed open the door and instantly wished she'd brought a flashlight. The corridor beyond had no windows, and it would be pitch dark when the door shut behind her. Not relishing the idea of creeping about the old manor in the dark, she propped the door open with a brick that lay nearby. Looking around, she was satisfied that the weak sunlight filtering in through the begrimed windowpanes in the great front parlor would be sufficient to light her way. Stealthily, she hurried down the dusky corridor to the narrow stairway she correctly remembered as being at the back of this wing that led to the basement.

There was not a sound in the house other than the rhythm of her footsteps on the wooden floor and the heavy whisper of her breathing that echoed off the walls. In spite of the stories she'd heard that the place was haunted, cursed even, she considered them nothing but childhood tales, good for raising goose bumps around the winter fireplace. She knew she was alone, that there was nothing to fear. Still, she couldn't seem to shake an illogical sense of foreboding.

She descended the stairs to the basement, where she found to her relief that the subterranean corridor was lit, although dimly, by light coming through small, ground-level windows. Picking her way through spiderwebs and curls of dust and debris on the floor, she proceeded toward the room she sought. She hoped her memory continued to hold true. She had not been here since shortly after the old man had died, when she was still a young girl. She and Cameron had crept onto the property unbeknownst to her father, who would have punished them severely if he'd known what they were up to. Claire grimaced. There was a lot that Father would have punished them for if he had known. But Cameron had learned early on to cover his tracks when he was up to no good, and she'd helped, willingly or not. She told herself she'd only done it because she didn't want their father to worry, but she knew in truth, it had been to save Cameron's backside.

Still distressed over Cameron, Claire worked at pushing those thoughts aside. That was all history. She wouldn't save her brother from his latest troubles, whatever they were, and she would cover for him no longer.

At last she came upon the two large dark doors she believed led to the room she'd stolen into as a child. She was certain she had seen them in her dream as well. Her pulse pounded thickly at her neck. In her dream behind these doors she'd witnessed some kind of obscene ceremony, and she'd been filled with terror and revulsion. With her psychic sensitivity, she worried suddenly that she might relive that if she stepped into the room. But she'd come this far. She must see if the symbol existed or if she was making it all up.

She touched the enormous knob set into the center of one of the doors and closed her eyes, tentatively testing the vibrations. Nothing. Relieved, Claire pushed on the door, and it opened into a circular chamber just as she'd thought. There were no windows, and the walls and ceiling were obscured in shadow, making it impossible to discern any details. She opened the doors as wide as possible, hoping the ambient light would be sufficient to reveal the symbol, but the room was large, the ceiling vague. Wrinkling her nose, Claire conceded she would have to step inside the room.

Again, she worried that the doors would close behind her, leaving her in darkness, but she pushed them open as far as they would go, and they obliged her by remaining there. She tiptoed further into the room. It was dank and chill, but she felt no untoward psychic vibrations.

It took a moment for her eyes to adjust to the gloom, but almost immediately she noticed the strange symbols painted on the walls. She had forgotten them, but the moment she saw them, she remembered how she and Cameron had tried to guess their meanings and their reason for being there. She moved slowly around the room, noting that it was divided into four distinct quadrants, each painted a different color and marked by symbols that resembled ancient Egyptian hieroglyphs. She tried to remember if she'd seen these walls in her dream, but she didn't think so.

At last, as she reached the very center of the room, she looked up, and her breath caught in her throat. Above her carved into the ceiling was the symbol that she'd seen on the two rings. Here, however, it was huge. The outer circle, created by the stem of a lily that reached around and came back into itself, was at least six feet in diameter. The shape of the eye extended from one side of the circle to the other, and there was a large, translucent gemstone of some kind in the center, giving her the uneasy feeling that she was being watched by a giant.

Claire stood in the silent chamber, hearing the rhythm of her heart in her ears, listening to her rapid breathing, when suddenly she heard another sound. She jumped, half expecting a ghost to peek into the room but then realized with sickening panic the sound was nothing supernatural. It was, rather, the very earthly sound of tires on the gravel of the car park at the front of the manor.

Michael twisted the ring round and round on his finger, fighting his rising anxiety. Beside him, in the rear of the stretch limo, Delilah rode in silence, and he could almost feel the hostility radiating from her. He knew why she was angry with him, but he simply couldn't do what she'd asked of him. Not yet, anyway. Maybe not ever.

He didn't know why. Any normal human male would have jumped at the opportunity to bed a woman like Delilah

Mason. But in spite of her beauty and allure, he was not attracted to her sexually. She was too strong, too demanding. He feared that once he'd slept with her, he might never be able to escape her influence.

He wasn't sure why he was with her even now, or why he had risen from bed before dawn, bathed, shaved, and dressed as if he were going to work, caught the first train from Montlivet to London, and been at Delilah's apartment before the city had begun to stir. It was as if he were being pulled there by an invisible tether. Once inside, Delilah had greeted him with no sign of surprise at such an early morning visitor. Instead, she'd commended him on his punctuality.

"It's good for a magician to rise early. The best magic is worked on an empty stomach and when the body is most refreshed."

"Are we going to work magic today?" he'd asked, his mind confounded and his thoughts confused. He had planned to return to Delilah's place, but at a reasonable hour. Something about all this didn't feel quite right.

In appearance, she was a different woman than he'd met the day before. Gone was the polished power broker in business suit and pumps and sensible hairstyle. That image had been replaced by a more sensuous version of Delilah Mason. This Delilah wore a flowing golden robe, and her hair fell in shimmering disarray around her shoulders. This Delilah had stroked the back of his hand and gazed at him with tempting, suggestive eyes. "We might," she purred. "What kind of magic did you have in mind?"

A warning flag shot up. This woman didn't want magic. She wanted sex. And somehow she'd drawn him here to use him, like a man uses a whore. Michael had moved abruptly away from her. "Look, Delilah," he began, but she'd riveted him with her hypnotic gaze.

"Don't be a fool, Nigel," she said. "You can have it all."

He'd looked at her, perplexed. "My name is Michael,"

he reminded her, and he saw her recoil, vexed that she'd made such a blunder. Nigel must be one of her other lovers, he had guessed.

"Nigel *was* a fool," Delilah replied coolly, recovering immediately. "He didn't understand what he was giving up. Don't make the same mistake."

"Who's Nigel?"

She turned and glanced at him, her head to one side. "You don't know?"

"Clue me." Michael's suspicion had mounted that the woman was out of touch with reality, and he was not exactly interested in hearing about another man's mistakes. But he'd thought it safer to keep her talking.

Delilah approached him again and ran her fingers down the length of his arm, as if sizing him up. "Nigel, my dear Michael, is the reason you are here with me."

Her logic eluded him. "I don't know anyone named Nigel," he'd said impatiently, "and I think it's time for me to leave. You can have the ring if you want it, but I'm out of here."

He'd tried to take a step toward the door, but his body wouldn't move. Delilah laughed.

"Foolish man. You're just nervous in the face of the great power that I am offering you. I understand your fear. After all, until now, until you came to me, you were nothing. You are still nothing, Michael." Her tone had turned hard, and her eyes gleamed fiercely. "You will always be nothing unless you become my High Priest. Only I can show you the way out of the pathetic little life you are leading. Only I can make you great, give you what you deserve."

Michael had longed to tell her that he wanted nothing from her but found he couldn't speak either. He was spellbound. Panic ripped through him. How was he going to get out of here? The only idea that came to mind was to play along with her, pretend to want to become her High Priest, and run like hell when she'd released him from whatever power was holding him.

But he'd remained unable to move. She loosened his tie. He began to sweat. She unbuttoned his shirt and ran flat palms over his chest. "Nice," she cooed. "Very impressive."

He was a prisoner. He could not speak, could not move, could not protest what she was doing. Which made it all the more disturbing and provocative. She'd slipped his jacket, shirt, and tie en masse from his body and let them fall to the floor. Then she stood back, like an artist studying her model, eyeing him critically.

"Michael, Michael," she'd chided, "you really must get it right this time. You are such a perfect specimen. You are the right man for this job. I've checked it out with the . . . higher authorities. It is such pleasant work. You needn't do anything much more than lay back and enjoy it. I'll do all the hard work."

With all his will, Michael had at last recovered his voice and his animation. "You're mad." He picked up his clothes and was gratified to see that she was clearly startled that he'd come to his senses.

She'd attempted to capture him again in her hypnotic gaze, but he averted his eyes. "How dare you defy me again?" she snarled. "You have no idea what kind of power you are challenging."

Remembering his plan to escape by going along with her, Michael had shifted his demeanor and smiled at her easily. "Oh, I think I have an idea. And I rather like it. But I will not be entrapped into anything, Delilah, especially something I know as little about as the power you claim to offer."

His words seemed to soothe her. "Oh, I do like a man who stands his ground. A man with a strong will. Perhaps we will get along after all, Michael."

He couldn't tell if she were mocking him or not. He

pressed on, curious about the man with whom she had him confused. "So, who's Nigel?"

She stood several feet away from Michael, her legs apart, and slowly she'd opened her gown, revealing to him all of her very beautiful, very naked body. "A fool," she said in a low, husky voice. "A fool who fathered a fool who fathered fools. Are you one of those fools, Michael?"

What was she talking about? Was she intimating that this Nigel was his ancestor? Suddenly she had his full attention. He'd come on this journey to learn the secrets of his family. Were those secrets somehow connected to this woman? He looked down at the ring on his finger. Delilah no longer had to bewitch him to hold him. Until he learned the secrets at which she hinted, he would go along with her.

"No. I don't consider myself a fool."

"Then come to me."

He wanted desperately to learn more, but he refused to become her toy, and as beautiful as she was, her ploy disgusted him. "Is that the bargain? Sex for secrets?"

She'd scowled and pulled her robe together again. "You're making this very difficult, Michael."

He knew he must do something quickly to soften his attitude and deflect her ire. He went to her and took her hand, summoning his most guileless manner. "Delilah," he'd said, employing a grin he knew formed a dimple in his cheeks. "I'm just a mild-mannered American professor," he protested in his best Clark Kent style. "You . . . you are . . . a little too much woman for me, at least until I get to know you better. You see, I'm a man of studies. Before I can act, I must know what I'm getting into. It's . . . what drives me."

He could not read the look on her face, but she'd appeared mollified, at least for the moment. "Very well, then, Michael. So be it. Consider yourself in school. You want to know what you are getting into? I suppose that's fair enough. But I must have your complete, undivided attention. And you must do as I say."

He'd raised his chin. "No deal. I will become your student, willingly, but not your prisoner."

She gave him a withering glare. "I never bargained for such a pain in the ass."

That had been four hours ago, before she'd insisted he accompany her on this little jaunt into the countryside to see the new property she was buying and attend the closing with her later in the day. As they drove, he tried to discern where they were headed. He wasn't certain, for he'd only taken the train to and from Montlivet, but he thought they were going in the same general direction. "Aren't we near Stansted Airport?" he asked, peering out the window of the limousine as the driver whisked them through London's suburbs.

"Very perceptive. How did you know?"

"I'm staying in Montlivet."

He saw one fine eyebrow lift. "How very coincidental. But then, we all return to where we've lived before."

He started to protest that he had never been here before, but decided that if he wanted to learn Delilah's secrets, he'd best keep his mouth shut and avoid being a further pain in the ass.

They arrived at their destination, a towering mansion of red brick and concrete that looked like a set for a Vincent Price movie. Michael expected bats to swarm from the upper windows at any moment.

"Where are we?"

Delilah looked at him with obvious disappointment. "You don't remember?" she said. "This is just part of what you once lost, Nigel."

Chapter Fourteen

CLAIRE'S FIRST INSTINCT WAS TO RUN. BUT TO where? She didn't know who might be visiting the old place. Probably a surveyor or appraiser getting the paperwork ready for the impending sale. Whoever it was, Claire did not wish to run into them and be charged with trespassing. No, she decided, it would be best to stay put. It was unlikely anyone would come down into the basement. Maybe if she just waited here, they would leave soon.

She left the round room and went to one of the basement windows. Standing on tiptoe, she was able to peer out, her eyes level with the gravel driveway. Suddenly, she clapped her hand over her mouth to stifle a scream.

A long, black stretch limousine was parked boldly in front of the door, and to her horror she saw Michael Townsend emerge from the far side door. He went around to the other rear door, opened it, and offered his hand to another passenger, who slid easily from the darkened interior.

It was the woman!

The red-haired woman from the dream who had writhed naked on the altar with the man named Nigel. What in bloody hell was going on here?

Claire thought she might be sick as a feeling of *déjà vu* swept over her. She'd seen the woman in her dream, here, in this very house. In that round room. Was she coming back in the flesh?

I've got to get out of here, she thought, panic-stricken. Was there another exit? She ran down the hallway to the far end, but found no second set of stairs. The windows were too narrow for her to wriggle through. She heard the pair enter the front door upstairs. Would she have time to race up the stairs and out into the back garden before they came this way?

Maybe they would tour the house. But why on earth would Michael be here, with *her*? Not for an innocent tour of the premises, she was certain. Her every psychic sense screamed at her—they were here to visit the round room, the temple room where the woman in her dream had worked her evil magic. Claire had no inclination to meet them on their way down the back stairs as she dashed for an escape.

Her only hope was the darkness.

She ran back inside the round room and closed the doors behind her, taking cover in the inky blackness. She positioned herself so that when the doors opened, one of them would swing back against her and she would be hidden behind it. If she held her breath and didn't sneeze or otherwise give away her presence, perhaps she could outwait their visit.

If she were lucky, she might learn something, too.

Like exactly how Michael was involved with that hellion.

She heard voices and the sound of footsteps approaching. The woman's tone was deep, throaty . . . familiar. It was the voice she'd heard on the phone.

Claire heard other words echo in her mind.

Warn him.

She had no doubt now that the ghost had meant Michael. But Claire *had* warned him. She had told him not to go, begged him not to meet the woman who had telephoned. Michael obviously had not listened. He was here with her, willingly it appeared, getting ready to take part in some awful . . . something. Claire's suspicions raced around her mind until she felt dizzy. Should she try to warn him again? When they entered the room, should she step from the shadows and call out to Michael to run? A scene from the dream sequence flashed before her eyes—Eloise confronting the sorceress.

Eloise, Claire believed, had died for her efforts.

Claire was heroic, but she wasn't stupid. She would stay in place and hope for the best. She couldn't help Michael, or anyone, if she were dead.

She heard the footsteps come to a halt outside the doors. The woman spoke. "This is the place, Michael. The temple of your destiny. Do you wish to enter?"

Claire willed her thoughts telepathically to Michael. *No!*

But he didn't hear. "We've come this far. I've told you I wish to learn your magic. If this is part of it, then I guess I'd better take a look."

Claire's stomach turned over as the doors were eased open. Fortunately, the door she hid behind stopped its swing before it pressed against her. She huddled as far behind it as she could. Then to her shock and dismay, lights flashed on, fully illuminating the room.

"Good," said the woman in a gratified tone. "I'd hoped the electricity had been turned on as I had instructed. Well, my darling, what do you think? Grand, isn't it? Or will be when I freshen the paint."

"What . . . what is this place?" Michael asked in a hushed voice.

"It is the Temple of the Circle of the Lily. See? Look on the ceiling. That is the symbol that you wear on your finger, Michael."

After a moment's silence, he replied. "Yes. I see the markings are the same. What do they mean, Delilah?"

Delilah. At last, Claire had a name. And it made her shudder. Was this woman about to destroy Michael just as the Biblical Delilah had destroyed her husband? *Oh, Mi-*

chael, get away from her, she cried out mentally. *Run!*

"As I've told you, my ancestors chose the lily because it represents purity, and they . . . we . . . only deal with power in its purest form. The eye is all-seeing. Those rays penetrate the universe. There is nothing we don't see. Or know. Knowledge is important, Michael. It is the key to power."

She went on. "The triangle is the connection between all things. And the circle, Nigel . . . Michael, is the joining of the masculine and feminine. See how the stem, the man, enters the lily, the woman? That is the secret of our magic. The joining of the most powerful energies in the cosmos. Sexual conjunction. Old Aleister Crowley named it High Sex Magick."

Claire gasped, and the sound was clearly audible in the silence that followed Delilah's last astounding statement.

"What the . . . ?"

Suddenly the door that had concealed her was pulled away, and Claire found herself staring into the fiercest, most angry face she had ever seen.

On a day that began in a most bizarre fashion and which had continued in that vein, little would have surprised Michael Townsend at this point. But surprise was an understatement when he saw the figure of Claire St. John revealed behind the door. The depth of his astonishment, unfortunately, was matched by the intensity of Delilah's rage.

"Who in the name of all the demons of Hades are you, and what are you doing here?" she shrieked, stunning Michael at the change that had instantly come over her. Her fury was an illogical overreaction that transformed her from a woman with complete self-control into a raging madwoman.

Claire's eyes were filled with terror as she looked past Delilah to Michael. She was frozen to the spot, unable to move, a rabbit in a trap, a fly in a web. Delilah stepped toward her, a snarl on her lips.

"Who are you?" she hissed. She reached for Claire with both hands, clutching the ruby shirt fabric in her fists. "Who are you?" she screamed into her face.

The shrill menace in Delilah's voice and the clear threat to Claire jolted Michael from his own state of shock, and he rushed to the two women and forced Delilah's hands from Claire's body. "Leave her alone," he commanded.

Delilah turned unbelieving eyes upon him. "What? You dare to defy me? Again? Wrong move, Michael. I destroyed Nigel. I will destroy you. And," she added, glaring at Claire, "I will take her along, too." She stepped away from them, and Michael put his body between the women.

"Leave her out of this," he warned. "She knows nothing about all this."

Delilah sneered at him. "Then why is she here?"

For that, Michael had no answer. He turned to Claire, beseeching her with his eyes for some kind of rational explanation. Instead, all she said was, "Run, Michael. Get out of here. Get away from her."

Delilah was enraged all over again. "You'll never run again. Anywhere," she threatened. "I'll break your legs, and your heart, and your mind. In the name of Althathea, demon of darkness, I curse . . ."

Suddenly, the woman choked. She reeled backward as if some invisible force had her by the throat. She was flung against the far wall and wrestled with an unseen assailant until at last she sank to the floor in a heap.

She raised her head to them, but her eyes were focused on Claire. "I don't know who you are, you bitch of a whoring hound, but I will see you in hell. Now go. Get out, both of you!" She filled her lungs and screamed out again, "Go-o-o!"

Michael wasn't about to argue. He grabbed Claire by the arm and thrust her through the doors, then ran, nearly dragging her down the hall, up the stairs, and out the front door.

"Which way?" She pointed past the limousine, toward an orchard, and he led their flight from the hysterical woman in the basement whom he now believed was beyond madness, more than dangerous.

They did not stop running until they reached the safety of Claire's house. They burst through the back door, sending cats flying, and after securing all the door locks, collapsed together on the sofa. Recovering from the shock and the arduous sprint home, they held each other for a long time, not speaking, hearts pounding, breath stabilizing. Michael was still surprised by Claire's presence in the old manor house, but he surmised it had to do with the symbol she'd seen on his ring—the same symbol Delilah had pointed out on the ceiling of the temple room.

Damn. He hadn't meant to, but Michael believed he had brought danger, perhaps disaster, into Claire's life by showing her that ring. He wished he'd never been so selfish to ask her to use her psychic powers in this godforsaken business. It was foolish enough of him to pursue his quest and become mixed up with the likes of Delilah Mason, but he should never have involved someone he loved.

His breathing was still heavy, and he felt hers equally labored against his neck. He held her closer, only then daring to reflect on what had just crossed his mind.

Someone he loved?

He felt her begin to shake in his arms, and he realized she was sobbing. He touched her cheeks and felt tears. "Oh, Claire," he whispered. "Oh, my God, what have I done to you?"

He raised her face and looked into its porcelain beauty, and he felt as if his heart were breaking. He'd spread his dark curse to this woman of light. He should leave her now. Instantly, before any more harm could befall her.

But he could not walk away from her now. He had involved Claire in his magical misadventures and believed she was now at terrible risk from Delilah Mason. He did not know how or when, but he knew the sorceress would seek her revenge . . . against both of them. Neither did he know how he would accomplish it, but he *would* protect Claire from Delilah's vengeance.

His heartbeat thundered and his arms closed around the woman he loved, and he wished with all his soul that none of this had happened. Was the curse—the one he didn't believe in—again about to destroy what he dared to cherish?

He would not let that happen. Not ever again. Curse or no curse, he vowed not only to keep this woman safe, but also to end the struggle between himself and life. He had the power to slay his personal dragons, for suddenly everything had shifted. With Claire in his arms, he felt the darkness that had been his life's companion begin to lift, and hope trickled in .to take its place. A remarkable sense of peace and joy surged through him, along with a desire to know in every way this woman who was the source of his deliverance.

Did he dare . . . ?

Searching the depths of her blue eyes, he saw in them a reflection of his own anxiety and hope, of fear and . . . something else he could not define. Something that his own hungry soul wanted desperately to be a reflection of his own love. He lowered his lips to hers, tasted there the salt of her tears. She ran her hands to the back of his head and drew his kiss deeper.

Michael had his answer. With the passion of her response, he lost all thought of his sorrow-haunted life. He was released from the unspeakable darkness that enclosed him. From her brightness, he drew light, courage, the strength of will to protect her from all danger.

Wanting her like nothing he'd wanted ever before, he ran one hand beneath the silken fabric of her tunic until he found the soft roundness of her breast. Moving the hard surface of the crystal pendant to one side, he felt the measure of her rapid heartbeat just beneath his hand. Was she still afraid of him? "Claire?" he whispered, seeking permission to travel the territory he longed to explore.

"Yes, Michael."

Her gentle reply was a statement, not a question, and the desire he heard in her quiet consent fueled his passion even more.

He lowered his lips to hers once again, and his heart rejoiced as he felt her press against him. She opened her lips and sought him with her tongue, sending a charge of pure desire straight through him. Slipping his hand behind her, he managed to unfasten the hooks on her bra, and he heard her give a little moan when he slid the garment away and held her bare skin against his palm. Her breasts were full, her nipples taut, and he longed to gaze upon them, unfettered by the layers of clothing that remained between them.

With a tender urgency, he helped her out of the tunic, removing the bra as well and taking the crystal from her neck. He lay down again beside her on the couch, cradling her in one arm, exploring her body with the other.

"You are so beautiful," he whispered, nuzzling a kiss near her ear.

She gazed up at him, her blue eyes wide and darkened with passion. "Make love to me, Michael."

He thought his whole body would explode from the desire she ignited within him. Without another word, he began to fulfill her request, lavishing kisses down her neck and across her breasts. He heard her quick intake of breath and felt her arch to allow him to pleasure her even more, and again he accepted her invitation.

With his lips worshipping at her breasts, he slid his hand down her belly and beneath the snug leggings and eased them away from her body, all the while thinking wildly that he must be having an erotic dream. Then he felt her hands at his waist, unfastening his belt buckle, releasing him as well, and he knew this dream was real.

He sought her depths and felt her encircle his waist with her legs. A honeyed warmth surrounded him as she drew him into her, obliterating every other sensation but his hungry need for her. Slowly, they began to move together, in a quiet rhythm at first but then with greater urgency, as if they were lovers reunited after a long separation. An exquisite energy blazed between them, and an intense and beautiful yearning took control of his spirit.

Her muscles tightened around him, and a small moan escaped her lips. He longed for the sensation to go on forever, but too soon the sheer delectable force of it surged beyond his ability to contain it any longer. Riding his passion into the beauty and power of his newly discovered love, Michael's soul shimmered with the brilliance of a million crystal shards, and his darkness was engulfed in a blaze of golden light.

From somewhere among the stars, he heard Claire cry out as she completed her journey as well, and in the moments following, his entire being was flooded with a wondrous sense of peace and power. He needed no magic to reclaim command of his life. All he needed was here, in his arms, this woman who was enfolding him, showing him the way back.

Claire lay very still in Michael's arms, awaiting a return to her senses, for she seemed to have slipped into an alternate reality. All that had happened in the past few hours seemed like something out of a movie or a surrealistic dream. Although she was accustomed to extraordinary, sometimes even preternatural events, such things had, until Michael Townsend walked into her life, happened only to others with whom she worked.

It was extraordinary not only that she was lying naked next to Michael in her sitting room, or that she had just made love to him, but that she was not afraid of him. She felt no darkness now, no anger. Something had changed. She could feel it.

As normal consciousness returned, she remembered how Michael had saved her from whatever evil the woman named Delilah had been about to fling at her. She shuddered involuntarily, remembering the horrific anger on her face.

"You okay?" Michael murmured from somewhere near her ear.

"I . . . I don't know," she answered honestly, deciding that whole incident must have been an hallucination or a bad dream. Or else that she must be mad. What on earth was Michael Townsend doing in the basement of Hartford Hall? "Michael, what is going on?"

She felt his chest rise and fall as he exhaled heavily. "I've made a terrible mistake," he said at last.

Her insecure heart sank, thinking he meant he'd made a mistake in making love to her. "I wanted it, Michael."

He laughed softly. "I don't mean about you," he murmured, kissing her ear. He offered no further explanation, but Claire felt tension stiffen his muscles, and she sensed he was struggling with some kind of inner conflict. She was assailed by a sudden doubt. Was he married? Had he come here, as Bitsy suspected, seeking a runaway wife?

Claire prayed it wasn't so. She loved being in his arms, feeling secure, protected. She wanted to stay here forever, but she knew it was possibly all an illusion. He was a man of darkness and many secrets. Although she did not want to break the spell that had just entranced them, she was too pragmatic to sustain a fairy tale.

"What mistake then?"

Michael pulled his body away from her and sat up at the foot of the couch, and Claire regretted the loss. Still, she must know what was happening, both with Michael and between them as well. She had just made love with this man, shared not only her human self but her etheric body as well. A part of her was now a part of him, and the other way around.

He reached for his shirt. "Make that plural. Mistakes. I shouldn't be here. I should never have involved you in this sordid mess. Maybe I should never have come to England at all.''

''Involved me in what? Please! Tell me what is going on. Who was that woman?''

He sighed. ''Her name is Delilah,'' he said with raw irritation. ''Delilah Mason. She lives in London.''

''She's a magician, isn't she? A black magician.''

''How do you know that?''

''I felt her evil over the phone. It is the same woman, isn't it?''

He dropped his head into his hands and rubbed his face. ''Yes. It's the same one.''

''Why did you go to her, Michael?''

He stood and finished dressing, and she donned her clothing as well. It was better this way. Less vulnerable. At last he answered. ''Because I thought she had something I needed.''

Claire felt herself go cold. What on earth could that black sorceress have that Michael would need, unless a part of his soul? Perhaps that was why his aura was black. She looked at him pointedly, concentrating on his aura, and she could see that although it showed a man with many worries on his mind, it was no longer black, but a muddy medium blue. ''What was that?''

His aura instantly darkened, and his expression hardened as the briefly opened door slammed shut again. ''I can't say.''

Claire's heart ached for him. What secret was he hiding that was so terrible he wouldn't talk about it? That he thought he had to go to someone like Delilah Mason to resolve it? She moved closer to him and took his hand.

''Look, Michael, whatever it is, it can't be that bad. Let me help. You mustn't go near her again. She is dangerous. Maybe even deadly. I've been told to warn you against her . . .''

''Warn me?'' He turned on her, his eyes suddenly fierce. ''Who the hell told you to warn me against her? What business is it of yours, or anyone's, what I do?''

Claire was stunned. Where was the tender, compassionate lover of only moments before? Where was the man who had risked his life to save her own? She stood up and straightened her clothing, her cheeks on fire. "So go to her then," she flared, striding to the far side of the room. "But that woman will destroy you, just as she destroyed Eloise. And Nigel."

He frowned, then blinked as if he were trying to register what she'd just said. "Who?"

"Never mind. It's only a bad dream I had."

But Michael was across the room in an instant, holding her by both arms. "Who are Eloise and Nigel?" he demanded.

"I . . . I don't know. Let me go," she said, jerking free.

He eyed her for a long moment before releasing her, and she guessed in that instant that his secret and Eloise's torment were somehow the same. Delilah had even called him Nigel. Her dismay deepened. As did her resolve to get to the bottom of this mystery.

Then she saw his face change, soften, and he let go of her arms. "I'm sorry," he whispered, shaking his head. "I didn't mean to hurt you."

"You are hurting me, Michael, by not letting me help you."

"You can't help me, Claire, and you mustn't keep trying. I don't want your help. Stay out of it. And make me stay away from you."

"You're not making sense."

His lip curled. "So what's new?" he retorted with bitter cynicism. "Nothing in my life has ever made sense."

"Michael, don't go to her."

"Don't *you* go to her," he retorted. "Don't ever go near Delilah again. You're right. She is dangerous. Stay away from her, do you understand?"

Claire struggled to hold on to her composure, but failed. The man was exasperating. "No. I don't understand, not one thing," she said, her voice rising. "I don't understand how you can make love to me one minute and tell me to make you stay away the next. I don't understand why you are compelled to get in cahoots with a woman you yourself just said is dangerous, a black magician, for God's sake. No, I don't understand, Michael. Help me."

His face was bleak, but he shook his head firmly. When he spoke, his voice was ragged. "Leave it alone, Claire. Leave *me* alone."

Chapter Fifteen

DELILAH MASON STORMED PAST THE CONCIERGE, UN-
aware of the man's existence. She pressed the elevator button herself instead of waiting for the servant to do it and
entered the ornate cubicle with impatience. As the elevator
rose smoothly and swiftly toward the penthouse, she
drummed her nails on the mirrored walls and caught sight
of her image there. Ghastly! Not only did she look un-
kempt, her face was lined with the fury that still raged
within her. Worse, there were bruise marks around her neck
where something from the Unseen had choked her and prevented her from casting the curse she'd intended.

Was the woman hiding in the temple a magician as well?
Or were there other forces afoot? She must discover what
had been behind that attack, for she could afford no op-
position in her upcoming Great Working.

She must learn the identity of the woman, and what she
was doing in the sacred temple. It was no accident. Delilah
had been an occultist far too long to believe in any notion
of coincidence. A woman, especially a woman like that,
who looked so ordinary, so . . . plebeian . . . did not go into
the basements of empty mansions, into magical territory,
unless she herself was a magician or had been sent there
by someone.

Sent to thwart Delilah's carefully laid plans?

Well, she would not be thwarted. Not again. Ever! The elevator door opened, and she charged into her suite. She would find out who this woman was and make quick work of her. Delilah was a master at psychic attack.

Her first step, however, was to rein in her anger. Anger was an emotion that got in the way of effective magic. She was above anger. Going into the private magical space she had created in the apartment, she sealed the door behind her and began the practice she knew would calm her. In moments, her heart rate was normal, her mind serene, her thinking clear. The first order of business was to telephone the estate agent and the architect and postpone their meetings until tomorrow.

Then she lay back on the priceless Victorian fainting couch she'd had installed in the room, which she used to support her physical body while her etheric body roamed the astral, and closed her eyes. In her mind's eye she conjured the image of the woman who had cowered behind the door before Michael had so foolishly rescued her.

Michael. Humph! Some High Priest he'd turned out to be. She would deal with him later. First she would concentrate on the woman.

Mentally she traveled back into the round temple room at Hartford Hall. Her inner vision was much like a video camera, and she zoomed onto the face of her nemesis. There was something familiar about that face. She concentrated even more intensely, and her efforts brought to mind, strangely, the face of Cameron St. John.

Yes. The woman looked vaguely like Sin-Jen. Was there a connection between them?

Cameron St. John was such a fop. He was vain and greedy, and she knew he had no compunction about illegally investing her funds. She'd learned that he'd tried it recently and gotten burned, but she'd never outright challenged him about it because he had found money from somewhere to make good on the margin call. Still, it was useful to know such things.

She remembered from the dossier that he came from beneath the station of those into whose company he had managed to insert himself. She'd chosen him to be in the High Court *because* he was vain and greedy. *Because* he wanted to climb the social scale so badly. Those traits gave her power over him, made it easy to control him.

She picked up the phone and dialed his office and within seconds had made a luncheon date. He promised to arrive at one o'clock. She would know shortly not if, but how, he was connected with the bitch who had her clutches on Michael Townsend.

Now about Michael. Delilah frowned. He was such a disappointment, but perhaps there was hope yet. Once she'd rid him of that blond, she would cast her strongest spell ever in an attempt to bring him back to her as High Priest. Give him one more chance. If that failed, he was not worthy of the position and would have to be destroyed.

Cameron St. John arrived promptly at one o'clock bearing a lavish gift of three dozen red roses. Delilah sneezed and asked her valet to take them. "I'm allergic to roses," she explained, "but thank you anyway. It was a generous gesture."

"I should have called and asked your man. I apologize for my thoughtlessness."

No problem controlling this one, Delilah thought with a cynical grin. "Please, come in. Our luncheon is prepared." She led him to the formal dining table and indicated where he should sit. "I'm delighted you could join me on such short notice."

"You are always my first priority," he said, reaching for her hand, but she moved it to the wineglass at her place.

"I'm pleased that you realize the importance of our work together. Tell me, have you been studying and doing the practices I've given you?"

"Every free moment," he assured her. "I have even recorded the chants on tape. I have a friend who works in a recording studio, and he's layered the chants twelve deep. It sounds like we are all together like that first night. I know everything by heart.''

''Commendable. But you must be careful. Those chants are powerful. You have much training to undergo before you will know how to safely use that power.''

He leaned toward her, his eyes gleaming. ''Delilah, I swore my loyalty to you with my very life. I want to prove to you I am worthy to serve you. Perhaps someday I might even become . . . your High Priest.''

Fat chance, Delilah sneered to herself. He was probably just sucking up to her, but she could not imagine giving her body to Cameron St. John in the act of High Sex Magick. She didn't believe he had the kind of energy she needed. But she allowed him to hope.

''That is a lofty ambition.'' She smiled in his direction. ''First, we must get to know one another better.'' She saw him glow. ''For example, I know little about your background,'' she lied. ''You're from Essex, I've heard?''

''Montlivet. Near Stansted Airport.''

''Oh. That is delightful country.''

''I hate the country.''

Delilah gave him an innocent smile as she probed deeper. ''Did you grow up there? Do you have family in the area?''

A look of disdain crossed his face. ''Unfortunately, I spent my entire youth in that back corner of the world. My sister, Claire, still lives there and loves it, but give me the rush of London any day.''

''You have a sister named Claire? What's she like? Tell me about her.''

He smirked. ''Why? She's just an aging spinster. There's nothing much to tell. We're twins, but as different as night and day.''

''Twins! How fascinating.'' Delilah grew more certain with every word that Cameron's sister was the woman who had been hiding in the temple room. "Does she look like you?"

Cameron shook his head. "Not at all. She's blue-eyed and blond. Short and, well, kind of dowdy."

That gave Delilah pause. The woman she'd seen, although lacking the kind of flair that appealed to Delilah, could not be described as dowdy. Perhaps it hadn't been his sister. She must be sure. "Do you have a picture of her?"

She could tell her protégé was annoyed that she was so interested in his sister, but he produced from his wallet a rather battered photo of her as she'd looked just out of school. "I don't know why I carry this," he said as he handed it to her. "I forgot I even had it."

The girl in the photo was pretty, in the full bloom of youth, without the sophistication of the woman, but Delilah smiled.

She'd espied her prey. Now to set her trap . . .

"You've sworn your loyalty to me," she said, running her long nail down the back of one of Cameron's hands. "Now you must prove it. Are you ready for your first test, Sin-Jen?"

An hour later, Cameron emerged from the high-rise building after his luncheon with Delilah. He didn't buy all her magical crap, but he intended to go along with it, because Delilah Mason could make him a wealthy man if he played his cards right. She was also a very sexy lady, and he was well aware that her secret rituals included an element of the erotic that tantalized him.

Although he was flattered that she'd singled him out for a "magical" mission, which if successful he believed would earn him high marks in her books, he was disturbed. What she'd asked of him involved his sister, and he did not want Claire, of all people, to know about his foray into magical activities.

It was a peculiar assignment, he considered, but then,

she was a peculiar woman. She'd asked him to bring her personal items of Claire's—hair and nail clippings if possible, which he doubted he could obtain in secret, or an item of clothing or jewelry. What she wanted with these things he couldn't fathom.

Claire wore little jewelry, but perhaps he could find out when she planned to be gone, use the key to the house which he still had on his chain, and swipe a blouse or something. He found the idea distasteful, but the thought of failing and incurring Delilah's disappointment was even more so. Big deal, he told himself, hailing a taxi to take him back to the brokerage. He could find some old T-shirt or a pair of socks. She'd never miss whatever he stole, for he wouldn't take something she normally wore.

On the short ride to his office, Cameron worked out a plan for insuring his sister's absence long enough for him to procure what Delilah had demanded. He wondered again briefly what on earth Delilah could want with Claire's things, but he didn't dwell on it. It wasn't important. What was important was pleasing Delilah. When he was around her, he could virtually smell power. He was heady with the promise of the power he believed she could bring his way, electrified at the thought of becoming as successful as Delilah Mason.

He would do whatever it took, even to pilfering his sister's underwear.

Back at his desk, he picked up the phone and dialed Claire's number. "Hello, Claire. Hi. Listen, I feel bad about the way we've been so estranged lately. I mean, it's like we're enemies or something. I don't want it to be that way."

He heard his sister gush her matching sentiments into the phone. She was so easy. "I know," he replied in sympathy. "So, will you let me make it up to you? Could you come into the city tomorrow and meet me for lunch? My treat."

She would like that very much, she told him, and he gave her directions to a restaurant in another part of town, near the offices of the House of Rutledge, one of the hottest fragrance manufacturers in Britain these days whose stock value was soaring. He hung up. Too bad he wouldn't be able to make lunch. It might be interesting to visit that company afterward. But he would be busy elsewhere.

Lady Sarah was exhausted from the psychic battle she had waged against Delilah Mason in the basement of the old manor house. The Watchers had alerted her from the astral just as she'd returned from the halls of the Akashic Records, and she'd had no time to recharge her energies before entering into the psychic fray.

She had won. This time. Because surprise had been on her side. But she had seen the fury on the face of the sorceress and knew it would not be long before she would be called to stand against her again. She had seen, too, the others who had been in that room and surmised that without protection from the Watchers, they would soon fall victim to Delilah's revenge. Claire had been there, had in fact been the focus of the woman's hatred. What was Claire doing in that room? Lady Sarah made note to call in her new recruit. Nothing must happen to Claire, for her psychic power was sorely needed.

Who was the man, she wondered, who had defied Delilah and placed himself in harm's way to protect Claire? Was it the tenant Claire had spoken of? He looked somehow familiar, his face like one she'd known before, although Claire had told her he was a stranger to the area. Perhaps his power could be enjoined in the battle as well if he wasn't on the wrong side. In spite of his heroic action, Lady Sarah was unsure if he had come there with Claire or Delilah.

She must warn Claire to be cautious. With forces of darkness, one could never trust external appearances. The likes of Delilah Mason could put on the most innocent of faces, appear the most solicitous of benefactors, if that served her evil purposes. So, too, could those aligned with her.

Before she did anything, however, Lady Sarah wanted to purify herself, for at the moment she was contaminated by the psychic contact with Delilah and could easily spread that filth. She went into the bathroom and filled the tub with consecrated water from special jugs she had prepared for just such emergencies. She lit incense in every room, leaving it to cleanse the atmosphere while she cleansed her body.

Taking off the white robe, she stepped into the water and felt a jolt as the magic began to work to remove the psychic soil. When the initial cleansing energy had passed, she leaned back against the tub and thought about what she'd read in the Akashic Records. It was troubling to learn why she had been called to this work those many years ago, but she was grateful for the chance to end the affliction once and for all. She might never know how it would affect the others, those she had left behind in her journey toward the Light, but she prayed from her heart that they, too, would be released from the darkness.

Michael returned to the cottage, tormented, confused, in a state of shock. It was difficult to believe he had arrived here less than a week ago, and in that short time he had managed to screw things up so badly. He had made little progress in the quest that had brought him here, for he'd allowed his search for his mother to take a back seat to his investigation into magic. With the exception of Delilah's claim that his mother had been involved in magic, which Michael found highly unlikely, he had not even pursued other avenues toward finding her.

He wished to high heavens he'd never gotten involved in the magic, for now not only had he royally pissed off the queen of the black magicians, he'd managed to involve Claire, placing her, he believed, in certain danger.

Claire.

Now there was something else he'd never intended to happen. He felt his heart constrict at the memory of what had just transpired between them. He wanted to love Claire, to be loved by her in return, but his conviction that he could take control and turn his life around had slipped in the reality that followed their lovemaking. His existence had been beleaguered for so long, he was unsure that he could shake the blight with a mere thought, impassioned as it had been. He didn't trust that he wouldn't touch Claire's life with tragedy as he had Kathy's.

In fact, at the death of his young fiancée, Kathy, Michael had vowed never to fall in love again, for he believed somehow he'd been responsible for what happened. On the surface he knew that was irrational, for it had been a car wreck on an icy highway that had taken her life. He had been nowhere near the car, and no one except himself ever sought to place blame in his corner. But to him, it was just one more example of his life's disasters, one more example of the dark destiny that seemed to be his.

Thoughts of Kathy led his mind directly to Alan Sandridge, his supposed best friend. Alan, a senior professor, had bitterly opposed Michael's affair with Kathy, for she had been seventeen years his junior and a student of Michael's. "Unprofessional," Alan had railed at him. "Cradle robbing is beneath you."

Michael had fallen for the brown-haired coed, for she'd offered him what no one else ever had—unconditional love. She never asked anything of him except that she could be his friend. She had been bright, a mentally stimulating partner despite her youth, and briefly she had brought joy into his life. He had grieved bitterly at her death, which had been a little over a year ago.

It had been Alan's disapproval of Michael's love affair that had caused him to cast the deciding negative vote when the department heads met to decide Michael's fate in academe. Even Kathy's death had not softened him, and Michael had to chalk up one more failure and disappointment on top of all the rest.

He was so sick of it all. Michael slumped into a chair

and held his head in his hand, massaging his temples. He thought back to the words in his mother's letter, claiming that she had brought a curse into the family. He looked at the ring on his finger and thought about Claire's statement that it had resonated a curse that went back many generations. In spite of his rational disbelief in such possibilities, at the moment, Michael felt that curse in the blackest corners of his being.

He forced himself to suspend his disbelief and briefly considered the possibility that he *was* cursed. Was there any way out of it? If a curse could be cast, was there some way it could also be lifted?

He recalled Delilah's claim that she could lift the curse that was defeating him. Had she just been using a figure of speech, or was she talking about breaking an actual curse? How would she know he was afflicted by a curse? He removed the ring and studied the symbol on it, knowing that it held the key to the mystery. He wanted desperately to know its secret, but he wasn't about to call Delilah up and ask her. He hoped he would never see that woman again.

No, he would find another way. He thought of the book Claire had lent him and went to the bureau to get it. He turned to the index and found there the reference he was looking for, then hastily thumbed the pages to the entry.

"Curses are the weapons of black magicians, black witches, and sorcerers," he read. "Curses are used to control their enemies, usually by instilling fear of their power in the victim's belief system. What one believes is one's truth. If one believes another has cast a curse upon him and allows that belief to control him, then indeed the curse is effective."

What one believes is one's truth.

Had he as a boy absorbed his father's malignant outlook and believed all along that his life was doomed? Had he allowed that to become a self-fulfilling prophecy? Surely he was smarter than that, but still . . .

He read on.

"There is another very serious form of a curse, however, wherein the sorcerer invokes the powers of astral beings, elementals, demons, and spirits of the darkness who execute the curse even if the victim is unaware that it has been cast. This type of curse is difficult to diagnose and even more so to exorcise, for the victim is rarely cognizant that it is the power of a curse that causes certain problems and afflictions. It is necessary to consult a trained occultist, preferably a magician of one of the high white orders, to determine if a curse is at the base of one's troubles, and then to rid oneself of its effects."

Michael stared at the pages, not knowing what to think. As an intelligent man, he could accept the first explanation from a psychological viewpoint. But the second was beyond him. What were astral beings and elementals? Were there such things as demons? He related to them only as mythological characters from literature and philosophy, the products of primitive imaginations and ignorant superstitions. Surely they did not exist in this day and time.

He knew in his gut there was more to what was going on here than either his own warped psychology or some ignorant superstitions. He had seen the ball of light in Delilah's hand. He had been frozen and imprisoned by some power she had cast over him. And today, he had seen *something* attack Delilah. He thought about that a moment, frowning. If he wasn't mistaken, he thought that she had been about to hurl a curse at him and Claire when suddenly she'd choked and was physically thrown back against the wall.

Michael closed the book and laid it back on the bureau, then took the signet ring with the symbol of the Circle of the Lily and returned it to the box where he had originally found it. Whatever had transpired, it had to do with the magical order Delilah had called the Circle of the Lily. It was bad news, and he wanted no part of it. He'd indulged his folly in "researching" the magical paraphernalia, and it had been a mistake. It was time for him to get on with the business he'd come here for.

The search for his mother.

He considered again moving to other lodgings to avoid the temptation of seeking out Claire's soothing company. He must not allow whatever curse followed him to touch her life. If he moved, he reasoned, he would not cast his shadow over her. But in his heart he knew it was too late. He'd already exposed Claire to the curse in the form of Delilah Mason. He must remain close by, a distant but vigilant guardian until he believed the danger had passed. He did not know what to expect, nor did he have any idea how to combat the forces of Delilah's black magic, but he would find the strength and the power to overcome any harm directed toward Claire . . . at the cost of his own life if necessary.

Chapter Sixteen

BEWILDERED AND UPSET, CLAIRE SETTLED THE phone back into the cradle after talking with Cameron, who called just as Michael stormed out. How could things be so right in one instant and so terribly wrong the next? She had been tenderly intimate with a man she loved and desired, and it was clear he had desired her, too. But afterward, almost instantly, Michael had flung up his emotional wall again that in their passion he had surrendered, if only briefly. In that short time, however, she had glimpsed the caring and vulnerable side of the man he kept hidden beneath his armor of darkness.

How she wanted to break through that armor, permanently, and heal what tormented him, but how could she heal anything if he wouldn't let her near?

It was curious that Cameron would have called just now, as if he knew his twin needed his comfort. She was glad he, too, was feeling badly about their alienation and wanted to make up. She looked forward to having lunch with him the next day. In the meantime, she was determined to discover what was going on with Michael without his knowing, and perhaps find some way to help him overcome his troubles. For only then could his walls come down permanently. Only then would he be open to the kind of love she wanted to offer him.

His problems had to do with magic, she was certain. Black magic, if he was involved with Delilah Mason. Even though Michael had dismissed her psychometric reading of his ring as a silly superstition, Claire believed he might be a victim of some kind of curse going back many generations.

Claire worked at sorting out the relationships that appeared interconnected and that must somehow be associated with that curse: Michael's ring was identical to the one worn by the skeleton buried beneath the tree, now in police custody. The symbol on the rings was also on the ceiling in the round room in the basement at Hartford Hall. Delilah Mason had called the room a temple of something called the Circle of the Lily. She remembered from her dream that there had been a strange ritual in progress in that room.

A mystical symbol.

A ritual ceremony.

A temple room.

Had Hartford Hall once been the meeting place of an order of black magicians known as the Circle of the Lily? Was that what Eloise's husband, the man named Nigel from her dream, had been involved in? A black lodge?

Claire shivered, wishing it were not so, but it was the obvious conclusion. What was even more alarming were the similarities between the past and the present. The woman on the altar in her dreams was the essence of evil. So was the woman named Delilah she'd seen today who resembled in every way the dream figure. Nigel had been the name she'd heard in the dream, and she'd heard Delilah call Michael "Nigel."

The woman who in the dream had taunted Eloise and caused her death had been in command in the temple room, just as Delilah had seemed quite at ease there today. Claire recalled her comment about having arranged to have the power turned on. How could she have done that, unless . . .

Claire was hit by the sickening suspicion that the "wealthy Londoner" rumored to have purchased Hartford Hall was none other than Delilah Mason.

Was history about to repeat itself?

Where did Michael, who had been wearing the ring of the Circle of the Lily when he was with Delilah, fit in with all this? An ugly thought entered Claire's mind. Was he innocent of involvement in Delilah's black magic as she'd wanted to believe, or had she been duped? Was Michael in league with Delilah in her contemptible enterprise? Was his rescue of her just a sham to get her out of the temple room before she could learn their scheme?

She sank onto a chair and covered her mouth with her hand. *Oh, please . . . no, God, no!*

But even as she wanted to deny it, Claire considered it a distinct possibility. Michael's aura was black. He carried darkness in his soul, a penumbra she had possibly misread as sorrow, but which might be evil instead. Black magicians were wizards at throwing people off their true nature.

She thought back over the past days when she'd been with him, and her suspicions increased. At the very first contact, he'd seemed to drain her life force. He had been secretive, aloof, and had exhibited unwarranted bursts of anger. Although he'd seemed naive about magic, that could have been a ruse to see if she had magical connections, and like a fool, she'd sent him straight to the Alchymical Book Shoppe. She cradled her head in her hands, heartsick. She wanted to believe in him, wanted to help him, but until she learned more about this whole business, she could not trust Michael again.

She wished to God she hadn't given in to her physical desires just now. Sexual union was one way in which an evil spirit could invade and contaminate another soul. Had he used her in this manner? Had she been infected by his darkness? She reached for the amulet and was horrified to find it was not around her neck. Claire closed her eyes, searching for it psychically, and remembered Michael undressing her. He'd probably removed it as well as her clothing. Had he known it had protective powers and taken it off it on purpose so she would be more vulnerable to his darkness?

Her glance darted to the sofa, where, to her relief, she saw the golden chain of the pendant dangling from beneath one of the pillows. She retrieved the talisman and slipped the crystal around her neck again and held it between both palms, saying aloud the prayer that Lady Sarah had given her in case she felt threatened. Then she added one of her own:

"Please, God, let it not be true."

Now that his loyalties were in question, Claire was forced to reconsider the danger of continuing to seek answers to the mystery that was Michael Townsend. He had warned her to stay away, that it was dangerous for her to go anywhere near Delilah Mason. How would he know that unless he was involved with her? But if he were under Delilah's power, why would he warn Claire away? Was he guilty or innocent?

The jury was out, Claire decided.

Her heart would not let go of its desire to pursue her own investigation, but her mind admonished her that if she proceeded, it must be with utter caution and open eyes. She must shutter her heart against the influence of her emotions, which were still squarely on Michael's side. If nothing else, she was determined to learn the truth behind the death of the ghostly Eloise. She had also committed her psychic powers to Lady Sarah's magical war, whether it was for real or not. Intuitively, she knew all of this was interrelated, but she did not know how. It was all part of a complex puzzle, and she was anxious to see the big picture.

Besides, she decided, taking action was better than sitting around with a knot in her stomach.

She reached for the phone again and dialed the number of the police investigator assigned to the mystery of the unearthed skeleton. "Yes, good afternoon. This is Claire

St. John. I'm calling to see if you have had any success in identifying the remains that were found on my property."

"Ms. St. John. I'm glad you called. Your name was on my list of people to contact today. No, we haven't come up with an identity, but our forensics people have discovered that the skeletal remains are fairly old, perhaps a hundred years or more."

"A hundred years," Claire murmured. The uprooted tree could easily have been a hundred years old, even more. Claire thought back to Maeve's original speculation. "Do you suppose whoever it was that died back then was buried and that tree was planted on the grave?"

"Could be," the police officer agreed.

"Have you gone back into the records at the turn of the century to see if there was mention of any incident, a murder or a disappearance in this area that was never solved?"

She heard him clear his throat. "Well, no, we haven't, nor are we likely to. Due to the extreme age of the bones, we are declaring the case closed. We'll likely never know the truth of the matter."

Claire was shocked and then outraged. "Surely you're joking. I mean, you can't just leave it at that. What are you going to do with the body? And the ring?"

"The body will be buried in a public grave," he said. "As for the ring, you may have it if you want. Since it was found on your land, and since it is unlikely that it will ever be claimed, we suppose it is your property."

Claire thought of the plaintive ghost. She . . . it . . . Eloise . . . deserved better than a burial in a public grave, a pauper's tomb. "Don't do that," she blurted impulsively. "Don't bury her like that. I'll . . . I'll pay for a decent burial in a churchyard in the village."

"Her?" She heard the curiosity in the policeman's voice. "Why did you refer to the skeleton as 'her'?"

But Claire wasn't going to tell this dispassionate policeman that she believed the bones belonged to a ghost named Eloise, who as a person just might have been murdered by magic. Somehow, she didn't think he'd understand. "Just my whimsy, I guess."

Claire agreed to pick up the ring at the police station and promised to call back when she had the burial arranged, then hung up the phone, discouraged that the police were so phlegmatic. Where were the keen inspectors that one saw on television? Obviously, these investigators considered the case of little consequence, but they didn't know the dreadful nature of the death, nor that in their very precinct, a similar evil was stirring.

The policeman had also told her they had found no explanation of the symbol on the ring, and when she mentioned an occult group called the Circle of the Lily, he made a note of it, but she got the impression that he really didn't care anymore.

Case closed.

But not as far as Claire was concerned.

Michael was unused to the role of private eye, and he felt more like a stalker as he followed Claire later that afternoon. Without a car, he would be limited as to where he could follow her, but he was lucky that she headed out toward the village on foot. As Michael made his way a discreet distance behind her, he wondered if he were following her as a protective measure, or if that was just an excuse to be near her even at a distance?

It was a question he couldn't answer.

All his life, he had avoided becoming involved with women, except once—the affair with Kathy that ended with such disastrous results. For all his life, he'd heard both with his ears and his heart the melancholy voice of his father repudiating love. Was it love that motivated him now? Or was it just a desire to clean up the mess he'd made in Claire's life? Did he even have the capacity for love? Maybe it was impossible for him to love, truly love, anyone.

And yet his feelings for Claire went deeper than just his

desire to protect her, far deeper than wanting to set things straight.

Far deeper than anything he'd ever felt toward a woman. Deep enough he'd already called it love. He loved Claire St. John. He loved her enough to do what was right by her, and then let her go.

She hiked past the center of the old village and up the far hill toward the newer section of town where, to his surprise, she entered a church. With her interest in the occult, he hadn't taken her to be much of a religious person, at least in the traditional sense. He waited, loitering behind some large bushes down the sidewalk. She took so long he half expected a neighbor to call the cops on him.

At last she came out again, a distraught look on her face. She turned and continued up the hill, then veered to the right onto the main roadway that went through town. He quickened his pace to follow and turned the corner just in time to see her going into a rather nondescript red brick building. He dared to go closer and was even more surprised this time to see that she had gone into the local police station.

What was she up to? Was she reporting the incident in the basement of the old manor house to the authorities? It was possible, he supposed, but to what end? She had no way of knowing that Delilah Mason had purchased the property and had every right to be there. It had been Claire who was trespassing.

She came out a short while later, and from his vantage point inside a launderette across the street, he saw her stuff something into the pocket of her tunic. She retraced her path to the intersection, but instead of going back down the hill to the village, she continued on about half a block to the Information Centre where he had first secured lodging in her cottage. Now his paranoia kicked in. Was she finding him other living arrangements? After his behavior, he wouldn't blame her.

The final stop on her jaunt proved to be the offices of

an estate agency, the English equivalent of a real estate company. She was inside barely five minutes, and this time when she came back into view her face looked positively grim.

As she headed back toward the village, the late afternoon sun kissed her golden hair, backlighting it and giving the impression that a halo surrounded her head. Michael's heart tightened. She was so beautiful, and he wanted her so much. But until he could trust that his unspeakable woes were behind him forever, whatever their source, she must remain off limits.

The shadows of the line of low trees at the western edge of the property of Fairfield House were stretching toward the front door by the time Claire, several minutes ahead of Michael, made her way down her driveway once again. Waiting behind the hedge for her to go inside the house, Michael was startled when a car suddenly raced past him and turned into Claire's drive. It was a nondescript mid-sized automobile with a single occupant. The car's horn sounded several times, then a woman emerged and rushed up the stairs and pounded on the door.

Michael watched as Claire emerged and the woman, gesturing wildly, grabbed her arm and virtually dragged her to the car. She slung the gears into reverse, sending a small cloud of dust and rock flying from beneath the wheels, then backed out of the driveway without regard to what was behind her.

Michael jumped back into the tall bushes to avoid being hit and caught a glimpse of Claire's blond hair behind the glass of the car's window just as the gears shifted again and the vehicle careened toward the village at high speed.

Stunned, he stared helplessly after it. There was no way he could follow or come to her rescue. Some bodyguard he was! He hadn't even written down the tag number of the car in which the woman he loved and had vowed to protect had just been kidnapped.

*   *   *

"What on earth is going on?" Claire finally managed to wedge her question in between Maeve's almost hysterical babbling. She was tired from her long walk and disturbed by what she had learned along the way.

"The war's on," Maeve heaved at last, and her words chilled Claire.

"Lady Sarah's war?"

"It's not her war. It's a threat to us all, but you in particular seem to be a target."

Claire recalled the acid hatred in Delilah Mason's eyes, and she could guess the source of the danger. Was Michael in danger as well, she wondered, or was he part of the threat?

"Slow down or we'll both be killed," she cried out as Maeve slid onto the roadway just ahead of a large lorry. She'd never seen her normally unflappable friend so perturbed. After her heartbeat slowed again, Claire asked, "Is it a magical attack?"

"I don't know exactly. I'm just responding to the strongest psychic summons I've ever felt. It was like Lady Sarah was screaming in my ear. She even instructed me to come get you. Didn't you get the message?"

Claire shook her head. She had felt nothing the last few hours except the numb pain that surrounded her heart as her suspicions of Michael's involvement with Delilah heightened. She had not been tuned in to receive psychic messages, but it still seemed odd that she hadn't picked up anything if the message was all that strong.

When they arrived at the little white cottage, it was apparent that the others from the séance circle had been summoned as well, for their cars were parked in front. Claire and Maeve rushed to the door, which Lady Sarah opened to them before they could knock. Jim and Audrey Amesbury stood close together, with Audrey casting a dubious eye around the all-white room. Bitsy was there as well, shaking slightly, and Claire decided that Lady Sarah's call must have just gone out, for she had been with Bitsy not long before. She must have closed the Information Centre early, as it was only now five o'clock.

Lady Sarah closed the door and performed a banishing ritual, sealing out all unwanted entities and energies before joining the group. When she took her chair at last and gestured for the others to be seated, her face, pale in the best of times, was white as tombstone marble.

"It has begun," she announced in a low voice. She turned her eyes to Claire. "You were discovered in the temple of the sorceress this morning, and now she seeks your destruction." Her voice held no malice, no accusation. It was just a statement of fact.

Claire's stomach turned nonetheless. "How did you know . . . ?"

Lady Sarah's eyes were dark and worried. "I was there, too. I was warned just in time and managed to fend her away. But you are in very grave danger." She turned to the others. "Delilah has sent out a call to all the forces of Darkness to support her. She is planning a magical working of the most diabolical kind, but first she must destroy anything or anyone who stands in her way."

"Destroy? You mean she's planning to kill me?" At Lady Sarah's nod in response, Claire cried out, "But . . . why? I have no power over her black magic."

"You have power over the man she has chosen to be her High Priest."

It was a simple statement, but one that stunned Claire speechless. So that was Michael's role. The High Priest of a black lodge. It seemed so improbable, impossible even. Yet she had just confirmed her suspicions at the estate agent's office that Delilah Mason was indeed the new owner of Hartford Hall. The pieces of the puzzle suddenly began to fall into place, and Claire did not like what she saw.

"Michael?" she whispered.

Lady Sarah looked at her intensely. "Is that the man who was in the temple as well?"

Claire could only nod in reply.

"What is his name? I must be able to identify him as an entity in this battle."

"Townsend," Claire uttered tonelessly. "His name is Michael Townsend. He is the tenant in my cottage I told you about." Claire's mouth was dry and her skin clammy. Her heart raged in denial even as her mind absorbed what Lady Sarah was implying.

The old woman gave Claire a curious look, then closed her eyes and sat in silence for so long Claire thought she had fallen asleep. When she opened them and spoke again, her voice was strained.

"Michael Townsend is not the willing High Priest that Delilah was expecting," she said as if reporting information she had just learned. "He is, however, of the lineage that Delilah wishes to have in service to her in this working, and she will pursue him until he either accedes to her wishes or dies."

Claire sucked in her breath. "Isn't there anything we can do? Can't we mount a preemptive attack or something?"

Lady Sarah gave her a patient smile. "That is not the way of the white magician. We do not attack, but rather deflect or absorb the dark energies. It is our job to rid the universe of the evil, dissipate it so that it will not re-form. There is much we can and will do. But I warn you that until this business is finished, you must stay far away from this man. I will do all in my power to protect you and, since he is an unwilling partner, to protect him as well, but you must not further invoke the wrath of Delilah."

With that, the white magician drew them into a formal magical circle and gave them secret instructions for coalescing their individual powers into an effective defense against the oncoming evil. "We must not fail," she warned them as they prepared to leave hours later. "Lives hang in the balance."

Chapter Seventeen

MICHAEL LOOKED AT HIS WATCH AS HE SAW THE headlights of a car turn into the driveway. One A.M. Where the hell had Claire been all this time?

Instead of attempting to pursue the car on foot, a futile effort, Michael tried to convince himself that Claire had not been kidnapped, but had gone willingly with whoever had come for her. There must have been some kind of emergency, he told himself over and over as he sat on the front steps, waiting. But as the hours dragged by and she hadn't returned, he considered calling the police.

A rush of relief swept through him as the car pulled to the front of the house and Claire emerged unharmed. Her voice was hushed as she bade her companion good night before closing the car door, but it held no fear. Only then did he feel like an intruder. Still, he must see her, talk to her, make sure she was all right. He waited until the car's headlights were aimed in the other direction before he stepped out of the shadows.

"Claire. Don't be alarmed. It's me, Michael."

Claire nearly jumped out of her skin anyway. She whirled to face him. "What are you doing here?"

"I've been waiting for you to come home." He decided

the simple truth was the best explanation for his interference in her life.

She glared at him. "What for? I thought you didn't want anything to do with me."

Michael winced. Nothing could be further from the truth, but he could not tell her that. "I wanted to make sure you were okay," he replied instead. "I saw you leave in a hurry, and I thought maybe Delilah had . . . well, kidnapped you."

The brief anger that had marred her face a moment before softened. Then she said in a matter-of-fact way, "She might try to do that, I suppose." The very calmness of her reply alarmed him. It sounded like she didn't believe Delilah would do any such thing.

"Claire, listen," Michael pleaded urgently. "I'm afraid you don't understand the power of that woman. I've possibly exposed you to her vengeance, and I'm not sure that she won't try to harm you. She is not in her right mind."

"Oh, she's very much in her right mind," Claire countered. "She is the proverbial woman scorned, unless," she added, eyeing him dubiously, "you are still her man."

Michael felt his face grow hot. "I never was 'her man.' "

Claire shrugged, indicating that she didn't know whether to believe him or not. "Are you afraid of her? Do you think she will try to harm you as well?"

It was a question he'd pondered all evening. He'd betrayed Delilah by defending Claire, and he thought it likely indeed that she might attempt some form of revenge against him, too. However, he had a nasty suspicion she might try to re-enlist him as her High Priest instead. Because he'd been the bearer of the ring, she seemed obsessed with him becoming her so-called partner in magic. He didn't know exactly what those plans were, but apparently they included raising magical power through the sex act. Delilah was a sexy woman, no doubt, but not to Michael's taste. Nor did he wish to indulge in crass intercourse with a woman he did not love. The act of making love was sacred to him, a beautiful, intimate sharing between two people who cared deeply for one another.

The way he cared for Claire.

No. He would never serve Delilah as her High Priest. Or in any other way. And for that, she would probably try to get even.

"I'm not afraid of Delilah," he answered Claire's question. He wanted to take her hands as they stood together on the small stoop in front of her house. She had not invited him inside, and even though he knew that was for the best, still he longed to reach out to her, to touch her and reassure himself that she was safe and sound. But she kept her distance, both physically and emotionally.

"You should be."

"What?" Her cryptic statement refocused his thoughts that had strayed in the wrong direction.

"Afraid of Delilah. She is planning terrible things."

Claire's rather dispassionate statement of fact sent chills through him. How did she know what Delilah was doing?

"What are you talking about?"

"All I can tell you, Michael, is that you must be very cautious if you don't want to be party to her evil. Stay away from her. And," she added, her face bleak, "you must stay away from me as well. Perhaps it would be best after all if you found other lodgings. I won't be able to serve your breakfast in the morning at any rate. And tomorrow I have to leave early for London. It's late now. I must go in."

With that, she turned the key in the lock and went inside, leaving Michael with his heart in a lump and his stomach in a knot.

Deeply disturbed, he went around the house to the cottage, pausing a moment to look up at Claire's bedroom window. She was so vulnerable it hurt. Her very nature left her open to the danger he'd brought her way, for she seemed to be the kind of person who wanted to help others, no matter what. She had some misguided notion that she wanted to help him, but she didn't realize the peril in her altruism. He must convince her to stay out of it until Delilah either forgot her or was in some other way placated.

Only one thing would placate that woman, he thought unhappily. His return to the role of her High Priest. The very idea sickened him. He hoped it would never come to that. He prayed that Delilah would find another man for her lascivious purposes and that she wouldn't waste her time and energy seeking revenge against him and Claire. In the meantime, he must keep his vigil over Claire as best he could, notwithstanding her coolness toward him just now, nor her warning that he must stay away from her. Her detachment, he thought, was her quiet way of paying him back for the hurtful things he'd said after they had made love. He didn't blame her.

But he wasn't about to stay away.

After yet another restless night, her sleep laced with erotic dreams about Michael Townsend, Claire arose conflicted and confused. She longed to be with him, yet she knew that Lady Sarah's advice was well-founded. *Don't further invoke the wrath of Delilah.* No, she must stay away and depend on the forces of Light that were operating even now to protect him . . . if he would keep his distance from the sorceress. Claire had been relieved at Lady Sarah's statement that Michael was an unwilling party to Delilah's scheme, but with the power Delilah had at her command, Claire thought he might be dragged into it even against his will.

Lady Sarah had also warned her against returning home, thinking it possible that Delilah could mount a psychic attack against her if she knew her whereabouts. Claire had pointed out that she doubted the sorceress knew her identity, much less where she lived. The white magician objected, too, to Claire's traveling into London the next day to meet Cameron. But again Claire had overcome her objections. There was no way she was going to miss her luncheon date with her brother, for she desperately wanted to restore the bond between them.

She bathed and dressed in a jade green suit that Maeve had insisted she purchase. She hadn't thought the expense of a suit was warranted, considering her casual country lifestyle, but today she was glad she'd bought it. She wanted to show Cameron that she was not the provincial bumpkin he believed her to be.

When she was fully dressed and ready, she reached for the crystal pendant, but it looked out of place with the conservative suit, so she decided not to wear it and placed it carefully inside a small, battered jewelry box on her dresser next to the ring she had retrieved from the police station yesterday. She didn't know what she was going to do with the ring. She surely didn't want it, but until she sorted things out and resolved the mystery that surrounded it, she decided to keep it in her possession.

The morning was brilliant as she set out on the short walk to the train station, and her spirits soared in spite of the troubles that surrounded her. She was thrilled at the prospect of patching things up with Cameron. She arrived at the restaurant early and waited with eager anticipation. Thirty minutes later, the maitre d' called her to the telephone. It was Cameron.

"I'm sorry, sis," he said, his voice sounding sincerely apologetic. "I've been held up here, and it looks like this meeting is going to last all afternoon. I've given the restaurant my credit card number. Please, at least enjoy lunch on me. I'll call you later and set another date. I'll make it up to you, I promise."

Claire was no longer hungry. And she was more than a little angry. It had taken a lot of effort to make the trip into the city. Cameron could be so thoughtless. She picked up her handbag, thinking she should have lunch anyway and order everything on the menu to run up his bill. But it wasn't her style. Instead, she left the restaurant and considered what to do next.

Somerset House, Britain's repository of records of births, marriages, and deaths, was a short walk away. Considering she only had first names and a vague idea of a time frame, Claire didn't know if she'd have any luck, but she decided that since she was here anyway, she might as well spend sometime digging through the archives, seeking the records of two persons who might have lived around the turn of the century in the village of Montlivet.

Eloise and Nigel. Surname unknown.

Two hours later she emerged, successful beyond her wildest hopes. She had found records of a man named Nigel Beauchamp who had been lord of the manor known as Hartford Hall in the late nineteenth century. He was born in 1865 and in 1890 had married a woman named Eloise McDowell.

Could this be *the* Nigel and *the* Eloise? Claire thought it highly likely.

There was no record of either of their deaths. They had one son, Joseph, born in 1895, but the Beauchamp family must have moved elsewhere, to another country, after Eloise's death, for the trail stopped there.

It did not matter to Claire. She'd found one piece of the puzzle—Nigel and Eloise had lived at Hartford Hall during the same time period that the police had guessed the body that Claire had discovered as a skeleton had been buried beneath the tree. She could scarcely contain her excitement.

Claire's dream of what had taken place the night of Eloise's death suddenly assumed new proportions, new meaning, especially since she suspected that Delilah had plans for reenacting the scene, possibly with Michael's participation. The thought turned her blood cold. Would Michael take part in such a despicable ceremony, willingly or not?

It was suddenly urgent that Claire find proof of what had happened to Eloise, for then she could show Michael tangible evidence of the danger of remaining within Delilah's sphere of influence. But where to look? She recalled Maeve's suggestion that she become a sleuth and wondered if Eloise's disappearance had been reported to the newspapers?

It was only mid-afternoon. She had time to give it a go. She took the underground to the newspaper office where a receptionist directed her to the morgue, the archives where the large daily paper stored copies of each issue.

This search was far more difficult, made further stressful by the fact that the office closed at half past five, giving her less than two hours. She carefully chose the dates of the microfilm she wished to look at and began her examination, rolling history dizzily before her eyes. She began in January of 1895, since Eloise had obviously been alive and present at the birth of her son. She searched only the front pages, thinking that the disappearance of a prominent person—which, as the lady of Hartford Hall, Eloise would have been—should have made front page news.

In the June issue four years later, a short piece caught her eye. The headline of the brief article read: FRIENDS OF MRS. BEAUCHAMP SEEK EXPLANATION. According to the report, several women friends of Mrs. Nigel Beauchamp, née Eloise McDowell, of Hartford Hall, Montlivet, Essex, had become concerned that she seemed to have suddenly disappeared. Upon inquiry, the husband, a wealthy merchant, stated that his wife had fallen seriously ill and that she was recovering in the family's holiday home in the south of France.

That summed up the entire report. There was no mention that she could find in subsequent issues of a scandalous disappearance nor the slightest whisper of suspicion that Eloise Beauchamp had disappeared under more mysterious circumstances.

The world had believed Nigel Beauchamp.

Only Claire, and Eloise's ghost, knew the truth. But she still had not one shred of evidence to support that truth. All she had was the claim made by a ghost that she'd been murdered, a skeleton wearing a ring that somehow connected the past and present, the memory of her obscene nightmare, and the eerie feeling that it was about to happen all over again.

If it hadn't been his own home, or at least his former home, Cameron might have felt like a thief when he entered Fairfield House. But its very familiarity eased his conscience for what he was about to do. It was no big deal, he told himself, a harmless caper, like he'd pulled to prove his loyalty once to a fraternal group in university. It was the same concept—if you wanted to belong to a secret society, you had to demonstrate your worth by obeying the leader of the group, in this case, Delilah Mason. Only Delilah was far more than the principal of a mere mundane organization; she claimed to be the High Priestess of a secret and powerful occult society. Whether he believed that or not, Cameron very much wanted to remain in her favor. To that end, he would steal his sister's socks, or whatever else he could find that would impress Delilah. He could not imagine what she wanted with Claire's things and guessed that it was the idea that he would steal from his own family that mattered, not what he took.

Heading for the stairs and Claire's room, Cameron swore as he tripped over a large black cat that crossed in front of him, brushing fur across his expensive slacks. How could his sister tolerate those beasts? There were so many of them, it was disgusting.

Claire's room was directly across from two smaller rooms on the second floor, one of which had been his, the other hers, as they grew up. She had moved into the main bedroom after the death of their father. She had redecorated it in shades of pale lavender and ivory, turning it from a farmer's place of rest into a feminine boudoir. It was unfamiliar territory to Cameron, and he felt suddenly ill at ease. Hastily, he went to the large armoire in one corner and opened the doors, revealing neatly stacked sweaters, slacks, lingerie, and accessories. The closet was in the same state of ultra-neatness, and there was no indication that one garment was favored over another. How was he going to determine what she wore and what she didn't?

He went to the dresser and eyed the bottles and jars of her makeup array. He guessed she would use these items daily, so he did not touch them. Then he spied the old-fashioned jewelry box he recognized as the one she had owned since childhood. Claire never wore jewelry. She'd used the box to house her rock collection. He opened it anyway and was surprised to find a pile of costume jewelry inside, on top of which rested a crystal pendant and . . . a ring. His eyes popped.

The ring was exactly like the one Delilah wore!

"Good God!" he exclaimed under his breath, and he picked up the ring and placed it on his finger. Instantly, he was filled with a sense of heady power, as if he were king of the world. Where on earth did Claire get this ring? Did she wear it? Or was it just a relic she'd come upon and stashed among her little-used jewelry?

It didn't much matter to Cameron where his sister had come by it or if she wore it, for he would have it for himself now. With the ring, he should be the one to serve as Delilah's High Priest, a role he expected would be incredibly sexually pleasurable. As High Priest, he would be on equal footing with the High Priestess, if not as committed to her cause. His ownership of the symbol would surely prove to Delilah that she could trust him implicitly—with her magic and her money.

His heart pounding, Cameron took the pendant as well, placing both items of jewelry in his jacket pocket and shutting the lid of the old jewel case. He then scrounged a pair of socks and a T-shirt from the bottom of the neat piles stored in the armoire.

Relieved to have completed his assignment, he was about to go back downstairs when he felt a cold draft on the back of his neck. Ice cold. He turned to investigate its source and jumped when he saw a figure standing in the room watching him.

"Who are you?" he demanded.

It did not answer. Indeed, it did not seem human, at least not like any human he'd ever seen. His flesh crawled as he saw it float and sway in thin air, its body insubstantial, a misty, shrouded form that seemed to silently recriminate him for the theft he'd been caught committing.

To his horror, the figure moved toward him. He backed away and ran into the dresser. "Leave me alone," he cried, edging around the piece of furniture and beating a hasty retreat to the bedroom door where he dropped the clothing. Just as he reached the head of the stairs, he felt himself suddenly thrust violently forward. He lost his balance and tumbled to the bottom where he lay for a long while, dazed. He peered up the stairs, expecting to find the specter or whatever he'd seen leering at him from above, but there was only the silence of the empty house.

A coward's fear nauseated him but also mobilized him to pick himself up and run for the front door. When he reached the safety of the Jaguar, he locked the doors and looked at his face in the rearview mirror. His eyes were wild, and there was a nasty gash on his forehead. Sweating profusely, he wriggled out of his jacket and started to fold it when he saw a white substance mucked all over the back. He held the garment away from him, thinking angrily that one of Claire's cats must have made this mess on his best cashmere coat. But the instant he touched it, he recoiled in disgust. That slime had not been wiped there by any cat.

Nor by anything of this earth, for that matter.

Cameron flung the jacket into the backseat and turned the Jag around in the drive with short, lurching maneuvers, then stepped on the gas and departed without a backward glance.

Chapter Eighteen

THE LIFE OF A PRIVATE EYE, MICHAEL DECIDED, could be very boring. He'd spent his entire day waiting and watching over Claire as she went about her business in London . . . hiding in the last car on the train into the city, staked out in a phone booth near the restaurant where she'd gone for lunch, and now leaning against a building across the street from the place he himself had gone only a few days before, Somerset House. What business she had in there he did not know, but he was tired, hot, and hungry, and he'd seen no sign that Claire was in any danger from Delilah. Likely, his paranoia was out of control and she was under no real threat.

Still . . .

The memory of the hatred in Delilah's eyes kept him resolute in his vigil.

It was three o'clock before he saw Claire emerge from the hall of records, and he dutifully trailed her to the subway. It was tricky to catch the same train and avoid being seen, even more so to keep an eye on her to see where she got off, but he managed. It helped that she had on such a stunning and easy to spot green suit.

Her next stop was the building that was home to one of the world's oldest and most respected newspapers. He considered waiting for her outside as he had in the other places, but with each stop he grew more curious to know what she was about, so he took a chance and went inside. He caught a glimpse of her just as she disappeared through a double door to his left. Ignoring the curious stare of the receptionist, Michael followed, going down a stairway and along a corridor which led to a glass-paned door marked LIBRARY. Through the glass, he saw Claire talking earnestly to the clerk.

What on earth could Claire St. John be looking for in the bowels of the newspaper office? His curiosity was raging and he was tempted to march through the doors and ask her what the hell she was up to, but his pledge was to be a guardian from a distance. What she was doing was really none of his business. All that should concern him was her safety.

He posted himself in an alcove next to a water fountain and continued his surveillance. He hoped after this she would return home. She was wearing him out.

It was nearly half past five when he saw the flash of her green suit pass by, and he raised the newspaper he'd been reading to hide his face. She was up the stairs and through the double doors before he could organize himself to follow, and he paused. Should he continue this apparently futile chase? Or was he being obsessive? He glanced through the glass doors of the library and saw the clerk straightening the desk, preparing to close for the day.

Deciding that Claire was probably already too far ahead for him to follow, he decided to see if he could find out what she'd been looking for in the archives. As he entered the library, however, the clerk disappeared into another room. He overheard a woman's voice coming from beyond the door. "We have just got to get that machine fixed," she complained. "It took me four tries to get a proper copy off the microfilm for that last customer. That paper is so expensive I can hardly bear to waste it, but the rubbish bin is full of it."

Michael eyed a trash can behind the desk. It was filled nearly to overflowing. He edged around the desk and was about to reach for the paper on top when he heard the footsteps of the woman returning to the front office. Without thinking, he ducked behind a tall bookshelf and hoped she wouldn't see him, and then he felt really foolish. Why was he acting like a thief? If he'd just approached the clerk and asked for what he wanted he probably would have got it. But it was too late now. All he could do was hope he wasn't discovered and wait for her to leave again.

In moments, she picked up her handbag and headed for the door with another person who had emerged from the back room. "Guess that'll do it for today. Want to stop by the Crown and Thistle for a pint before we go home?"

The other person agreed as they walked out the door, and then to Michael's horror, he heard a lock slide into place. Good God. Some private eye he was. He was trapped in the basement of the newspaper building.

Angry at his predicament, he considered what to do next. Surely there would be a cleaning crew in later. Maybe he could make his escape then. In the meantime, he had ample opportunity to forage through the trash bin. He sat at the desk and plucked a crumpled ball of thermographic paper from the top of the pile. The image was smudged but readable, and he knew instantly it was the one he sought, for the article was about a woman who had seemingly disappeared from the village of Montlivet in Essex.

It was an odd little clipping, dated June 1899. Almost a hundred years ago. That in itself was intriguing, but even more so was the fact that the missing woman, a Mrs. Nigel Beauchamp, was the lady of Hartford Hall, the manor house presently under contract for purchase by Delilah Mason.

Michael became more troubled than ever about Claire's recent activities. She'd been snooping around Hartford Hall only yesterday. What was she looking for? What was so important that she'd spent over two hours in front of a microfilm machine to obtain this article that had to do with the old manor? He read it again, trying to find some reason for her interest.

Suddenly, something from the newspaper story jumped out at him. He knew of no one named Beauchamp, but . . . Nigel! That was what Delilah had kept calling him.

Nigel.

It was an unusual name. Could she, in her obviously warped mind, have confused him with this Nigel Beauchamp? That made no sense at all. Nigel Beauchamp, the wealthy merchant from Montlivet mentioned in this article, had lived a century before. There was no way she could have known him. Likely, there must be a descendant of the same name.

He closed his eyes and concentrated, trying to recall what else she'd said to him when she took him to that old house. She'd acted almost surprised when he didn't recognize the place. That was impossible, of course, when he'd never been there. But she'd made some other comment as well, when they were en route: *"We always return to where we've lived before."* Michael had never lived at Hartford Hall, but perhaps the Nigel she had him confused with had lived there. He groped for further recollection of Delilah's seemingly illogical conversation and came up with another bewildering statement. *This is just part of what you once lost, Nigel.*

Michael's mind suddenly spun with a frenzy of questions, about Delilah and Nigel Beauchamp and Hartford Hall and Montlivet, Essex. But most of all about Claire St. John and why she had traveled all the way to London and made the effort to uncover this article.

Obviously, she was not heeding his warning. She was not staying away from his affairs as he'd urged. In fact, it appeared she was doing exactly the opposite. She was deliberately nosing into things that were best left alone.

With mounting anxiety, Michael folded the paper and secured it inside his jacket pocket. He looked around, slightly panicked, for a means of escape. Claire was playing with fire, and he had let her slip out of his sight. He had to get out of here.

Michael tried the front door, but as he'd suspected, the clerk had locked it behind her. He thought about calling out, or using the telephone, but he didn't want to have to explain why he had ended up locked in the newspaper morgue. Surely there must be another exit.

He made his way through the maze of storage shelves that housed the news of bygone days in microfilm cans, like so many mini time capsules. Turning a corner, he saw a dim sign at the far end of a corridor. Exit. Hoping against hope, he hurried through the quiet toward the door, which he opened by pushing against a bar and which shut and locked behind him. He climbed the stairs and pushed out of another door at ground level and found himself once again in the heat of late afternoon London. He headed for the train station.

Perhaps Delilah posed no more of a threat than your average commonplace lunatic, but she was one strange and deluded woman. Claire had not kept her distance, and he feared that she might eventually meddle to the point that she would encounter Delilah again. If nothing else, Delilah Mason was rich and powerful, and he doubted that she would think twice about hurting Claire in some way, just for sheer meanness.

He must not slacken his vigil again. And somehow, he must convince Claire to drop all this snooping. Nothing good, he was certain, would come of it.

"You look like you've been in a bit of a scrap." Delilah entered the room where Cameron waited, pacing restlessly. He had a bloody cut on his forehead and was dressed in a shirt and tie, but no jacket. "What happened?"

Cameron, although obviously agitated, took a deep breath and assumed an arrogant stance, his hands on his hips. "It was nothing," he replied. "I just took a little fall for you." He moved closer, and Delilah sensed a change in her cavalier initiate. He seemed possessed of a new confidence, some previously hidden inner power. She didn't like it.

"Did you bring me what I need?"

His smile was both sardonic and sensual. "I believe you will find my booty interesting." He raised his right hand and extended it toward her.

Delilah was astounded. He was wearing the signet ring of the Circle of the Lily. "Where did you get that?" she demanded.

"Let's just say I . . . found it."

Delilah's mind worked furiously. To her knowledge, Michael Townsend possessed the only other ring in existence. Had this idiot somehow stolen it from Michael? Or, she wondered, suddenly alarmed, had she been mistaken in believing Michael was the one sent to serve as her High Priest? Had the higher powers, witnessing Michael's reluctance, taken things into their own hands? Delilah knew the forces of Darkness were impatient: Had they destroyed Michael and awarded the ring, and the assignment, to Cameron St. John?

She hoped it wasn't the case. She was not in the least attracted to Cameron, although she supposed he could serve her purposes, and she was not going to defy the dark legions who were backing her in the Great Working. He was a virile male. His sexual desires seemed strong and his interest in her undeniable. He wasn't her choice for a magical partner, but at this point, she would do anything to achieve her ends, including working High Sex Magick with Cameron St. John.

She remained aloof. "Do you know what it means?"

He came to her and touched her cheek. "I have been your most ardent pupil," he replied. "I have read everything you asked, and then some. I know that the man who wears this ring should be your High Priest. Allow me." With that, his lips brushed hers, and she had to work to refrain from withdrawing from his touch. Perhaps the powers would send Michael back to her. Perhaps not. Until she knew what was transpiring, she must keep all options open. Nothing must stand in the way of total success.

"We'll see," she replied stepping away and remaining noncommittal. "What else did you bring me?"

Cameron scowled at the rebuff, but answered mildly, "No clothing. I couldn't tell what she would miss if I took it, but you might like this." He held before her a heavy crystal pendant mounted on a gold chain.

Delilah held out her hand, and he dropped the cool stone into her upturned palm. Perfect. Crystals retained energy better than any other material, and she was well practiced in scrying them to learn what energies had been recently active with them. For her, it was as easy as viewing a television screen.

She held the crystal in her open palm and brought it closer to her eyes. She softened her focus, blurring the outside world and giving her a clear vision of the world inside the stone. She saw, and felt, the presence of two people, a man and a woman, both in the state of heightened passion. Delilah looked more closely and saw the face of the man, reflected as if from above. It was Michael Townsend. And below him, naked in his arms, was Claire St. John, Cameron's sister. She felt the pulse of their blood, the rhythm of their union, the heat of their sex, and fury enflamed her.

"Damn them!" Delilah flung the crystal across the room with a shriek. "They will pay for this," she snarled. "I will make them pay." She whirled to face Cameron, who had lost his earlier élan and was eyeing her with fear and apprehension. "You. You want to be my High Priest? Do you have any notion what that entails?"

His expression relaxed. "I believe I do."

"Are you ready to serve? Now? This very night?"

Cameron loosened his tie. "Instruct me, my High Priestess. Your wish is my command."

Delilah smirked at his cliché. He'd damned well better mean it, for he had no real knowledge of magic, no real concept of what was about to transpire and would have to follow her lead to the letter. She was glad he seemed eager to perform without asking the purpose of this particular magical working. She had earlier decided Cameron had no love lost for his sister, but she didn't know how he would react if he knew that by surrendering his body and his sexuality to Delilah, he was infusing her with his power, and that she would use it to destroy his sister.

Claire returned home from London tired but gratified that at least her day had not been wasted. With what she had learned during her impromptu visits to Somerset House and the newspaper, she'd been able to piece together a clear picture, at least in her mind, of what had happened to Eloise. The poor woman had been trying to save her husband, Nigel, from some sort of black magical ritual. She had been killed by the force of the power that had been raised in the temple room, and her husband, probably in his panic, had buried her in the meadow and planted a tree on the grave to cover up the deed. When her friends came snooping, he'd made up the story about her serious illness and her retreat to the south of France. And he'd gotten away with it for almost a hundred years!

Although it satisfied her curiosity to know the ghost's story, she still did not have a clear understanding of the relationship between that event and what was happening in the present. She'd confirmed yesterday at the real estate agent's office that Delilah Mason was the new owner of Hartford Hall, and from what Claire had overheard in the temple room, she guessed Delilah was planning to use the old manor house for the practice of black magic once again. Lady Sarah had told her that Delilah was the sorceress who was orchestrating the evil magical working that was afoot, and that she wanted Michael to serve as her High Priest. Even though the white magician claimed that Michael was reluctant to do so, Claire couldn't help but wonder how he became involved with Delilah in the first place.

Where did he get the ring?

Claire entered the house and threw her handbag on the couch. Cats jumped, stretched, or merely yawned at her in greeting. "Anything interesting happen around here today?" she asked, petting those who presented their furry bodies for her attention. Lefty yowled for dinner. "All right, all right." Claire went into the kitchen and refilled the animals' bowls with food and freshened their water. Then she went upstairs to change into something more comfortable, wondering if Michael had found another place to stay.

At the door to her bedroom, she saw a pair of her socks and a T-shirt lying on the floor. "That's odd." She frowned and bent to pick them up. Maybe she'd dropped them on the way from the laundry, she thought, but it had been a couple of days since she'd washed clothes. The items hadn't been on the floor that long. Must be the cats, she decided, refolding the shirt and placing both pieces back where they belonged in the armoire.

Claire slipped into a comfortable robe and lay down on the bed, hoping for a short nap to restore her energy. Her mind found it difficult to relax, however, jumping from one thought to another like a bee in a garden. The first flower it visited was Michael Townsend. She wanted to remain there and drift on the sweetness of remembered intimacy, but a breeze of intellect shook her off and sent her spinning to another thought-flower, this one wearing the face of Delilah Mason. The word "danger" flashed through her mind, which then flitted to the warning issued by Lady Sarah to stay away from Michael.

As at last she began to drift into sleep, Eloise poked her head into Claire's waning conscious thoughts, bringing a troubling warning of some kind of betrayal by Cameron. Must be my anger at being stood up surfacing from my subconscious, she thought drowsily, and then was overcome by her fatigue.

The animal that approached her looked like a large, feral cat, with fierce eyes and pointed teeth that flashed menacingly when it opened its mouth and hissed at her. It stalked her, following her as she made her way through the darkness. She began to run, and the cat leaped onto her back, and she could feel the tear of her skin beneath its claws. With a voiceless scream, Claire fell to the ground and rolled to her back to face the assailing animal. But the shape of the creature shifted, and it became a giant snake. She could feel the icy scales against her skin as it slithered around her body. She realized to her horror that she was naked. She rolled away, but not before the ugly fangs pierced the skin of her arm.

Running. She was running for her life, but going nowhere. The snake was a horrible, repulsive creature now, like an ancient demon with a grotesque face, claws, and wings. It flew at her and tried to peck out her eyes. She covered them with her arm just in time, taking the bite on her hand instead. Enraged, the creature lashed at her with his long tail, which entwined her like a whip and knocked her down again. She fought against the bindings that cut into her wrists, but she couldn't move. She heard a hideous laugh and looked up to see the demon standing over her, his male member hard and erect, ready to pierce her.

"Claire!" A voice sounded in her consciousness. "Wake up! It's not real. Fight it." With a violent jerk, Claire pulled free of her beastly assailant and opened her eyes. Her heart pounded so hard and fast it felt as if she had actually been running to escape the nasty creatures in her dream. It was nearly dark outside, and the room was in deep shadow. Claire sat up on the bed, shaking convulsively, wondering what had conjured such a nightmare. Damien, her black cat, jumped onto the bed, but when she reached out to stroke him, he swelled to the size of a tiger, arched his back and hissed loudly. She screamed and leaped from the bed, frantic to escape the phantasm. In spite of her terror, she managed to recall some of the brief training she'd been given by Lady Sarah.

"Delilah's psychic attack may come in the guise of vile creatures who appear real but who are nothing but thought-forms," she'd told her. "The power she wields is strong enough to project whatever loathsome ideas come into her head and make them appear real to you. You must remember, they are not real. They are nothing unless you give them power through your fear. Face them, banish them, and they will disappear."

That's easy for you to say, Claire thought grimly, but she did as Lady Sarah had instructed. "You don't exist!" she said aloud to the beast. "Go! Get out of here!" To her immense relief, she saw the cat figure shrink until it looked again like Damien. It kept on fizzling until it popped and became nothing, leaving Claire staring at the spot on the bed where it had appeared.

"Holy Jesus!" she swore, more an invocation than an expletive. She flicked on the bedside lamp and hurried around the room, turning on all the lights until at last every corner was illuminated. No demons confronted her, at least for the moment, but she dared not go to sleep again.

Then she remembered that Lady Sarah had told her one of the ways such a psychic attack could be successful was to deprive the victim of sleep, eventually causing him or her to fall ill. Another effect was to convince the victim that he was insane. According to the white magician, some attacks had been so effective that the person being attacked eventually sickened and died or else committed suicide.

What could she do, she wondered in panic, to ward off the demons and keep them from entering her thoughts and dreams? The amulet would offer some protection. As would her own sound mind, as long as it stayed that way. She went to retrieve the crystal pendant, but when she opened the jewelry box she stared at the contents, appalled. The crystal wasn't there. Claire was certain she'd left it there on top of the costume jewelry she'd bought to go with her new wardrobe. Her heart dropped like a rock when she realized the other item that was missing as well.

The ring.

Someone had been in her house. In here, in her bedroom. Her skin crawled, and she felt violated. She searched the room for evidence of other missing items, but besides the absence of the ring and the amulet, everything appeared in order. She thought about the socks and T-shirt and wondered if the thief had dropped them in his hurry to leave. But what would a thief want with things such as that?

Claire fought back the nausea that rose in her throat. She had been an occultist long enough to know that some practices, especially of the dark arts, required the use of personal items for the spell to work. Practices like voodoo. The casting of curses.

Did psychic attack work that way as well? Had Delilah come here and taken her things in order to evoke the horrible images into Claire's dreams? It seemed unlikely. A more reasonable assumption would be that she sent someone else to do her dirty work. Someone who was in her power and would do her bidding without question.

Someone near to Claire.

Someone like Michael Townsend.

Chapter Nineteen

SWEARING THAT SHE WOULD NOT BEND TO THE PSY-chic assault of Delilah Mason, an attack possibly abetted by Michael, Claire began a regimen of magical rituals taught her by Lady Sarah that were supposed to protect her from the thought-form attacks. The main defense lay in recognizing that the demons, both in her dreams and in her conscious waking, were but creations of Delilah's mind, powerful thoughts transferred telepathically from one mind into another. They appeared to be real, but they only achieved reality if Claire allowed them an existence in her own mind.

With each exercise, Claire's anger heightened. She would not be held hostage by a psychic terrorist. She called Maeve and Bitsy and the Amesburys and told them what had happened, and all agreed to pool their energies to raise a psychic barrier around her against further thought-form attack. She would have called Lady Sarah, but the white magician had no phone, so the best she could do was try to reach her mentally. With the powers that woman had developed, Claire figured she already knew anyway.

By the time she retired later that night, Claire was confident that no more demons would invade her dreams. Now, if she could just stop thinking about Michael Townsend, quit accusing him of the theft of the ring and her talisman, her mind would be at ease. But his collusion with Delilah seemed the only logical answer to the disappearance of those particular items.

Her dreams, if she had any, were benign, and Claire awoke refreshed and clearheaded about her choices concerning the magical actions that were afoot. She could not back out now from her commitment to Lady Sarah, for after last night's thought-form attack she knew she was involved in the magical conflict whether she wished it or not. She must maintain her psychic defenses at all times, for she did not know when another attack might be launched.

One of those defenses must be physically staying away from Michael.

For whether he committed the theft or not, he was obviously a part of all that was taking place, and Claire could not afford to be vulnerable in any respect at the moment. She hadn't seen him since she told him to find other lodgings, but since he hadn't returned her key, she believed he was still residing in the cottage.

She rose and dressed and went into the kitchen. From the side window she could see the door to the cottage, but she couldn't tell if Michael was there or not. She'd told him he was on his own for breakfast henceforth, so he wouldn't be stopping in for his full English today. The kitchen seemed empty without him. She had liked the way he seemed so at ease at her small table.

Claire began to prepare breakfast for herself, and when she went to the stove, a shadowy movement outside the window caught her eye. It was Michael leaving the cottage. Her stomach did a little somersault. She watched him turn onto the path that led away from the house toward the village, and her heart constricted. Why did it have to be this way? He was the first man in years . . . ever . . . who had claimed her heart like this, and yet she couldn't trust him.

Had he taken her possessions? She just couldn't believe

it. An idea struck her. It wasn't quite her cup of tea, but she did have a key to the cottage . . .

Before she could talk herself out of it, she grabbed the key and ran to the apartment. If Michael had stepped out for breakfast, she would have a little time to search through his things. Of course, even if she didn't find the ring and the amulet it didn't mean he hadn't stolen them. He might have already delivered them to Delilah. But if she found them she would know for sure where his loyalties lay.

The apartment appeared almost uninhabited. There were no newspapers on the table, no dirty dishes in the sink. The bedroom was the only room that gave evidence that there was a tenant in residence. Claire stood at the door, nerves on edge. The bed was unmade. She walked slowly to it and put her hand against the pillow. There was a slight indentation where his head had lain, and she wished the pillow were still warm. She wished, in fact, that he was here with her, beneath the covers, and that all this other madness simply didn't exist.

With a sigh she drew away from her fantasy and looked around, wondering where he would have stashed the stolen items. His suitcase was balanced on the arms of a chair near the closet. She opened the lid and was surprised to find that he had not unpacked everything. Or, she thought gloomily, remembering that she'd asked him to leave, he was in the process of repacking.

Inside the case she saw a curious-looking box. It was wooden, painted a dark, military drab green. There was no lock on it. With bated breath, Claire opened it.

She choked back a cry of astonishment and dismay at what she saw. Even though Claire was not herself a magician, she recognized the implements and insignias in an instant. Oh, my God, she thought, slamming the lid and withdrawing from the box. He *is* a magician. All that innocent talk about starting from ground zero in a research project was just another of his lies.

Near tears, she closed her eyes. Well, she'd wanted proof . . .

But she allowed herself only a short moment of grief. Pulling her emotions together again, she became even more resolved to find her missing belongings.

For now she was convinced that Michael Townsend, magician, was the thief.

With determination, she opened the box again and sorted through it. She came upon a ring, but from its vibrations she knew this was the one Michael had worn, not the one he'd stolen. There wasn't another, at least not in the box. The amulet was not there either. She ran her hand carefully beneath the folded clothing in the suitcase, but nothing hard or metallic met her touch. Instead, she felt an oblong piece of paper. An envelope. She slipped it out and studied it a moment. It was yellowed and battered, dog-eared on one corner. Nondescript in every way. Yet she could psychically feel a sadness in the vibrations of the paper as intense as what she'd first sensed in Michael.

The hair at the back of her neck prickled as she also sensed suddenly that she was no longer alone in the room. Wheeling around, she found herself the object of Michael's angry gaze.

"Isn't breaking and entering against the law in this country?"

Claire wanted to die. She couldn't believe she'd let herself get caught in such a situation. But his mocking tone raised her hackles. "Yes, it is, Dr. Townsend. And you ought to know about breaking and entering. I only came here, legally with a key, to reclaim what you stole from me."

"I beg your pardon?" Michael came to where she stood and jerked the envelope out of her hand. "This," he held it up, "is not your property. Nor is anything else in this room. I don't know what you are talking about."

"I'm talking about what you stole yesterday while I was away in London."

Michael glared at her. "I stole nothing from you or anybody else."

But he offered no alibi, no further explanation of his activities that might have proven his innocence. Only a challenging gaze.

"I'd like to believe you," she snapped, "except I keep running into contradictions that lead me to think you have been less than honest with me about other things. Like your claim that you know nothing about magic when you have a box full of things that even the most fledgling of magicians would recognize."

She saw him glance toward the box. Then his gaze returned to her. "What's in that box is none of your damned business."

"It's my business when a tenant in my cottage uses magic to attack me in the night." She hadn't meant for that to slip out, but anger strained her control. She was amazed at the abrupt change in his expression.

"Attack? How could you have been attacked? I was watching ... I mean, I was awake most of the night. I didn't see anyone ..."

If he was feigning innocence, he was doing a highly effective job. His slip of the tongue unsettled her, though. What did he mean, he was watching? Was he spying on her?

"What attacked me, as I'm sure you are well aware, was not in the physical. It was sent as a thought-form by someone wishing to frighten me, perhaps even harm me."

Michael stared at her, remaining speechless. His gaze probed hers, and in his eyes Claire read anxiety and concern. For what? For her? Or that she had rightly accused him?

"It's worse than I ever dreamed," he uttered at last, putting his hand to his brow. "Good God, I'll kill that woman if she harms you."

"Are you talking about Delilah?" Now they were getting somewhere.

"Yes."

"Are you . . . her High Priest, Michael?"

The revulsion on his face was undeniable, as was the anger. But he didn't answer her question. Instead, he retorted, "How do you know about that?"

Claire was uncertain how honest to be with him about her knowledge of Delilah and her magic. A part of her wanted desperately to believe that he was repulsed by the sorceress, but the box of magical paraphernalia taunted her from the corner of her eye. "How on earth did you ever become involved with Delilah?" she asked, avoiding his question in turn.

"That, too, is none of your damned business. I told you to stay out of this."

"It *is* my business, because you've brought it to my doorstep. And I can't stay out of it. There's . . . there's more to Delilah's magic than you can even imagine, Michael. She is a horrible, horrible woman." Claire wanted to tell him everything, to warn him of the danger of being anywhere near Delilah Mason when the magical war erupted. But if he was on the wrong side, if his innocence *was* feigned, then she would be betraying Lady Sarah and the forces of Light by providing vital information to the enemy.

Which was he? Friend or foe?

Claire's heart was painfully cleft in two.

As if he'd read her thoughts, Michael's expression softened, and he gathered her into his arms. "Oh, Claire, I wish to God I'd never heard of Delilah Mason," he whispered into her hair. "I wish I'd never brought you this trouble. Yes, she is a horrible woman, and I want nothing more to do with her. I was hoping she'd back off, but I was afraid she might try to harm you. So, well . . . I've sort of been keeping an eye on you."

His words were earnest, and when she looked up into his

eyes she saw the truth. He was as afraid for her as she was for him. "Keeping an eye on me?"

He gave her an abashed grin. "Yeah. That's where I was yesterday when somebody broke into your house. I followed you to London."

Claire didn't know whether to be angry that he would presume to invade her privacy like that or pleased that he cared enough about her to do it.

If it were the truth.

"Where did you follow me to?" His accurate answer was proof of his alibi, and Claire melted into his arms again. "Oh, Michael, I'm so relieved. I'm sorry I mistrusted you, but knowing you have been involved with Delilah and that you had access to the house . . ." She grew silent, then asked, "If you weren't the thief, who was?"

Michael took her hand, and they sat down together on the unmade bed. At first Claire thought perhaps her earlier fantasy was about to come true, but Michael remained all business. "What was stolen from you?"

Claire hesitated. "The crystal pendant I wear often," she said, "and a ring."

"Valuables?"

"Not really. I think the thief was after things of a personal nature. My instincts tell me that somehow Delilah was behind it and that she's using those items to focus her magical attacks against me."

Michael's arm tightened around her waist, and he tipped her chin to bring her gaze to his. "I wish I knew what to do to protect you better," he told her, his frustration evident in his words and expression. "I know you might not believe it, but I don't understand all this. I am not Delilah's High Priest. I am not even a magician, black or white. I have only recently learned that those items"—he gestured toward the box—"were used for ceremonial magic. They aren't my tools, Claire. I found the ring I showed you in that box as well. It was all hidden away . . . in my father's attic."

Claire was astounded. "Your father's attic? Was he a magician?"

"Not that I know of. But that's not the point. The point is in my eagerness to understand some things about my family and my past, I got mixed up with Delilah and now, because of me, you're being threatened by her wickedness as well. I never meant that to happen. I swear it. And I swear I'll do everything in my power to protect you from her."

With that, he bent and pledged his vow with a kiss that began as the seal of his promise, but almost instantly turned into a promise of the fulfillment of needs of a more immediate nature. He eased her down onto the bed, and Claire's head nestled into the pillow that only a short time before had evoked a fantasy for exactly what was happening now.

Be careful what you wish for, she thought with a lazy smile as she drew him into her arms. But he was exactly what she longed for. He was strong, virile, and protective, and his touch transformed her doubts and fears, making the madness go away, if only for the moment. She allowed herself to relax and forget the terror and to luxuriate beneath his caresses. She helped him rid themselves of the clothing that restrained them, and when they were free, she made love to him with an abandon that bespoke her need to forget the evil and to reawaken herself to the sweetness of life.

He surrounded her with his strength, his body possessing hers with a desperate passion as fierce as her own. There was no time, or desire, for gentle tenderness. They were two souls struggling to become one, for in that oneness lay their power to conquer all.

She savored the taste of him in the hungry kisses she scattered over the skin of his face, his neck, his chest. She inhaled the essence of him, sending his scent into the well of her memory. She explored the strength of his muscles as she ran her hands across his shoulders and down his back. When he entered her, she instinctively thrust toward him and dug her nails into his flesh. Never had she experienced the hunger, the drive, the need for a man that now commanded and controlled her body.

They met one another in an explosion that rocked her to the core, sending her into another realm, where there was no evil, and where the only power was the power of love.

Much later, Michael reluctantly let Claire ease out of his arms, for when their passion was spent she'd become worried that by being intimate they risked invoking Delilah's further wrath. It seemed a useless concern to Michael. The attacks had already begun, and he felt he could protect her better if he were with her.

She was adamant that she must return to her own house, however, so with a feeling of deep misgiving, he'd walked her across the flagstones and kissed her before closing the door behind her. He'd told her to forget any notion of him moving to other lodgings, insisting on remaining physically nearby in case she needed him. Claire had smiled and kissed him—with a sigh of patience, he thought—but she'd followed his wishes in locking the house, although she pointed out that thought-forms weren't deterred by locked doors.

Michael bathed and dressed, still dazed at the intensity of the passion that had erupted between them. This was a side of Claire St. John he'd never dreamed existed. A side he would like to get to know better, he decided with a grin. *Would* get to know better when the rest of this was safely behind them.

He was troubled by all that she'd told him and dismissed any last remnant of his former prejudice against what he'd once called "hocus-pocus." After hearing of the vicious and macabre nature of the psychic attack against Claire, he believed it was indeed magically induced and that it was the malicious brainchild of Delilah Mason. She had vowed to destroy both of them, and Michael suspected this was but the first of her efforts. He believed Delilah had stolen Claire's things, too, either herself or by proxy, and it turned his blood cold to think of her dark evil invading Claire's home.

He had vowed to protect Claire, but he was not sure exactly what it would take to keep that promise. Delilah's weapons were unfamiliar to Michael. Claire had attempted to ease his mind as to her safety by revealing that some of her psychic friends, led by the white magician known as Lady Sarah, were keeping a magical watch over her. But Michael couldn't depend on magic. He could only depend on himself and his wits. He was a rational man. There must be a rational solution to this most irrational situation.

Michael dressed as he had the first time he'd met Delilah and considered his plan of action. Facing her wrath did not faze him. He'd rather look the enemy in the eye than try to second-guess what she was planning. Perhaps he could reason with her, defuse her anger, change her mind. He drew in a deep breath and looked in the mirror.

What if it didn't work?

He had an ugly suspicion only one thing would propitiate Delilah Mason. His return to her chambers in the role of High Priest.

By the time he reached Delilah's apartment, Michael's nerves were on edge, and he vacillated between forced composure and unrestrained fury. The concierge in the lobby of the high-rise building recognized him and stood to greet and politely detain him according to the usual protocol. But Michael pushed past him and strode to the elevators. "Tell her I'm in a hurry." The doors closed in the man's startled face.

Delilah herself awaited him when the doors opened again at the penthouse level. "Well, darling, I'm glad to see you've come to your senses," she said. He heard the triumph in her voice, saw the determined gleam in her eye. She wore a long black robe that clung sensually to her lush body beneath its silken folds, but if she'd meant it to be seductive, the effect was lost on him. Instead of appealing, she looked hard and mean.

Michael had come here with the intention of trying to reason with Delilah, but he saw from the mad glint in her eyes that there was going to be no reasoning with her. He opted for a direct approach.

"Lay off, Delilah."

"I beg your pardon?"

"Lay off your attacks on Claire St. John."

She studied him for a long moment, then an amused smile touched her lips. "Whatever do you mean, Michael?"

"You know damned well what I mean. Leave Claire alone. She has nothing to do with you and your magic. It's me you are angry with. Take it out on the right person."

Delilah made a sweeping gesture, indicating for Michael to precede her into the apartment. "Let us go inside and discuss this like civilized magicians." Once in the luxurious living area, however, she turned on him in fury. "You're damned right I'm angry with you. You are my High Priest, Michael Townsend. I will not have you tainted by the attentions of that insipid creature."

At the insult against Claire, Michael's blood boiled and his barely restrained anger exploded. "I am not your High Priest or anything else. I owe you nothing, Delilah. I wish I'd never laid eyes on you. I will have nothing to do with your so-called magic. It, and you, revolt me."

Michael saw Delilah Mason's imperious manner evaporate. Her face turned deadly white, and her eyes widened in rage. "How dare you . . ." She reached to claw him with her nails, but he caught her arm and held it firmly.

"How dare *you*?" he returned. "How dare you think you own me? How dare you hurt an innocent person like Claire?"

"Innocent? Like hell she's innocent. She's meddling in my affairs." Delilah wrested her arm from Michael's grasp. "She's out to thwart the Great Working that is my destiny," she snarled, "and it would appear that you've chosen to become her accomplice." She shook her head. "Bad choice, Michael. I will destroy you both."

Michael glared at her and dared to push her rage a notch higher. He didn't believe it matched the intensity of his own yet. "No you won't. From what you've told me and what I've read of your High Sex Magick," he uttered the last three words with disdain, "without the right High Priest, you are powerless. You claim that by my lineage I must serve that role. Well, I refuse. You have no High Priest. Your magic is impotent."

Her face flushed and her nostrils flared, but she only stared at him in stony silence. In a moment she turned away and went into the private room that served as her magical headquarters. When she returned, she carried something in her hand. She held it up, letting it dangle between her fingers, and Michael recognized it as Claire's crystal pendant.

"Where did you get that?" he asked, not letting on that he'd suspected she had it.

"There are others more loyal to me than you and who do my bidding without question. Others who will serve eagerly as my High Priest. You think I need you, but you are sorely mistaken. You were offered the opportunity because you came bearing the ring, but you have betrayed the Circle of the Lily." She gave a low laugh. "Seems more of those rings are around than I thought. Another has turned up, alongside this pendant. I have awarded it, and the position of High Priest, to the loyal protégé who acquired them for me." She laughed scornfully. "It doesn't really matter who serves as High Priest as long as he can get it up. I would have preferred you, but one man is as good as the next if I can stand prolonged sexual contact with him."

Her last comments disgusted Michael, but he was taken off guard by what she'd just said, that another ceremonial ring existed and that it had been pilfered along with the crystal from Claire's house. Claire had mentioned that a ring was stolen, but she hadn't told him what kind. Why? And where did she get such a ring? Had she lied about not being a magician? His sudden uncertainty about Claire defused the anger that had sustained him so far against Delilah. His gaze bore into her as he stood before her clenching and unclenching his fists.

"What do you want from me?" he asked at last.

Victory gleamed harsh and golden in Delilah's eyes, but she shook her head. "Nothing, Michael. Nothing at all. I wanted you to accept your heritage, but you refused. Now it's too late. All I want from you is your absence."

Michael suddenly perceived what a terrible mistake it had been for him to come here. He had done exactly what Claire had warned him against—invoked greater wrath from this madwoman. Instead of protecting Claire, he had probably increased the danger that threatened her.

"I'll go. But I implore you, leave Claire out of it. She is innocent of trying to thwart your schemes. She knows very little about magic."

"You are the innocent, Michael, if you believe that. Didn't you see her attack me in the temple room?"

Michael had seen *something* attack Delilah, but he found it impossible to believe it had been Claire. He shook his head and turned to go.

"Fool," he heard Delilah utter behind his back.

From out of nowhere, a cat darted in front of Michael, tripping him and knocking him off balance. He didn't fall but was thrown awkwardly against the wall. When he looked for the animal, however, it seemed to have vanished. He raised his eyes toward Delilah, who threw her head back and laughed mockingly. When she recovered, she shot him a warning glance.

"You'd better watch your step, Michael."

Chapter Twenty

CAMERON MADE UP A LIE TO EXCUSE HIS ABSENCE from work that afternoon, telling his supervisor that he was meeting an important client for an extended lunch and not to expect him back that day. It was only a partial lie, he convinced himself. If he could please Delilah Mason, she could become the largest client in the brokerage.

He smiled. What a job. Taking off in the middle of the day to be with, in the most unbelievable way, the richest woman in London. He shivered in anticipation of what he expected the afternoon to bring. If it was anything like last night's ritual . . .

He was ushered to the elevators without a call to the penthouse. "Miss Mason is expecting you," the concierge said, his face professionally unreadable. Cameron's nerves tingled. She was waiting for him. Eager. He grew hard at the thought. What had transpired between them the night before, although bizarre, had also been highly erotic. As she'd become his tantalizing tutor, she'd explained to him that the rituals of her High Sex Magick employed techniques used by the ancient Tantric masters. She had also insisted that he remain the passive partner, for she'd said he had much to learn and if the magic was misused it could be dangerous.

He grinned in amusement. That wasn't it at all. Delilah was a control freak, and she wished to maintain control in their sexual relationship. Cameron didn't mind. In fact, with her in command he'd enjoyed the most fantastic erotic experience of his life. Great, if kinky, sex.

The elevator doors opened. He hoped it was about to happen again.

The servant showed him through the hall of mirrors, as he'd dubbed the magical entrance to her apartment, and taken him directly to the private chamber where he indicated for him to assume the proper attire. "Miss Mason will be with you directly."

The "proper attire" meant nothing at all except a ceremonial robe. Naked. He slipped out of his business clothing and hung everything in the closet as she'd instructed the night before, then donned the red velvet floor-length robe. His erection was so strong it hurt. He paced the room, anxious for the High Priestess' to come and relieve him of his exquisite misery.

Last night she had taken her time to raise the power she said she needed for some magical working, and her sexual prowess had extended Cameron's pleasure beyond belief. Never had it lasted so long. Never had he been able to exhibit such control with a woman.

But then, he'd never been with a woman like Delilah.

What was her secret?

He'd seen her reading from a book, a manual or something. Maybe it contained instructions for the High Sex ritual. He saw a cabinet on one side of the room which he knew contained candles and incense and the like. Perhaps the book was there. With a furtive glance in the direction of the door, he decided to check it out. If she caught him, he could just tell her he was reading it because he was eager to please her.

It was there on the top shelf. An unbound book with ragged yellowed pages. He took it in his hands and turned through several pages. It was as he'd suspected, an instruction manual, not only for High Sex Magick but for many other kinds of spells as well. He wondered briefly if the rest of her magic was as delicious as her sexual rituals.

He heard a noise outside and quickly replaced the book and moved away from the cabinet just in time for Delilah to make her entrance. He'd noted she was fond of framing herself in a doorway and holding a pose for all to admire. It was good showmanship, for she had a body worth admiring.

"I'm pleased you could come," she told him, flowing into the room in a silken black gown.

"I've told you where my loyalties lie," he replied, taking her hand and kissing her fingers, noting with satisfaction that they both wore the ring of the Circle of the Lily. He believed it was the ring that had opened the door for him to become her High Priest. He hoped it was just the first step in a long, sensual, and profitable relationship for them both.

"I have an urgent mission for you," she said, brushing past him and setting candles around the altar. Cameron watched her, his arousal intensifying in anticipation.

"Just name it."

She lit the last candle, placed and lit incense in a holder, spoke some magical words, and made some secret gestures. Then she held out her slender arm and beckoned with fingers he knew could work magic with his body. "First, let us raise power."

She led him to the altar where she removed his robe and laid it across the cushioned table. Her eyes roamed from his head to his toes, stopping to admire the hard evidence of his desire. "Very nice," she grinned wickedly. She turned on a tape recorder, and as the sound of the familiar male chanting reached his ears, Cameron began to feel a glow suffuse his skin. It seeped into the muscles beneath as he followed her lead into the rituals of High Sex Magick.

As she worked, his desire reached a fevered pitch, but instead of ending in orgasm, she managed to maintain the exquisite sensations at their peak until he thought he would lose his mind. The fire that burned intensely in the core of his sex seemed to grow until it flamed outward from his body, filling the room. It flared around Delilah who knelt above him on the altar. Her body was golden in the candleglow; her hair became part of the fire. Consciousness ebbed as he heard her chanting words that sounded strange in his ears, but she recalled him into the moment.

"Deum Nocturnus," she called to him. "God of Darkness. That is now your magical name."

Cameron writhed beneath her, barely hearing her. "Yes, my queen."

"You have pledged your loyalty only to me, your High Priestess. Now pledge that you are my servant, that you will do as I say without question. Swear it! Swear it on your life, and all power shall be given unto you."

His breath coming in short, heavy gasps, he swore the vows she demanded, hungry for her to end the sweet torture even as he wished it to go on.

She rewarded him by bringing him to still more incredible heights before allowing him release at last. The power of his climax was so strong he lost consciousness.

When he awoke, Delilah was sitting on the Victorian couch, watching him.

"Come," she beckoned. "Put on your robe and come sit by me. I am pleased with you."

No one could be more pleased than himself, he thought, still partially in another realm of delight. He went to her, his body weak, his mind dazed, his virility spent for the moment.

"You took a sacred oath during that ritual. Do you remember?"

"Yes," he said, vaguely recalling that he'd sworn to be her servant and to do whatever she asked. For that kind of sex, he would do anything.

"I am ready to assign your next magical task."

"I am ready to serve you."

"You brought me the items I required for your first test. Things belonging to your sister. Now I want you to bring me . . . your sister."

Night began to fall, and Claire paced her sitting room like a caged tiger. The tension of waiting, not knowing what to expect next, knotted in her shoulders. She'd called Maeve five times that day, hoping to learn what was happening in Lady Sarah's war, but the calls were answered by a machine. Only on the last effort did she remember that Maeve was in London at Belgrave Square that day.

As reluctant as she was to become embroiled in a battle between the magicians, Claire had committed her psychic resources to Lady Sarah and was ready to get it over with. She was also more willing to fight the magical battle than she had been at first because she believed that if Lady Sarah and the forces of Light were victorious, the sorceress who lay claim to Michael, despite his reluctance, would be vanquished, and he would be freed from her influence.

After hours of mental debate about Michael, Claire had decided that she could no longer continue to harbor doubts about his loyalty. She chose to believe him when he denied that he was under Delilah's influence and when he told her he wanted nothing more to do with that evil woman. Once Claire had believed that Delilah might have been the source of his dark aura, but he claimed he'd never met her before coming to England. If that were true, the darkness emanated from some other source, probably the curse she had felt resonating in his ring.

With each minute that dragged by, Claire became more resolved that once the clash between the magicians was over she would get to the bottom of Michael's curse and help him break it, whether he wanted her to or not. Because until he was free of that inner darkness, there was no hope for the two of them to be together. After his tender love-making this morning, Claire wanted him to be her partner forever, and she was unwilling to give up on him without a fight.

But what lay between them was a dark and dangerous abyss. Would the forces of Light triumph? Would Lady Sarah's magic, supported by their small group of psychic mediums, be sufficient to overcome the power of Delilah? Would Michael drop his emotional barricade and let her inside his heart at last? All day Claire had resisted using tools of divination to discern the outcome, for if it was not a good one, she didn't think she wanted to know.

Unable to stand the suspense any longer, however, she picked up the pack of tarot cards.

The spread fell before her in an unsettling lineup. At the basis of the matter was the Magician, the first card in the major arcana, the card of manifestation. That was not surprising, but which magician? Delilah Mason or Lady Sarah?

The second card was the Two of Pentacles, showing a jester figure juggling two golden discs while treading water. Shaky. Unbalanced. Undecided. That was in the position of the present state of affairs.

In the slot of hopes and fears fell the Lovers. Not always indicative of love, but in this case, Claire read it as her hopes for love between her and Michael and her fears that it would never be.

The Fool stepped into the recent past position. Had she been a fool for falling in love with Michael? Or did the card represent some other force, someone who had foolishly "stepped off a cliff" or "gone over the edge?"

Covering the present card was the Devil. How Claire hated that card! She shuddered, not wanting to think what it might mean. Was their magical war bedeviled? Did the card represent the evil forces that surrounded Michael? Or was it Michael himself?

In the position of the near future she laid the Eight of Swords, and the impact of that card sent a shiver through her. The card depicted a blindfolded woman imprisoned by eight sharp swords that formed a barricade behind her. Claire considered the irony of that card—although the woman is bound, she is not really imprisoned and can set herself free if she wants. She hurried on to the next card, not forming her opinion of what that might mean until the entire spread was on the table.

The Death card came next, and at that Claire almost put away the cards. In the position of the near future evolving, the Death card indicated not necessarily a death as much as a change or transformation. It could also, however, portend a physical death, and with all the currents ebbing and flowing around her in the magical realms, and with the battle between Light and Darkness imminent, Claire psychically sensed that the latter could very well be the meaning in this case.

The card representing the effect of others on her was the Queen of Swords. The mental queen, a woman of great mental powers. It gave Claire some small comfort, for in this card she saw Lady Sarah, the magical warrior in a pose of serene victory.

Next she drew the Chariot, a card indicating strong willpower. It fell into the position of herself in the environment of the future. Whatever was about to happen, she would need every ounce of her will to succeed.

The final card, the outcome, was the most distressing of all. The High Priestess. Her immediate reaction was that Delilah, the only High Priestess she knew of, would win out in the end. But it was a resolution she could not accept, so she kept her focus on the card for many moments. The High Priestess represented the inner self, the intuition, the feminine, and what gradually seeped into Claire's mind was that this card was telling her to follow her inner guidance in the matter of Michael. To trust her feelings.

Was that the real meaning? she wondered, staring at the layout morosely. Had she read the outcome accurately or only as what she *wanted* it to mean? She turned away, confused about the entire pattern and wishing Maeve would come and help her interpret it.

The phone rang, startling her. News at last?

It was Cameron.

"Hi, sis. Listen, I'm bloody sorry about missing our luncheon yesterday. Please say you'll forgive me and let me make it up to you."

His voice sounded unnaturally brittle, a little nervous even. What was he up to now? Claire wondered. "I'm not making another trip into London, if that's what you're proposing."

There was an extended silence, then Cameron said, "Would you invite me to tea tomorrow? It's Friday, and I could take off early. After tea, maybe we can take a walk like we used to across the pasture. I feel like I've lost touch with reality sometimes in the heat of my job. I'd like to breathe some fresh country air again."

"I can imagine," Claire replied cynically. His proposal appealed to her, but she wasn't getting her hopes up that he would actually show. "Come if you want. I'll make fresh scones and Devon cream."

"My favorite. Great! I can be there as early as three. Will that suit you?" Not waiting for her answer, he barged on, a little too eagerly, Claire thought. "I know! We should walk up the path and break into Hartford Hall, like we used to do when we were kids. I've heard the old place has been sold. This will likely be our last chance before the new owner takes possession."

Claire was mortified at the thought of ever returning to the manor house. "I . . . I don't think that's a good idea, Cameron. Come for tea but forget about breaking into Hartford Hall. We're grownups now, remember?"

He ignored her barb. "See you at three tomorrow then. Think about it. It would be a harmless adventure. Maybe you'll change your mind."

"Don't count on it."

*   *   *

Banished from Claire's presence by her fear of provoking Delilah, Michael continued his watch over her as best he could from the frustrating confines of the cottage. Returning from his disastrous mission in London, his own fears engulfed him as Delilah's threat echoed in his mind.

I will destroy you both.

Michael could accept the threat against him as Delilah's revenge for being spurned. But she had no right or reason to threaten harm to Claire. None that he could think of at any rate.

Delilah's claim that Claire had owned a ring bearing the symbol of the Circle of the Lily bothered him. He was also disturbed by Delilah's apparent conviction that Claire was somehow trying to abort her Great Working. He was not sure exactly what a working was. It was obviously an important magical event to Delilah, who'd called it her destiny. Important enough that she'd bought Hartford Hall to gain access to the old temple room. Important enough that she'd shared some of the secrets of her High Sex Magick with Michael in her efforts to draw him into the Circle of the Lily. Important enough that now she was threatening both their lives.

Again he tried to reason through her motivations for making such a dire threat. He'd refused her sexual overtures, but only a psychotic would kill someone for that. It had happened, of course, and Delilah could easily be described as psychotic. But what had Claire done to invoke her murderous wrath?

She'd been trespassing. In the temple room.

Michael paused, considering that. What *had* Claire been doing in the temple room? Had she owned a ring like his own? If so, why hadn't she told him? Other recollections crossed his mind that he found odd. Claire had said she'd been told to warn him, and in fact she had tried desperately to keep him from his first appointment with Delilah. How he wished now he had listened! But *who* had told her to warn him? Did she hear voices, or was she, too, involved in magic?

As a man of reason, all of this occult business seemed irrational and impossible, and yet he had witnessed first-hand the power Delilah claimed for her magic. She'd once asked him if he had power. He gave a heavy sigh. At the moment, he felt entirely powerless against her, because he knew little about the forces she wielded.

What was power anyway? Was it Delilah's kind of ma-nipulation of others? If so, Michael didn't want it. To him, the quintessential scholar, knowledge was power. If he un-derstood something, he could face it head on.

But there was much he didn't understand, about magic, about Claire, about his life. There wasn't much he could do about the latter two at the moment, but . . .

He went to the stack of books that lay on the table, the occult books he'd bought at the Alchymical Book Shoppe. It was time he began his real research.

He read late into the night, and as his knowledge of the forces of the occult grew, so did his trepidation. He read accounts of psychic attacks such as Claire had experienced. He read about the concept of sexual intercourse being among the most powerful means of raising the energies of magicians. He read about curses. What once he had dis-missed as childish abracadabra, he now considered seri-ously, not just because of his involvement in recent events, but also because these books were written by scholars, not wizards, people who like himself held doctorate degrees from famous and respected universities.

They believed in it. Now he did, too. And despite her concerns about being with him, Michael desperately wanted to see Claire. He needed other answers. He needed to know if the ring that was stolen indeed was like his, and why she'd been in the temple room. Three A.M. was not an hour to go calling, however, and he was exhausted. Turning out the light, he fell asleep in an instant.

Delilah's face was twisted in mirthless laughter as he entered her apartment. She invited him through the mirrored hallway, past the living area and into the private magical chamber. Fear and anxiety clutched at him for he knew she was planning something diabolical. Around him the room seemed to shimmer in a fiery aura, and it was very hot. Delilah closed the door behind him, and he was imprisoned in her lair. She willed him to look in the direction of the obscene altar where she'd tried to seduce him, and to his horror, he saw Claire naked and bound on the table. He wanted to rush to her and save her, but Delilah's magic rendered him unable to move.

"I thought you might want to watch," she taunted him. "I will be rid of her soon, and then it will be your turn. This way, you will know what to expect."

Michael's fear turned to sheer terror as Delilah drew out a dagger with a yellow handle and brandished it in the firelight. He recognized the knife. It was the one in the box from his father's attic. Somehow, he had provided the instrument of Claire's death.

"No! Don't . . . !"

But Delilah only laughed and raised the athame high. "You wanted to know about power, Michael. I'm about to show you power. Sacrificial blood is even more potent than sexual energy. Watch."

The air around him turned foul and he stood transfixed in horror, watching as Delilah slowly lowered the knife to Claire's throat.

"No! Delilah! No . . . !"

Michael came out of the dream drenched in a cold sweat. As he returned to consciousness, he realized with relief it had been only an unholy nightmare, his subconscious spilling over with fears concerning Claire.

Or had it?

Was his dream, like Claire's, part of Delilah's efforts at

psychic attack? Was the venomous woman giving him a preview of what she had in mind for them? He bolted from his bed and threw on a pair of jeans and a shirt. Then despite the hour he raced across the covered walkway and hammered violently on Claire's back door.

"Claire! Claire! Answer me! It's Michael. Are you all right?"

Chapter Twenty-one

CLAIRE AWOKE TO SOMEONE POUNDING FURIOUSLY on her door. She leapt from her bed and pulled on her old terry robe. Who on earth would be making such a racket at this time of night? She took the stairs two at a time, noting that night had nearly flown and that dawn was already on the horizon.

"Michael?"

"It's me. Open the door."

She flung it wide and found herself looking into a face that was filled with both terror and concern.

He pushed her backward into the house and locked the door behind him. Then he drew her into his arms. "Oh, thank God!" he whispered hoarsely. "It was only a dream."

Claire thought she must be dreaming too as his arms enclosed her and she leaned into his strength. "A nightmare?" she asked quietly, embracing him in return. She felt his nod where his chin rested on the top of her head.

"She's going to try to kill you. I saw it in my dream." He didn't go into the details, but Claire surmised his dream must have been intense and realistic.

"It's your worries coming to the surface, Michael,"

Claire suggested. But she knew it wasn't the case. His dream likely portended Delilah's intentions.

Michael led her into the sitting room and they sank into the couch where only days before they had discovered the depth of their love . . . and the beginning of this terror. He held her closely, and she inhaled deeply of his scent, wanting every impression of him to be written on her soul.

"It could be that I'm so afraid for you my own fears played out in my dream," he agreed hesitantly at last. "But I have done a lot of reading since yesterday morning . . ."

He paused, and Claire knew he was thinking about the hour or more they'd spent in his bed. She nestled closer and waited for him to continue.

"From my new understanding of the occult, I think it might be that she sent that dream telepathically, just to frighten me."

"It's possible."

"Claire, I have to tell you something."

The edge in his voice scared her.

"I did something really stupid that makes me believe the dream was a deliberate thought transference," he said, kissing her forehead and running his hands through her hair.

A premonition made Claire's blood run cold. "What, Michael?"

"I went into London yesterday. I went to Delilah's to try to reason with her and get her to call off her warped revenge attacks."

Claire stiffened. "You what? What happened?"

"She wouldn't listen, and I only ended up making her angrier than ever. She's insane, Claire, and I've made her even more determined to take vengeance against us."

"Oh, my God." Claire exhaled and dropped her head into her hands. It was exactly the kind of confrontation Lady Sarah had warned her against. But it was done, and there was nothing that would change it. All she could do was surround them both with the protection of the Light and pray that Lady Sarah knew what she was doing.

She also decided it was time to let Michael in on the bigger picture, for she saw clearly that he was in danger now as well.

"I could use some coffee," she said, easing herself from him. What she had to tell him could not be said in a lover's embrace. It was possible that he would think her as insane as he believed Delilah to be. "Join me?"

"Yeah, sure," he answered bleakly.

Claire took heart that Michael had read enough on the subject of occultism to at last begin to take it seriously. Over coffee, eggs, and toast, he told her about the materials he'd read in the night. "I would still find this all difficult to believe, except that the authors of those books were scholars, like myself."

She reached for his hand and gave it a squeeze. "Remember I told you that 'the occult' merely means 'the hidden'? There is much that scholars and scientists just haven't yet discovered or dissected to their satisfaction, things that can't be explained in known terms. Like electricity was hundreds of years ago. And gravity. There are creative forces available to us all, but only a few have the knowledge to use them. Some of these people we call wizards and sorcerers and magicians, but spiritual leaders know of these forces as well."

"Forces?"

"Mental forces. Creative powers. They are what drives us all. You've heard of books like 'As a Man Thinketh' and 'The Power of Positive Thinking?' They're talking about these forces." She drew her hand away to pour him another cup of coffee. "Unfortunately, these powers are not always used for positive results and not all thoughts are good. The forces I am speaking of are impartial. They are not just forces for good. They simply exist, like electricity, and in the same way can be used for good or evil. It is the manipulation of these forces that comprises the practice of magic. White magicians use them for good, black magicians use them for evil."

Michael studied her for a moment. "Are you involved in magic, Claire?"

She sighed. "I wasn't. Not until you arrived." She gave him a rueful smile. "Now I'm up to my backside in it." She told him at last about Lady Sarah and the magical war that loomed in the astral realms as well as on earth. "I know that all sounds incredible," she concluded, "but believe me, it's real."

"That's ghastly." Michael stirred his coffee absently, his expression deeply troubled. "My God, how I wish I'd never brought you into all this."

"Actually, you didn't." Claire gave him a small grin, wanting to ease his mind. "You only stirred the pot a bit. I would have eventually become involved anyway. Eloise would have made certain of it."

"Eloise?"

If he suspected she was nuts, this would provide him with final proof, Claire thought as she prepared to tell him her next fantastic tale.

"Remember last week, the first day you were here, and I went all hysterical?"

"It would be hard to forget."

"It was silly of me, of course, to be so frightened, but then I'd never encountered a ghost before."

He looked across at her, his eyes reflecting the skepticism she'd expected.

"Ghost."

"Ghost." She told him about finding the skeleton and the ring, and of Eloise's spectral visitations. "She brought me a present once," she added, just for full effect. If she was going to put him off, now was the time to do it. Before she lost her heart to him any further, he must know that he was involved with someone who respected all possibilities regardless of how absurd they might seem to the rest of the world. She brought the crucifix to the table, then proceeded to tell him about her dream of Eloise's death.

"That's why I was at Hartford Hall," she finished. "I

wanted to confirm my recollection that the symbol on the ring was the same as I thought I had seen as a kid in the basement of the manor house.''

''Eloise,'' he said slowly, as if trying to sort something out. He turned to her and gave her a sideways glance. ''You wouldn't be talking about Eloise Beauchamp by any chance?''

Claire's eyes widened. ''How did you know that?''

Michael enjoyed her astonishment, glad that he had brought one little surprise to the table considering everything she'd just laid on him. ''Wait just a minute.'' He went back to the cottage and returned with the wilted scrap of paper that contained the old newspaper article. He read the headline aloud.

''Friends of Mrs. Beauchamp Seek Explanation.''

She reached for the paper. ''Where did you get this?''

Michael grinned sardonically. ''Well, I didn't steal it from you. I stole it from the trash can at the newspaper library just after you left the building.'' He came around to the back of her chair, laying his hands on her shoulders and massaging the tightness he felt there. Claire was putting on a good face and acting as if she were not perturbed by the events going on around her or the threat to her life, but Michael knew better. ''I told you I followed you. I couldn't imagine what you were looking for at the newspaper office.'' He kneaded her muscles. ''What were you looking for, Claire? Answers for the ghost?''

''Maybe. And answers for myself as well.'' She rolled her head against his hands. ''Mmmm. That feels good.''

Michael knew what would feel better, but he thought making love would be inappropriate at the moment. There was still too much to unravel concerning the danger they faced.

''Do you know anything about the man in the article named Nigel Beauchamp?'' he asked.

''No hard knowledge. Only what I remember from my

dream. I think Nigel Beauchamp must have been involved in a black lodge. From what I gather, it was known as the Circle of the Lily. He was knee-deep in the kind of ceremonial black magic Delilah is using, and he practiced it in the temple room at Hartford Hall. I suspect Delilah is somehow trying to resurrect that lodge for her black magic.''

Michael paused, unsure how or whether to tell Claire that Delilah's magic included sexual rituals. But he didn't need to. Claire continued.

"In the dream, the man I think was Nigel was participating in . . . sexual intercourse with a woman who looked a lot like Delilah,'' she told him. He was glad she couldn't see the color he felt rising to his face.

"High Sex Magick,'' he said in a low voice.

"Is . . . that what Delilah wanted of you?''

Michael was disgusted at the thought that he had even remotely considered it. "Yes,'' he said. "But she never got what she wanted. That's one reason she's so furious.''

Claire turned in her chair and looked up at him, her luminous eyes filled with joy. "Michael.''

He sat down again in the chair next to hers and took her hands. "I could never use my body like that,'' he said. "Making love is reserved for the most special person in my heart.'' He leaned forward and kissed her gently on the lips.

She closed her eyes, and they leaned together, foreheads touching. "I think history may be about to repeat itself,'' she told him. "I guess you know that Delilah is the one who's bought Hartford Hall, and from what I overheard, she plans to refurbish the temple room.''

"She has a problem, though,'' Michael replied. "She has no High Priest.'' He hoped to God he was right, that because he refused to play the role, her power would be diminished even if she used another man's body in the vile act.

"What made her think you were her High Priest?''

"The ring. She told me that it proved I was of a lineage destined to serve her in that capacity."

"She called you Nigel."

"More than once."

They grew silent. Then Claire spoke. "Nigel Beauchamp? Did she think you were Nigel Beauchamp reincarnated or something?"

"She's mad. She might think that. I figured she had me confused with someone named Nigel. Do you think there might be a descendant of Nigel Beauchamp with that name?"

"Somewhere maybe. But there are no Beauchamps in Montlivet," Claire told him. "When I discovered proof that Nigel and Eloise had actually lived at the turn of the last century, I kept digging, trying to find their descendants. But I got no further than the birth of a son, Joseph. I checked the records up to World War I, but there was no mention of any of them. It's my guess Nigel left the country and took Joseph with him."

A faint memory buzzed in his head, but Michael couldn't quite hold it still long enough to look at it. Something about Nigel and lineage.

Lineage. He had come to Montlivet in the first place seeking information about his lineage. He'd looked it up as best he could at Somerset House, and his search had taken him as far back as his grandparents who'd lived in the first quarter of the century. He tried to recall their names but couldn't. He had them written down in his briefcase. He made a mental note to check that later.

"So where does all this lead?" he asked Claire.

"I think Delilah Mason, insane or not, is going to resurrect the Circle of the Lily. From what Lady Sarah has told me, it is a magical working of the most intense evil. The Watchers have told her that if it is not stopped, Delilah will obtain enormous power that would allow her to influence and manipulate all kinds of people to do the will of the dark forces."

Michael was having trouble once again academically assimilating all this. "Who are the 'Watchers?' "

Before she could answer, they heard a knock on the door. Claire glanced at Michael, pulled her robe closer about her, and went on bare feet to answer the front door. He followed and stood in the arched doorway between the dining room and the sitting room. This morning she was not dressed in the stunning manner he'd seen her in the past few days, but she nonetheless stirred his desire.

She opened the door. On the stoop stood the woman who had come tearing after Claire the first day Michael had begun to follow her. A stout woman of middle age, she bustled into the room, then stopped short when she saw Michael.

"Meet my tenant, Michael Townsend," Claire said, blushing slightly. She turned to Michael. "This is my mentor and friend, Maeve Willoughby."

Michael saw bewilderment on the woman's face, followed by annoyed chagrin.

"What's he doing here?"

Claire was unhappy that Maeve had arrived to find her with Michael when both of them knew that Lady Sarah's warning had been serious. She was also embarrassed her friend had caught her wearing only her bathrobe in the company of a man. But more than either of these, she was alarmed. It was barely six A.M. "What's happened? Why are you here?"

Maeve gave her a scowl. "You called five times yesterday. I didn't listen to my messages until this morning because I was so late getting back from London last night. I sensed something must be wrong, and rather than call you, I decided to come right over. What's going on?"

Claire winced at having to relate Michael's dream, for she knew it would upset Maeve. But it was best she know the truth, for she would understand why she'd gone against Lady Sarah's dictates and allowed Michael into her house.

Maeve shook her head when told about the dream. "I believe our confrontation is very near," she said. She turned to Michael. "I know you mean well, but your continuing presence here could put Claire in great danger."

Michael didn't flinch, but he glared at Maeve. "I've already put her in great danger. I didn't mean to, but I'll be damned if I'm going to stand around helplessly and let something happen to her."

Claire heard the frustration in his voice, and she was warmed by the emotion she saw on his face. It wasn't just that he felt bad about the present situation. He wanted to protect her because he cared about her. "He's right, Maeve. She's already launched her attacks. Nothing we do now can make it any worse."

Maeve looked from Claire to Michael and back again, her expression doubtful and worried. "Will you excuse me a moment?" She pushed past Michael and went into the dining room where she took a seat with her back to them. Claire motioned for Michael to join her in the kitchen and shut the door behind them.

"What's she doing?" Michael asked.

"Asking for directions." She saw his confusion and laughed. "She's going into trance, where I think she'll get directions from Lady Sarah."

"Isn't the phone working?"

"Lady Sarah has no phone."

"But how . . . ?"

"They meet on the astral plane." Claire figured if he was willing to accept all she'd told him before, he would at least consider the possibility of minds meeting in other dimensions, and besides, it gave her something to do besides worry what Maeve was really up to. She made tea while she talked.

Several minutes later, the senior seer joined them in the kitchen. She looked drained and drawn. When she spoke, it was to Michael, not Claire.

"You have been welcomed into our efforts," she said

wearily, sinking into a chair. Claire set a cup of hot tea in front of her. Maeve nodded in thanks, then continued. "Lady Sarah is aware of what has transpired, and she trusts that your loyalties lie with Claire, not Delilah." She leaned toward him slightly. "I hope her trust is warranted."

Michael frowned at Maeve's skepticism and came to stand behind a chair opposite her, his large hands enveloping the ridged back. "Of course it is. What can I do?"

Claire was amazed at how easily he offered his help without really knowing what he was getting entangled in.

"You can get some rest." Maeve said shortly.

"What?" Michael's hands tightened on the chair until Claire saw the knuckles turn white. "What do you mean, get some rest?"

Maeve turned her own tired eyes on him. "God knows we're all going to need every ounce of energy in this business," she told him. "You haven't slept much tonight, have you?"

Michael shook his head. "That doesn't matter. What matters is Claire's safety."

"What matters, my dear boy, is that we are prepared when Delilah engages the battle. According to Lady Sarah, that will be very soon now."

Michael held her even gaze for a long while, as if assessing whether or not Maeve was as loony as the rest of them, and Claire suppressed a smile. "What does Lady Sarah want of Michael in the magical war?"

"She didn't say." Maeve glanced at him dubiously. "She was adamant that he had a role to play, and . . ." she added pointedly, "that he must be rested if he were to be effective." She looked directly at Michael. "Will you respect her wishes? In this case, she is the leader, the high command, so to speak."

Michael let his head drop between his upper arms, raising it again a moment later. "I won't leave Claire alone."

"I'll assume your vigil," Maeve told him. "I will sit with her . . ."

"You are both being silly," Claire objected. "Nothing's going to happen now. It's broad daylight." But she was silenced by Maeve's look.

"Either we stay the course we promised Lady Sarah, or all is lost," she said, daring Claire to defy her again. It was the first time Claire had known her mentor to be so unrelenting. Stubborn even.

Claire turned to Michael. "Go on," she said. "Get some sleep. Maeve'll keep me company, and maybe by the time you wake up we'll know better what is going to happen."

The expression on Michael's face told her that he wouldn't mind getting away from this circus. It also held a warning that she had better wake him up if she needed anything at all. It was a new sensation that a man was so determined to protect her. Claire liked it. A lot.

"You know where to find me." He started toward the door.

His action galvanized Maeve suddenly from her chair. "Wait. I almost forgot."

Claire watched as Maeve performed a ritual of protection around Michael, and she saw the mixture of amusement and annoyance in his eyes. He remained silent, however, and allowed the older woman to complete the procedure. Claire was glad, for even if Michael thought it was silly, she knew he would need every benediction available to protect him from the forces that were about to descend around them. She went to him when Maeve was done and raised on tiptoe to kiss him gently. "Get some sleep."

After he'd gone, she turned to Maeve. "You don't have to stay around. I'm not afraid."

"You should be."

The solemn answer sent chills up Claire's spine. "What's going on?" she asked, slipping into the chair Michael had just let go of, wishing she could feel his strong hands on her shoulders again.

"Lady Sarah has called the others to her house. She thinks an attack is imminent, although she says she doesn't believe it will come exactly as the Watchers thought it would. Something is skewing Delilah's plans.''

"Michael's refusal to become her High Priest?''

Maeve nodded. "That's part of it. Also, I think her own jealousy is getting in the way. She's furious that Michael refused her and has fallen in love with you.''

The words rang in Claire's ears. "In love? What makes her believe that?''

"Even black magicians know the truth when they see it.''

Was it true? Did Michael love her? He hadn't told her so. She knew from his protective actions that he cared very much about her. But love . . . ?

"I am in danger, aren't I?'' she asked Maeve, realizing that if Delilah's jealousy was strong enough to get in the way of the working she considered to be her destiny, it was dangerous indeed.

"Yes, my dear, you are. That's why I came, and why Lady Sarah instructed me to stay here.''

"Why don't we just go to be with her?''

Maeve shrugged and shook her head. "She insisted that you remain here. I must admit I don't understand it and I don't like it.''

Claire made breakfast for her friend, wishing it were Michael at her table rather than Maeve, regardless of her fondness for her mentor. "I'm glad you are here,'' she said, serving their meal, "but you only need to stay until this afternoon. Cameron's coming by at three for tea. He can give you a break, and maybe by then Lady Sarah will call us over to her house.''

Maeve looked uncertain. "She told me not to leave you unguarded.''

"I won't be unguarded, for God's sake. Michael's right next door, and Cameron's my brother. I'll be safe enough with him.''

Chapter Twenty-two

TO HIS SURPRISE, MICHAEL SLEPT SOUNDLY AND awoke refreshed just past noon. Outside his window, the summer day was clear and bright, belying the ominous occult storm that threatened from realms unseen. He found a clean shirt and got dressed, but his mind was preoccupied with that storm. Could the magical war Claire had told him about be real, or had he landed in the midst of a bunch of nutcakes?

He wanted to go to Claire, to hold her in his arms and reassure himself that things were all right, but going to the end of the covered walkway, he saw that Maeve's car was still in the drive. Drat.

His stomach growled. Deciding that Claire was safe with her mentor, he went down the steps and walked briskly into the village for lunch. Forty-five minutes later he returned.

Maeve's car was still there.

He sensed that the woman didn't like him, or perhaps didn't trust him, so he went back into the cottage and tried to resume his reading. His mind refused to remain on the material in front of him, however. It kept jumping instead to Claire and the danger from Delilah he believed surrounded them both.

Just before three o'clock, he slammed the book shut, unable to restrain himself any longer. He needed to see Claire, if only to reassure himself of her safety. He peeked around the side of the house again, and although Maeve's car was gone, he was astounded to see a sleek black Jaguar just pulling up. As he watched, a darkly handsome man stepped out carrying a full bouquet of red roses and a bottle of wine.

Michael stared at him, bewildered. Who was this guy? He looked for all the world like a man who'd come courting. Did Claire have another lover? She didn't seem the type to be seeing two men at the same time, especially when she was intimate with at least one that he knew of. A familiar darkness descended over him again. How could he have so misread her nature?

His lunch roiled in his stomach. Now what? The woman he loved and had vowed to protect was inside her house with another man. Was she safe with him? A chilling thought occurred to him. What if the caller were someone sent by Delilah? Michael paused by the back door, wanting fiercely to be on the other side of it, to run the guy off, to demand Claire's loyalty only to him.

But even though they had shared precious intimate moments, he'd never told Claire how he felt. Maybe he hadn't wanted to admit even to himself how much he loved her, for a part of him still felt it was dangerous for any woman to get close to him.

The funk deepened, as did the self-recrimination. It was too late to worry about the dangers of her becoming involved. She was already involved. Or so he'd thought.

Longing to know who his rival might be, he leaned his ear to the door when he heard the doorbell ring at the front of the house and heard Claire greet her caller affectionately and thank him for the flowers. Obviously, it was someone she knew and cared about.

Damn it.

This put a whole new slant on things. He wasn't about to knock on the door now. Or intrude in her life further if she had another lover. He would remain in residence only long enough to assure himself that Delilah had called off her attack and that Claire was safe from the influence of his miserable existence. Then he'd pack his bags and head back to the States. His father had been right. Life wasn't a bowl of cherries, and you couldn't trust a woman.

He returned to his rooms where he spent the next hour in sheer hell. At last, he thought he heard the back door to Claire's house open, and he listened through his own front door. He heard the lilting sound of her laughter, and the very joy it carried turned him to stone.

"Cameron, we can't . . ." She giggled like a young girl.

Can't what? Michael didn't want to think about it.

"Oh, come on, Clary. Don't be such a worrier. No one will catch us. You know there's no one there. It'll be fun. Like old times."

"I shouldn't have had all that wine," she said, her statement ending in a hiccup. "I feel dizzy."

"It's about time you loosened up. Now come on."

Michael winced at the obvious. The man . . . she'd called him Cameron . . . had gotten her drunk, and it appeared they were off to the woods, "for old times' sake." Was it Claire's choice to go with him? Or had the wine stolen her good judgment?

The big question was—should he follow them?

If Claire were with this man by choice, it was none of Michael's business what they did in the woods. He doubted they were going there for a picnic, and he had no taste for voyeurism. Nor did he at the moment think she was in danger. She was with someone she'd known for a while if there were "old times" to be remembered. He watched them from one of the small windows in the cottage as they made their way arm in arm along the same path down which he and Claire had run when making their escape from Hartford Hall. Claire's steps were uneven, and his heart lurched when he saw her weave and almost fall. She might not be in present danger from Delilah, but he knew she was very vulnerable to any advances the man might make toward her.

He went out onto the back stoop and watched from the shadows until they disappeared over a rise. A part of him wanted desperately to run after her and wrench her from the other man. The more reserved side of his nature reminded him that it appeared she was with him by choice.

It was beneath his dignity to impose himself on her. With more pain in his heart than he had ever known, he acknowledged the truth. She had chosen another lover.

The curse strikes again . . .

Claire had anxiously watched Maeve's car drive away, and she was glad that only moments later, Cameron's arrived. Although she claimed otherwise, she was unsettled being alone after what Maeve had revealed had come to her in her trance.

Things were getting really nasty in the astral realm, and it was about to explode over onto the Earth plane. Only nobody knew just when. Michael was in it now, too, solidly on their side, but curiously, Lady Sarah had continued to insist that Claire keep her distance from him. It seemed moot at this point, but Claire had learned not to question the white magician. There were reasons that would be revealed when the time was right. Still, she was glad that Maeve had insisted on returning after Cameron's visit, to spend the night if necessary. Claire's nerves were growing increasingly raw from apprehension.

She was glad to have her brother's visit as a distraction. "Cameron! Hi!" She greeted him with a warm hug, gratified to see he'd brought along some guilt presents. She liked roses, and although she didn't drink much, she appreciated the wine. "I thought you came for tea," she teased, taking the bottle from him.

"We can do tea, then do wine. We're grownups, remember? I'm not in any hurry. The place looks great, by the way."

Claire watched him survey the sitting room of their child-hood home, and she sensed instantly that he was afraid of something. He saw her watching him and laughed nervously. "Seen any ghosts lately?"

"Funny you should ask," she told him. "I think we have one who's come to visit, hopefully only temporarily."

Cameron went into the dining room and glanced at the tarot cards still spread on the table. He scowled. "How'd that happen? Did you invite him?"

"Her."

He gave her a disdainful look. "Get serious."

"I am. I've seen her twice now, in the kitchen." Claire would have liked to share the story of the skeleton and the ring and the ghost with her brother, but his attitude irked her. He still didn't take her psychic abilities or her work seriously. So she changed the subject.

"I have fresh scones, and the water's hot for tea. Want some?"

"Uh, sure." He seemed reluctant to follow her into the kitchen, and Claire wondered suddenly if Cameron was afraid of ghosts.

They sat at the kitchen table, chatting amiably about mutual friends and life in the village, but Claire never lost the sense that Cameron was on edge. After tea, he opened the wine bottle, pouring them each a generous glass while Claire cleared the dishes. "Do you usually drink in the middle of the day?" she asked over her shoulder as she rinsed the plates in the sink. She was concerned that her brother's new life might include some unhealthy habits.

"Only when there's something to celebrate."

She turned and gave him a smile. "What are we celebrating this afternoon?" she asked, taking the goblet he handed to her.

He gave her a self-deprecating smile. "That you've forgiven your brother for being such an ass?"

It was the Cameron she knew and loved, the one who could never bear to hurt her and who, when he went too far with his pranks and mischief, always came back and asked forgiveness.

"Sounds like something to celebrate," she said, taking a sip. The wine was delicious, red and fruity, perfect to go with cheese and fruit, which she dug out of the refrigerator.

"So, we slip from tea into cocktail hour. Very good." Cameron appeared pleased. He nibbled for a few moments, then cracked one of his mischievous grins. "Want to have an adventure after this?"

"Not if you're talking about breaking into Hartford Hall."

"Oh, don't be a spoilsport. Someone's bought the old place, I hear, and soon we won't be able to visit it anymore."

Claire didn't mention that she knew the new owner, or that she doubted seriously that Delilah Mason would be a very good neighbor. Nor would she tell Cameron about her narrow escape from the round room in the basement. There was no reason for it. Indeed, such a bizarre incident would likely only whet his appetite for the adventure he was proposing at the moment. There was no way Claire was going back to Hartford Hall, now or ever.

"Doesn't matter," she said, sipping deeply of her wine. It tasted sweet and seemed to take the edge off her earlier anxiety. "I don't want to go there this afternoon."

Cameron topped off her glass and edged the cheese and fruit platter toward her. "Why not? Afraid of ghosts?" His manner was taunting.

"If I want to see a ghost, I can stay at home," she remarked. "Can't we just enjoy our time together right here?"

Cameron stood and stretched and went to the window. "It's just such a gorgeous day, and I don't get the chance to come to the country often. I was looking forward to the walk to the old manor as much as the roguery of breaking in."

A glow began to suffuse Claire, and she realized she was

feeling the wine. "If you want me to take a walk, you'd better stop pouring the wine," she said with a giggle.

"You're a cheap date," her brother laughed, turning to face her. "Don't you like the wine? It's very expensive, you know."

"You wouldn't drink anything that wasn't. But I mean it, I'm feeling a little woozy."

"Well, come on then," he said, dragging both her and her chair away from the table. "Don't drink anymore. I don't want you getting sick. Let's go up the path toward the Hall. We don't have to break in, although no one would know the difference." He led her to the back door and out into the fresh air. "Maybe you'll change your mind by the time we get there."

"Cameron, we can't . . ." Claire protested, her tongue feeling thick. He admonished her not to be such a worrier and insisted again it would be fun, just like old times.

"I shouldn't have had all that wine." She hiccuped. "I feel dizzy." Cameron took her arm, and together they wove their way up the path. She was happy to be on good terms with her brother again, but she wished she hadn't drunk his expensive wine. She didn't think she'd had but a couple of swallows, but she felt as if she'd consumed the whole bottle. She breathed in the fresh air, trying to regain sobriety, but her head was spinning. "What'd you put in that wine?" she asked, teasing.

"You're just out of practice. You really should drink wine more often."

About halfway along the path, Claire was suddenly seized by a terrible suspicion that Cameron *had* put something in her wine. That was ridiculous, she told herself, but bright sparkles of vertigo began to dance before her eyes. Her knees weakened, and she fell. From waning consciousness she felt her brother pick her up.

"Take me home, Cammy. Please. I don't feel so good."

*   *   *

Cameron regretted that the chemical he'd laced his sister's wine with had made her feel ill, but now that she had passed out, she should be in sweet dreamland for quite a long while. When tonight's events were over, he would carry her back to the farmhouse and remain with her, ever the solicitous brother, until the chemical wore off. He'd been assured she would come out of it with no lingering side effects.

When Delilah had insisted she wanted to meet his sister and had asked him to bring her to Hartford Hall as his next magical task he had almost balked, for he did not want Claire to know that he was dabbling in the occult. But the High Priestess had assured him that she wouldn't mention anything about their magical activities to her. She'd explained that she had recently purchased the old manor house and thought it would be a good idea for her to meet the sister of her High Priest, who was also going to be her new neighbor.

A reasonable enough request, but still, he was uncomfortable about the two women meeting, so he'd taken matters into his own hands and changed the plans just a bit. He would deliver Claire, and more . . .

He'd had to think fast to figure out how to pull it off, but he was pleased with the outcome so far. He just wished Claire had lost consciousness a little closer to Hartford Hall. Even though a small person, she was like dead weight in his arms, and he was gasping and perspiring heavily when at last he entered the round room in the basement and laid her carefully upon the altar he had prepared earlier.

Before arriving at Claire's, Cameron had gone to Hartford Hall. He recalled from his childhood that there was some sort of mysterious round room in the basement, and when he'd entered it, he knew why Delilah had bought the old house. The room had obviously once been a temple for some sort of magical practices. It was perfect for his plan, and he'd set everything up in the room according to the instructions he'd read in the unbound diary he'd taken from Delilah's supply closet. It was a strange little book, filled with all sorts of spells and incantations, most of which he didn't understand. It didn't matter. He didn't need to understand anything except the rituals of High Sex Magick, which had its own large section toward the middle of the book. Although the ritual called for the sex act to be performed on the altar, Cameron had decided it would be more dramatic if Delilah entered to find Claire in the center of the circle. They could move her for the serious part of the ceremony.

Cameron's whole body tingled at the thought of what was likely to transpire later when Delilah showed up. He was certain the High Priestess would be impressed with the surprise her new High Priest had arranged for her, and he expected tonight's Sex Magick to be of the most sensational kind. He looked at the ring on his finger and was filled with a sense of great power. Although he didn't understand how she worked the magic on his body, he could not deny that the power they raised together was almost palpable.

Cameron checked his watch. It was early yet. Delilah was not scheduled to arrive for at least another hour. He decided to practice. He wanted everything to be just perfect when his magical mate entered the temple. He lit candles in the places specified by the diary. There were thirteen in all, long red tapers designed to burn for many hours, arranged in a wide circle around the altar. When their glow filled the chamber, he turned off the electric lights. He removed his clothing in the flickering light, anticipation flushing his skin and building a hard erection. He donned the long red robe and placed a golden crown on his head, then punched the PLAY button on the large tape player he'd brought.

The room reverberated with the haunting rhythm of his chanting, as his one powerful male voice, layered on the recording by the audio technician, sounded like a roomful of men. The effect was incredible, and his skin prickled. He glanced at Claire. Would the sound awaken her? He went to her, but her shallow, even breathing showed she was still deeply under.

And so he began. Reading the unfamiliar words from the ancient diary, he practiced the incantations he'd heard Delilah utter during their sexual unions. Although the exercise lacked the intensity of the real thing, the words conjured the promise of what was to come, and he felt his temperature rise. The sound was stimulating, pleasurable, and he repeated it over and over, reaching an altered state, feeling the magic of Delilah's power begin to course through him.

Time became suspended as his consciousness narrowed into tight focus. He never heard the car drive up. He never saw the door to the temple room swing open until it was too late. He became vaguely aware that someone else had entered the room, and as his mind cleared he looked toward the door and saw Delilah staring at him openmouthed.

She'd ruined the surprise, but it didn't matter. He was prepared to pleasure her tonight, using her own tools of sweet, sensual torture. Soon she would be begging for him. He turned to her and raised his head, allowing his robe to fall open in front.

"Welcome, my Priestess."

Chapter Twenty-three

ARRIVING EARLY AT HARTFORD HALL, DELILAH MADE her way to the temple room, eagerly anticipating the evening's work. Shortly, Claire St. John would be history, as would her driveling brother. Their demise would clear the way at last for the Great Working, and she believed she could cast yet another, even stronger spell and compel Michael Townsend to return to serve as the true High Priest of the Circle of the Lily. She was annoyed at this interruption in her plans, but it was necessary now, and she was anxious to get it over with.

As she reached the basement, she heard a familiar sound and knew instantly something was wrong. It was the chanting of the men she'd been training for her High Court. Her face contorted in anger. What were the men doing here? She had told Cameron to bring his sister, not the whole damned lot. There were to be only the three of them.

"That silly bastard!" she uttered and raced toward the double doors that sealed the sacred temple room.

She stopped abruptly outside the doors and heard Cameron's voice, loud and strong, invoking the awesome powers of the unseen gods, the forces of Darkness of which he was dangerously ignorant. She froze in shock. How in hell had he learned that ritual? It was a secret only the Delilahs knew, written in a book that she kept locked in her private inner sanctum in the penthouse. The book with no cover. The last Delilah had stripped away the binding and flung it in the face of the High Priest who had betrayed her, just before she'd stripped him of his magical powers and invoked a terrible curse upon him.

An uncomfortable suspicion struck her. Had Cameron found the book and somehow managed to steal it?

Rage surged through her at the thought, and also at the notion that someone other than herself was attempting to make magic in her temple. How dare he? Cameron would die for this. They would all die. She reached for the large knob on the door, but stopped before her hand touched the metal.

There was danger here.

Even those untrained in magic could raise immense power using the invocations coming now from Cameron's lips. She must be very careful, for one misstep could lead to disaster. Power in the wrong hands could destroy everything. She quickly performed a magical ritual designed to protect her from the forces that might be out of control in the temple, then tentatively touched the door in case it was charged with stored magical power. It was safe, and she pushed it slowly open.

The scene before her eyes both revolted and angered her. Standing in the center of a circle of lighted candles, naked beneath his ceremonial robe and crowned as the High Priest, Cameron St. John stood, his eyes glazed, his arms extended. On his finger he wore the ring of the Circle of the Lily. When he saw her, he smiled wickedly. "Welcome, my Priestess."

There was no measure in hell that could register the outrage that burned through her. The presumptuous upstart! Then she saw the body of the sister lying on the altar, which fueled her fury even more. He had defiled the altar! The sacred altar of High Sex Magick.

She was relieved that the chanting was not coming from

a circle of her initiates as she'd feared, but only from a tape recorder. At least one thing had gone right. They were alone, the three of them. She could proceed as planned, except that her torture of them would be more excruciating, their deaths more prolonged. She wanted to savor the look on Cameron's face as he edged slowly and painfully toward his harrowing death, knowing that it was his own greed that had caused it. She was not sure how he had gotten so out of hand. She had known Sin-Jen was power hungry, but she'd underestimated his avarice. One would think Cameron, not Michael, was the descendent of Nigel Beauchamp—both had been such fools.

Delilah drew herself to her full height and assumed the magical glamor of the High Priestess that allowed her to virtually shimmer in the eyes of others. She saw she had captured Cameron's astonished attention. She dared not step closer, however, for it was possible the dolt had raised enough power to give her a nasty shock if she attempted to breach the circle. It was not necessary at any rate. She could accomplish her work from a distance.

"You have been a very naughty boy, Sin-Jen," she said. The triumphant expression vanished from his face. "You must be punished. No one steals my magic and lives to tell of it." As a taste of things to come, she raised her hands, and bolts of energy slashed out like lightning from her fingers, lashing the man's body. Cameron screamed and fell to the floor, writhing in agony. Delilah laughed. "You want power? I'll give you power, you weasely little money-grubber." With that, she gave him another jolt that sent his body across the room where he slammed into the wall and convulsed in spasms.

"You should have listened to me, Cameron," she chided as if scolding a small child. "You had the chance to know power, but you have abused your privileges and now you must die." To underline her words, she grazed his groin with another flash of power, and Cameron doubled over and cried out again.

Delilah's attention turned to the figure of the woman on the altar. She was clad in a lovely sapphire-blue dress. Perfect to meet her Maker, Delilah decided. "Now it's your sister's turn," she said aloud.

"No, please, don't . . ." Cameron pleaded weakly.

His earnest whimper gave Delilah an idea. "Perhaps you'd like to watch." She skirted the circle and kicked him in the rear. "Get up."

Cameron made a motion as if he was attempting to stand, but he was unable to get up. Disgusted at his weakness, Delilah placed both hands on his shoulders and raised him to his feet like he weighed nothing. "When I said I wanted to meet your sister, I didn't mean like this. I had expected a more respectful—and conscious—meeting. Wake her up."

"I . . . I can't. She's drugged."

"Drugged? Too bad. I would have liked to have seen the fear in her face again. But drugged is a wonderful state for her torture at any rate. She'll feel everything more intensely in her dream state. Want to watch?"

"Please, Delilah, don't hurt her. She knows nothing of all this, I promise."

She spat on him. "You know nothing, you nincompoop. She knows everything. She's been poking around in places she doesn't belong, and now she's going to pay." She raised her arms high above her head and directed her fingers toward Claire.

However, instead of shooting into the sleeping woman, the force of the lightning power backfired into Delilah and sent her reeling backward, where she fell through the circle of energy. The air crackled, and she was wracked with pain. She lay on the floor, stunned, and when she regained her senses, her knees were weak and her hands shook. She looked at Cameron with pure hatred.

"I don't know how you did that, Sin-Jen, but you are a dead man . . ."

*   *   *

After an hour, Michael had begun to worry when Claire and her friend had not returned. After two hours, he was nearly sick with anxiety. Thinking he might have somehow missed their return, he decided to risk looking like a fool and barged out the door, across the covered walk, and pounded on Claire's back door.

He had not been mistaken. There was no one home. Still, he felt compelled to go inside.

"Claire? Anybody home?"

He was answered by a cat or two, but no human voice greeted him. Michael sensed something was wrong. Dreadfully wrong. He didn't know where the feeling came from, but it crept over him like a shroud. Who was that guy in the Jag? Where had he taken Claire? He went into the kitchen where a dozen red roses nodded from a vase on the drainboard. An open bottle of wine and a plate of cheese and fruit sat on the table.

The wine confirmed his suspicions of the reason for Claire's tipsy behavior; the roses led him to believe that the man was a romantic interest.

At the moment Michael didn't give a rat's ass if the mystery man were another lover. He was the source of the sense of dread and foreboding that had now lodged like a chunk of lead in Michael's heart.

Despite the heat of the afternoon, Michael suddenly felt a chill in the room. That's odd, he thought, looking around to see if perhaps Claire had air conditioning. He saw no vents and heard no hum of equipment, but the chill grew stronger.

She is in terrible danger! Run to her!

Michael just about jumped through the ceiling. "Who's here?" But no answer came, and he got the distinct impression that although he'd heard the words as if the speaker were directly behind him, they had not actually been spoken. It was his own imagination working overtime, his own fear telling him what to do.

Hartford Hall. The basement of Hartford . . .

This time he was certain he had heard audible words. But who was speaking to him? And what on earth would Claire be doing in the basement of Hartford Hall?

Suddenly, the truth shattered through him. "Oh, my God!" The man was someone Claire knew and trusted, but he was not her friend. He was Delilah's agent, sent to charm and persuade her to come to the black magician's lair.

And Michael had stood by and watched!

Grief and guilt and frustration and anger all flared through him. He had to save her! But was he too late?

Hurry! Hurry! Run to her! Take the cross!

"Who are you?" he cried out, whirling in a circle to find the source of the disembodied voice. The coldness seemed to encircle him, and it felt as if he was being propelled by it toward the shelves in the kitchen.

The cross!

He was standing in front of the jeweled crucifix Claire had shown him, which she'd claimed, to his utter disbelief, had been given to her by the ghost she'd run into in the kitchen.

The ghost.

"Eloise." He murmured the name he remembered from the newspaper article. That triggered the recollection of all Claire had told him about Eloise and Nigel Beauchamp, which brought the rest of the horrible possibility crashing down around him.

Claire believed Eloise had been killed in the temple room by black magic. She'd also told him that she thought Delilah was about to resurrect the black lodge that Nigel had been part of, the Circle of the Lily.

The voice in his head virtually screamed at him.

Hartford Hall! The basement of Hartford Hall!

Picking up the crucifix, Michael did not stop to question the source of the voice again. He knew where to go, even if not exactly what to do, to prevent history from repeating the tragedy of a century before.

Run!

The path seemed longer than it had when they'd escaped Delilah's wrath on that ill-fated morning. Tall grass lashed at his legs, and his breath came in hard, short, painful bursts. He prayed to whatever gods were out there that he was not too late.

He arrived at the edge of the woods that bordered the old manor house and stopped with a lurch. There was a car in the drive between him and the house. A long, black stretch limo with a driver behind the wheel. Delilah's driver, who would as soon kill Michael as look at him if his mistress had ordered him to do so. He scanned the area, hoping for some other way into the house, but it occurred to him like a flash out of the blue that he must first take care of this potential adversary.

Michael was not a dramatic man, nor one attracted to violence, but the scene that now flashed in his mind seemed neither ludicrous nor impossible. He knew exactly what he must do. Keeping at an angle where the driver wouldn't see him in the rearview mirror, he sprinted across the pebbled drive and opened the car door, startling the unsuspecting man. He crashed the crucifix into his face, stunning him, then hauled the considerable bulk from behind the wheel and threw him facedown on the rocks. Another blow to the back of the head and the driver lay inert. Michael hoped he hadn't killed him. The force of his anger had given him greater strength than he'd ever thought possible.

Tucking his unlikely weapon beneath his belt, he ran into the house and took the back stairs two at a time. At the bottom, he stopped to catch his breath, trying to remember how far along the basement corridor the temple room lay. That was when he heard the chanting.

The voices were low, deep, mesmerizing, and Michael's confidence wavered. There were more people in that devil's den than he had reckoned on. He'd expected to have to take out Delilah and her henchman, then get Claire safely away. He hadn't counted on a chorus.

Another of those strange thoughts filled his mind.
It's not what it seems.

Michael hoped that was true because he wasn't going to stop now. Claire was in there, and he was going to get her out.

Hopefully alive.

He heard a crack, like the sound of lightning splitting the air, followed by a scream so horrible it made his flesh crawl. "Claire!" He raced toward the temple room. One door stood partially open, and without hesitation he stepped boldly into the darkness beyond.

When his eyes adjusted to the dim light, he saw a circle of candles flickering in the room. Delilah stood just outside the circle with her back to Michael. A man apparently contorted in pain lay on the floor just in front of her in the center of the circle. The same man Claire had accompanied from the farmhouse. Was it his scream he'd heard?

Then his eyes focused on the image of Claire's inert body lying on the altar and his heart almost stopped beating. Was she dead? Had she been a sacrificial victim in Delilah's sick scheme? He stood frozen to the spot, alarm electrifying his body, fear contracting his heart. He waited, horrified at the scene that unfolded before his eyes. Delilah played with her victim, attacking him with some kind of unseen force that emanated from her hands. He heard her threaten to impose her torture on Claire, who the man revealed was not dead but only in a drugged sleep. A small relief in the face of her hideous threat.

He must save Claire! But how? What powers did he have that could face down and destroy the magic of Delilah Mason? He saw her unleash a bolt of power intended for Claire, and in that brief instant the image of a mirror rose up clearly in his mind. A mirror, placed directly in front of Delilah's hands. A mirror that reflected and reversed the direction of the power, sending it back into her with full force. He watched in wide-eyed amazement as Delilah fell into the center of the circle where she apparently became enmeshed in a maelstrom of current. The air sizzled and turned hot, after which Michael felt a distinct release of power. He hoped it was over, that Delilah had been destroyed by her own evil, but to his dismay, he saw her rise up like a copper-headed Phoenix and face the cowering man across the room.

"I don't know how you did that, Sin-Jen, but you're a dead man," she murmured. "You and your sweet sister."

The body of Lady Sarah was still as a stone in the armchair that supported it, but her life force was elsewhere. From the astral plane, within the Palace of Light and surrounded by the energies of the Watchers, she looked down upon the temple room with anguish in her heart. It grieved her that she had been forced to use Claire as bait in the opening battle, but she needed Michael Townsend's mind to ground her mental attacks as they came onto the Earth plane. She had known he would follow the woman he loved and try to rescue her. She knew as well that it was his destiny to play a critical role in this conquest, for if . . . when . . . the forces of Light were victorious, his life would be changed forever.

Her plan was simple. She would send small attacks against Delilah, like the one she'd just launched, which would chip away at the magnitude of her evil power. Each attack would discharge some of the sorceress's negative forces, which Lady Sarah would then magically attract, absorb into herself, process, and eventually release as harmless, neutralized energy.

She knew if she tried to absorb all of Delilah's evil at once, it would be too much and would likely kill her, even with the resources of the Watchers at hand. The Delilah energy was ancient and strong. Lady Sarah was unsure if she even had the strength to absorb it in small increments. That was why she had called on Maeve and the others to sit with her earthly body and take on and process any negativity that might escape.

She felt the impact of the first of the energies released by the mirror technique and was stunned by the foul stench as well as the raw, hateful power. She braced herself and closed her eyes, allowing it to sift through her being. She felt it diminish as it passed through her center of Light. She smiled to herself and nodded as the wave of evil passed and was dispossessed of its power.

But she could already tell that the first attack had used up some of her own power as well. Was she strong enough to sustain the entire war?

She opened her eyes and saw a figure approaching. It was a woman in a flowing sapphire gown. Claire St. John came toward her with open arms and a look of deep love and concern on her face.

"Let me help," she said.

"You must not stay here. It's dangerous. You've not been trained . . ."

"I must stay here. I know what you are doing, Lady Sarah. Yours is a sacrifice of great love for humankind. I, too, have a great love, and I wish to use it—to help you and to free Michael from the curse."

Her knowledge caught Lady Sarah by surprise. "You know about the curse?"

Claire nodded. "And I know that I am useless on the Earth plane at the moment. In my drugged state, I'm on the astral whether I wish to be or not. Please, let me help."

Lady Sarah admired the insight and courage and, most of all, the unconditional love of this young woman. "Very well then," she said, heartened herself and re-energized. "I could use your help." She sent an immediate visual image of the strategy of the war into Claire's consciousness, and the younger woman nodded. "I am young and strong. I can take whatever she flings at my body on the Earth and absorb the evil as it is deflected to the astral. But Lady Sarah," she added in despair, "I see that Michael has followed me, and I don't know how to protect him."

The old wise woman smiled as Claire took up her position beside her. "Leave that to me."

Chapter Twenty-four

As michael looked on in incredulous dismay, he saw the scene from his nightmare become reality. Although not bound, Claire lay helpless and unconscious on the altar, and Delilah drew a long dagger from beneath her cloak. She motioned to the man to come to her, and he staggered toward her as if he were being drawn by an unseen magnet. She held his head between her two hands and murmured incomprehensible words. The man nodded, zombielike, and accepted the short sword. Michael recognized it as resembling the one in the box from his father's attic. The man from the Alchymical Book Shoppe had called it an athame and said it was used in magical ceremonies.

Like murder?

"You know what to do, don't you?" she crooned to the man. "You want to please your High Priestess, don't you now?"

He nodded in response to both questions and slowly began to lower the knife to Claire's neck.

"Stop!" Michael left the protection of the shadows and rushed toward the ghoulish tableau, but he was stunned when he ran into a force as concrete as a brick wall that surrounded Delilah. He attempted to reach out and knock the knife from the man's hand, but he was paralyzed, like he had been once at Delilah's.

The sorceress gazed at him in surprised satisfaction. "Well, Michael, you've come after all."

"Leave her alone." He glared unflinchingly into her eyes. Once she might have had the power to mesmerize him, but he willed himself not to fall under her spell. If only he could move!

Delilah's answer was a familiar evil laugh. She looked at the other man who wavered uncertainly at the interruption of his murderous deed, then swiped away the dagger from him. "I've changed my mind. I'd rather have the pleasure of killing her myself and let the both of you watch."

"Delilah, don't!" Michael had no idea how he might overcome her power. The only defense he could think of was to give her what she wanted. "I'll . . . I'll do as you wish. I'll become your High Priest. I'll do anything you want. Only don't hurt Claire. Let her go."

Her lips parted in a derisive smile. "It's a little late for that, don't you think?"

"I mean it, Delilah. I swear it."

The smile vanished. "Prove it."

"What do you want me to do? Just name it."

The smile returned, partially. "Come to me, Nigel. Kiss me."

The thought utterly revolted Michael, but he'd made a bargain. Perhaps if he kept his promise, Delilah would not harm Claire. He tried to take a step toward her, but his feet wouldn't move.

"Well? Aren't you going to do as I ask?" she demanded.

"Let me loose, Delilah. I know you have me under some kind of spell. You did it to me before."

She frowned fiercely. "I have no hold over you at the moment."

"Then why can't I move?"

"What do you mean you can't move?"

Michael tried again with all his might but the best he

could do was strain and move his head. "I can't come to you because I can't move."

He could almost see a shimmer of darkness emanate from Delilah's body, waves of simmering hatred directed at him. Illogically, he thought of olden days and saw himself as a knight protected by a shield. Before the waves reached him, they seemed to glance off something, and the dark power was deflected. As had happened earlier, her own evil forces were repelled and returned to her. He saw her physically struck as if someone had slapped her.

She came toward him, enraged. "What . . . ? How . . . ?!" She reached out to touch him, but her hand encountered a solid force that jolted her on contact. She retreated. "Why, you son of a bitch."

Michael was dumbfounded, but panic rose within him. He didn't know how he was repelling her advances, but it was sending her into a manic fury. He was terrified that she would retaliate by murdering Claire right before his eyes.

"I'm . . . I'm not doing this, Delilah. I thought it was you . . . your power holding me."

She stood before him, seeming taller than he remembered, her eyes wild and streaked now with red. Her breath came heavily, and she appeared to be working to regain her composure. Then she turned to Claire, who was sleeping peacefully through the madness.

"It's her," Delilah snarled. "She has the power. She is the one . . ." She approached the altar and raised the athame over Claire's throat.

"No!" Michael cried, and tears of fear and frustration and regret stung at his eyes. How could he have ever let this get so out of hand? He was the one with the curse. He should be the one to die, not the innocent woman who was about to be butchered. "Please, no . . ."

But Delilah's knife descended slowly and steadily until it touched the fair skin of Claire's throat. An image came unbidden to Michael's mind. He saw a large snake, a fierce, powerful serpent jump from between Claire's lips onto the knife. With fangs seemingly as long as the dagger's blade, it struck Delilah's arm. She dropped the weapon and recoiled into herself, rolling in pain against the wall and sinking to the floor. The snake vanished into nothingness.

Michael stared after it, his heartbeat thundering. What was going on here? Was that snake real? It couldn't have been. And yet . . . Still unable to move, he considered the pictures that had sprung into his mind—the mirror, the knight's shield, the snake. They weren't real, but they were more than mere mental images. They were forces of some kind of power he could not see. It sounded crazy, but he felt as if he were part of some kind of counterattack against Delilah.

The black magician staggered to her feet and with great effort regrouped once again. But this time she did not approach either Michael or Claire. She went instead to the man who had remained in frozen animation throughout the long and terrible moments. She took his hand in hers and whispered into his ear. He nodded.

She opened his robe and placed one hand over his heart, the other on his genitals. She closed her eyes, threw back her head, and shrieked strange and alien words into the darkness. Then, before Michael's horrified eyes, he saw the color drain from her victim. The man twitched violently, as if his soul were being torn from his skin, and after a long, terrifying moment, he collapsed in a heap at her feet.

Michael's eyes met Delilah's and he understood what had just transpired. Delilah had stolen the life force from the man to replenish her own depleted energy.

After the pain of the snake attack subsided, Delilah began to suspect what was happening. Something was actively thwarting her plans. She'd come to perform a simple magical procedure to remove the obstacles to her Great Working, but instead, something . . . she wasn't sure what . . . was not only preventing her from accomplishing her goal but was also seriously draining her energy. Her attacks had been turned against her, depleting her resources and rendering her magically debilitated. At the moment, she was not powerful enough to even cast a spell, much less undertake the Great Working. It would take days, weeks maybe, to recover her strength and renew her efforts.

What was going on? Had her plans for the Great Working become known? Were her enemies in the astral and beyond responsible for her present weakened state? Or was it the three in the room with her?

She suspected a coalition between them. Damn! Her fury returned and with it renewed determination to achieve what she'd set out to do. Only now, instead of just getting rid of Claire and Cameron St. John, she would destroy Michael Townsend as well.

But she was too weak to proceed. She needed an infusion of energy, new life force. She turned to Cameron who stood silent and cowering before her. She was going to kill him anyway. Why not absorb his vitality in the process?

Still dazed by his own magical injuries, Cameron agreed to the plan she whispered into his ear, thinking it was part of the High Sex Magick. He opened his robe and offered himself up to her, even managing a simpering smile, never knowing it might be his last.

His life force entered Delilah's body in a rejuvenating rush. She hoped it would be sufficient. She turned to her task with icy resolution, and it occurred to her that the deaths of Claire and Michael could serve her as well. She could kill them by draining their life forces and incorporating them into her own, making her stronger still. She must proceed with caution, however. Unlike with Cameron, she was afraid to touch them physically, believing that such an attack, like the others, would be somehow deflected back upon her. She would have to find another approach.

Delilah turned to the pair and considered who to do first. Claire in her drugged state would be simple and not very dramatic, although Delilah would enjoy watching Michael squirm through it. But she decided she would do her beautiful High Priest first. Too bad, she thought with some small regret. He really was a stunning specimen. But the powers of Darkness who supported her efforts in the Great Working had been sorely mistaken to send him her way. The ring must have come into his possession by some other means than inheritance. He simply wasn't the right man for the job.

With confidence born of her renewed energy and with the clear head of an experienced magician, Delilah began her assault. She walked slowly in a circle around Michael, vocalizing a powerful chant she'd often used to bend difficult subjects to her will.

Her will at the moment was to reach through the invisible protective shield that surrounded Michael and suck dry his life essence. The draining of a life force didn't necessarily require physical contact. Nor did she need the permission of her victim. That served only to expedite matters. If she could just break through the barrier, she could achieve her goal in a matter of seconds.

She was halfway round the second time when a thought abruptly occurred to her. If Michael Townsend happened to be the rightful heir to the ring and the High Priesthood of the Circle of the Lily, then likely he still bore the curse which the last Delilah had cast upon her own wayward High Priest, Nigel Beauchamp and his descendants. Even though Delilah was uncertain that he was the legitimate heir, she must use caution in absorbing his energies, just in case. Otherwise, she could be infected by his curse as well. The safest thing to do, she decided, was to break the curse herself, an easy enough chore.

The Delilah energy had invoked the curse; the Delilah energy could remove it.

But first she had to get to him.

"Michael," she said aloud. "Come to me." She was testing the spell that held him bound in place, not really expecting him to do as she said. But he moved. She reached out, tentatively feeling for the barrier, but there was none. Very well, she thought, satisfied that her magic must once again be in control. Now was the time. She would break the curse, and then she would break him.

"In the name of Bamathael, I cleanse you of the curse placed upon you by my ancestress," she intoned, following this statement of her intention with other words of power. She knew she was succeeding for she saw a cloud of darkness seep from the very pores of his skin and dissipate into the air. She waited until she believed every trace of the curse had disappeared, and then she smiled at him malevolently.

"The curse that has plagued you your whole life is now gone, Michael. Poof, just like that! Isn't magic great?" She gave a throaty laugh. "But it's too bad you won't live to enjoy it." She prepared to finish her business with Michael when she was disturbed by a noise nearby.

She turned and saw Claire St. John sit up on the altar. At first Delilah wasn't sure it was really the same woman. This creature was not the fearful little ninny who had cringed before her in this room a few days before. This woman had fire in her eyes, and pure power radiated in a brilliant golden aura all around her.

Delilah recoiled in spite of herself. Something had shifted in the universe, and she no longer trusted that her forces of Darkness were more powerful than all the rest. Doubt beset her. Fear encroached upon her. And anger returned.

Claire was reluctant to leave Lady Sarah alone, for the elderly magician was terribly weakened by her efforts at neutralizing Delilah's negative energy. But the old woman had taken Claire's hands firmly between her own bony fingers and insisted that if they were to be successful, she must return to the Earth plane immediately. She issued specific instructions and placed a blessing upon her, and the next thing Claire knew, she was awakening in a strange and eerie place.

Facing the formidable sorceress herself.

Claire was no longer afraid, for she knew she held the only true power that existed in Heaven or on Earth. She looked beyond Delilah and saw Michael, and her heart was filled with that power.

It was called love.

No matter what happened, nothing could destroy the love she felt for him. She had seen from the astral the sacrifice he'd been prepared to make to save her from Delilah's evil. He loved her as well. She believed it with all her heart. Lady Sarah believed it, too, and in her final directive had told Claire how to use that love to once and for all vanquish the Delilah energy.

She slipped from the high platform upon which her body had been sleeping, and a feeling came over her that was nothing short of euphoria. She was strong, fearless, powerful. Claire had no idea how she was going to fight the sorceress, but she knew the forces of Light had accrued major victories while she sat with Lady Sarah, and she understood that it was her job to engage the final battle. It was a battle she had every intention of winning.

Cautiously Claire skirted the momentarily startled Delilah, holding the tawny animal gaze of her enemy with her own. She reached for Michael's hand and immediately felt a flow of power between them. She glanced at him out of the corner of her eye, and her heart leapt to see that there was no trace of the black aura around him. She also saw the golden-white light of Lady Sarah's protective blessing enlarge until it surrounded them both.

She knew they were ready.

She squeezed Michael's hand, and he returned the signal, as if he understood. They moved as one toward Delilah. The power of their love joined together was immense, and it was magnified by their determination to rid the world of Delilah's evil at last.

* * *

Claire wasn't sure afterward exactly what happened that night. One moment they were marching confidently toward their foe, the next they were fleeing for their lives from an unholy inferno.

Delilah had spun out of control at being so boldly confronted, and Claire guessed that she must have become so angry she let loose the very demons of hell. She must have conjured every wicked, obscene power in the universe and hurled every curse in the book at them. Claire remembered the room turning red and beginning to spin and Michael's hand closing fiercely around her wrist, pulling her, drawing her away from the scene and taking her to safety.

They ran up the stairs, through the now-darkened house, out the front door, and into the safety of the woods before Claire remembered.

"Cameron!"

Her brother had been in there. Her brother had brought her to this place. She must save her brother!

She broke free from Michael's grasp and lurched toward the house.

"Claire! No! Stop!" he yelled, but she paid no attention. All she could think of was saving Cameron.

She made it only to the edge of the woods when she felt Michael's body close in on hers, knocking them both to the grass. She screamed for him to let her up, and she kicked and struggled against him.

"Claire! Stop it!" he commanded, holding her firmly. The sound of a mighty explosion suddenly rocked the night as the virtual hatred of hell came belching from the bowels of Hartford Hall. Michael's body shielded her from the debris of brick, mortar, wood, and steel that rained down around them. Only the full branches of summer saved them from injury.

Claire lay still, stunned and sickened. Surely this couldn't be happening. In a few moments, she felt Michael's weight shift, releasing her, and she rolled from beneath him and sat up. "Oh, dear God," she cried when she took in the devastation before her. Michael put his arms around her and pulled her close to him. The once-grand old mansion was ravaged. The limo had been tossed like a toy car, and what was left of it had landed in a heap of twisted metal on the far side of the car park. But surprisingly, there seemed to be no fire.

"Oh, dear God," she repeated as the horror sunk in. "Oh God, oh God, Michael!" She felt the edge of hysteria at the back of her throat. "Cammy's . . . Cameron's in there."

Michael drew her even closer. "I'm sorry, Claire." They sat paralyzed in silence for a long while, then Michael asked, "Who was he?"

Her eyes filled with tears as anguish flooded her heart.

"My brother," she managed. "He was my brother."

Chapter Twenty-five

"THEY DIDN'T BELIEVE US, YOU KNOW." CLAIRE huddled miserably beneath the protection of Michael's arm in the back of the taxi on the way home from the hospital. The earlier fair weather had given way to a nasty storm, and the night was pitch black, pierced occasionally by a slash of lightning. Rain streamed against the windows.

She was exhausted, her energy completely sapped. Her emotions vacillated between hopes and fears.

The police and fire departments had descended on the scene only moments after the explosion, and miraculously, they had managed to find Cameron amongst the wreckage. Even more miraculously, he was still alive, although barely.

There was no sign of Delilah Mason.

"Would *you* believe our story?" Michael pressed a gentle kiss into her hair.

They had been transported by ambulance from the devastation at Hartford Hall to the hospital, where after being treated for cuts and bruises, they had been interrogated at length by the police. They had decided beforehand to tell the truth about what had happened in the basement of Hartford Hall, as unbelievable as it sounded.

The first policeman to question them not only disbelieved them, he became hostile, thinking that Claire and Michael were making up the story of a magical attack to cover some other heinous plot. Only when the officer who had investigated the discovery of the skeleton in the tree arrived did Claire have hope they wouldn't be arrested.

Despite her almost unbearable anxiety over Cameron's condition, she managed to tell the investigator everything she knew about the Circle of the Lily, the ring, Nigel and Eloise Beauchamp, the temple room at Hartford Hall, and Delilah Mason. What she didn't know, what she couldn't even begin to fathom, was her brother's insistence on taking her to the old manor house in the first place.

She heard Michael tell the police of Cameron's participation in the magical practices that had taken place and how Delilah had become angry with him and attacked him. It was clear that Michael believed Cameron had been part of Delilah's conspiracy to resurrect the black lodge.

But Claire couldn't conceive of that. Not now. Not yet. Maybe not ever.

Neither did she mention anything to the officer about Lady Sarah and the magical war. There was a limit to what most logical policemen would believe, and she figured she was already rather past it.

The investigator dutifully wrote everything down, however, withholding his own opinion on the matter and kindly fending off the other officers. At last the head nurse intervened and insisted that Claire was in no condition to continue and gave her a sedative with instructions to go home and rest. She was reluctant to leave her brother, but he was in intensive care, and there was nothing she could do for him now but pray.

Claire knew they weren't through with the police, but she was glad to get away from them for the moment. Michael had tried throughout the difficult night to run interference for her, answering questions whenever possible and shielding her from the media who began to trickle in, chasing the ambulances. But her brother had been seriously injured in the explosion, and the police wanted to talk to Claire more than Michael.

The taxi pulled up to the front of the house, and Michael paid the fare and helped Claire out of the cab. Her knees felt like rubber and her head throbbed. She was grateful for his support, and she leaned into his strength as they hurried through the rain to the front door.

Inside, she allowed him to carry her upstairs to her room. He drew a warm bath for her while she eased her out of her torn and tattered clothing. She cried for the ruined garments as they fell into a sapphire blue puddle on the floor.

It had all gone so wrong.

She drew on the comfortable old terry robe and headed for the tub. Michael was standing in the hall outside the bathroom, waiting for her. The look on his face was both tender and quizzical.

"Do you want me to go?"

Her eyes filled again with tears, and this time she made no effort to stop them from flowing. "Go? Oh, Michael, please, don't ever go. Don't ever leave me."

She rushed into his arms and held him as tightly as he held her, and both cried until there were no more tears left.

"Your bath is getting cold," Michael murmured at last.

"I'm too tired to take a bath."

Again Michael lifted her into his arms. He carried her to the bed where he settled her gently beneath the covers.

"Michael, don't go," she said again and turned back the comforter on the other half of the bed. "Stay with me."

He turned out the lights. The red letters of the digital clock glowed through the darkness. One forty-eight. Claire felt the weight of his body as he sat on the edge of the bed. She ran one hand up the middle of his back and discovered that he'd removed his shirt. She swallowed over the hard knot that kept forming in her throat, fighting the tears that threatened to surface once again. Only this time they were not tears of sadness. They were tears of joy and gratitude.

Michael was here. He was not going to leave her.

Not everything had gone all wrong.

Michael held Claire in his arms throughout the night. Her sedative took effect almost immediately and she drifted off to sleep just after they went to bed. He'd refused medication, thinking that he needed to be alert in case of emergency. He slept only fitfully, his thoughts and dreams intermingling in a montage of surrealistic images of the horror he had witnessed. Nothing seemed real. Nothing seemed rational. He felt as if he'd been an actor in a B-grade movie.

He awoke at dawn, certain of only one thing. The woman in his arms. He lay quietly, thinking of her words, spoken in quiet desperation as they faced one another in the small hallway outside her bathroom.

Michael, don't leave me.

He never wanted to leave her. But doubts remained about his own gloomy history, and he felt that many of her present troubles had been precipitated by his arrival on her doorstep.

He shifted slightly, and Claire moved her body with his, as if following his lead in a dance. He gazed down at her slumbering form. She was so incredibly beautiful. Her hair looked like spun silk, her cheeks like fine porcelain. Her lashes brushed against her cheekbones in a smoky sweep of gray. Her lips were full, and he longed to kiss them, but he refrained, not wishing to steal away her much-needed rest.

God, she'd been through so much. He hurt for her. He hurt for her physical pain and for the agony she felt about her brother. Her twin! He hadn't known she had a twin, and the man he'd seen get out of the Jag yesterday had looked nothing like this fair-haired beauty. He'd seemed dark, threatening. Michael thought about that a moment. He'd seen nothing other than the man, but something about him had given Michael the impression of darkness, of impending danger. Was that what an aura was? Although he hadn't seen any sort of cloud or haze around him, nonetheless he knew instinctively that the man wasn't someone Michael wished to be around Claire, simply because he seemed . . . dark.

Is that the way Claire had seen him when he knocked on her door? Dark? Michael chewed on that for a while. He'd never thought of himself as dark, but then again, when he'd come here, he'd been hurt, angry, bitter at the many betrayals life seemed to have sent his way.

Maybe he *had* been dark.

The question was . . . was he still dark? He looked into his heart, searching for anger. Looking for resentment, fear, sadness. He thought of his mother. His father. His fiancée. His former best friend and his denial of tenure.

None of it mattered anymore. He found no anger or any of the other negative emotions that had lodged in his heart for a lifetime. He found no darkness, no reason to believe he was cursed.

All because of the woman who slept intimately in his arms. All because of the love she had given him unconditionally. And the love she'd drawn out of him. He'd never believed he was capable of the feelings of openness and wonder and joy that suffused him at the moment.

If Claire wanted him to, he would stay with her. Forever. He couldn't even conceive now of ever returning to the world of his academic post at Strathmore and the small, narrow-minded people he'd left behind. He had no idea what he would do next, but it didn't matter. He was strong, self-assured, empowered in a way he'd never been, and he could do many things to create a new career. To create a new life with Claire by his side.

But between now and then there was much for them to face. There was the police investigation, the possibility that her brother might die. As for himself, Michael needed to put closure on his search for his mother, one way or another.

His mother.

He'd never told Claire the real reason he'd come to England. He remembered the notes he'd taken during his research at Somerset House, and he wondered if Claire would know of any of his ancestors who had lived in the area. If she was feeling up to it later, he decided he would tell her about Stella Townsend and show her his notes. At least she would know the reason at last for his visit to Montlivet. He doubted if she would be able to shed much light on his search, but like the rest of the ghosts in his closet, that simply didn't seem to matter so much anymore.

Unwilling to end the magic of the closeness of their entwined bodies, Michael remained in bed until the urges of nature could no longer be ignored. Once he was up, however, reality set in, and he decided to prepare himself for whatever the day might bring. Closing the door quietly behind him, he pulled on his jeans and went to the cottage where he bathed and changed into clean clothing. Then he returned, checked on Claire, who was still sleeping soundly, and went downstairs again into the kitchen.

The roses were still there, their heads no longer proud, but hanging now as if in sorrow. The wine bottle remained open on the table, along with the overripened fruit and crusty cheese. Together, the gifts her brother had brought served as a bitter reminder of his betrayal.

Michael had no doubts whatsoever that Cameron St. John had been in Delilah's employ in one way or another. According to what Claire had told the police, Cameron still had a key to the farmhouse. It would have been easy for him to steal the things from Claire's jewelry box. Michael supposed that Delilah had used them to somehow focus the attack of the demonic thought-forms that had come into Claire's consciousness, both waking and dreaming.

Also it was obvious from Cameron's mode of dress, or undress as it were, in the temple that he was serving a role in Delilah's black magic. Was he the new High Priest she'd taunted him about? Probably.

He started to throw away the flowers and pour out the wine, but then he decided against it. The flowers were Claire's, a gift—perhaps a final gift—from her brother, no matter how evil his intention. Michael felt he had no right to get rid of them without her permission.

The wine was something else. Michael suspected it had been poisoned or laced with something that knocked her out. He was thankful in a strange way that her brother had arranged for her to miss most of the macabre event. The wine should probably go to the police for testing, but that was up to Claire. He hated to add salt to Claire's wounds, but she had to know—and accept—her brother's complicity in what had taken place and understand that he had brought about the circumstances that in the end could have cost him his life.

He found the cork still in the wine opener, and he stuffed it back into the bottle and put it out of sight. Hearing a sound behind him, he turned to find Claire standing in the doorway watching him.

"Is there coffee?" she asked. Although rested, her countenance remained strained, her eyes sad.

"There will be in a minute. Come. Sit down." He held a chair for her and whisked away the fruit and cheese plate as she sat down. Claire told him where to find the coffee and filters, how much water to put into the machine. They looked at each other in silence from across the room, their eyes locked in mutual disbelief of all that had happened. The only sound in the room was the sizzle and drizzle of the coffeemaker pouring black liquid into the carafe.

When the brew was ready, Michael filled two cups and brought them to the table. He sat across from Claire and reached for her hand. She did not pull away, but instead brought his hand to her lips and kissed his fingers. "Thank you," she whispered. "Thank you for saving my life. And thank you for staying the night with me."

Michael's throat constricted and he tightened his fingers

around hers. "I want to stay with you every night, forever, if you'll let me."

She looked into his eyes, and a tremulous smile spread across her lips. "I . . . would like that very much."

Claire had awakened when Michael slipped out of bed, but as consciousness returned, so did the memory of the night before. As much as she wanted to be with Michael, she was not eager to begin the day. She lay beneath the covers for a long while, thinking.

She thought about Cameron. Had he intended to sacrifice her to gain Delilah's favor, as Michael had claimed? Could her brother have been part and parcel of Delilah's black magic? It was too horrible to consider. Yet Cameron had been stubbornly adamant that they go to Hartford Hall. And he'd drugged her wine.

She forced those thoughts from her mind and shifted her consideration to Michael. If it hadn't been for Michael, she would likely be dead. Although a part of her felt as if she was dead, memories of Michael's strength and support renewed her spirit.

Michael.

He'd stayed with her through the grueling hours of the police interrogation. He'd fended away hounding reporters. She remembered Michael hustling her to the taxi. Michael carrying her upstairs. Michael holding her in the dark hours, asking nothing, just offering his love and protection.

Michael.

She wanted Michael.

She got out of bed, took a quick bath and dressed in one of her new outfits. With fresh makeup and brushed hair, she looked in the mirror and decided she looked better than she felt. Only one thing could make her feel better.

Michael.

She found him wandering about the kitchen, acting as if he wanted to clean up the place. She liked having Michael in the kitchen. She liked the idea of Michael living here, being family.

Sitting now at the table with him, holding his hands, hearing him say he wanted to be with her always, Claire believed she could be strong again. With Michael's love, she could face the uncertainties that lay ahead.

"I owe you some answers," Michael said after a long while. "If you think you might be willing to marry me, you deserve to know what you're getting."

"Is that a proposal?" she said, hoping like hell it was.

"It is. But before you give me your answer, I want to tell you some things about my life that may make you change your mind."

Claire doubted it seriously. Even though she was at present desperate to divorce herself from anything occult, she could not shed her natural sixth sense. And it was screaming at her loud and clear that Michael Townscnd was the man created to be her perfect lifemate.

But she listened patiently to what he had to say anyway.

Her heart ached for him as he told her about his childhood, his belief that his mother was dead, his feelings toward his father. She felt his pain when he talked about his fiancée's death, his best friend's betrayal, his loss of tenure. "And then you told me my aura was dark, and that I carried around a deep anger and sorrow. I tried to deny it at first, but you were right. I did feel all those things and more. I began to believe in the curse my mother wrote about . . ."

"Your mother? But I thought you just said your mother was dead."

His face was grim when he answered. "I thought so, too. Until I found this." He produced from his pocket the soiled envelope she'd run across in his suitcase. "It's a letter she wrote to my father when she left us. I was two years old. My father told me she was dead, and I never knew the difference until I found this in that box of magical tools in the attic. I still don't understand if there is any relationship between this and the other items, but apparently my mother firmly believed that she was cursed. After you began talking about curses, I guess I started to believe it was possible myself.''

He handed the letter to Claire, who again psychically felt the despair that resonated within the pages. Before she opened it, she looked at Michael, studying his aura. There was not one hint of black, not one flash of red. "If you were cursed," she said softly, "it's gone now." His aura glowed the healthy colors of an individual who has found deep inner power and a feeling of self-worth, and who is filled with love. It all made Claire smile, but she was especially overjoyed at the implications of the last item. Love. Was he filled with love for her? She felt it was so.

Claire returned her attention to the envelope. She read the letter carefully, then looked at the picture. "Is this your mother?"

"I think it is." Michael handed her another slip of paper. "I came to England to see if I could find her. I went to Somerset House, and I traced the family as far back as I could, thinking I might come across somebody who would know her, but the records broke off in the mid-twenties.''

Curious, Claire looked at the paper. Her heart picked up a beat, then began to pound harder as she looked over the list of the names of his ancestors. "Michael, look! Didn't you see this?"

She pointed to the name he'd written as being that of his maternal grandmother. "Margaret Grisham. Née *Beauchamp*! Michael, that's just too much of a coincidence. There aren't that many people named Beauchamp around here.''

She saw his stunned expression. "How'd I miss that?" he asked aloud. "I guess I forgot about it after all the rest of the magical things got started.''

"If you are a descendant of Nigel Beauchamp..." Claire began to put it all together. "... That explains how your parents, your mother in particular, might have come by the ring. She inherited it.''

"And that's why Delilah thought I was 'destined' by my lineage to become her High Priest." Michael sighed and ran his fingers through his dark hair. "Oh, I don't know, Claire. It all seems so impossible."

"It isn't though. It's all quite possible. I don't understand exactly how the pieces fit, but they do fit, Michael, trust me." She held up the faded photo again and stared into the face of the young woman captured by the camera.

"Michael," she said slowly, an astounding realization dawning on her, "there's somebody you need to meet."

Chapter Twenty-six

MICHAEL RECOGNIZED ONE OF THE CARS PARKED IN front of a strange white cottage a few miles out of town as belonging to Maeve Willoughby, Claire's mentor. Only yesterday she had insisted he stay away from Claire, exposing her to the danger presented by her own brother. He shifted uncomfortably in his seat. "Will you please tell me what this is all about?"

Claire shook her head and gave him an enigmatic smile as she shut off the ignition. "You'll see very soon."

With a grave look on her face, Maeve ushered them into the house and put her finger to her lips. "Lady Sarah is very weakened," she told them. Glancing around, Michael was startled at his surroundings. The inside of the house was as white as the outside. It suddenly registered with him that Maeve had said "Lady Sarah." Was this the home of the reclusive white magician Claire had once mentioned to him?

"Is . . . is she going to be all right?" Claire asked. Michael saw the worried look on her face and put his hands on her shoulders. She brushed her cheek against his fingers in acknowledgment of the unspoken support he was offering.

"We don't know. She took a terrible hit there at the

last." Maeve glanced uncertainly at Michael and then looked back at Claire. "Does he know?"

"Some of it. I haven't had time to explain everything. Please, can we see Lady Sarah? It's very important."

Maeve nodded hesitantly, but laid her hand on Claire's arm. "Are you all right? Lady Sarah told us what you did from your drugged state. That was very brave, Claire, and very dangerous."

"It was all very dangerous. Please tell me it's over."

The older woman let out a heavy breath. "We hope so. There's no sign of either Delilah's mortal body or the energy of this most recent incarnation, but the Watchers think it's possible a fragment of the Delilah energy might have escaped. However, if it did and it tries to regroup, it will take longer than another millennium."

Their conversation made no sense to Michael. What were they talking about? What had Claire done that was brave and dangerous? He wasn't sure he wanted to know.

They entered a small bedroom which, like the rest of the house, was decorated all in white. An old woman lay on the bed, eyes closed, her long white hair splayed out against the white linen pillowcases. If he hadn't been told otherwise, Michael would have thought she was dead. Sitting in chairs close by, three people maintained a vigil over her. He recognized the redhead from the Information Centre, but the others were strangers. Claire led him to the bedside.

"Lady Sarah," she whispered and softly touched the wrinkled skin of the woman's face. "Lady Sarah, it's me, Claire. I've brought Michael Townsend."

At the mention of his name, the woman's eyelids fluttered, and very slowly she opened them. She didn't look at Claire. Her entire attention was focused on Michael.

"We meet at last," she said in a weak, strained voice. She studied him for a long while, then added, "You are a brave man. We have much to thank you for."

Michael was certain he'd never seen the woman before, but something about her face seemed familiar, comforting.

There was also an air of peace about her, a deep serenity of spirit that put him instantly at ease. She seemed somehow . . . holy. Yet he did not know what she had to thank him for.

"I'm afraid I don't understand."

A smile crinkled across her mouth. "I watched you from the astral in the battle last night. I used your mind to ground the thought-forms that I sent to destroy Delilah by turning her own evil magic against her. Do you remember a mirror, for instance? Or a snake?"

Michael was shaken. He wasn't sure he liked the idea of a total stranger invading his mind and using it, even if it was for the highest good. He was also not sure he believed her.

"I seem to recall those things," he replied tentatively.

She moved her arm on the bedcovers. "Do not be afraid, Michael Townsend. Because of your courage and your actions last night, you will never have to be afraid again. Come, sit here and I will tell you a story . . ."

Michael looked doubtfully at Claire, who urged him to follow Lady Sarah's instructions and who took her own seat on a chair next to him. The rest gathered around, and he sensed they were as eager as he was to hear what she was about to reveal.

Her voice was ragged, aged, tired, but she seemed to summon energy from within and began:

"The woman you came to know as Delilah is more than a mere mortal. Her physical body was a vessel for an energy, a force of evil that has been increasing and coalescing for centuries, like a gathering hurricane. The Delilah energy has incarnated from time to time to test this power, and each time it has wreaked havoc within that particular Delilah's sphere of influence on earth.

"Until this Delilah incarnation, the power was limited to one person's effect on the material plane, but this Delilah wanted more. She was planning a Great Working with the forces of Darkness in the astral that would make her the conduit for evil of unthinkable dimensions to enter the world. We had no choice." She sighed. "We had to stop her."

Lady Sarah spoke as if it all made perfect rational sense, but to Michael, her explanation was melodramatic and bordered on the insane. The claims made by Delilah Mason, however, had sounded that way, too. He didn't know what to believe, if any of it. "What happened last night?"

The old woman laid her frail hand on his. "We went to war." She then told him an unbelievable tale, relating her travels to the astral plane as if they were normal, everyday occurrences and speaking of her visit to the Akashic Record like it was a trip to the local library. She told him about her affiliation with and commitment to the Watchers, speaking of them as real people. "They are great beings of love and light who watch over the worlds of the universe. Long ago they asked for my help in this fight, and I committed my life to this struggle."

"But if they're so powerful, why couldn't they just take care of her . . . out there?"

"It doesn't work that way. The Delilah energy was incarnated on the Earth plane, so they had to use Earth forces in the war against it. They had to involve humanity in its own salvation, so to speak. I chose to volunteer for this many years ago."

"But why?"

Lady Sarah gave him a sad look. "It's a long story, but one you deserve to hear." Maeve brought a glass of water and the old woman took several small sips. "Thank you." She returned her gaze to Michael. "I volunteered because I could not bear for the darkness to continue. For generations my family seemed to have borne a curse, and I wanted to put an end to it. At first, of course, I didn't understand what caused the curse or know anything about the Delilah energy or the forces that govern our universe. I just prayed daily for an end to the sadness that weighed heavily in my heart. I prayed for guidance and understanding. I prayed for a way out. That's when I first heard the voices."

"Voices?"

"I thought I was going mad. I began to hear voices inside my head, directing me, answering my prayers in effect, but I didn't know it at the time. I tried running away, but that didn't work. Finally, I started listening to them, and they told me exactly what I had to do if I truly wanted to gain release from my torment. I wanted freedom from my agony more than life itself. I had in fact given up everything in my life to fight the evil. I no longer cared that others thought me mad; I knew what I had to do. So I trained with the Watchers for nearly thirty years for the battle we engaged in last night. With the grace of God, we've won."

Something about her story gave Michael pause. "You mentioned a curse . . ."

"The Delilah energy has cursed many people over the ages and many reincarnations, but it came to roost on my family about a hundred years ago. Delilah then was known as Delilah Freeborn. As a mortal woman, she fell in love with my great-grandfather, Nigel Beauchamp, and enticed him into the practice of black magic."

Michael's heart lurched, and he felt Claire's hand slip into his. Lady Sarah continued.

"When Nigel's wife, Eloise, attempted to thwart Delilah, she was killed by a tragic magical accident. Nigel realized his horrible mistake and denounced Delilah, but it was too late. As a scorned woman, she cast a spell on him and his son and all his descendants down through time."

Michael was staggered by the woman's tale, but he remained silent and allowed her to continue, although a thousand questions assailed him.

"The story of how the curse afflicted the family is long, and I haven't the energy to go through it, although I learned it all from the Watchers. Suffice it to say that until last night, every descendent of Nigel Beauchamp lived a miserable life. Most of them died tragically."

Michael recovered enough to ask the question that burned foremost in his mind. "Besides yourself, are there . . . are there any other surviving descendants of Nigel Beauchamp?"

The telling of the story had cost Lady Sarah a great deal of energy. Her face was ashen, and her eyes seemed even more sunken. Michael worried that his question had upset her and perhaps had caused her to take a turn for the worse. He saw one of the strangers in the room, a man, approach the old woman and take her hand. No one spoke for a long while, and Michael was puzzled. Everyone in the room seemed to know what was going on except him. Claire squeezed his hand and motioned for him to put his ear to her lips.

"He's sharing energy," she whispered.

Michael had witnessed Delilah's forced transfer of energy from one body to another, but this was altogether different. This man was freely giving of his energy. It was an act of love. In a little while, Lady Sarah was strong enough to pick up her story.

"There are two living descendants at the moment," she told him. Her gaze penetrated his. "I am one. You are the other. We have both suffered from the curse of this Delilah. For years I prepared myself for the battle that took place last night, for I knew that if it was successful, the curse would be broken at last. When you arrived in Montlivet, I knew that it was your destiny to participate as well. That's why I allowed Claire's brother to take her to Hartford Hall, for I knew you would follow, and I needed you on the scene." She gave him a faint smile. "I believe we were successful. But as far as breaking the curse is concerned, Delilah did the work for us. Do you remember?"

Michael's thoughts collided in a mind already on overload, and he vaguely remembered Delilah raving something about the curse. But he was confused.

"Why would she want to break the spell?"

"She was about to absorb your energy, the same way

she took that of Claire's brother. But she remembered that you were cursed, and she didn't want to take a chance on contaminating her own energies. So she lifted the curse. I sent Claire back down to Earth at that moment, to distract Delilah from what she had planned and to launch the final attack.''

Michael stared at the old woman. Her whole story was unimaginable, inconceivable. Then an even more impossible thought occurred to him. She had said they were both descendants of Nigel Beauchamp . . .

''Who are you?''

Lady Sarah's chest rose slowly and fell again in a silent exhale. ''I am your mother,'' she uttered at last, her voice almost gone. ''The mother who deserted you, Michael.'' Her eyes searched his even as her consciousness faded. ''I did this to break the curse and free not just myself, but you and any descendants you might have from its power. Now that you know why I left, I pray that you will forgive me. I did it because I loved you, son.''

Then her eyes closed. Michael saw his mother take in another long breath, let it go, and die.

Epilogue

CLAIRE AND MICHAEL STOOD HOLDING HANDS, GAZing down upon the graves that lay side by side in the churchyard. Emotion tightened Claire's throat as she silently read the names on the simple headstones.

Eloise Beauchamp.

Stella Townsend.

Both victims of the Delilah energy who had bravely fought the evil in their own ways.

Claire prayed that their sacrifices had not been in vain.

It had been two months since the night of the terrible magical war, but neither Claire nor Michael had totally assimilated the enormity of what had taken place. Perhaps they never would.

After Lady Sarah's quiet death, they had returned to Fairfield House, stunned at what they had learned from the old white magician, Michael especially. They'd hoped to have some time alone to start sorting things out, but they arrived to find the police investigator already on the doorstep.

"I've just come from the hospital," he told them, looking at Claire with sympathetic eyes. "Your brother's condition is grave, but he is going to make it."

Relief washed through her and she leaned into Michael's arms. "Oh, thank God."

"He's got a lot of explaining to do, though."

To both of us, she thought ruefully.

Claire invited the inspector inside where, over hot tea, they learned that Scotland Yard had taken over the investigation. "Your story is not as unbelievable as you may think, Miss St. John," the officer said. "Scotland Yard has known about Delilah Mason's occult involvement for a while. They have a . . . friend, shall we say, in a certain occult bookstore in London who keeps them apprised of such activity in the London metro area. Although practices such as hers are not illegal, they are . . . questionable, especially when they might be involved in the accrual of such enormous wealth as hers. The Yard believed she might be using occult threats to pressure vulnerable people into making certain . . . deals."

Claire wondered if that was how Delilah had seduced Cameron into participating in her black magic. Undoubtedly, he had recently been vulnerable to people of great wealth and power.

She was relieved to learn that she and Michael were no longer suspect in any way. Scotland Yard considered them merely witnesses to what so far was reported only as an accidental explosion.

"Until we learn the cause of the explosion, we won't know whether or not it was the result of criminal activity. It's odd," the inspector added with a frown and a shake of the head, "an explosion with no fire."

He confirmed what Claire had already known would be the case, that Delilah Mason's body had not been found among the rubble. The police surmised she had escaped. "There is a warrant out for her arrest," he concluded. "She's charged with attempted murder. We'll be in touch as soon as she's apprehended. You both can expect to be subpoenaed in the case."

Claire doubted that any subpoena would ever arrive, for she believed that Delilah Mason no longer existed, either on the Earth plane or elsewhere.

The officer told them that unless and until Delilah was found, Cameron's culpability in the affair remained uncertain. Until she implicated him, his criminal exposure was limited to any charges that might be brought against him by Claire or Michael. Although she'd sworn she wasn't going to bail him out of trouble ever again, Claire couldn't bring herself to inflict any further punishment on him. He had, after all, suffered horribly and almost lost his life.

After the investigator left, she poured the remaining tainted wine down the drain and threw away the bottle.

Days later, when they were finally admitted to his hospital room, Claire sensed before she spoke to him that Cameron was a changed man. Something altogether different radiated in nearly palpable waves from his complex psyche. It didn't stem from despair or defeat, but rather from a dramatic shift in values. Claire smiled. Maybe her dark twin had at last seen the light.

But his psyche appeared to be in better shape than his body. He lay against the white pillowcase, his skin nearly the same shade as the linens except where ugly contusions lashed his arms. These were not the petty bruises of intravenous needle punctures, but the grisly results of Delilah's brutal attack. Claire grimaced.

Cameron's eyes opened when he heard them enter the room. "Hi, sis," he whispered. In spite of the change she sensed had taken place deep within him, his eyes were dark and sad, and they pleaded with her for forgiveness. She came and sat next to his bedside.

"Don't talk, Cammy. It's all right."

"I . . . I have to . . . tell you . . ." Tears filled his eyes. "I . . . never meant for it to happen."

"Shhhh. I know you would never intentionally do anything to hurt me."

"I had no idea . . ."

She stroked his hair away from his forehead. "You just get well. We can talk later." She saw his gaze move to someplace above and behind her, and she realized he'd just noticed Michael's presence. "We have a lot to talk about, Cameron." She smiled. "Including a wedding. This is my fiancé, Michael Townsend."

Cameron was discharged from the hospital a week later. He was still weak, and Claire insisted he stay at the farmhouse to recuperate. Together the three of them—Michael, Claire, and Cameron—talked for days, unraveling from three points of view the incredible web spun by Delilah Mason that had ensnared them in its evil. Each in his own way and for his own reasons prayed that her evil was behind them forever.

When Cameron was recovered enough to attend the ceremony, Claire and Michael were married in the village chapel. Neither of them wanted to remain in Montlivet, however. The village held too many horrible and traumatic memories.

To Claire's delight, Michael expressed his wish to reclaim his English heritage rather than return to the States. He applied for and was accepted as headmaster at a boys' boarding school in Dorset.

Although Cameron found a different job and divorced himself entirely from his once-coveted circle of rich friends, he still wanted no part of the country life, so Claire sold the Fairfield property to the farmer who had been leasing the land. She never once regretted letting go of her childhood home.

It was time to let go of the past.

Claire decided it was time to let go of her occult work as well. She wasn't sure exactly what her next career might be, but at the moment it didn't matter. Soon they would leave Montlivet and embark on the future together. Michael was by her side, and their love had created a new life that grew within her. The only career she wanted right now was to become the best possible mother to their child.

Michael had been torn by his own mother's deathbed revelation, and Claire knew he felt cheated in a way. For

even though he'd learned the truth about her, he never got
to know the woman who had given birth to him, the
stranger named Stella Townsend. Perhaps having a child of
his own would help heal that wound as well.

Claire turned away from the graves and squeezed Michael's hand. "Let's go," she said softly, looking up at
him with a tender smile. "Life's waiting on us."

Haywood Smith

"Haywood Smith delivers intelligent, sensitive historical romance for readers who expect more from the genre."

—*Publishers Weekly*

SHADOWS IN VELVET

Orphan Anne Marie must enter the gilded decadence of the French court as the bride of a mysterious nobleman, only to be shattered by a secret from his past that could embroil them both in a treacherous uprising...

_____ 95873-0 $5.99 U.S./$6.99 CAN.

SECRETS IN SATIN

Amid the turmoil of a dying monarch, newly widowed Elizabeth, Countess of Ravenwold, is forced by royal command to marry a man she has hardened her heart to—and is drawn into a dangerous game of intrigue and a passionate contest of wills.

_____ 96159-6 $5.99 U.S./$7.99 CAN.

Start a love affair with one of today's most extraordinary romance authors...

HER SECRET AFFAIR

BARBARA DAWSON SMITH

Bestselling author of *Once Upon a Scandal*

It is Regency England. Isabel Darling, the only child of an infamous madam, is determined to exact revenge on the scoundrels who used her late mother—and uncover which one of these men is her father. As she sets her sights on blackmailing the Lord of Kern, his indignant son Justin steps in to stop the headstrong Isabel—and start a passion from which neither can escape...

"Barbara Dawson Smith is an author everyone should read. You'll be hooked from page one." —*Romantic Times*

HER SECRET AFFAIR
Barbara Dawson Smith
0-312-96507-9___$5.99 U.S.___$7.99 Can.